Adam Smyer is an attorney, martial artist, and mediocre bass player. He lives in the San Francisco Bay Area with his wife and two cats. *Knucklehead* is his debut novel.

Knucklehead.

Knucklehead.

BY

Adam Smyer

BROOKLYN, NEW YORK, USA
BALLYDEHOB, CO. CORK, IRELAND

This is a work of fiction. All names, characters, places, and incidents are the product of the author's imagination. Any resemblance to real events or persons, living or dead, is entirely coincidental.

Published by Akashic Books
©2018 by Adam Smyer

ISBN: 978-1-61775-587-3
Library of Congress Control Number: 2017936110

Akashic Books
Brooklyn, New York, USA
Ballydehob, Co. Cork, Ireland
Twitter: @AkashicBooks
Facebook: AkashicBooks
E-mail: info@akashicbooks.com
Website: www.akashicbooks.com

For Malcolm

~

and for Dee

But this ain't the eighties, brother, it's the nineties!
And shit's a whole lot more intense.

—XB

Drop Squad (1994)

Once, when I was very young, I did an experiment. I was at my grand-mother's house upstate. I found a moth stuck to some flypaper hanging near the screen door out back. It was still struggling. And I prayed. I said to God, *God. I know that You can hear me. I need You to do something. I am going to take the matches out of my pocket and I am going to set that moth on fire, unless You stop me. I know that You know I am telling the truth. I'll do it. Please stop me.*

Nothing happened. I stuck my hand into my overalls and pulled out the little box of wooden matches. *I know You saw that, God. I know that You are watching. I need to know that You wouldn't let this happen. Please. Stop me from doing this.* Nothing. I lit a match. *I have to actually do it, God, because if I don't then I was bluffing, and You will* know *that I was bluffing. I need You to know I am not bluffing. Last chance, God. Stop me. Please stop me.*

The match was almost out by then, but I tilted it downward and touched the tiny triangle of flame to the tip of the moth's wing. It burned like paper.

I

A Slight Relapse.

"**E**verybody needs to move the . . . fuck . . . back!"

Frat boy in a suit at the front of the bus. It was obvious from his giant red baby head that six months ago this kid was crippling quarterbacks and raping cheerleaders on some campus. Now he was here, on his way to a job his daddy got him, and mad at us about it. It was barely 7:00 in the morning and we were all getting yelled at. Not to mention, we were packed in pretty tight back there already; there was noplace else to go.

"Move!" He actually put his hands on the man closest to him and pushed him into someone else. I tried to watch the fight, but there was none. *This bus is full of sheep.*

"GOD . . . DAMMIT! Listen! *You people need to get to the back of this . . . fucking . . . bus!*" The herd quivered.

I told myself that I was trying to be funny.

"Looka here, chief," I called to him. The sheep froze. "If you got off the bus, it would be a lot less crowded. A *lot*." Laughing, I looked around for support and found none. "That's what you want, right?"

I'd expected us to banter more. I was going to suggest that, if he was having trouble getting to work on time, he consider taping *Letterman,* or eating breakfast the night before. But instead Frat Boy asked, "Why don't you get off the bus with me?"

We thudded to a halt. In the middle of the street. The doors snapped open and, just like that, everyone but Frat Boy had their backs to me. *Cut from the herd!*

"OK. Let's go. You and me are gonna sort out this city's bus problem!"

I scootched toward the back door. "*Baaaaaaaaaaaaaaaaaaaa!*" I bade those around me. They made room.

I worked my way down the little stairs. Frat Boy was already on the side-walk. The bus peeled out, doors still hanging open. "Let's go," he said over his shoulder as he headed up the street. For a moment, I wondered if maybe we really were going to find a café somewhere and sit down and figure out what the mayor needed to do about mass transit. Then I looked ahead and saw that he was just leading me over to a little alley down the street for my beating.

I followed him toward the alley. I followed him closely. He had his back to me.

Frat Boy wasn't dumb. And he was fast for a big guy. He spun around as soon as he heard something. But what he heard was me pulling my collaps-ible baton out of my bag and telescoping it open to its full length. So when he turned around, all he got to do was watch me hit him in the neck.

The baton was made of thick metal wire, coiled into progressively nar-rower sections about three feet long end to end. I swung it as hard as I could. The coil was stiff, but as it flew across that short distance it curved into al-most a semi-circle. The middle of the club smacked him in the large muscle over his left shoulder. Then the thing wrapped itself around the back of his neck, and the little metal ball on the tip hit him in the throat.

I took a step back. Frat Boy's hands went up to his neck, but otherwise he was still. He stared into space. I wouldn't have thought his face could get any redder.

For a minute we just stood there in the early morning, me with my arms at my sides, him doing the universal sign for Some Motherfucker Just Hit Me in the Throat With a Fucking Baton. I thought about hitting him again, but he was done. I collapsed my club and put it back in my bag and walked away.

When I got where I was going, I pulled out a pen and my notepad, and flipped it open to the back page, the one that had the heading "DAYS WITHOUT AN INCIDENT." I crossed out the "73" that had been written last on the page. And under the crossed-out "73" I wrote "0."

Q and A-hole.

Tuesday, October 11, 1988

Professor Lakin stood over me. I held still and pretended to read. But he wouldn't leave, so I looked up.

It's funny: In high school, you're a kid. In college, you are almost no longer a kid. Then in law school you're a kid again. Calling us all "Mr." and "Ms." only reinforced the point.

"*Mister* Hayes," Professor Lakin boomed down on me. Then, softer, "You did a remarkable job yesterday. Thank you."

All I did was get you off of me, I thought. Apparently I said it out loud as well.

He smiled a bit. "That's what I needed. A little back and forth. It engages the others." Law school is one of the worst, last bastions of the Socratic method, possibly second only to boot camp. "You made my job much easier. Again, thank you."

I nodded and tried to smile. It seemed like I'd gotten some capital out of it, at least. Professor Lakin nodded back and finally went away.

A few minutes later, class began. "When last we met, ladies and gentlemen, *Mister* Hayes was good enough to educate us on the finer points of the tort of Tortious Inducement of Breach of Contract. Today we will look at the related torts of Tortious Interference with Prospective Economic Advantage, and Tortious Interference with Contractual Relations."

Professor Lakin began his annoying habit of pacing slowly back and forth across the stage at the front of the classroom while staring straight up and talking at the ceiling, like he was dictating the Constitution or the Torah. It was excruciating. "Now, obviously, what distinguishes these two torts is that the latter is a disruption of an existing, ongoing contractual relationship, whereas the former is a disruption of a relationship that contains only the potential for future business. The cases that you were assigned to read—and that I assume you all *have* read, carefully—make that clear." He scolded us with his eyes.

"The real question," he continued, "is what distinguishes Tortious Inducement of Breach of Contract from Tortious Interference with Contractual Relations?"

We fidgeted.

"Mister Hayes!" he shouted, whirling around. "Can you give the class concrete examples that distinguish these two torts?"

"Probably not."

Professor Lakin oozed up to his little podium and leaned over it and showed me his teeth. "Oh, come now, Mr. Hayes—surely *something* comes to that razor-sharp legal intellect of yours." He blinked expectantly.

Everybody was staring at me. "Alright. So, the time Spacely Sprockets signed that big contract with Mercury Rockets, and Cogswell Cogs tried to mess it up." All I got were blank stares, but there was no way people my age didn't know exactly what I was talking about.

"Yeah. Cogswell builds a robot that looks like the president of Mercury Rockets, and he sends the robot to go have dinner at Mr. and Mrs. Spacely's house. And the robot disses Spacely in front of his woman and tells him that Mercury Rockets is backing out of the contract. That's tortious interference of contract." Fewer blank faces now.

"But, if Cogswell had built a robot of *Spacely* instead, and sent it to the president of Mercury Rockets' house to diss *Mercury* until *he* backed out of the contract, *that* would be inducement of breach."

Now everybody was staring at him. "And why, Mr. Hayes? Why is that?" I wondered if he thought I couldn't explain my own example. Maybe he was actually asking me why.

"Well . . . because, in the first situation—where the Mercury robot disses Spacely—the reality is that the parties are still in contract. At the end of the night, actual Spacely still wants to do business with Mercury. And actual

Mercury is somewhere still wanting to do business too. But in the second situation, there's a real repudiation of the contract, by a real party, when actual Mercury dude gets mad at the Spacely robot and says, "Screw you guys and your contract." Even though it's all a big misunderstanding, induced by fraud, there's been a repudiation—a breach—by an actual party, and not a robot."

I couldn't read the silence, so I talked some more. "I mean, the damages would be calculated the same either way. But it could matter, down the line, if the date of the breach became relevant."

More silence.

"Depending on the facts."

Finally, Professor Lakin spoke. "*Thank* you, Mr. Hayes." A smirk. "And kudos on reading ahead in the syllabus. We don't get to the tort of 'dissing' until next semester."

The class bathed in Professor Lakin's smugness. I didn't get it. All around me, these people were forgetting English as fast as they could, trying to sound "lawyerly." This is why people hate lawyers. Me, I was going to talk to juries. These chuckling snipsnaps wouldn't be capable of talking to anyone but each other.

Then he moved on to someone else and left me alone for the rest of class. But once class ended and Professor Lakin left and we were all wearily packing up our stuff, Carolyn Hirsch, some judge's kid from Long Island, speed-walked up to my desk and barked, "I saw that!"

Sometimes I get a hard-on when I fall asleep in class, so I said, "Saw what?"

"*I saw him give you the answers!*" Her face was quite red. "Before class. I saw him approach you and *tell* you the answers to the questions he asked you!" A crowd started forming around us. Some of the faces looked confused, but most looked angry.

"You're joking." I took another glance at the mostly mad faces. "You're not joking."

"He *prompted* you!" She appeared to be seconds away from angry tears.

I almost could have laughed, except that I was mostly mad myself by then. "What? OK. Just so we're clear," I said to the jury of my peers, "you are saying that the exchange I had with Professor Lakin today in class was scripted."

"Yes!" It was the shrill kind of tone that can, by itself, get a brother arrested. Or worse. Carolyn was attacking me. We were fighting, she and I.

"You are saying that—in plain sight of everyone—Professor Lakin walked up to my desk and said to me, 'Today I am going to ask you to explain the difference between inducement of breach and tortious interference. Use that episode from the fucking *Jetsons* where Cogswell built a robot in your answer.' You're saying *that*."

I didn't get a response, so I continued. "Did you *hear* him say that?" Silence. "Of course not, 'cause you sit way the fuck over there." I waved the back of my hand toward her desk like where she sat was the ghetto. "But you *saw* it. You saw him tell me something. Right in front of everybody. So we are dishonest and dumb. Me and Professor Lakin both. We perpetrated a fraud on all of you, for no reason. Badly."

The mob now looked like it felt pretty stupid, but still I said it:

"Either that, or some black guy is smarter than you."

We sat with that for a moment.

"Hey—think what you want," I said as I finished packing up my shit. "Believe whatever you need to believe. I wouldn't want you all to go home and hang yourselves or anything." I met eyes with each and every one of them as I said that. "You know, from the shame. You go and tell yourselves whatever you need to keep on truckin'." I picked up my bag and turned back to Carolyn Hirsch and looked into her creepy green eyes. "You do whatever you've got to do."

I pushed my way out of the circle of classmates. "You people are crazy," I said, to all of them, before I turned and walked away.

Professor Lakin was standing right outside the lecture hall, off to the side of the open door. He'd been listening the whole time.

"Well done, Mr. Hayes," he murmured. His eyes danced.

"Crazy," I repeated. Then I left.

The Study Supergroup.

Friday, November 4, 1988

My cockles warmed by my classmates, I decided to put together a study group and crush them.

I had, of course, read the book *One L* as soon as I got accepted into law school. We all had. The genius of Scott Turow's account of his first year at Harvard Law lies not in its compelling prose, although it is compelling; the genius lies in having written a book that is guaranteed to be read by a fresh crop of thousands every year. You have to read *One L* the summer before you start law school the same way you have to get a lap dance at a stag party. And *One L* tells us that once you are in law school you have to be in a study group.

Ordinarily, the primary purpose of a study group is to study. I was starting a gang. Good grades weren't enough for me anymore. I needed to run this place I had come to hate. We would get good grades. We would make it look easy. And we would laugh at them while we did it.

I assembled my team with great care.

I selected my first recruit, Rachel Katz, in Property class. Professor Tucker was introducing us to the idea of *de minimis* litigation. Basically, some disputes are too small or minor to be worth a court's time. They are *de minimis*. But drawing that line can be difficult. "What about a boundary dispute?" Professor Tucker asked. "Between two neighbors, say. A little strip of land. How wide a strip should they have the right to sue over? Two inches wide? . . . How long a strip, then?" We went on like this for a while.

Professor Tucker asked, "Ms. Katz—is six inches *de minimis*?"

"Not on a Jewish man."

Impressive.

After class, I touched her shoulder as she stashed her books in a huge Gucci bag. She glanced up through dark crinkly hair. "Hey. You're pretty cool. Wanna be in my study group?"

She did.

The only person at NYU I was sure was smarter than me was Alejandro Velez. It wasn't because he looked smarter than me, but he did. If Alejandro ever tired of the law, he could always have a career playing smart people in the movies. He looked like the scientist who discovers, a bit too late, that the new supercollider is tearing a hole into another dimension. Except brown. He was a Puerto Rican Jeff Goldblum.

Alejandro also had that constant low-level panic many high achievers seem to share. I had noticed this panic early on and resolved not to catch it. But it certainly didn't disqualify him from conquering the world with me. He didn't talk much in class but, when he did, his statements were information laden and agonizingly nuanced. I soon learned to replay his words in my mind a few times to try to get all that I had surely missed the first time. Before long I was writing down his comments verbatim. If I could understand something Mr. Velez said on a subject, then I understood that subject.

I had to have him. The day after I got Rachel I rolled up on Alejandro after Contracts and followed my proven formula: "Hey. You're pretty smart. Wanna be in my study group?"

He did.

I needed a fourth; all the best study groups are quartets. Pickings were slim. Most of our classmates were those "lawyerly" snipsnaps and/or Mayflower trash. But two days after I'd acquired Alejandro I was gathering up my books and turning to leave class and there were dimples in my face. I'd seen those dimples before. On soft brown cheeks flanking a tiny gap between perfect front teeth that lived beneath huge brown anime eyes peering out from under dark bangs.

She was too cute to talk to. I don't know how else to put it. The sight of her shut down my ability to form words. On more than one occasion I had walked up to her, opened my mouth, and walked away. Her name was Amalia Stewart.

"Do you want me to be in your study group?" she asked, smiling.

I did.

Closer.

Thursday, January 12, 1989

There was a knock on my door. I'd been watching TV at the time, so it was a miracle I even got up. I squinted through the peephole. It was Amalia Stewart. I put on some pants and opened the door.

"Whatcha doin'?" She peered past me into the tiny university apartment, openly scanning for intel.

I stepped aside. "Oh, you know. Drinking brandy and reading the Constitution."

The study group had only met twice so far, and we'd been all business. But Amalia had no business tonight. She didn't bring any books with her; she didn't have some question she could have asked over the phone. She came with no cover whatsoever. Amalia Stewart had basically just knocked on my door and told me she liked me. What moxie! Of course, the odds I didn't like Amalia Stewart were quite low.

Then I remembered the TV. *Fuck.* I'd been watching *Cops*; it was still playing on the screen. Worse, I was *not* watching *The Cosby Show*.

I don't think you heard me: I said that *The Cosby Show* was on, and that I was not watching it. And I was black. And it was 1989. If being black has rules—and it does—then in 1989 *Thou Shalt Watch* Cosby was easily Rule Number Two, after *Thou Shalt Keep It Real.* I was doing neither.

I wasn't watching *Cosby* because the shit wasn't funny. It was just normal. I understood that America likes to pretend that there is no such thing as normal black people, so it was revolutionary or whatever to show some in prime time. But *I* was a normal black person, and the novelty was wasted on me. Honestly, I found it mildly insulting. I was down with *A Different World*, and I would soon be down with *Fresh Prince*. They were funny. Watching *Cosby* was like watching an ant farm.

But my opinion didn't matter. All that mattered was that Amalia Stewart was about to walk into my bedroom and see 16 Philly cops stomping some brother instead of Theo and Rudy laughing at the Cos's bit about pajamas. I bit my lip. *I done did it now.* I'd never minded not being tall enough, and I'd learned to live with not being cool enough. But not being black enough was something I'd dragged behind me my whole life. And it was about to drag me down.

Amalia floated past me into my room. "Cool—*Cops*." She plunked down on my bed without asking. "They're showing a marathon tonight, aren't they?"

They were. *Is this a trap? Is Amalia Stewart Black Police? You can usually spot the kente cloth. Is she working undercover?*

"Uh. Yeah." I felt my eyes darting around, searching for the exits. If Amalia Stewart was Black Police, she was working deep cover. Amalia was a full-on prep, old school, all headbands and pearl necklaces. This evening she was sporting a purple polo shirt with a red sweater tied around her shoulders and what my brain was telling me were called "boat shoes." She wore shit like that every day. *Definitely not Black Police.* You couldn't get Black Police to dress like that once, not even for The Cause.

I took a breath and tried to relax. Even with being outed as a *Cops* fan, this was still pretty much the greatest thing that had ever happened to me. I went to the bed and sat down. I didn't touch her.

We watched the rest of that episode, then another. "People say this show is racist," she remarked at one point. "I don't think so. Sure, they show folks getting arrested, but there are a lot of them too." She gestured at the screen. At that moment, a 30-year-old white man with no teeth was removing his shirt. Two suburban Jersey deputies alighted from their vehicle and administered his beating.

When it was over I got up to get us a couple of sodas. I checked my face in the toaster to make sure I didn't have anything hanging out of my nose. When I came back into the bedroom she was studying my notepad. The back pages.

"What's this?"

"Oh. Just what it says. Days without an . . . uh . . . incident. I . . . keep track."

"What kind of incident? Do you turn into the Hulk?"

I couldn't decide whether to respond *Sort of* or *I wish!* so I didn't say anything.

She moved closer to me. "What kind of incident?"

I looked away. "Oh, you know. Bullshit. The kind of bullshit that happens on the street."

"I *do* know. It isn't as if I've never been to New York, but living here is crazy. People back home think Manhattan is nothing but investment bankers, but it is more like a mob of drunk investment bankers fighting in the street."

"Heh. Ye."

"But why do you need to keep track? Count the days?"

Here was the thing about this conversation: I could detect no hint of fear, of judgment, of anything negative, in either her tone or her demeanor. Only curiosity. If we had known each other a long time, that would have made sense. But we hadn't.

"I'd like to go a year without . . . without getting into it with anybody. That seems kind of impossible right now. But other people do it." Not for the first time, I was grateful that black people don't blush. *Why isn't she leaving? Why isn't she excusing herself and never talking to me again?*

She stared right at me. "You start fights?"

"No. Absolutely not. I've never had a problem with anyone who wasn't being aggressive toward me. Or someone I care about. Or someone helpless. But I'm trying to find other ways of dealing with people. Even aggressive people. Trying to. I'd like to."

She glanced down at my notepad. "A hundred and twenty-two. Days. Is that good?"

"Yes. It's really good." I couldn't meet her eyes anymore. "For me."

"Hm. Good luck with that." She put the pad back down on the desk and closed the distance between us. She grabbed a soda, then took my hand and led me back over to my bed. Now short-sleeved Cuban officers were beating down shirtless Cuban drunks in Miami. We sat and stared at the screen an hour or so longer. At least, she did. Mostly I stared at her.

The Door.

Saturday, February 25, 1989

It was about 11:00 p.m. and we were walking through Alphabet City, on our way to a performance art thing on Avenue D. Mohawked punks huddled in doorways smoking. Skinheads marched along in packs. Today there's probably some fake nice name for the long letter-named streets at the far east of upper lower Manhattan. Something like Kenwood, maybe. Gardenside. Bullshit. It's Alphabet City. It's crazy, but I still look back on dirty, violent, corrupt eighties Manhattan fondly. Even though I should have died there.

I was determined to make her think I was hip. It was our third date—our third *real* date, anyway, by Amalia's standards—and I was literally praying that the Three Date Rule was in effect. As we picked our way through the vomit and dog shit and used needles, I dazzled her with my critique of the upcoming film *Do the Right Thing*. Spike had favored his alma mater with an advance screening the week before.

"The film itself is brilliant, but its true greatness is in the context of its time. Our times."

"I think I agree," Amalia said, smirking. Those anime eyes were smiling. At me. "My Bull Meter just came on by itself. But continue," she waved her slim pretty hand at me. Her eyes were like two brown puppies under a shiny black Christmas tree. "Please."

"A'ite. So, the way the press has been bugging out about the movie and it's not even out yet. Almost all the advance coverage Spike's getting includes—no, *features*—a warning not to see the fuckin' movie. 'It's gonna cause riots,' they say. 'Race riots in the streets of New York. Across the country. Around the world.'"

"That is the fantasy, yes." She crinkled her nose and pursed her lips. *Her lips. Her mouth. Focus!*

"Right. That's their fantasy. That black people are clueless. Spike is going to tell 20,000,000 black people something about our own lives that we don't already know. Nobody ever says that that something isn't true, mind you. Just that, somehow, none of us know it yet, and when we are finally told we will promptly lose our damn minds."

Amalia wasn't smirking anymore. She was walking and staring down at the sidewalk. Granted, in Alphabet City you really did need to watch where you were stepping, but also it was clear that she was listening very closely. That Amalia Stewart was listening to me run it down made me unspeakably happy.

A man who looked an awful lot like Pete Townsend got out of a cab and walked over to a pay phone. We and everybody else were too cool to notice.

"All they can imagine us doing is what *they* would do. Since we have not yet burned this entire disgusting country to the ground, we must have no idea how fucked we are, right? They think that they can know this about us. As if their consciousness, their experience, encompasses all others, and the rest of us are just subsets of whiteness. How else could you have groups like Creedence Clearwater Revival playing bad blues with a straight face in front of huge crowds listening with a straight face? How else could they write those same tired roles over and over on TV?"

"'I ain't be got no weapon,'" Amalia said softly.

"Right. How else could they talk about 'minorities,' as if white people are the majority race on this planet, or in this city, or anywhere?"

Now she was frowning. I felt bad that I had made her frown. "People at school speak of 'women and minorities,'" she said. "As if I cannot be both. As if only they can be women. It would be easier to interpret that some other way if they did not deny my womanhood a thousand other ways as well."

"OK. That was deep. I never thought about that one before."

We slipped through a forest of dealers at the corner of 6th and C.

"But . . . um . . . so, the movie," I went on. "This mindset . . . this God complex, whatever you want to call it, well, it's what *Do the Right Thing* is about. Sal had it. That's why he was so surprised by what happened. He thought that, even though those people had lived in Bed-Stuy their whole lives, somehow they didn't know where the hell they were. Their view of him was so different than he thought it was. They thought of Sal like a neighbor, and Sal thought that he was their king or a missionary or Tarzan or something. Sal is them—the media. The media is Sal when they freak out over *Do the Right Thing*. They are freaking out over their own reflection, like a parakeet."

Amalia was staring across the street. I followed her eyes just in time to see a young woman in a motorcycle jacket slap a large, hairy man in the face. The man was wearing an ill-fitting wedding dress.

She was smiling again. I kept going. "It's funny. Everybody says that black people are obsessed with racism. We are—because they are obsessed with race. Sal never forgot who he thought he was and who he *thought* they were. Not for one day. He was sure he was doing them a favor by being there, making money. And they had simply accepted him. Sal lived among us for a generation—well, he worked among us—and he never really knew what we were like, or wondered, or even wanted to wonder. It never even occurred to him to wonder. Because we were not real."

That sounded lucid to me, so I shut up. Amalia ruminated with her eyes and her mouth.

Sure, I saw dude coming. And I admit that I noticed we were on a colli-sion course. And no, I did not try to get out of the way. Maybe I thought that if Amalia saw me scoot out of a dude's way it could negatively impact my whole getting-laid agenda. I guess I figured that if we bumped shoulders as we passed, then we bumped. Happens all the time in New York. I didn't care.

He was big, but I was pretty skilled in the ways of NYC Bump Fu. We bumped. Hard. Neither of us yielded. A tie. I was fine with that.

A moment later, dude started calling, "Ay, mang!" to my back. I took a few steps more but he kept calling me out, and something in his voice put me on notice that having my back turned would in no way alter his response. It wouldn't have altered mine.

I was wrong. Dude wasn't big. He was huge. The man was the size of a door. Even now, sometimes when I look at a door I think of him. That was what stood glaring at me: a door in some sort of jersey with a head on it. My shoulder must have hit him in the nuts. But by then I was pissed too. This punk was calling me out in front of my woman!

Pathetic.

The door said something to the effect of, "What the hell?" For the life of me, I can't remember his exact words. I do remember what I said in response, though. I said, "Ey, man. *You* bumped into *me!*"

I still do not fully understand why those were not my last words.

As soon as they left my mouth, even before The Door started moving, everything slowed down. To a crawl. Almost to a stop. My brain knew that something important was happening before I did. There is a name for that phenomenon, when everything slows down. I can't recall what it is. But it's not uncommon. You're on a commuter bus, speeding across a bridge in the rain, on your way to work. There's barely time to settle down and read two stories in the paper before you are off the bus again. But let that bus hit a puddle, hydroplane, and go sliding toward the guardrail, and suddenly there is time to make peace with your Maker, say goodbye to each of your loved ones, draft your will, and carefully replay each regret, not the least of which is taking the bus that morning when you knew you should have taken the train. Anyway, the scientific name for it escapes me. But I know the feeling well. I get it a lot.

Slowly, The Door shook his head at my stupidity, and then he started walking toward me. Incredibly slowly. And, as he walked, he reached into the duffel bag he held in his left hand.

I stood and stared. On paper, I was fully capable of knocking that bag into the street and delivering several punches to his head. Or, if I couldn't reach his head, I could have hit him in the nuts some more. It felt like it took The Door five minutes to close the short distance between us. But it never occurred to me to do anything. Instead, I gawked, frozen, and wondered what he had in the bag.

It was shiny. Not chrome-shiny; stainless steel. I know this now. I also know that it was a Smith. Looking back, I recognize it. A Smith & Wesson .45 auto, stainless. Years later I would own one. But back then it was just Huge Gun in My Gut.

My life flashed before my eyes. Sort of. What happened was, I remembered every ass whupping I didn't get in my life. Every time I got away. Every fight I'd gotten lucky and won. I had been quite lucky. But I realized in that moment (which felt much longer) that I would have been better off taking more thumpings every now and again, because now my tab was about to be settled all at once, in one unsurvivable lump-sum payment. My life had caught up with me.

I don't know what my face looked like, but I can guess. Because instead of squeezing the trigger and blowing my chitlins all over Avenue D like he was supposed to, The Door only sneered and shoved me with his non-gun hand and turned his massive bulk around like a giant column of living smoke and blew down the street. I watched him. It was puzzling. My body was confused that it was not dead. Death had come and then just floated away. I watched it go.

And my dumb ass, my crazy dumb ass, picked up where I left off and started talking at Amalia again. "So, anyways, by the time the movie finally does come out—"

"Marcus. What the heck. What the hell, Marcus." I flinched. Amalia didn't cuss. I don't have enough *motherfuckers* in me to match that one *hell*.

She was staring down at the ground again, only now instead of puppies they were laser eyes cutting deep into the earth. "*Don't* . . . touch me," she said, even though she wasn't looking at me and I hadn't even realized I'd been reaching for her.

"Marcus," she murmured, "I did not know this needed to be said. But. You cannot be that way around me. You just can't."

"What way?" She shot her laser eyes at me. I really wanted to touch her. I didn't.

The lasers were cutting into me now. Blowing right through. "What were you *just* talking about. About people not seeing people. About people not being real. I do not see you? I am Sal?" I started shaking my head no like crazy. *No. No.* "I see you, Marcus. And I am telling you that you can *not* be that way around me. Not ever. This is not negotiable. Are we clear?"

I looked away. "Yes." Fluffy clouds of shame muffled the word. She was right. I hadn't thought about it, not consciously, but yes, I guess I thought I was fooling her. I guess I thought she must be fooled, because she was with me.

She turned and walked on. It seemed like she was walking away from me but I followed. I figured she knew how to tell me to stop if she wanted.

"The next time that happens," she said to the ground, her back to me, still walking, "*every time* that happens, from now on, this is what you do. You take a deep breath, and you unclench your fists, and you say to the person you have offended this word: *Sorry*. In the situation you were just in, you say 'I'm sorry' to the person, as sincerely as you can, and you get on with your life."

"Really?"

She didn't respond.

"OK."

She walked on, me trailing behind. We were leaving Alphabet City. Guess she'd had enough performance art for one night. She didn't speak, which scared me. I almost could have laughed at that. *Sure—now you're scared.* When she led me back to my university apartment building and stood aside so that I could open the heavy lobby door I felt confused and relieved and still a little scared. But grateful. And confused.

I came to think of The Door as my guardian angel. You wouldn't have known it from how I acted those next few years, but the reality check he delivered unto me that night probably saved my life down the line. That's guardian angel shit.

Later that night, while Amalia was in the bathroom, I snuck over to my desk and pulled out my notepad. I opened it to cross out the 166 and start my day count over. But she had already written the word "ZERO" large across the bottom of the page.

Home.

Wednesday, March 22, 1989

It wasn't cold, but I was wet, so I engaged my afterburners and moved down Broadway at Maximum New York Walking Speed. It was almost 6:30; most places, people would be coming home from work. But in this neighborhood of Lincoln Center and the Met it seemed like most people were going *to* work. Divas and ballerinas glided alongside musicians and teamsters, everybody ignoring everybody.

I'd loved growing up here. It was so out of step. Everywhere you turned, there was someone who had proverbially made it here. Artists who'd forgotten to take their vow of poverty. No one would ever pay money to see me dance, but I could relate. This was my scene. I'd known little else. I slalomed through the crowd on autopilot, trying not to hit anybody with my gym bag. At 134 West 66th, I ducked into the lobby.

"Marcus! Hey!" Luis smiled and waved from the mailbox area with his free hand. He balanced three packages on the other. The consistently best-dressed man in my building was the doorman. Today Luis was rocking a beige three-button I'd never seen before, complete with the Puerto Rico flag lapel pin I'd seen most of my life.

"Luis! How you been?"

He shrugged. "You know. Runnin' shit." The little old Jewish lady getting her mail six feet away pretended not to hear. Because, in my building, Luis Ruiz ran shit.

"Cool. Would you let her know I'm on my way up, please?"

"No prob."

Mom opened the door while I was unlocking it. "Honey, you know you don't have to buzz up. This is still your home, baby."

I hugged Mom, arms set to that familiar power level, As Hard As I Can Without Hurting Her. She sighed.

I dumped my duffel. "You mind if I take a quick shower?"

"This. Is. Still. Your. Home."

"A'ite, a'ite." I glanced around. "Where do you keep the towels now?"

"Same place they were when you lived here, fifteen minutes ago."

I took a long, hot shower. Buildings have no water pressure anymore. Probably to conserve water. I get that. I also get that a long, hot shower after a workout is one of the things I am going to miss most about life on Earth after I am dead.

A half hour later I went into the kitchen, wearing sweats I got from a bedroom that admittedly still looked a lot like it did when I lived there. A feast waited for me at the table, along with my smiling mother.

"Whoa. Hey, you didn't have to—"

"My son is home! I just heated up some leftovers."

Even more than hot showers, one day I will miss my mom's cooking. Collards. Wings. Corn on the cob. I sat down and got to grubbin'.

"Where are you coming from all sweaty?"

"Dojo. Karate school."

"Really?"

"It's new. Kind of a condition of my probation."

"Excuse me?"

"Amalia." I was distracted by the comfort food; the information was coming out in a way that was neither helpful nor politic. I stopped eating. "That woman I've been telling you about. Amalia Stewart. She kind of ordered me to take up a martial art."

"And you're going to tell me a good reason why she would do that, aren't you?"

"Yes." I ate a forkful of collards for strength. "'Cause I almost got us killed. She says I need 'an outlet.'"

"Hmm." Mom sat, hands on the table, and waited for me to figure out how much to tell her.

I told her everything: the date, The Door, the bump, the gun. Amalia's reaction. I wish I had been paying closer attention to Mom's reaction; I was sitting there, bascially telling her, *Hey, the other night while you were watching* Murder, She Wrote *the phone was supposed to ring and regret to inform you that the rest of your family was gone now too.* But she took it well. At least, she didn't freak out. Mom wasn't the freakout type. I think that with me she always knew to act like whatever I was saying was normal. It kept me talking. She'd have made an excellent lawyer.

I was done. She gave me another minute to make sure I had nothing to add. Then, "And how do you like karate?"

"Mom. I love it. Did you know, the whole time we've been living here, one of the greatest martial artists of our lifetime has had a dojo not 10 blocks from here? On West End, near 72nd. Yan Su Academy. Sensei, the founder, still teaches there. Akira Tanizaki. Back in the day, in the golden age of modern martial arts, you know, in the early seventies, when countries used to challenge each other in tournaments, Sensei was the cat Japan used to send to kick other country's dude in his—the butt. When he was

19, he knocked Thailand's best fighter *out.*" I showed her my fist. "*Out.*"

Mom seemed less impressed than she should have been. "And what are you getting out of it?"

"Well, I just started a month ago. They don't let the white belts fight or anything. Mostly push-ups and crunches some days, then they'll show us a little something. But I've been going three or four times a week, and I'm getting kind of hooked. It's fun, and, I think I feel . . . better. Even after I'm not tired anymore. Just, you know . . . calm, I guess."

She patted my hand. "Calm is good, baby. So when am I going to meet your friend?"

"We could do it this weekend, if you want. Mom, you're gonna love her. She's wicked smart."

"Of course she's smart. She picked you."

"Pretty sure that *I* picked *her*, Mom."

Mom just smiled.

The D-word.

Thursday, April 6, 1989

"There are inherent limitations in the state's power to regulate private conduct," Amalia said. Professor Lohmann urged her to continue with a raising of his bushy eyebrows.

We were in Constitutional Law. Our assignment had been to read *Bowers v. Hardwick*, which the United States Supreme Court had handed down three years earlier. I can sum up the facts and the holding of *Bowers* with this popular paraphrase of the majority opinion: "There is no constitutional right to sodomy." Even for a periodically corrupt body like the Supremes it was unprofessional, at best.

Gay folks around school were pretty militant. No surprise there. In New York in the eighties, everybody was militant. Even the capitalists were militant. And *Bowers* had, understandably, pissed the gay militants the fuck off.

"There are limitations in theory, and there are even more in practice," she went on. "Sexual activity is inherently private. Any attempt by the state to regulate deviance . . ."

The room got frantic. All over, people began to flutter. Classmates—the gay ones—started wagging their fingers at her. "Don't say 'deviance'! Don't say 'deviance'!" they cried.

I was amazed. *Don't say? In a Con Law class about civil liberties? Really?* The irony was lost on them. They were literally hopping mad—some had left their seats and were jumping a little, like they had to pee.

We were sitting in the front row. Amalia turned fully around in her chair. She swept those eyes over the would-be correctors behind her. They stopped hopping.

"You don't have the market cornered on deviance," she said softly.

The activists contemplated this statement. And, almost in unison, all the faces turned slightly and regarded me. Everybody knew we were a couple.

And I nodded at them. Slowly. Gravely. I considered saying, *And how!* or something like that, but I thought I might laugh. This was serious theater. Little preppie sister had just blown the minds of folks who were used to blowing other people's minds. So I nodded, and we let the silence grow. Rachel sat all the way in the back; she was hiding her face behind her awesome curtain of curls but her shoulders were shaking. Really glad we didn't make eye contact. I'd have lost it.

Professor Lohmann, the only openly gay member of the faculty at that time, savored the tension. Those eyebrows waggled obscenely. He couldn't have been happier. I had to crack a little smile at that. Man, we were doing those people's jobs for them. The university should have been cutting us a check.

For me, the funniest part was that we hadn't even made love that many times yet, let alone gotten freaky. I knew that, going forward, the whole school would now assume that Amalia was making me eat dog food and slamming me nightly with a strap-on. They were mistaken, but still I made a mental note to have us agree on a safe word the very next time we were alone.

Mongoose.

Saturday, June 24, 1989

I swear to God, we'd been discussing whether to go to antiquing. That's how much we were minding our own business. That's how innocent I was. *Antiquing.*

We were driving around Berkeley, California in a rental car. Rather than work summer jobs, we had both opted to live off of student loans. Next year, the summer job we got would likely be the same job we took when we graduated, thus plotting our course for the remainder of our careers. We'd agreed to have some fun while we still could.

And now she was showing me Berkeley, the place of her birth, for a week. Amalia's memories were organized around fashion the way history books are organized around wars, so the tour through her childhood had turned into a buying trip. We were getting clothes and knickknacks and shipping them home. That way, she explained, if anybody asked where we got something, we could just say "California" instead of actually answering.

It was a sunny, beautiful day and we were cruising up Telegraph Avenue, near the university, gabbing. I was driving and Amalia was navigating.

"Ooh—make this right," she said as we came up on Parker.

I made the right. Safely. I did not cut those boys off. I signaled, got over to the right-hand lane, signaled again, and made the turn. I did notice that, when I first signaled, a car behind me sped up, as if to prevent me from getting in front of them. But it was too far back to catch up and I got over easily, with plenty of room between us.

But it was 70 or 80 degrees in Berkeley that day. The streets were clogged with young women wearing very little clothing. And whenever the streets are clogged with young women in very little clothing, the streets are also clogged with packs of young men half out of their minds. I understood. I'd been one of them, seemed like yesterday.

The response by the driver of that car was completely out of line. The honking, sure. Once, twice. OK. I ignored it at first. Then, when it kept up, I waved—an insincere, Queen Elizabeth on parade–type wave that was just going to have to do. But it didn't. Still behind us, he started doing this weird thing with the gas and brake like he was going to rear-end us but would stop inches away. The passenger in the car was making a gesture I did not understand. I was getting annoyed.

Then they cut left into the oncoming lane, zoomed past us, shot back into our lane, and came to a tire-screaming stop just in front of us. A roadblock.

I now considered rear-ending them. I could say it was an accident. But returning a damaged rental car would be a hassle, and the insurance company might tell those boys where we lived. So I decided to get out and beat their ass instead.

I put the car in park and glanced at Amalia. She was staring ahead at their car. "I'll be right back." She did not respond. I unfastened my seat belt and got out.

Both of the guys in the car had already gotten out and were waving their arms at me like young gorillas in mating season. They were maybe 20. That age is strong enough, and stupid fast, and invincible. At 25 I was probably stronger, but also a little less fast and a lot less invincible. One of them, the Asian dude, was my size. The brother was bigger. Both looked like jocks, puffed up and fake angry; my mom would have said that they were "smelling themselves."

Hurt the big one, fast; get rid of the other one for good; then take your time with the big one. It was doable.

I closed my door and began to walk toward them. And the young men jumped back into their car and peeled out.

I waited a minute. They weren't circling around the block or making a U to run me over. They were in the wind.

I looked around at the dazed bystanders on the sidewalk. "Did you see that?" I yelled at a couple who were pretending that that had not just happened. "They blocked our car like they all wanted to fight but when I got out to fight they ran away! *Ah-hahahahahahahaha!*" Neither responded. Sheep.

I got back in the car, still pumped. I had been happy to pound those dudes, but watching them run was even better. I gave Amalia a big smile and reached past her to our glove box and pulled out my little pad. I was going to cross out the *119* that I'd written there yesterday and put down a *0*. Which was fine. It was worth it. But Amalia put her soft little hand on mine and said, "You did not do that. They did that."

I stared at her for a long time, to make sure I understood. I wasn't smiling anymore, but I still felt good. I put the pad back in the glove box.

"I don't even know why you still carry that thing around," she said as I started the car.

We went antiquing.

Dr. and Dr. Stewart.

Sunday, June 25, 1989

Because we were "back home," as Amalia called it, like we were in Alabama or something, I had to meet the parents. We'd had very few conversations about *us* but that was only because we didn't need to.

We parked in the driveway. It was where she'd grown up—a big Victorian in North Berkeley. We had just rung the doorbell when Amalia turned to me and said, "Address them each as 'Doctor Stewart.'"

"What?" The door opened and a woman who could only have been her mom stood there smiling at us. Behind her the place looked like the set of the Pat Boone Christmas Special, only with black people, which I guess means it didn't look like the Pat Boone set at all. Also it was summer. But there was a very fancy light fixture, almost a chandelier, hanging above our hostess, and a wide staircase to the right. Behind her was a long, bright hallway lined with paintings and photographs, leading to what appeared to be a large living room. The kitchen was to our left. I could only glimpse a corner of it from outside but it looked big and professional, and when the smells coming from there hit me in the face I had to work not to drool. And in front of it all, smiling, was Amalia in 30 years. A little heavier than her daughter, but that only brought out her dimples and her boobs. Party dress. Pearls. Heels. Beaming. Mom was killing it, and I knew that she knew it, because she just stood there smiling at us for at least five seconds while I was properly bowled over and maybe a little bit intimidated.

Amalia stepped forward and clutched her mother and squeezed. Her mom closed her eyes and let go of the door and squeezed back harder. I silently rehearsed my introduction while they hugged. It didn't sound right in my head. Too "Dr. Livingston." The Stewart women released their grips at the same time and Amalia slipped past and inside, leaving me alone. I felt a whiff of panic coming on, until Dr. Stewart turned her warmness to me and extended a bejeweled hand. "Marcus," she said. That's all.

I took that beautiful hand and we gazed at each other. It was pretty intense. It should have felt phony—we were, after all, strangers—but it didn't. "Doctor Stewart." Not like how I'd planned, but OK. More than OK.

I offered her the bouquet of flowers in my other hand as if I were courting her. Which I was. Mothers are easy. You woo them in much the same way you wooed their daughter. If it works, they approve. It's like an audition, or a sample.

"Dinner is almost ready. Harold is setting the table."

"Cool." *Oops.* I should have said *Lovely* or something. But she didn't seem to notice.

Amalia had only gotten a 30-second head start on us, but by the time we walked into the kitchen she was already working, setting a covered dish onto the dining room table. Amalia's mom gave me a little pat on the arm and walked away, picking up one of those long lighters and heading over to three candlesticks waiting on a counter. They were all busy, and kind of ignoring me.

I scooted past Amalia to the kitchen sink and washed my hands and dried them with a paper towel from the roll hanging nearby. Everyone hides their garbage can someplace different so I stuck the wet paper towel in my pocket. Then I walked over to Amalia's father, who was on a step stool taking a stack of heavy-looking plates down from a cupboard. "I'll take that."

He handed me the plates and went back for a gravy boat on the top shelf. He didn't respond—he barely acknowledged me. But it seemed efficient, not rude. The man was, after all, a surgeon. They are not known for saying, "Scalpel, *please*."

I wanted to rinse the plates. That's what we do at my house, but it occurred to me that it might offend them if they took it to mean that I thought the plates were dirty. I knew that the plates weren't dirty. You rinse the plates before you use them because you do, that's all. So I rinsed each plate and gently shook it dry, and then I dealt them all around the table. I turned back toward the kitchen and saw Amalia's mom heading to the table with a big bird on a platter. I took it from her and put it down in the middle of the table.

It went like that for maybe ten minutes. No *Oh, you must be Mr. Stewart* or *Marcus I've heard so much about you* or any of that crap. Maybe it was because I knew and loved Amalia, but it felt like I knew her parents. Maybe that's what it was like for them. Everyone else's family is a little creepy, like a weird parallel-universe version of your own. Everyone else's family smells a little funny. But these people hardly smelled funny at all. And it wasn't superficial familiarity, either—I was upper-middle class too, but that looked different in Manhattan than it did here. They just smelled right.

When our team-building exercise was over we sat down to a large formal dinner. I knew we would say grace—the female Dr. Stewart was the pastor of a large AME in Oakland—so I had sense enough not to just dig in. But

I did get a little blindsided when she asked, "Marcus? Would you like to do the honors for us?"

"I'd love to," I lied.

I thought on it a bit, and ended up going the same route I had when I rinsed the plates: I did what I felt.

I glanced around the table. "Would you all mind if we prayed silently? To be honest, I don't really need another person to talk to God for me, and I wouldn't presume to do it for anyone else." None of them seemed particularly rocked by this, but father and daughter did turn to Pastor Stewart. She said, "I wish more people felt that way. Yes. Let's."

Although that food merited serious, single-minded eating, we got to the Twenty Questions part of the evening as we were starting to tuck into our seconds. Nobody was fat, but these people could eat.

"Amalia says you are an only child?" Mr.—I mean, Dr.—Stewart asked.

"Yes sir. Just me and my mom."

"What happened to your father?" Too often that question has sounded to me like an accusation, but this time it felt like a good and natural question. I didn't know if Amalia really hadn't told them much about me or if he was playing dumb to be polite.

"He died before I was born." Nobody responded, so I added, "He was killed."

Their faces changed. They really hadn't known. They stared at me—didn't press, but didn't change the subject either. Alright.

"He was killed in the ring. Beat to death. He was a boxer." My answer to this simple question contains a lot of information. I have learned to take my time and spread it out a little. "Madison Square Garden. I was there. I mean, my mother was there, pregnant with me. Eight months pregnant."

We ate in silence for a while.

"This is what I understand, from what my mom has told me," I continued. Even Amalia hadn't heard this part. "My dad was six feet even, 175 pounds—a solid light-heavyweight. But he chose to fight above his weight class. That was allowed . . . no one did it, but it was allowed. So he fought heavyweight. I'm not sure why . . . Maybe the money was better. Maybe ego. Maybe both. Maybe just because he could. He did pretty OK against larger men. He told my mom he would quit and get an office job after I was born. Go to night school, all of that. I don't know if he was telling the truth.

"Anyway, boxing was kind of chaotic in the sixties. That night, I think his fight got canceled and then another fight got canceled, and he was offered the chance to fight a contender—a serious, ranked heavyweight." I didn't give them a name, and they didn't ask. "And my dad agreed to do it. Again, ego, money—I don't know. Maybe because his woman was there and he wanted her to see him fight. We're like that." By *we* I meant guys; they nodded, so I think they understood. "But what was different about this fight was that my dad was still kind of coming up, making a name, learning his craft, and this other guy . . . well, he was already there. He was an experienced, seasoned fighter, *and* he was bigger. It's just a reality of combat that between men of equal skill, the larger one has the advantage. And that's *equal* skill.

"I don't blame the other guy. Not really. Mostly I blame the ref, for not stopping the fight sooner. The guy beat on my dad's head for three rounds, and only after my dad didn't come out for the fourth did they stop it."

Amalia was crying, quietly but hard. Her mom seemed close to it. Maybe her dad was too, and just not showing it. He muttered something about a hematoma.

"And, frankly, I kind of blame my dad. He chose to climb into that ring. You sell your motorcycle as soon as your wife tells you she's pregnant. You never ride it again, and there's an ad in the paper the very next Sunday. That's one of the Man Rules, right? That's in the Man Constitution. Well, also, you stop boxing. You just do." I considered licking the gravy off my plate but fortunately did not. "Maybe it was going to be his last fight, or one of his last. I don't know. But, just like that ref, he waited too long. And he got himself killed, while his wife watched." I swallowed and turned away. "And I listened, or whatever."

"He bit off more than he could chew," Mr. Dr. Stewart said, matter-of-factly, after a while. "We all do that sometimes. It's how most of us die, one way or another. You know how Elvis Presley died?"

"Wasn't he on the toilet?" I said, brightly.

"That's right. 'Straining at stool,' they call it. It is not uncommon. See, when you strain that way, the vena cava—well, suffice it to say that it does funny things to your blood pressure." It was the most animated I had seen Mr. Dr. get. *God—my girlfriend's dad is a goth.* "If you have an existing blood pressure problem, or a heart problem, that spike in your BP can be too much for you. Fatal. But who knows this about himself? No one. Not if you haven't experienced any symptoms. You're thinking, 'A little constipated today. I'll muscle it out.' You've done it before. Hundred times over your life. Maybe even yesterday. But today"—he shook a mushroom, impaled on his fork, at me—"today you have bitten off more than you can chew." He popped the mushroom into his mouth.

"I get that. I do. I've thought about the fact that my last thought on this earth, however old I am, will probably be something like, 'I can totally make that light.'" I laughed. "If we were animals in the wild, or even people in the wild, we would all lose a step some time around 40 and something would eat us. I get that. And I get that people make mistakes. But still. Fighting above your weight class is, like, a *metaphor* for foolishness. And I just question whether it was wise to do anything that is proverbially foolhardy when you are expecting a kid. I mean, spitting in the wind would be OK . . ." I laughed again. They were real laughs; none of this was new to me.

"And getting high on your own supply would not." We all turned to her. Mrs. Dr. was a trip.

"Yes," I said, still laughing. "Exactly. All I'm saying."

We ate.

"It did work out, though. In a way, I mean. He at least had a lot of insurance. Between that and help from family, my mom was able to raise me, full time, until I started school. I still kind of remember some of that. It was nice.

And as soon as I started school so did she, and she got her undergrad degree, and then she started some entry-level job at New York Telephone. By the time I was in high school she was a project manager at AT&T. Now she's a senior manager and about to retire. She's 55. People don't really get to retire at 55 anymore. So, in a way, he took care of us. Either that, or we didn't need him to begin with." I plugged my mouth with stuffing.

Eventually, all of the air came back into the room. We had thirds and dessert and seconds of dessert. We talked. We laughed. We even sang a little.

Mrs. Dr. had just suggested we have thirds of dessert. And I said, "I lied." And just like that the air was gone again and we all sat in our little vacuum and stared at me.

"About my dad," I said. "His death." The vacuum kept sucking the words out of my mouth and pulling them apart into nothing. Everything I said just got swallowed up. I needed more words. "Not that he died. He did die. Long ago. But not in the ring. Like I said."

All three of them sat motionless, staring. You could really see the family resemblance in their stunned faces.

"He just died. That's what I was told. I was really little. Heart attack, I guess. Not 'straining at stool.'" I laughed toward the wax statue of Mr. Dr.— *Too soon?* "And that's the truth. That's the truth," I repeated.

Mrs. Dr. was the first to speak. As a pastor, she was probably the one most used to fucked-up confessions. "Why did you lie?" she asked. She looked so sad. I was expecting anger. Hoping for indifference. I didn't understand sad. Maybe that was just her face.

"I don't know." I did know. "People always ask about that stuff sooner or later. About your parents. They read so much into it. I can't help how many living parents I have, or how they died. No matter what you tell them, when you're done they always give you this look like they know something new about you. But it's not new. Not to me. I'm the one who told you!" I knew I was getting a little too excited. They still seemed pretty shocked. I needed to be gentle.

"It's like being black," I said. Mr. Dr.'s eyebrows rose slightly. "You talk to someone on the phone, about an apartment or a job or whatever, and you hit it off a little, and you even talk a little longer than you needed to to do business. And the person on the other end says, 'Yeah, come on down, let's do this.' And you say, 'OK!' and you're all excited because you finally caught a break. And you get all dressed up and go on down and you knock on the door and they open it and they look at you. And then they get confused. Even if you are wearing a nice suit they just gape at you for a second like, *I didn't order a pizza.* And it takes way too long to explain to them that you are the same person who exactly one hour ago told them that you would see them in an hour. And then it dawns on them that you have deceived them. You can see it on their face. Like, now they're thinking that an hour ago when you were talking about both loving Dungeons & Dragons when you were kids, they were talking about D&D the *game* and you had been talking about actual dungeons or something. Then they get weird. Like I'm a different person than I was an hour ago." I was starting to lose my train of thought. "Because . . . because they didn't know I was black. Like that matters. Like what they knew or didn't know had anything to do with who *I* am. But *I* knew that I was black! Right? Right? We've all been there, right? You want to say, 'Why are you acting like this is some new dramatic development? I'm the same motherf—I'm the same dude I was an hour ago. I was black when you met me. *You* didn't know. But I was. I swear that I've been black a long time now. So this, this is your trip. Yours. So stop acting like it's mine!" I scanned the faces of the jury. Mr. Dr. was gone. He was in his happy place, probably the place he goes when he is cutting people's spleens open. Mrs. Dr. still looked very, very sad, but at least she was present, engaging me.

I couldn't read Amalia to save my life. Even though she was staring right at me. She had an expression on her face; I could see it; I just could not figure out what that expression was.

"Anyway . . . what? Anyways, so, that's what it's like." I'd completely forgotten what I was talking about. "And it's a real problem, sometimes, because

. . ." *You are losing it. You are losing them. You are losing* her. "Right! It's just like that, because, a little while ago, when I met you, my dad was already dead. You just didn't know it. People meet you and, later when you tell them your father died, you see them go back and write 'ORPHAN' in all the margins of everything that has already happened between you. And if you're *black* and you tell someone your father is dead, the odds of ever getting them to believe that he wasn't shot robbing a liquor store are damn near zero. Honestly, saying that he just died sounds like a lie even to me." That was true.

"The story I tell . . . the story I told you . . . I like it because it kind of takes the focus off of me. I mean, I don't like it . . . I prefer it to the truth. I mean . . ."

Fifty billion years from now, when the universe contracts and implodes and existence everywhere ceases, it will still be louder than it was in that room.

"It gives people something to do," I said finally. "They're gonna do something with whatever I tell them, so I give people that."

Now Mrs. Dr. was watching me like I was a bug that made her sad. She turned to her daughter. I think I actually heard her neck creak.

"Did you know about this?" she asked. I guess she meant, did Amalia know the real story about my father's death. She didn't.

"Yes," Amalia said. Only, she never looked at her mother. She just kept staring at me. "Yes, Mama, I knew."

I didn't know if her mother believed her. I didn't know if she believed me. And I couldn't tell if Mr. Dr. was even listening. He was still clearly, visibly in his happy place.

I bet his happy place is awesome. Mine sucks.

Discovery.

Saturday, May 5, 1990

"OK," I opened the meeting, "Professor Greenlee—Bankruptcy. What can we expect?"

"Greenlee is lazy," Alejandro said. We all nodded. "I pulled every one of his final exams, and it is clear that the man has not written a new question in 20 years. In fact, for most of that time he has given up on even recombining different questions from past examinations, and instead gives the exact same finals, rotating over a six-semester cycle. Which means that it is likely—highly likely—that the final exam Professor Greenlee will give us next week will be identical to the exam he gave on May 28, 1987." He handed copies of the exam all around.

"Doesn't Professor Greenlee know that the law library archives every past examination, and lends them out to students?" Amalia said, amazed.

"He knows," Alejandro replied. "He doesn't care. Lazy."

"We're all in agreement on that?" I asked. We were. We tucked next week's exam into our bags. "Who's next?"

"Employment Law," Rachel said. "Professor Betts. Last week. Talking about how the statute of limitations starts over again each time a new act of harassment occurs. And then she goes, 'So . . . that's kind of a big deal . . .' Didja see that smirk? Anybody else catch that?"

"I noticed it," Amalia said. "It irked me."

"Yeah. Smug prick. But I'd bet good money that was a tell. The exam's gonna turn on that issue."

"I agree," Alejandro said. "Betts likes to bury a critical fact in a question that changes the analysis completely. Last semester it was the fact that the defendant was no longer the plaintiff's direct supervisor at the time of the conduct alleged. The court applies a different test in such a case. The people who didn't catch that probably got a B-minus, at most."

The three of them shuddered visibly. I was the only one in the group who'd ever actually gotten a B-minus in anything, ever.

"Recurring harassment," I said. "Concur. Everyone?" Amalia nodded. "Next?"

Amalia stood up. She always stood when she made any sort of presentation. "Antitrust. Professor Finke has a history of using examination questions to promote his political agenda. Each semester, he writes a fact pattern that compels the student to take the position that some practice, while anticompetitive, is nonetheless legal. He seems to believe that this will indoctrinate us."

"He's probably right," Alejandro mused.

"OK," I said. "What will he force us to defend this year?"

"Price fixing," Amalia announced. "Finke taught the recent *Needham* opinion as if he were appealing it."

"That's right," Rachel said. "That case did *not* go his way. He's gonna wanna fix that."

"He is trying to fix it now," Amalia responded. "Two days ago, the spring edition of the *Michigan Law Review* was published. It features an article by Professor Finke arguing that *Needham* should be reexamined, and why." She passed out copies of the article.

"How did you know to check Michigan's law review?" I asked her, but she only smiled.

"So," said Rachel, staring at Professor Finke's latest publication, "this is basically what he considers the A-plus answer to the question he's gonna give us."

"With his ego, it is doubtful he considers it an A-minus," Alejandro replied.

"Agreed," I said.

We covered all six classes, and we were right all six times.

We were already lawyers.

No, You Probably Can't.

Monday, August 6, 1990

It was the week before any classes started anywhere at NYU. The law school had taken over one of the undergraduate dorms, a massive apartment building on Bleeker, for law firm first-round interviews.

Rather than all of us taking time out of our studying during the school year to beat the bushes and law firm partners taking time out of their billing to recruit, we all came together under one roof each year before classes began for a huge interview orgy. The orgy imagery was made no less apt by the fact that each desk in each room was three feet from a bed. If you and your credentials made it past this initial hurdle, the next round or two of interviews were much more likely to yield an offer. It was very efficient.

So, that was the situation. There was no other activity taking place. The entire building was being used for one purpose: job interviews. It was filled with two kinds of people: (1) young people in blue suits; and (2) old people in blue suits. That's it.

I wasn't messing around. I had eight half-hour interviews booked for that first day alone. Baby's First Briefcase was stuffed with résumés and transcripts and references and writing samples. I was rocking a navy pinstripe three-piece and wingtips. I was rested, caffeinated, and not too gassy. I was ready.

My morning went well enough at first. I made my little speeches and tried to get used to the half-hour format (which back then seemed like a very long interview). I learned where to linger and where to keep it moving. I got better at making my face appear interested, like Arsenio. I was making moves. Then my 11:30 happened.

It was 11:29. I knocked on the closed dorm room door and entered when I heard a grunt. Wedged behind the tiny desk was a large middle-aged gentleman stuffed into a blue suit. It was a nice suit, but because it didn't cover the man's face his Boston was showing. I was trying to figure out how to make that work in my favor as I smiled warmly and said, "Mr. O'Donnell?"

Mr. O'Donnell did not smile back. He didn't glare either. He just looked at me.

"Can I help you?" he said.

When I think back on this moment, Me Now wishes that Me Then had answered, "No, you probably can't. Thank you for your time," and turned my back on the inappropriate racist some firm had seen fit to send to a Top 5 law school. Me Then could have used the reclaimed time to bounce back from that bit of surreality and rest up and practice and go into his remaining interviews with renewed vigor. That is certainly what Me Now would do today, knowing what I now know, what I then only suspected, or feared.

But my next thought is that, had I done that, perhaps I wouldn't even be Me Now now. Maybe that would have been a mistake. Maybe the man was legally blind and thought that the blue of my three-piece was actually a jumpsuit and that I was making the rounds emptying trash cans. Or maybe the angry Irish gentleman would have been offended by my militant self-respect and complained about me to the school, blackballing me. Or maybe it was some sort of test and it was actually a great firm. I just didn't know. I couldn't know. And so the second thought that Me Now has is great admiration for Me Then, for being prudent and taking the high road and not shooting off the retort I have carried around for 25 years but rather saying, sweetly, "I am Marcus Hayes? I'm here for my 11:30? Interview?" and upon getting absolutely nothing in return taking tentative steps to the ugly chair on the other side of the desk and sitting on the edge of it and having a little staring contest and, upon realizing that the man was never, ever going to commence the interview, commencing it myself and asking the big red face questions about the firm and receiving yes or no grunts and head gestures for the full 30 minutes before thanking Mr. O'Donnell and backing slowly out of the room.

Push-ups.

Wednesday, October 31, 1990

Things were in full swing at the dojo.

I'd barely been training a year and a half and already I had been "invited" to test for brown belt. Most of the people I'd started with hadn't tested for green yet. The test wasn't for another month, but you were under the microscope long before that. I could feel Sensei's eyes on me when his back was turned.

We were doing basic exercises—crunches and such. We started doing knuckle push-ups. That sounds macho, but knuckle push-ups are better for your wrists. They condition your knuckles, but overall they are not any more difficult than palm push-ups.

We were knocking those push-ups out. The room was steamy and everybody was kiai-ing like crazy. I knew I was in the hot seat, and I welcomed it. I was a lion.

Sensei had crossed the large room in the seconds since I'd last peeked at him, and now he was standing right in front of me. Before I could wonder what was about to happen, I felt weight on my back. Hands. He was leaning down on my back. While I did push-ups.

Sensei's not a big man, but he's not a small man either, and if I were to sit even a little baby down on your back when you were 30 push-ups into some unknown number you might be bummed. But I was in the zone. At that moment, it felt like it wouldn't have mattered if he had stood on my back. I knocked those motherfucking push-ups out. At some point I noticed that my kiais were somewhat louder than those of the students around me, but I didn't care.

I don't know how many more push-ups we did. Maybe just five. But before we stopped I could have gone forever, and as soon as we stopped I could have died.

Sensei gave us a few seconds to recover, and then announced, in an accent so thick that it was basically Japanese, that we were now moving on to one-fisted push-ups, starting with the right fist.

Fine. But I made the mistake of glancing down at my knuckles first.

It is not enough to say that the skin was gone. Of course the skin was gone. And I'd had no idea that there was room for anything you might call "meat" underneath the skin of the knuckle. But on my right hand, middle knuckle, I was looking down into something white. It wasn't bone. Too fleshy. I think it was maybe tendon. Maybe ligament. I forget the difference.

I stared at it. And then. I put. My fist. Down. On the floor. I took. The naked raw bloody. Tissue. That I had just. Looked at. And I put it. Down. On the dirty. Gritty. Wooden. Floor. And I did push-ups on it.

I wasn't *kiai*-ing anymore. I wasn't even just screaming. Rather, my soul was flying out of my mouth. Fleeing. My fellow karatekas stared. I don't know why I did it. I mean, yes, traditional Japanese martial arts training is largely about digging as deep as you can, when you don't have to, so that if one day you really do have to dig deep you can, quickly. But this wasn't traditional Japan. It wasn't even modern Japan. We were in midtown Manhattan in 1990 and I was a law student and I could have just said, "Osu, Sensei. I can't do it. My hand is busted open," and no one would have faulted me. Not even Sensei. But, for whatever reason, I did what I did.

After class had ended, getting ready to leave, I wasn't tired and I didn't hurt. And I had a thought: *This is* my *dojo now. My flesh is ground into the wood. It's mine.*

A few Saturdays later, I spent the afternoon doing katas and sparring and I got my brown belt no problem.

I guess that at the time I figured I was deliberately over-preparing for my life. You know, in an abundance of caution, so that my life would be easy. That's probably what I was trying to do.

Minority Fare.

Monday, November 19, 1990

This is what it's come to.

I scanned the huge room. Naked folding tables filled the space. It was the kind of place where they hold gun shows. We were not on campus. We weren't even in Manhattan. We were in Queens. I felt my face wincing. *Why didn't they just send us to fucking Jersey.*

The big New York law schools collectively put on a Minority Job Fair every year. It was always a few months after the regular job fair, presumably to give us minorities a little time to figure out what was going on and our place in it. Most of our classmates of pallor had stopped interviewing long ago. Almost everyone still wearing a suit to class was swarthy or better.

If the looks on their faces were any indication, my colleagues were as bummed and insulted as I was. For the most part, I was surrounded by the cream of the crop. The Talented Tenth—not just the Talented Tenth of black people; the Talented Tenth of everybody. Smart-looking motherfuckers in the right clothes with the right slim little leather portfolios with their two-page résumés inside. But here we were, in Buttfuck Heights, and we needed jobs. The stakes were high. The job you got your second summer set the high mark for the opportunities that would be available to you the rest of your life. Amalia had snagged her second-summer job weeks ago, but that was at the district attorney's office. It had been her first choice. But the public sector was different. Plus, everyone loved Amalia. Everyone did not love me.

I searched around the room for the table bearing the name of the firm that was my first interview. I found it and hovered nearby. I was a little early, but there was not another interview going on there, and when my eyes met those of the grownup seated alone at the table, he beckoned me over with a smile.

It was an unremarkable interview. Which was what was so remarkable about it. It was pretty much what I had initially expected, way back before Mr. O'Donnell and his brothers and sisters who'd followed. It was normal. The partner who interviewed me, a white guy in his forties, glanced at my credentials—which, judging by the underlines and tiny comments in the margins, he'd already read at least once before I got there—and asked me about them. I gave the answers I'd planned to give. I asked my insightful but standard questions about his firm, and his responses were predictable but enthusiastic. He was friendly. I made him laugh a couple of times. When our time was up we shook and thanked each other, and I got up and left. It wasn't like a scene out of a Spike Lee movie at all.

All of my interviews that day went well. I even had a great interview with the San Francisco office of O'Donnell's "can I help you" firm. They sent a black attorney—a compact, prosperous-looking brother named Evan Madison. Sure, it was pandering to send a black partner to the Minority Job Fair, but they still got props. Most firms that large and well respected had zero black partners to send, even if they wanted to.

By the end of the day, I felt much better. I was downright happy. I think we all were. Our futures *were* assured, just like everyone had always told us. I got it now. They called it the Minority Fair because if they called it the Less-Racist Law Firm Fair someone would complain, maybe even sue. That's just how it was.

This Christmas.

Tuesday, December 25, 1990

In hindsight, she had makeup on. I didn't think much about it. Cute chicks look like they have a little bit of makeup on.

I opened my eyes and her face was about six inches from mine, on the other end of my pillow. She was giving me that "Are you awake yet" look cats give you after they wake you up. I felt vaguely kicked.

"Good morning!" She was laying there, face resting sweetly on folded hands, but she was putting out more heat than I give off when I'm awake. "Merry Christmas!"

"Merry Christmas, baby." I moved in and planted one on her juicy bullseye lips. Cherry lip gloss. Odd.

Shit. I hadn't wrapped her gift yet. I'd only gotten her one thing. But it hadn't been easy, and it hadn't been cheap. Beanie Baby unicorns were more rare than real unicorns. After a month of classified ads and letters back and forth, I'd found a dealer in Iowa. "Dealer" was a fitting word. He knew what he had, and he knew it was Christmastime. So he fucked me. Hard. And I let him. For Amalia.

But that was over now, and there was an exceptionally cute unicorn waiting for my love in my porn drawer. All I needed to do was avoid the whole gift exchange until I'd had a few minutes alone. I decided to make extra coffee; maybe I'd get lucky and she'd have to go poop.

But she had my hand and was pulling me out of the bed. "Come on," she said while she batted her eyes. "Let's see if Santa came."

Shit.

She pulled me into the living room.

Oh.

Santa indeed had come.

Whoa.

Santa had been up for hours.

All of the furniture and other junk had been cleared away, and the floor was covered with a fluffy white blanket that actually did resemble snow. Foot-high gingerbread houses formed a town. I knew that we could and would eat those houses; they probably came from Balducci's. Tiny gingerbread men and women swept off their porches with candy canes.

At the center of Christmasville was what appeared to be the actual Charlie Brown tree. Not only was it real, it was alive. Potted. I wondered what we were going to do with a pine tree. For now, though, it was damn cute. A single red ornament kept it busy.

Next to the Charlie Brown tree, and almost as tall, was a battery-operated dancing Santa. I'd never seen one before. He was black, and doing the hoochie coochie to some fifties-era rockabilly Christmas song I did not recognize.

Santa was doing his bump-and-grind in the direction of a colossal pile of impeccably wrapped packages.

Aw. Shit.

I looked one last time for an escape, but this was happening. Now.

"He came!" She ran the rest of the way into the living room. "Oh, boy!" She plunked down beside the Charlie Brown tree and and handed me a package.

Santa was good to me. Turned out that all of my gifts were actually one gift: a new set of pads. One time—just once—I came home from the dojo and mentioned that my pads were getting worn out already. I'd been sparring a lot.

She'd gotten me everything: headgear, mouthpiece, gloves, shin guards, foot pads, and the biggest goddamn cup I'd ever seen. "Gotta protect my interests," she smiled.

They were all exactly what I would have bought myself—better than I already had. It was perfect. Of course it was. Chick did her homework. In fact, it was entirely possible, I realized—likely, even—that she'd gone to Yan Su and asked Sensei what kind of pads I would like. I tried to deal with that.

There was one more package. "What's this?" she queried to no one. I was about to cop to her gift not being ready. She set upon the box and ripped it open.

"Omigod!" She squeezed the unicorn and buried her face in it. "He's *soooooooooo cuuuuuute!*" She snuggled it until I was jealous. "How did Santa know?"

I just smiled. Amalia was no joke, but neither was I. Mrs. Dr. had been happy to help me brainstorm the perfect gift. Apparently, unicorns had been her thing when she was little. I'd loved this woman since before she was born, before I was born. I wanted to love her then, now, always. And Mrs. Dr. knew it. I'd only called her because I had no one better to go to, but I now think it went a good way toward rehabilitating myself in their eyes.

Amalia pushed me down and lay on top of me and put lip gloss on my face, our Beanie Baby mushed between our bellies. Her mom had kept our secret, but Amalia just knew things. She went and got her gift and wrapped it.

There would be no hiding anything. That was fine.

Stars.

Thursday, January 17, 1991

The restaurant was called Stars. It was a big deal. I'd never heard of it, but I wasn't from here.

The West Coast had changed everything. Whether the people there actually were different or just wanted to appear different didn't matter. All I knew was that, out here, I had the same credentials my classmates had back home.

One minute I'd been riding the Long Island Rail Road out to some tiny firm in Whiteflight, New York for coffee and an apologetic rejection; the next I was at a big round table near a sunny window in a breathtaking restaurant on a street clean enough to eat off of, in a city full of parks and pastels and two cute women making out with each other at an outdoor table across the street.

Except for Evan Madison, who sat opposite me, my six lunch dates were all giant blue-suited white guys. They were easily the nicest giant blue-suited white guys I'd met so far. All were partners at the San Francisco office of Can I Help You?, which was usually called Clay, Conti & Dixon, LLP. The SF office was the headquarters of one of the largest firms in the country, with 500 lawyers worldwide. And Clay Conti—the home office, anyway—wanted me.

The partners were having a good time. I'd come to understand that recruitment season was probably known in some quarters as free lunch season. They whispered like teenage girls, starstruck by other diners. They were particularly enamored of a well-dressed brother two tables over, and it did not appear to be for my benefit. They said he was the speaker of the state assembly. When he glanced over I gave him a nod, which he saw but did not return. Seemed like an asshole to me. Still, a town where it was possible for a brother to run shit was someplace I needed to be. It was almost like I'd imagined Atlanta, only not boring.

Once the partners were good and lit on red wine we opened our menus. Mine didn't have any prices in it. A lady menu. *Is it that obvious that I'm not paying?* Of course it was. I was a baby.

My mom performed the single largest socioeconomic migration I am personally aware of. And this was why she did it. For me. You can be as smart as you want, but if the employers and other shot callers of the world can't smell their own class on you, you won't get as far as you might have. And class cannot really be acquired. It is not a dollar amount; it is a set of expectations. We form our expectations shortly after we arrive on Earth. That is what my mother gave me. I hadn't eaten at a lot of places like Stars, but no place was too good for me.

A waiter appeared, and everybody ordered quickly. I'd been fretting over my pants. *Why does such a fancy restaurant have such linty linens?* When it was my turn to order I wasn't ready. So I skimmed my lady menu and ordered something called "calamari." Sounded Italian. Something with tomato sauce on it, probably. How bad could it be.

"Have you been to Mount Tam yet?" Bill Hughes asked.

"I don't think so. What's the difference between a mountain and a hill?" This got a big laugh. It had been a real question but I let it go.

"Oh, you *must* hike Mount Tam while you're here," Bill said. "There are some fantastic trails out here. Spectacular views."

"Spectacular," Dick Agretelis echoed.

All I must do is stay black and die. And FYI we came in from the spectacular views like 50,000 years ago. If you think that living outside is better than this, you are out of your fucking mind.

"Indeed."

"Yes—enjoy the sights on your vacation," Gilbert Price said. "Because there's no way a New York City kid like you would ever come to California to stay."

Gilbert was the bad cop in my recruitment process. The others paused, watched.

"Of course," I said. "You know, Gil, you being a psychic and all, I would think you'd be an investment banker, not a lawyer. Or at least have bigger clients." Stunned silence, and then hearty laughter all around. Big Bill Hughes pounded the table; he was full-on drunk. Evan laughed too, but he looked more relieved than amused.

"It comes in handy here as well," Gil said, smiling slightly.

I yukked it up with them. I was one of the boys.

Someone put a plate of fried spiders down on the table in front of me.

I examined them. For just a moment, I considered the possibility that the partners were playing a prank. And then I ate the spiders.

I smiled and I bantered and I told my little stories and I daintily ate the most disgusting thing I had ever eaten, seen, heard of, or imagined in my life. And I did it without a trace of ambivalence. I ate those spiders like they were good. I cleaned my plate.

I got an offer in the mail the next week.

A Thousand Words.

Monday, March 4, 1991

If you were black, it was the only thing there was to talk about. A half-dozen LAPD just whaling on some poor guy. A brother. The video was dark, it was grainy, but also it was plain as day.

We watched it over breakfast. Amalia ate and shook her head at the screen. "Typical. Shameful."

"Well—yeah, but . . . look at the bright side, though."

This earned me the blankest expression ever to grace a face.

"We got it on video! On *video*!" I pointed at the screen. Brotherman was still rolling around on the ground. I withdrew my finger. "Look. I feel bad for dude. I do. But, this happens, and also, it happens all the time. Like you said, it's typical. And we got one on tape!"

Her expression didn't change.

I gestured around my glorified dorm room with my spoon. "This is law school, right? We are all about evidence here. This thing between black folks and cops has never been our little secret. But most people in this country don't believe it happens."

"They choose to believe it doesn't happen."

"Yes. True. They choose not to know. They turn a blind eye, because that's part of it. Agreed. But—" and I pointed at the screen again; couldn't help it—"good luck ignoring *this*!" We both looked at the TV. The cops had gotten tired from thumping on this guy. They were standing around, clubs at their sides, like golfers. Then one or another of them would have a flashback about getting picked on in third grade and start swinging his baton on the brother again, back and forth, like crazy.

Amalia took another bite of Angry Flakes and stared at the screen. "They will watch this. And they will say, 'Thank goodness someone videotaped this the very first time it ever happened! Now we can make sure it never happens again.' They will imply that."

"Well, look at you, all cynical!" I laughed. "All cynical and cute and right. Yes, they will say that. But it doesn't matter. Because that's a much less good lie to tell yourself. It's a lot like the thought, 'My boyfriend will never hit me again' compared to 'He'd never hit me at all.' It is a lower-quality idea. It won't hold up as well. But now it's all they have. And it will rot their brains."

She didn't respond, so I guess she gave me that. I turned off the TV anyway.

Alejandro and I huddled in the hallway after our morning class. "I heard that the guy who shot the video is getting death threats," I said.

"Yes," Alejandro replied. "He said that in an interview. Death threats from police."

"White cat, yeah?"

"Yes."

"Well, he's a brother now."

Alejandro nodded.

"All they have to say is that they thought you had a gun," I murmured. "They don't even have to plant one. Pretty sure they used to have to at least plant one on you. Like, back in the sixties. Now they can just say."

Alejandro nodded. "Maybe police don't have access to as many throwaway guns as they used to. Maybe they need to conserve."

"Fuckin' gun control."

It was the talk of the school—sometimes. Like I said, among black folk, it was the only news. And frequently I heard others discussing something in hushed tones. I heard words like, "Terrible!" Something was being roundly condemned. But not to me. As if I hadn't heard? Didn't know? I don't think three white people made eye contact with me that day.

They weren't all cowards. Rachel came up behind me after the last class of the day. "I know it doesn't change anything, not really, but *those* cops will have to be sacrificed. For the sake of the system."

"Yes. Because they got caught."

"Which is the only thing that makes this special. I know . . . it's the exception that proves the rule." She started to walk away.

I touched her elbow. "Yes. But all I've ever known is the rule. So, an exception is actually kind of nice."

I immediately regretted the word *nice*, but she seemed to understand.

As soon as classes were over I went home. *Home* home; where I grew up. I needed my mom. I bet a lot of us needed our mom that day. We sat in the kitchen and drank coffee in the evening for no reason.

"Your day sounds a lot like mine," she said, after letting me unload. "Our neighbors have been as skittish as your schoolmates."

I had not seen that coming. "That's insane. I only just met those fools at school. These people have known us for decades."

"Well," Mom said, "*we* know *them*. This morning, when I was coming back from step aerobics, Doris Kane was walking into the building in front of me, and when she noticed me behind her she broke into a little run to get to the elevator. The elevator door was still open when I walked into the lobby. Doris was smiling at me. But she was also pushing the Door Close button like a madwoman. I smiled back at her and went to the mailboxes and let her go. I knew the mail hadn't come yet. I didn't want to be on the elevator with that any more than she wanted to be with me."

"Wow."

"Mm-hmm. And a little while before you got here, I went down to the laundry room. I stepped out of the apartment with my basket, and while I was locking up, Joan McClendon opened her door. And our eyes met, and she closed the door back. And locked it."

"They're scared of you," I marveled. "Little five-foot-tall business lady. Scared."

"Yes. I haven't seen anything like this since *Roots*. It was on every night for a week. You were still in . . . grade school? Junior high? I don't remember."

"Junior high. Seventh grade."

"That's right. I remember you talked about it in school. I asked you. Your teachers taught *Roots* all that week. That was good for you children. But out in the work world?" She let out a hard chuckle. "Those crackers left us alone. That's how I knew they were watching it too."

We sipped our strong-ass coffee.

"This was before VCRs. Everyone watched a show at the same time. Each night, someone would get raped, or maimed, or killed. And the next day, black folk went to work, like always. But we *wished* someone would say something to us! There was real unity that week." She stared into her cup. "They were united too—united trying not to get jumped on!" Now she laughed for real. "Mm-hmm. They felt guilty. Just like today.

"But here's the thing, baby," she went on, softer. "Here's the thing: *they've* got something to feel guilty about." She reached for my hand across the table; I immediately felt sleepy. "I know, when a drug addict hits a lady over the head and his face is all over the paper and he looks like you, how you feel a little bit responsible sometimes. We've talked about that. And I hope you know that you've got nothing to do with that hoodlum. You didn't raise him. *I* certainly didn't raise him. And he's not raising you. You didn't grow up on the money he took out that lady's purse. He's not a part of you. It's got nothing to do with you. Not with who you are or where you are or how you got there. You don't do it. You don't benefit from it. You wouldn't tolerate it. That's what makes that so different from this. Do you understand what I'm saying?"

I told her that I did.

I did not enjoy watching that video. I was truly sorry it happened. But I was glad that this wasn't just another invisible, forgettable incident. This time, we would see a little justice. They had been exposed. This time, the system would work. It had to.

Another Thousand Words.

Sunday, March 17, 1991

Un. Real.

Not two weeks later. Another grainy video. This one's indoors. A little store. Back east it would have been called a bodega, with Puerto Ricans or some other sort of brown people running it. But they didn't call them bodegas in South Central, apparently, and this one was run by an Asian woman. We see her standing behind the counter, where the security camera is pointed. We see someone wearing a backpack walk into the store, past the counter, and out of the shot. We know that her name was Latasha Harlins. She was 15 years old.

We see Harlins approach the counter, a plastic bottle of orange juice in her hand. The woman behind it—her name is Soon Ja Du—snatches away the girl's backpack. They trade slaps over the counter. Soon Ja Du stumbles, stands, picks up a stool, and throws it at Latasha. She misses. Latasha grabs her backpack with one hand and throws the plastic bottle with the other; she too misses. Latasha says something snarky and turns to walk away.

And the woman reaches under the counter, pulls out a gun, points it at the back of the schoolgirl's head, and fires.

Latasha is dead immediately, before she's even finished falling. You can see it. By the time she hits the floor she's just a doll.

It was on every channel, not quite as often as the video two weeks earlier but often enough that I could watch it every 15 minutes or so for two hours across the various network and cable news shows. I couldn't stop. I couldn't believe that you were allowed to show that on TV. You can't show fake sex but you can show real murder. In prime time. I felt Amalia's concern for me radiating from various parts of the house. She wanted me to turn off the TV and be with her. To be happy. I couldn't right then.

My disbelief faded. As I got used to it, I attempted to focus on the fact that the woman had been arrested. She would be tried and convicted and sent to prison. It wasn't enough; it was hardly anything. But it was all we were going to get. I told myself that it was enough.

Of course, we didn't even get that.

Soon Ja Du was tried, and the video was admitted into evidence, and the jury watched it. And the jury convicted her of voluntary manslaughter, which was fair. Heat of passion, like if you walked in on your wife with another man. And the jury recommended a sentence of 16 years. Which also was fair, considering.

But then the judge—Judge Joyce A. Karlin—disregarded the jury's recommendation and sentenced Soon Ja Du to probation. No prison. Not a day. Five years probation, 400 hours of community service, and a $500 fine.

That night, watching the video over and over, if I had known all that, I don't know what I would have done.

Backup.

Tuesday, July 23, 1991

'Twas the night before the three-day California Bar Exam. Downtown Oakland has a Chinese takeout place every six feet. "You hungry?" I asked. "Maybe you want we should get some takeout?"

"Sure. Do you have any money? I left my purse at the hotel."

"Naw, man, I ain't got no money." I scouted the rest of the block. "Cool—there's a coke machine across the street."

She rolled her eyes. "Why do you still call them that?"

"Takes me back to the good old days. On The Street. All that junk-bond money. Up my nose." I winked. She rolled her eyes again.

I started to jaywalk. "I've got my card. Pick a place."

"That one."

"Bet." I trotted across the street and hit the coke machine.

I went into the takeout joint Amalia had picked and slipped her a twenty. She was the only customer, being served by a little old Asian man. An even littler old Asian lady peeked over the counter at me.

I don't think they realized that we were together.

Amalia seemed to be having the normal experience: *Hi, I'd like the _____, please / OK / That will be $____ / Here you go / Here is your change / Thank you.*

I enjoyed the Special Treatment: *What you want / Hi, can I have the _____ / You got money / Obviously / Show me / See, so can I have the _____ now / We are out of that / OK, can I have the _____ then / It's very spensive /* etc. Granted, the Special Treatment was what I got in New York Chinatown too, but they didn't know that.

Eventually, I was permitted to buy some old-looking shrimp fried rice and a few sad dumplings. I paid and left without fuss. Getting preemptively shot in the head seemed a real possibility.

Silently, we regrouped outside, unstapled our paper bags, and stared down into our takeout cartons, surveying our respective takes. After a moment, I closed my bag and started to head back to the hotel. She caught my arm.

"Hold this." She handed me the bag and her change and went back inside.

I stood outside and listened to a different kind of special treatment: Angry Sister Putting People Through Their Paces. *My food is cold / But / The rice is hot but I think you nuked it / No / Was that beef range-fed / What that / You didn't give me a fork / Yes / No, you didn't / This one's dirty / How long has that dead chicken been hanging there / Let me see your last health inspection certificate* / and on and on and on. She busted those old folks' balls a long time.

Eventually, she came back out, holding three plastic forks, a thick wad of paper napkins, and two cans of Pepsi. She hadn't taken any money in with her. She grabbed her bag from me and dropped in her extorted loot. "Let's go."

We walked awhile.

"Once we move and get settled in and stuff," I said, "we should get married."

"Yes."

West.

Wednesday, August 21, 1991

We'd all seen Rachel off to LA two weeks earlier, and Amalia to San Francisco a week after that.

Now Alejandro and Mom were at the airport with me. A stewardess opened the door to the gate and announced that we were about to board. At that, all pretense of good spirits disappeared.

I took my mother's hands and she squeezed mine really hard.

"Mom . . . I've put this off as long as I can."

"I know."

"I've never been away from you before. Not really."

"Baby, you've got to go. You have to leave here like I had to leave Alabama. You're too good for the life you'd have here."

"Yeah." It was absolutely true that in the city of my birth, I'd gotten one callback interview and zero offers. And all the way on the other side of the country, where I knew no one and had never lived or even visited until a year ago, I'd gotten offers from four top-tier firms, including Clay, Conti & Dixon, the firm I'd signed with. I ate spiders for them; they owed me.

Still. I didn't want to go. I did and I didn't. My bright future waited for me. My beautiful fiancée. Piles of money. Freedom. Nothing on the other side of the scale but this one little lady and if I could have figured out how to bail on the whole thing right there without looking like a punk, I would have. If Mom would've let me. She wouldn't have.

The stewardess announced that my section was boarding. I hugged Alejandro. I hugged my mom a long time, until I felt those little pats she did on my back when she was ready to be done hugging. "You go do this," she said into my ear. "You go get 'em."

We were all smiles again. "Go."

"I'll talk to you tonight."

"OK."

"I'll call you as soon as we land."

"We'll talk soon enough. Go!" She laughed.

I went.

Years later, she told me that her heart had been thoroughly, irreparably breaking.

Life swept us up.

We each spent 12 hours a day at the office, five or six days a week. We worked hard but it all felt very glamorous, very *LA Law*. In January, we did our taxes; when we saw our taxable incomes in black and white we laughed and laughed. And that was for just four months.

We finally started to live together full-time. We wanted to buy a house, but with our newborn careers there just wasn't time to hunt or do all of the business involved. So we rented a little cottage on Steiner, near that row of colorful Victorians on the hill overlooking downtown, the one on all the postcards and the one that everyone who ever comes to SF always takes a picture of like it's the first time. Amalia called it our "Dream Deferred House."

At some point we got married, in a small ceremony at Mrs. Dr.'s AME. Mom already loved Amalia but called her "daughter" for the first time. Our parents met. Mom approved. Dr. and Dr. were visibly relieved.

At work, Evan created opportunities for me, and I took them. On smaller cases, he let me conduct depositions and argue motions. On big cases, he took the lead and I had his back. We were unstoppable.

As a baby DA, Amalia met the expectations her grades had created by winning her first trial two months after she got there. Then she exceeded them by winning another trial a month later.

When we weren't working or playing, we nested. We adopted kittens, a litter of three that could amuse each other when we were at work. The five of us spent entire Sundays in bed.

Money wasn't real. We had everything that could be delivered to us delivered. At night we went to concerts and four-star restaurants, and on long weekends we stayed at B&Bs in beach towns with no other black people in them and terrorized the locals with our smiles and cash.

The world was brighter. The air was sweeter. Everybody loved everybody.

Bizarroworld.

Wednesday, April 29, 1992

It was just after lunch. I was writing a brief. I was trying to explain to the Ninth Circuit why they should make Bank A eat a huge loan that had gone bad, rather than Bank B. The trick was to think of reasons other than *Because Bank B is the one that's paying me.*

The phone rang.

"Marcus."

"Baby! Baby? What's wrong?"

"Do you have a minute?"

"What's the matter?"

"Are you alone?"

I tried to relax. "Yes."

"Have you heard?"

"No. What."

"The jury acquitted those policemen."

I can't really describe how I felt when I heard that. Best I can say is that I felt bad. I felt so bad.

"I wanted you to hear it from me."

"Thank you. I love you."

"I love you too. I am going to let you go now."

"Alright. Thank you, baby." My hands were shaking. "See you soon."

I hung up and sat there.

I had waited so long. We all had. We'd made it through the initial horror of the video and the betrayal of non-black people around us denying what was right in front of them or avoiding us or simply not caring. We sat through all the spin by the pundits and the press going after Rodney King for being an asshole, as if the Penal Code provided that the penalty for being an asshole was to take the beating of a lifetime in the street. We survived the change of venue, when the trial was moved from LA, where the crime occurred, to Simi Valley, former Reagan stronghold and future Trump stronghold. We watched while that classic piece of Americana, the All-White Jury, was impaneled. We sat through the trial, which the press called "the Rodney King trial" even though it was those cops being prosecuted but then actually turned out to be the Rodney King trial after all.

We trusted. We didn't want to trust but we'd had little choice. We trusted and we waited. And this was what we got: not guilty on all counts. Those cops were home by now.

I stood up. I would take a walk around the office. I wasn't thinking clearly—I wasn't really thinking—but it felt like the whole world had just changed, completely, and I wanted to go check out the fishbowls on the ceiling and the potted plants made of feathers and the paintings that were alive.

But it was all exactly the same. Everybody was walking around, or sitting, or standing. Content, or at least resigned. They were all acting like everything was normal.

I went by Evan's office but it was empty and dark.

I wandered down almost every hall in the building—our seven floors of it, anyway—searching for one single thing that made sense. People either ignored me or gave me the too-big smile reserved for the One Black Guy in the Office. I must've been staring at them like they were ghosts.

I made my way back to my office and fell into my chair and stared out the big window for I don't know how long. Maybe an hour. Eventually I swung my chair back around and saw that the *Message* light on my phone was blinking. I hadn't heard it ring.

It hadn't rung. The message was an alert sent to everyone in the firm, in every office, every city, from sea to shining sea: "This is a Clay, Conti & Dixon Telephone Emergency Response System alert to all locations," said a prim female voice that sounded vaguely familiar. The head of HR, maybe. "Rioting has broken out in parts of Los Angeles, and may be starting in other areas, in response to today's Rodney King verdict." Even through my haze I bristled at that term. "All personnel are to conclude their business and proceed to their homes immediately. Contact the managing partner of your office for information regarding transportation in your area, as well as other emergency information. To repeat: all firm locations are hereby closed, immediately and until further notice. Please follow the firm's Telephone Emergency Response System procedures for further instructions tonight, to-morrow, and subsequent days until the current crisis is resolved. Thank you." The message began to repeat. I hung up.

I couldn't believe it. There were cats here billing $400 an hour. All this place did was make money. That was what it was for. And they were telling us all to stop. It was odd enough they were telling us to stop making money in the San Francisco office because there was a riot in LA; they were telling them to stop making money in New York. This was going to cost untold thousands—tens of thousands? Hundreds of thousands?—and they were eating it, *con gusto*. Still, I didn't look a gift horse in the mouth. I left imme-diately. You know, because of the riots.

We stayed up all night, watching the news and talking to friends and family on the phone. It sucked, but it was exciting too. The Revolution meets New Year's Eve.

Unfortunately, the next morning, the Telephone Emergency Response System message was less auspicious: "All of you, get the fuck back to work"—something like that. I wouldn't have showered but Amalia made me.

I returned to the office spent yet refreshed, having vicariously let off steam. I felt better.

I was the only one who felt better. It was the exact opposite of the day before. Today, it was everybody else who looked haunted. They'd been up watching TV all night too. People I'd been around daily for months stiffened when they saw me, or wouldn't look at me at all. At first I was like, *Hey! It's me! Me!* But by lunchtime I was more like, *Boo, motherfucker! Boo!* I went home early to watch more rioting.

They got over it, or whatever they did with it, eventually. But, for me, a certain feeling never went away. It was the realization that that place wasn't just alien; it was positively opposite. From that point on, I thought of the firm as *Bizarroworld.*

Snuggle Sex.

Tuesday, June 30, 1992

"Let's get under the covers!"

My rap had atrophied to this. I didn't have that much game to begin with, and Amalia, being basically down for whatever, ruined what little game I had.

We hustled back to the bed we'd only gotten out of to call in sick. I'd woken just before she had, and we stared at the thick, wet fog blowing past our kitchen window for a while until Amalia spoke for both of us: "No."

It was June and we were bundled up like hobos. I was wearing a full set of sweats over a full set of thermals, and two pairs of socks. Amalia was making some sort of social commentary in two pairs of stirrup pants and an unknown number of Cosby sweaters.

We burrowed into the covers from opposite sides of our king-size bed and came face-to-face, an inch apart, inside our blanket fort. Usually I hate breathing another person's exhale; it's gross, and I think I might asphyxiate. But I wasn't thinking about that. For some time we just stared at each other, grinning like bad children. Her eyes were so shiny.

I kissed her nose and started tugging on her clothes. "Why are you wearing so many *pants!*" I whined. *Shmooooove.* We took off some of our pants.

She pulled off one of my socks. I kissed her on the cheek, put my hand on her waist, and smushed her against me. Then my hand slid down to her butt.

"Bananorama!" she cried.

Turned out, the only thing around our house that needed a safe word was our safe word. It was abused on a regular basis.

I laughed and slid my hand back up to her waist. I kissed her on the lips. Again. The third time I felt her tongue so I barked, "Bananorama!" She laughed into my mouth but then the tongue went away. I got one of her Cosby sweaters off, but when I went for a stirrup I got the safe word so I left it alone. We kissed and rolled around awhile. When she slid her hand down into my remaining pair of pants I unleashed a torrent of *Bananoramas* the likes of which Bananorama themselves have never heard. We howled.

We started getting to it a little more seriously. After a while I noticed I was being touched in places that Amalia wasn't touching. I poked my head out from under the covers. All three cats were lying across us. I've never been sure what cats think people are doing when they are messing around. Maybe cleaning each other. Maybe just cuddling. Anyway, it was a group scene now.

Cuddling is as satisfying as sex if you do it right, and I was happy to do our "pile of kittens" thing for a while. But we were pretty far down the sex path. Not to the Point of No Return, but probably the Point of Uncomfortable Return.

I didn't care, and I suspected Amalia felt the same way, but I still wanted to check. So I went back under the covers and peeked at her. "It's *all* love," she replied. We smooched a little more, then shifted waistbands and other elastic bits to places that were more sustainable. We popped our heads out of our love fort and looked at the babies. The purring immediately doubled in volume and intensity. We were literally a pile—Amalia was half draped over me, Jimi and Suki were sprawled across both of us, and Nia was on me with her head on Jimi's belly. My limbs were twisted and random, like someone who has fallen out of a moving car. We purred. I think I fell asleep.

Two Papers.

Monday, July 6, 1992

I started reading two newspapers a day. This was back when San Francisco had a morning paper (the *Herald*) and an afternoon paper (the *Inquisitor*). This was also before the *Inquisitor* became a piece of shit. I had subscriptions to both.

I started reading two papers as soon as I realized that another way the partners were hazing us associates, besides piling on impossible amounts of work, was by quizzing our awareness of current events. This came in the guise of small talk.

They knew that we were all spending 80% of our waking hours doing billable work. In fact, had they known that any one of us was not spending 80% of their waking hours doing billable work, that person would have been fired. But at the same time, we were not allowed to become law monks, tunnel-visioned mole people with no awareness of the world around them. We'd be less profitable to them that way.

If those were the rules, that was fine by me. No way those fools were going to catch me sleeping. If they wanted to play Trivial Pursuit, we'd play.

So every morning I read the *Herald*, on the bus on the way to work, or sometimes first thing in my office. Reading it in my office was not ideal, because much of the quizzing took place on the elevator up to work at 7:30 in the morning. "Marcus! Think they're gonna filibuster that reform bill?" "Morning, Dick! I don't think they have the votes. It'd look too bad if they try and it passes anyway. Personally, I think the president has the moderates locked up and they're keeping that quiet. Have a great day, Dick!" I was pretty sure that partner was named Dick. Most were.

Unfortunately, I was thorough. I didn't just read the watercooler stuff. I read the whole paper.

The most fucked-up stories in the paper are the tiny ones. Usually they are in the back, but occasionally they are perfect for plugging in a blank space at the bottom of page 3. Sometimes they are mindblowing, like FIRST CYBORG CREATED (seriously—there was a story about a petri dish somewhere that contained a few living cells and a tiny microchip, living together as a single integrated organism). But usually they were horrible, like GRANDMOTHER SHOT BY POLICE (seriously—her name was Eleanor Bumpurs).

The paper was full of those. Every day. December 29: FAMILY FREEZES TO DEATH IN VAN. May 3: WOMAN CONVICTED OF MURDERING 3 CHILDREN SENTENCED TO PROBATION. July 16: HANGING WAS NOT A HATE CRIME, SAYS SHERIFF. October 12: STUDY SHOWS MOST AMERICANS READ AT A THIRD-GRADE LEVEL. And more. And more. Every single day.

My attempts to chat with the partners about those stories always failed, and I soon stopped trying. But I kept reading them. And I came to think of them as the real stories, the important ones, despite the fact that no one else read them. *Because* no one else read them. Someone had to.

Duck Season.

Monday, November 16, 1992

"Which way is Columbus?" No *Hello* or *Excuse me* or preface of any kind.

The cop turned to me. He was smiling. Wasn't expecting that. And he didn't stop smiling when he saw me. Really wasn't expecting that.

The cops here were better than they were in New York. Couldn't deny that. I'd been robbed by cops in New York. And even though I'd barely been in SF a year I was a respectable adult here, whereas back east I'd been a schoolkid. So my relationship with the police was changing. But cops were still, for the most part, cops. Even here. After all, it had been right here in San Francisco, just the day before, that Jarrold Hall had an exchange with Officer Fred Crabtree like I was having now.

Yesterday, Jerrold Hall was a smartass, like me, in the Bay Area, like me. And, like me, Jerrold had a talk with a cop. Unlike me, Jerrold was a teenager, and not a corporate attorney in the business district in broad daylight. Also, Jerrold didn't start it. Nonetheless, at the close of their conversation, Officer Crabtree decapitated Jerrold Hall with his shotgun as the young man walked away. Crabtree told investigators that he'd thought Hall was going to get a gun and come back. And that was that.

And about a week earlier, two police officers in Detroit beat a man's skull open with their flashlights for no reason. Well, I would call it no reason. The reason the officers gave was that the man—his name was Malice Green— had refused to open his hand and show them what tiny object he held in his palm. It might have been crack. So they broke his head into pieces on the street. Nobody cared.

I glanced pointedly at the cop's nameplate: *OFFICER C. CREELEY.* His smile wavered a bit, but held. He looked away and up over my shoulder, and pointed. "Columbus is about five blocks that way, up the hill. It runs almost parallel to this street—"

"What time is it?" Back then, a lot of us brothers referred to the times in which we lived as Duck Season. We were the ducks. And if *I* knew that Officer C. Creeley could kill me and probably get away with it, he sure as hell knew. But that didn't mean I had to accept it. I wasn't going to hide.

Officer Creeley regarded my face with mild disbelief. His eyes moved to my wrist, and the large Movado on it. It cost a week of his pay and looked like it. I was in gray flannel, with a Brooks Brothers trench and a fancy umbrella. I should have been wearing a bowler.

He didn't appear angry. I'd expected him to get mad. I didn't want him to beat my ass or kill me, but I knew that if he did, he wouldn't get away with it. I knew too many people. That was the most I could ever hope to expect from the law: not protection, but revenge.

But Officer Creeley didn't want to kill me. He just wanted to go home. The cop sighed and lifted his wrist and looked at his Timex. "One-thirty."

"Thanks," I said. I walked past him, away from Columbus. I felt his eyes on me. I think I heard him sigh again.

That went OK. Next time, I won't say thanks.

Yuppie Flu.

Monday, January 4, 1993

"Can you go without me, please? I made a list . . ."

This was not the first time, but it was the first time it annoyed me. This had almost become our routine: Amalia and I would make plans to run errands together and then, at the last minute, she'd bail. Because she was "tired."

I'd never thought of her as lazy before. But I was tired too. In fact, I hadn't even known that being tired was a reason not to do something. I wondered why she was comfortable laying the "tired" explanation on someone working 60 hours a week.

She'd worked 60-hour weeks too, for a while, and had been kicking more ass than I was. Then, after less than a year and without talking to me about it first, she dropped down to an 80% schedule. I didn't mind. We were fine on money. A couple of months after that, she dropped down to 60%. Again without talking to me. No one at the DA's office asked her any questions about it, apparently; maybe they'd assumed that she was pregnant. She wasn't.

She started researching things. Health things. One day I came home from work and she told me she had allergies. Another day, she was environmentally sensitive. "I'm sensitive too," I'd responded, but she thought I was joking. Then she'd told me she had something called Epstein-Barr virus. I'd never heard of it, but apparently my wife was, as usual, on the cutting edge, because soon after that I started to hear about it everywhere. As part of the pop media takeover of the issue, the name was changed to "chronic fatigue syndrome" and then, simply, the "yuppie flu." I liked that name best.

And, frankly, I was a little bit hoping I'd catch it. At my job, a 40-hour workweek was considered part-time. Literally—you had to go to HR and get written permission to work 40 hours a week, and you probably wouldn't get permission unless you were pregnant or dying. And, whether you got permission or not, just for asking you could kiss partnership goodbye forever. But two yuppie flu cases working two days a week each would still make more money than my mom ever did. So, yeah, I was looking forward to catching the buppie flu too. But I never caught it. I was fine.

Amalia was sitting up in our bed, surrounded by large pillows. She held a slip of paper out to me and tried to smile. I nodded and walked up to the bed and took the carefully prepared shopping list and I gave her a kiss on the cheek and left and did the shopping.

I did not nag her; I did not complain. I did not call her lazy. I kept my mouth shut. That was pretty much a first for me.

Nice Try.

Friday, February 26, 1993

I was making dinner in my work clothes. Amalia was sleeping. She'd been sleeping when I left that morning. The TV was on. Dinner was almost ready; I was trying to decide whether to wake her when the mindless crap I wasn't listening to was interrupted by a Special Bulletin. The World Trade Center had been bombed!

I stopped slicing garlic and turned to the screen. False alarm, pretty much. Car bomb in the underground parking lot. Six dead. Cabbies kill more than six people in a Manhattan afternoon.

I went back to my garlic. *Alright, terrorists! Way to swing for the fences.*

We're from Marin.

Wednesday, March 3, 1993

A *baby!* In a wasteland as sterile and joyless as a law firm, a baby is an irresistible beacon of cuteness. I pulled up to the edge of the crowd and started working my way inward, like a sperm.

Carlos Lopez was officially coming back from paternity leave next week; this was just a quick recon visit. Carlos was my hero because he was the first man I'd ever heard of risking his job to take paternity leave. But also Carlos was most certainly *not* my hero because he insisted on pronouncing his name *Carliss*. Carliss Lopes. At first I took this as an insult to the intelligence of everyone in the building. But later I learned that when white people like you, they pretend that you are white too. So that they don't have to hate you. Carliss was just getting with the program.

Carlos had also come by to show off his good-looking family. Marie was gorgeous. Glamorous. She dressed like Mayflower trash, and she acted like it too, and she almost *almost* looked like it but for what real Mayflower trash might call a vaguely "ethnic" complexion. I harbored a strong suspicion that Carliss's lovely Marie was really *Maria With a Silent A*.

The baby was ridiculous. Eleanor (*Eleanor?* Seriously?) was a perfect six-month-old, happy and drooly and fat. She was wearing a red sundress. You knew that somewhere there was a matching hat.

Being yuppies, Carliss and Mari(a) had all the cutting-edge baby technology. As we stood around adoring the baby, Mari(a) scooped some organic apple sauce into a large plastic bowl and slammed it down on the tray of Eleanor's travel high chair. Eleanor (seriously—Eleanor?) immediately grabbed the bowl with both hands, presumably so that she could throw it at us. She struggled with the bowl. I was starting to think that those thick guns she was rocking were just for show, until I saw that the underside of the bowl was a huge suction cup. I felt proud to be an adult. *They still have all the power, but at least we're smarter.*

"If this law thing doesn't pan out, I'm selling baby accessories," I said.

"I'm in. Let me know when I should pack up my office," Dick Morrison said. Pretty sure his name was Dick.

"And I'll take one of everything," Mari(a) smiled at me. I suppressed a shudder. *The only thing scarier than that perfect face smiling at you every morning would be taking it for granted.*

Eleanor gave up on trying to throw her glop at us and regarded the crowd, digging the scene with a gummy grin. Like me, many of my colleagues seemed to think that a baby looking at you is good luck or something. When her eyes landed on someone, they would make a surprised, delighted sound. People who'd barely spoken to me were making fools of themselves over this fat baby. I was liking them a little better. I searched for Evan, but he wasn't there.

Eleanor's eyes met mine and stayed there. After a few seconds it became evident that she was no longer scanning the crowd but was now staring at me. At *me*! I tried not to make too many cooing noises as I stared back and sucked up the baby rays that Eleanor was beaming at me from her giant eyes.

We must have been locked like that for 30 seconds—me trying not to coo, Eleanor fixated with a blank expression. I was about to start asking her who was a little baby when Mari(a) lifted Eleanor out of her chair and began fussing with the sundress. She seemed different now. I looked around. So did the others. They all had the same blank gaze the baby did. Which was odd—she had been smiling a moment ago. So had everybody else. Before the baby noticed me. Until she noticed *me*.

Oh.

The others had beat me to it. Suddenly the educational children's song *Which of these things is not like the others / Which of these things just doesn't belong* started playing in my head. Only faster. And it sounded kind of evil. While Mari(a) fake-fussed over the baby, I thought for the first time about the implication of that song: that which is not the same does not belong. *Never too young for that, I guess.*

After a little while, Mari(a) got the baby and herself together. She put Eleanor back in her high chair, then lifted the whole thing up and rotated it 90 degrees so that the baby couldn't see me anymore. And she turned to me and looked me straight in the eye and said, "We're from Marin."

Just a hint of apology. But not too much. It was simply an explanation.

It took me a minute. This was relatively new for me. In New York City, there are black people everywhere. Not in Bensonhurst or Howard Beach, obviously, but those places are not in Manhattan, and so they are not New York. There are black people in New York, everywhere you go. Upper east side, upper west, lower east—even Chinatown. We may or may not be running shit, but we are at least physically present. But in the oh-so-liberal San Francisco Bay Area, there are neighborhoods and cities and entire counties with zero black people in them. Amalia and I had seen them. Places like Marin County. Or like this building on days I called in sick.

I smiled at Mari(a) and shrugged, as though her explanation was reasonable and not insane. She didn't seem that cute anymore. Neither did the baby. I stood around another minute. Then I went back to work.

Night Night.

Sunday, March 28, 1993

At least things were good at home. No, they weren't. But we didn't know it yet. One particular memory stays with me, although it was not, for us then, unusual. It's just a flash of a memory. A few seconds. Us kissing good night and turning out the light and going to sleep. I went to sleep lying down. Amalia went to sleep sitting up. She could no longer lie on her back. Hadn't been able to for some time. Weeks? Months? All we knew on that night was, if she did lay back, she would immediately be overwhelmed by a feeling of panic and some pain. And so, like the old joke, she didn't lay back.

I don't know why we didn't question this further, or at all. I mean, we were two legal eagles (one on hiatus), young, gifted, and black, from savvy towns and with savvy parents, and we questioned everything. But the inability to lie down, this routine of sleeping sitting up, propped on pillows like the Elephant Man—this, somehow, was a given. We didn't know what was wrong, but I guess we thought we'd figure it out eventually and, until we did, this was our solution. Problem solved! There wasn't anything wrong, really. Not really.

Today, I have no illusions about how wrong I can be. I know how wrong I can be.

Siege.

Monday, April 19, 1993

The siege in Waco, Texas was ending badly.

There were tanks—tanks!—rolling into buildings, knocking down walls. Fires raged. Gunfire popped and cracked.

The talking heads providing voice-over support for the siege were beating the Ruby Ridge comparisons to death. About a year earlier, the FBI had raided some white separatist's "compound"; people got hurt. A few got killed. The public was outraged.

I lived my life a little worried that I would be shot in the head by a cop or a cashier or just some nobody who saw me running to catch a bus. Generally, black people aren't outraged when another black person is killed while committing a crime. We don't love it, but it doesn't offend some sense of how the world should be. All our spare outrage gets taken up by the murders of black people guilty of walking, or standing, or sleeping.

This was before I'd ever heard the term "white privilege." But I now know that it describes the anger of those shrill newscasters over the gunfight at Ruby Ridge. How shooting at some nazi who'd shot at you first was even newsworthy was beyond me, what with all the genuine atrocities that get reported exactly once, or not at all.

Waco, however, seemed a somewhat different story. Freaking tanks!

Taking in the carnage at Waco, I had no idea that Randy Weaver, the nazi who'd gotten himself into the gunfight at Ruby Ridge a year earlier, would become the poster child for a movement. I didn't know that exactly two years after Waco, Tim McVeigh would mark the anniversary in his own way. But I remember that I did not like how things were looking. I did not like the feeling in the air.

It was a spectacle, at least. Dinner was late that night. Amalia was sleeping anyway.

Crossing the Street.

Monday, June 28, 1993

Both finally and suddenly, things came to a head.

"Baby? What's the matter?"

Her fork was on the table. Her hand was on her chest. She was staring down at her omelet.

"I. Can't. Breathe."

I called a cab.

Thirty minutes later, we were in the office of Sandra Fallstich, Amalia's primary physician. Thirty minutes after that, Dr. Fallstich confessed that she had no idea what was wrong. So I called Saint Ignatius Medical Center, which was across the street, and told them to expect us.

We were on our own getting across the street to the hospital. Something about liability. And so my wife threw her arm over my shoulder and I pulled it tight around my neck with one hand and held her waist with the other and we jaywalked across Divisadero, one of the biggest, busiest streets in San Francisco. I wanted us to go down to the corner and cross at the light, but Amalia wasn't having it. She said she wouldn't make it.

Limping together across Divis, huffing and puffing, cars whizzing by, hospital both right in front of us and impossibly distant, our denial finally fell away. We left it lying in the street. In hindsight, she'd been sick for almost a year.

Call, Interrupted.

Thursday, July 1, 1993

Amalia was all I could think about. But life went on, dragging my body with it. I had to let it. If nothing else, we needed my health insurance. Amalia was now a guest at one of the most expensive hospitals in the country, and we had no idea what was wrong with her.

So I went through the motions. I left my wife in a hospital and I did what I had to do.

Twenty minutes into a meeting at the offices of another firm, a smoking-hot secretary strutted into the main conference room, gracefully laid a note down in front of one of the partners, and fled. The note was upside down from where I sat, and it was written in loopy script, so I didn't get to read all of it before the partner snatched it up. I did, however, make out the following: *There is a sniper in the bldg. across the street.*

I scanned the room. Their temple resembled ours. Big. Brightly lit. Long, shiny wooden table with a dozen cushy armchairs around it. And a honking-huge picture window. Floor-to-ceiling, wall-to-wall, looking out onto another tower filled with identical people. Only that tower also had a guy with a rifle.

I waited for the partner who got the note to say something. Something like, "Let's get out of here." He didn't. He just sat. The meeting droned on. *Is this fucknut really going to let us all hang out in the crosshairs?* It appeared that he was.

I considered my options:

1) I could say something. *Hey, Dick. Couldn't help but notice that some-one just told you there's a fucking sniper across the street. You wanna wrap this up?*

Negative. I was the most junior person at the table. My job was to sit there and look pretty, then go back to the office and do all the work. If I said something, even if the room got shot up the second we left, no one would appreciate my candor. It would be said that I spoke out of turn and disrupted the meeting. Interfered with billable business. I could get fired. A year ago, angry black people in LA had everybody running home. But a (probably) white guy actually shooting people across the street right now required more deliberation. That's just the way Bizarroworld was. And losing this job was no longer an option. The health insurance.

2) I could discreetly tell John (the partner I was with) and pressure him to leave, or at least to let me leave.

This too did not seem promising. For one thing, he might not want us to leave. John was something of a thrill-seeker. He put in a lot of pro bono time suing, and bankrupting, hate groups, which was what I liked about him. But, as a result of that, he was on a lot of hit lists, which was what he liked about himself. If anybody ever even just smacked John he would realize how not cool being on a hit list is. But it was too late for that now. No. John might tell me to sit tight.

3) I could just pack up my briefcase and go.

I was liking this option better. I could say—whatever. My pager went off. Sudden, explosive diarrhea. Had to get home for Shabbat. Didn't matter. Only, they might try to stop me. I could not rule out the possibility that one of these millionaires would respond to me with some statement that began with the word "Nonsense!" and tell me it would only be a few more minutes and make me sit in front of that big window for another hour. Or two. *Make me.* Ugh.

Whoever this guy was, the sniper, he was downtown because he hated lawyers. That was obvious. There was nothing downtown but lawyers and bankers and places for us to eat lunch. And we were lawyers. That too was obvious. A dozen men and women, mostly men, all white but one, in navy pinstripe suits, some with our jackets hanging on our chairs behind us and our sleeves cutely rolled up like we were working. Hell. *I'd* shoot us.

My head felt very big.

I mouthed the words "Excuse me" to no one in particular and scooted sheepishly away from the table and tiptoed toward the door. I all but said, "I have to pee."

I stepped out into the hall and the heavy frosted-glass conference room door closed slowly behind me. I did have to pee. So I wandered down a hallway until I found the Men's. Then I left.

The elevator was a tomb. The lobby was a madhouse. The police were using it as a staging area. Or maybe they'd have called it a "command center." The 10-foot-high glass lobby doors were propped open and the noise blew in, along with scraps of paper and the exhaust of a dozen trucks with motors running. Older cops in fancy uniforms conferred with men in suits. The lit glass "You Are Here" building directory was covered over with a blueprint of the building across the street; geeks and stormtroopers pored over it. Nobody paid me any mind. I tried to look official.

Jacket and briefcase still upstairs at the table, I crossed the lobby and stepped out into the street, where it was all megaphones and dudes in tactical gear and good-looking people talking at cameras. The yellow tape keeping out the rubberneckers was a block away. A giant Aryan holding an assault rifle stood to my left. He smiled at me. Dude had been waiting for years to break out his toys for real. To my right stood one of the more established newscasters—Tamara Jones, who'd been on one of the affiliate news shows back east when I was a kid, and thus had been a major depositor at my teenage spank bank. She still looked good. I sidled up close enough to hear but not so close as to be a jerk.

"Sue, we are hearing reports that the death toll so far may be as high as six—six dead, and counting," Jones said into the camera, with just a touch of glee. "And we now understand that the gunman is moving through the building, opening fire on occupants. Police are moving to intercept, but the location . . ."

So, not a sniper. Cool. I took off.

I was lucky that my wallet was in my pants pocket and not my jacket. I hopped a bus. Traffic was a clusterfuck; a 20-minute ride took over an hour. I called Amalia at the hospital as soon as I got home.

"I am *so* glad to be talking to you. I've been lying here watching this craziness. It's on all the channels. I assumed you were safe, but . . ."

"I'm alright. We're alright. Neither of us is anywhere near that mess anymore."

"Anymore? Your office is on Montgomery. Where were you today?"

I told her.

"Oh, Marcus. Oh, Marcus. You could have just as easily been meeting in *that* building. He is attacking a law firm. They say he was a client."

I hadn't thought about that. Across the street was close enough. But the people inside really couldn't leave. They were hiding—some of them unsuccessfully. Suddenly I felt a whole new level of tired.

"Baby, if you don't mind, I know I was supposed to visit you tonight . . ."

"Don't you dare leave our house. I need to know that you are home. It isn't only this one sick man. He doesn't have long. But it is a war zone out there. I saw soldiers. Actual soldiers. I need you to stay put. Mama and Papa are both here with me."

"Thank you, baby."

"Promise me you'll stay put."

"I promise. Now you promise me."

We both had a good laugh over that one; she wasn't going anywhere. "I promise too."

"OK then."

"Hmm? Marcus, Mama wants to speak to you."

"Marcus?"

"Mrs. . . . uh, Dr. . . . ?"

"Call me Mama."

"OK."

"You were going to try to make it to the hospital tonight? After . . . that?"

"Yeah . . . ma'am . . . ma?"

"Marcus?"

"Yeah?"

"You're a stand-up guy."

My chest quivered. I felt more relief than I'd felt when I escaped the kill zone.

"Yes ma'am, I am. I try to be. Whatever I am, it's hers."

"I can see that. Thank you."

"No. Seriously. Thank *you*. For her. I don't even know how you did that."

She laughed. I hadn't heard her laugh in some time. "We didn't do much. I'm going to give you back to her. Good night, Marcus. Be well."

"You too. Good night, Mama."

Amalia said she was tired, so we said our good nights and hung up.

The kittens and I watched the news all night. The cops didn't get to kill the shooter; he killed himself, eventually. Eight dead, not counting him. An absolutely anemic death toll by New York standards, but it was too much for San Francisco.

All of the talking heads blamed the guns. They didn't seem to notice the crazy fuck attached to them. I think they might have held a black shooter somewhat more accountable. But as it was, one person killing several other people was somehow society's fault.

When I showed up at work the next day, my jacket and briefcase were sitting in the guest chair of my office. John must have brought them back with him. We never spoke of it.

Pamphlets.

Friday, August 6, 1993

When doctors have bad news for you, first they give you a pamphlet. There seems to be one for every occasion. The bad-news-pamphlet industry must be a billion-dollar business. Hallmark for hospitals.

As Amalia's primary physician, it was Dr. Fallstich's job to deliver all the bad news of the specialists. The first pamphlet she gave us was entitled, "So You Might Have Cancer." I'm sure we were supposed to read that in a solemn, firm, compassionate tone, the way Linda Hunt or Morgan Freeman might read it. But, after a lifetime in New York, all I could hear was Old Jewish Lady: *So you might have cancer? Oy! I know from cancer!*

On the cover of the pamphlet was a picture of a tree.

Dr. Fallstich fulfilled her legal and ethical obligation to say words to us in a room. Mostly I stared at the tree. I was supposed to be taking notes and asking questions. But that tree held some strange hypnotic power. I wondered if there was something hidden in the drawing, the visual equivalent of a subliminal message, firing up unknown synapses in my brain. It felt a lot like being high.

The Talking Stick.

Monday, August 9, 1993

Another week of going through the motions. Amalia was home from the hospital at least. Mama and Mr. Dr. were with her every moment they could be, which was a lot of moments. They understood I had to keep the health insurance going.

I needed to hustle. I'd run out of work. By now, most of my fellow associates had bonded with one or more partners, and they got their billable hours in by working on whatever cases their partner was working on.

But I had chosen badly. Lately Evan was in the Dubai office more often than not, doing financial stuff with some other associate. I couldn't blame him for avoiding these people, but he had stuck me with them. Sometimes I wondered if he had recruited me to be his replacement.

I was struggling to keep up. More and more, when Evan was not around, I was going to Anne Shimoguchi, the firm's official staffing partner, for work.

Anne's door was open. I stood in the doorway and tapped on the wood. The expression on her face after she saw me made me wonder if I was still sporting the mask from that *Alien* costume I'd worn in the Castro last year. Then she smiled. A lot.

"Oh! Marcus! Come in!"

I did. "Hi, Anne." I sat.

We smiled at each other but nothing much else was happening so I said, "Well, it's that time again."

"I'm sorry?" She seemed more confused than sorry.

"Time for another assignment?" *You know, the only reason you and I ever talk?*

"Already?"

"Yes. Dick Buckley and I filed that motion to dismiss in the patent case. It was granted last week."

"Really?"

I kept smiling, but that took all my energy, so I just sat there until she got off her butt and walked over to the file cabinet where she kept the dregs. The staffing partner's inventory was made up of the cases that my colleagues viewed as beneath them, or that required working with partners no associate would ever deal with voluntarily.

She flipped through files a long time. *Is she searching for a case that's hard enough? Or one that's easy enough?* Eventually, she settled on one—she closed the file cabinet—but she continued to stand there and read it. She turned around and looked at me, then turned her back again and read some more. I passed the time by staring at her legs. Finally, she returned to her seat.

"An employment case!" she announced without handing me the file. "Maddox versus Western Industrial." She didn't bother saying which party we represented; we didn't do people. "Harold Maddox alleges that he was wrongfully terminated by his supervisor, one Helga Petrov." I would have gotten that from the first paragraph of the complaint. I focused on my breathing and practiced patience. I got to practice patience a lot.

Anne stared at me so long I started to wonder if she was going to ask if I wanted to fuck. But then she said, "You would be perfect for this case. Mr. Maddox, the plaintiff, is a black . . . I'm sorry . . . a black . . . gentleman. He is alleging racial discrimination." She stared some more. "You would be perfect for this case because—it would just be good if, when people looked at the . . . you know, the parties and the lawyers sitting at the tables in the courtroom, that they couldn't automatically tell which side was which. The jury, for example. Or a reporter. It would look better. For us."

I have to come to believe that my poker face is my greatest professional asset, more valuable than my ability to digest large amounts of information or my problem-solving skills or my writing. Because I could have all of those other abilities but, if people could see on my face what I think of some of the shit they say to me, they wouldn't want to work with me. People don't want to be around a mirror all day.

Anne finally handed me the file. I thanked her and left.

Back in my office, I reviewed the file. I had a dozen or more witness statements spilled out across my desk, even though we'd only received the complaint five days earlier. It was as if Western Industrial had been building a file on Maddox for most of the six months he'd worked there.

I was bored at first, skimming the statements of Maddox's colleagues, until it dawned on me that pretty much everything Maddox's employer was saying about him, my employer could say about me.

Mr. Maddox was moody, sometimes even surly. He did not participate in all of the social events at the company. (Not "any"; "all.") He sometimes had political disagreements with his colleagues. His coworkers didn't feel that they had a sense of the person, or his personal life. He wasn't fitting in. This was why they fired him, they said.

His work was fine.

Then there was the stick.

The file contained statements from three different employees at Western, two of them managers, stating that on a certain date three months earlier they had witnessed Mr. Maddox on the elevator or in the hallway carrying a large stick. Apparently, he didn't threaten or attack anyone with it; if he had, I think they would have mentioned that. He didn't brandish it in any way. He just entered the building, rode the elevator, and walked down the hall to his cube. Carrying a stick.

A goddamned talking stick. I knew it was a talking stick because I had one too.

My in-laws knew that I was struggling. One day I came home from work and Mrs. Dr.—I mean Mama—had left me a flyer for a support group at her church. A support group for black men. For the last couple of months, when I could, I was making a little pilgrimage to Oakland after work on Tuesdays. (The prohibition on Negro congregation was still unofficially in effect in most parts of San Francisco.) Mainly we talked about the challenges of being black in this insane motherfucker. We didn't talk about how to change it or anything. More or less we just looked around and said, "Shit is crazy, man," and then nodded. Or, better, "They are crazy, man." And nodded. There was this older cat who used to say things like, "Hello, my people. I'm Wazir, and I am recovering from slavery." "Hi, Wazir!" we'd respond. It sounds silly. But, much like the dojo, it turned out to be just what the doctor ordered. These people, the Stewarts—they got me.

Anyway, we had a talking stick. *Support group* + *black people* + *nineties* + *Bay Area* = *talking stick*. I loved that stick. It was a long, polished piece of knotty old dark wood decorated with beads and strings and a couple of feathers. One of those brothers had gone all out making (or buying) that talking stick. It had good mojo. We took turns taking the stick home after a meeting ended and bringing it back the next week. It was an honor, as well as a way of making sure you came back.

About a month ago it was my turn. I brought the talking stick home. Amalia made *us* use it all week. When Tuesday rolled around again, I put on a black double-breasted suit and some oxfords and I picked up my briefcase and my big African talking stick and I went to the office. I would take the stick to the meeting after work.

I sat there at my desk with the Maddox file in front of me and I flashed back on riding the elevator at work with my stick. It had been crowded and more than a little tense. At the second floor, I moved aside to let a woman out and a tall, pinched-up-looking man to my side raised his arms in a sad and impotent block. Even though we had not yet coined the term "workplace violence," at the time it felt a bit like folks thought I was fixing to go crazy and swing my stick at them and fuck up everybody on the elevator for no reason. At the time, I largely dismissed my impressions as exaggerated. Also, I thought it was funny.

And now, here I was, reading about myself. A plaintiff with absolutely no chance of winning. The fix was in on every level. Judge and jury alike had been thoroughly bred not to believe Harold Maddox, or to care if they did. And the state of the law made the facts almost irrelevant anyway. Without a doubt, this case would not survive our first motion. Maddox v. Western Industrial was an easy win for whoever took it.

I returned all the papers to the file in the order I'd found them. I closed the file and carried it out of my office and back to Anne's. Her door was still open. I knocked on the jamb.

Anne glanced up at me and jumped again.

"I can't do this," I said, walking in uninvited. "This case. I can't do it."

For some reason, I expected her to argue, to ask me to explain why. But she just took the file and said, "OK!" more brightly than I'd ever heard her say anything to me before. "I'll find something else for you! Can I get back to you?"

"Sure!" I said. "Thanks!"

I went back to my office and read the paper.

The Introduction.

Thursday, August 19, 1993

Ignatius was becoming my second home, and Amalia's first.

It had not been hard to figure out that there was something inside her chest; it pressed down on her heart when she lay on her back. And after the X-ray we knew it was the size of a softball. But we still didn't know what the fuck it—or "the mass," as they called it—was.

My first thought was surgery—go in, look at it and, ideally, remove it. They didn't want to do that. Lots of doctors tried to explain why. The only explanation that made sense to me came from a nurse: "We don't want to make it mad."

It was the beginning of the long rite of passage known as Watching Doctors Shrug at You. They literally shrug. On TV, doctors always know. Always. And if they don't know, they look you in the eye and they vow to find out. And then they do find out, and they fix it. In real life, they look you *almost* in the eye and say, "I performed the procedure. I met the applicable standard of care. The results were inconclusive." (This is when they shrug.) "That'll be $35,000." If you haven't seen a doctor shrug at you, you will. And then you will die.

Mr. Dr. was, of course, her unofficial primary care physician. But there's only so much a colorectal surgeon can do about a softball in his daughter's chest. So he worked behind the scenes, getting referrals, vetting said referrals, and having unofficial follow-up meetings where he asked the questions we didn't know to ask. His reports to us were warmer, and infinitely more reliable. But basically he was shrugging too.

At this point, though, there were still more tests they could do, and now we were getting an MRI. I mean, she was getting one. It had taken two weeks for a slot to open up. That's a long time to wait when you have a softball in your chest. Or when your wife does.

Even though the appointment was for 11:00 they came and got us at 9:00. Mama and Mr. Dr. had to wait in Amalia's room, but the nurse let me follow when she pushed Amalia's wheelchair to the on-deck waiting area next to the MRI room in the basement.

The place was a mill. Whenever I hear folks talking about GMOs and power lines and pesticides and plastics leaching into food, I remember that MRI room. Business was very good. By 9:30 a considerable line had formed behind us. The customers covered almost the entire spectrum of ill health: from standing outpatients to seated inpatients to short-timers lying on gurneys. Most were accompanied by a single companion in street clothes; we covered pretty much the entire spectrum as well. To this day, when I hear people talk about side effects and free radicals and secondhand smoke, I think of that room. That long line of sick people. One after another, badda bing badda boom, world without end.

The staff kept things moving, and by 10:45 we had next. An MRI machine looks like a Stargate. A huge off-white plastic ring with a table coming out of the center, all by itself in the middle of a large, sterile-looking room. A tech operates the ring from a lead bunker nearby. You lay the patient down on the table and walk briskly into your bunker and, from there, slide the table into the Stargate. So far so good.

Then the noise starts. The deafening pounding. The rhythmic, nonstop metallic clanking that is immediately the loudest thing you've ever heard, until it gets louder.

If you could hear anything underneath the clanking, you would hear the whirring. Instead, you sense it. Something huge and heavy inside the ring is spinning around you, over and under your head, fast, like an electron accelerator. With the pounding, though, it's more like a defective electron accelerator spinning out of control.

One of the big disadvantages of teeing people up so far in advance for their scan is that it gives them a lot of time to watch and to think about it. We were all penned in behind thick glass, gazing out onto the MRI room. One by one we watched people get shoveled into that thing and terrorized. No one seemed prepared for it, emotionally. Preparation did not appear possible.

It goes without saying that you mustn't move. That is a standard feature of medical torture: the more painful and horrible whatever it is they're doing to you, the more you have to hold still. If you move, they have to start over. And, given that you have consented to all this, it also goes without saying that if they don't perform the horrible procedure on you at all you will die for sure.

The middle-aged woman currently in the hot seat was having a hard time. Once they slid the table into the Stargate, all we could see were her feet sticking out, and they kept wiggling desperately. They were in drab green hospital-issue slipper socks.

Things were running late. 11:00 came and went. The woman wouldn't hold still. *Couldn't* is probably more accurate, but the staff, I think, would say *wouldn't*, because they kept telling her to hold still, as if that would help. They grew impatient. The woman was talking, but I couldn't make out the words, and the people inside the room didn't seem to be listening.

The machine would come on, pound for a while, and then stop after the woman moved. Eventually an old doctor went into the room and stuck his head into the Stargate and straight-up yelled at the woman. The slipper socks became still. The doctor left.

The terrible thing started up again, and now it ran for a long time. When it stopped, I thought they must be finished; I hadn't seen the woman move at all.

A nurse ran into the big room, and then another. Then two more. Then the grumpy old doctor from before. They shoveled the woman out of the Stargate and worked on her. CPR, I guess. At some point a nurse became aware of us and walked quickly to the window we were all cowering behind.

After glaring at us for some reason, she reached off to the side and pulled a white curtain over the glass, blocking our sight.

"Now why the fuck didn't they do that before?" someone behind us said.

We hid and listened. There was much barking of orders, and then a lot of beeping and yelling, and then silence. No one inside our room spoke, and nobody came in from the outside to tell us anything for a long time.

We all jumped when the door opened. A different grim nurse, wearing that tight smile that is not a smile at all. "Miss Stewart? Um . . . Amelia Stewart?"

"Yes?" Amalia said, reaching out and grabbing my arm.

"We're ready for you now."

"You're joking, right?" Amalia asked, but the nurse did not answer. She just not-smiled and stepped away from the door, apparently expecting us to follow.

"Ready for *what?*" Amalia said, louder. She did not move; neither did I. But the nurse waited us out. Again: you are there to do something that, if you don't do it, you *will* die. Definitely. Badly.

She didn't want to go, but she did. She got up from the wheelchair and walked out of the waiting room. I was behind her. The nurse blocked me before I could get into the big room. "You can't go in there," she said, not-kindly. "The radiation."

"Don't care." I tried to get around her. "I don't care about the radiation. *She's* getting it. I'll be fine."

"I'm sorry, sir." Sterner now. "We cannot allow—"

"Is there something I can sign? A waiver? No problem. Gimme. You want me to write one for you?" It hadn't occurred to me that she would have to do this alone. But when I thought about it I realized that I hadn't seen a single loved one in the actual treatment room.

"No. Sir."

"What happened to the woman?" Amalia asked from just inside the big room. "The woman who was in here earlier?"

"She had a—she had a heart attack." The nurse glanced down.

"Did she die?"

The nurse said nothing.

"Oh my *God*. Marcus . . ."

And then they took my wife from me and closed the door and left me standing in the waiting room, curtain still drawn so now I couldn't even watch. And I knew that if I barged in they would just start over.

I imagined them marching her over to the machine and laying her down on the table. Telling her to lie *very still*.

For the longest time, it was dead quiet.

"What's that smell?" Amalia called out.

And then the pounding started.

"Wait!"

The pounding got louder. It went on and on and on.

That was how Death introduced himself to us.

Working the Phone.

Monday, August 23, 1993

Home from the hospital. Alone. Jacket still on. Dark. Sit. Phone. List of numbers. Dial. *It's cancer*. Wait. Hang up. Dial. *It's cancer*. Wait. Hang up. Repeat. Repeat. Repeat.

Everybody's Farrah.

Wednesday, September 1, 1993

The circle of chairs was ridiculously large for the number of people sitting in them. Maybe 30 chairs for 10 people. That was just part of the cycle, some-one told me. People came in waves. Nobody could explain why, but I saw that it was true.

Mr. Dr. found this group for me. They come in just like I did, scared and overwhelmed. There is a swift and harsh indoctrination: *Your loved one has cancer. Yes,* cancer *cancer. And she could die from it. Yes, people still die from cancer. Yes, we did put a man on the moon, but she could still die. And yes, it is your responsibility. We realize that you are not a doctor, or a nurse, but you caught this one. You're up.*

Then, the training. Once they break you down, they build you back up, like the Marines. *This is what a phone tree is. This is what you keep in a bag by the door. Clean technique: learn it; live it. This is how you give an injection. This is how you stay sane. This is how I do it.*

Soon you are a veteran. Proven in combat. And it becomes like any war: a job. Maybe you live that way for months.

Then you start to lose. Battles turn and go wrong at the last minute. There are intelligence failures and sneak attacks and ambushes. Things you will never unsee. By now, Death is sitting in the trench next to you, eating hash out of a can with a knife. You learn, all over again, that you are powerless.

False hope kicks in. I had seen it already. The doctors here give up, so you go to Mexico. You spend every last cent you can get on a Hail Maria in some clinic down in TJ, and you come back with a bunch of books and Naderesqe talk about the FDA and the AMA and how they for some reason don't want to cure cancer. And you try to talk us into taking our loved ones down there for treatment too, because, you say, your loved one has gotten better. And she has, a little. The placebo effect is real.

Then we never see you again.

A nondescript white guy had the floor. He was saying what he always said.

"We should have never gotten married in the first place. My family was furious when I told them I was going to marry Kathy. My friends thought I was joking!" He laughed the bitterest laugh ever. "I almost left her on our *honeymoon.* I should have left her. I never should have married her in the first place. We just didn't get along. Fought all the time. I really almost left her last June. I almost left. She hit me and I hit her back and I knew that now I could leave without wondering if we could have saved it. We shouldn't even try anymore. But I didn't. I didn't leave, you know? And then, next thing I knew, she was sick."

Gah. I turned away. At least I was taking care of someone who would have taken even better care of me.

"So now she's sick, and I can't leave. You know? You can't leave your wife while she's got *cancer*! You just don't do that. Can't do it. Who does that? You know who leaves his wife when she has cancer? Newt Gingrich." He snorted that ugly laugh again. "Newt made his wife sign papers in her hospital bed. I can't do that! You can't do something *Newt Gingrich* would do? Can you?"

He waited for an answer.

"I should have never married her in the first place—"

"Marcus?" Jason, the facilitator, interrupted; this was where we came in. He tried to catch my eyes. "Would you like to share today? You seem . . . kinda deep in thought."

We were all at different stages of this death march, but I was the newest to join. Everyone was staring at me like Pennywise was behind me with a mallet.

"Sure," I said. "OK." I knew I couldn't talk about what I had been thinking about. I had been trying to imagine staying here if Amalia left. Staying on Earth. I was having trouble imagining it. But I couldn't say that; we were in a hospital basement and I didn't want to get locked up on a 5150, which happened to folks at these meetings from time to time. So I talked about what I had been thinking about before that. "OK. Spending all this time inside the hospital is changing how I see the rest of the world."

I glanced around the room. A few people were nodding. "I realize that hospitals are inherently morbid places. People only come here if there is something seriously wrong with their body. But, see, something is seriously wrong with *everybody's* body, sometimes. Hospitals are where most of us began and where most of us will end. It's natural." I sat awhile. It was dead quiet except for a vending machine in the corner. The air was stale.

"But, that's the thing—there is *no* sign of that natural fact on the outside. None. I stagger out of Ignatius onto the street after a day or two in Oncology, and it's blinding." Somebody groaned. "Everything's shiny. Even at night. Even the people. *Especially* the people. Folks strut past this place like it's got nothing to do with them. And never will. Like they are going to live forever." Now everybody was nodding like crazy. "One minute I'm in her room, or in the halls, and everybody around is either a little less sick than Amalia, as sick as Amalia, or dying. And then I step outside, and, suddenly, everyone's young and healthy and strong and beautiful. Everyone has huge grinning teeth and long shiny yellow hair all fluffed out like that Farrah poster that was everywhere when I was growing up. Everybody. Brothers. Old people. *Everybody*. Farrah."

The woman sitting directly across from me was staring at me hard. She was one of those sisters with reddish curls and freckles that I always assume are from Louisiana or one of those other places with particularly complex race rules. I'd met her the day I joined; her name was Debra something. I looked back at Debra and tried to get the rest of it out.

"If I was a visitor from another world, and I hadn't done any research or anything, I would think that most humans don't die, ever," I said. "Only the unlucky, or the stupid, or the weak. You see all those peacocks out there, it seems impossible that each and every one of them is going to shit themselves and stop breathing, sooner rather than later. They all sure seem to think that they're immortal."

I glanced down at my hands. "I know that, just a little while ago, I was immortal too. But now I know. And I know that I'll never *not* know again, ever. I know I'll never be the same.

"That's good, I guess."

Nobody was nodding anymore. We just sat.

Then Debra spoke.

"My parents had six boys and four girls. I'm the only one taking care of our sister."

I peered up at her. We all did. Debra didn't talk a lot.

"Yup. Mr. and Mrs. Jesse McGee had ten children. Nine lived. Five live in the Bay Area. One has breast cancer. One takes care of her. The other three? The other *seven*? Not bloody loikley!" She chuckled, sort of.

"It's bad. She's not going to make it. Everybody knows that. She knows it. She's not stupid. She's greenish brown, but she's not stupid. High on morphine, yes. Stupid? No.

"But she's still in there, you know? She's sick. She won't be in there forever. But neither will I. Or you," she said to me. "Like you said—all that matters is if you are still here now. That's all that can matter. And Abby is still in there. Nobody else can see that. Nobody else cares. But I care."

"I care," I said. Our eyes met again. You weren't supposed to respond directly to people in the group. No cross-talk, they called it. But Jason didn't scold me for it.

I wished the meeting were over. I needed to get home and see my love.

Whirled Peas.

Monday, September 13, 1993

There was all this fuss about who stuck out his hand first, who shook whose hand, when, how long, lefty or righty—it was silly. But none of that could change the fact that Yasser Arafat and Yitzhak Rabin were shaking hands. In public!

The three of them stood there, Clinton in the middle, and Israeli and Palestinian shook hands for all the world to see. Never thought I'd live to see that. Cameras were going off like crazy. Yasser had a huge grin; Yitzhak seemed decidedly less comfortable.

I'd been an Arafat fan my whole life, in part because my mom was. But in recent years I'd developed a tremendous respect for Rabin. Throughout the forties, fifties, and sixties, he'd killed more Arabs than anybody but Moshe himself. Which I did not respect. But, when this guy said, "Enough already with the killing," nobody could call him a pussy. And when he stood up in the Knesset and said that those brown people they all hated were just that—people, like them—I couldn't believe it.

None of it was going to make Amalia well again. But I remember standing in the kitchen, watching the ceremony on the tiny TV, a pot of frozen peas boiling furiously on the stove, ignored. I felt hope—deep and muted, but hope. Who knew what the future could bring? You can't make this shit up.

Now I wonder if Rabin had that expression on his face because he knew he was a dead man.

At the time, it all felt like it meant something.

Now He Tells Me.

Friday, September 17, 1993

"They'll never accept ya," he said.

Carlos Lopez was draped over the steering wheel. He didn't look like he was really driving. That was because he wasn't really driving. The foot on the gas worked fine, but the brake was forgotten. Also, he was steering with his forearms. Also, he was staring at me.

The night wasn't going as I had hoped.

Desperate for any relationship that would get me out of Staffing Partner Ironic Assignment Hell, I had been courting Carlos. Evan was basically gone, clearly preferring his two-man Dubai satellite—imagine that! Carlos was the only other lawyer in the building with any melanin at all, with the exception of the Asian partners, who wanted even less to do with me than the white ones did. The fact that I was now also Cancer Boy somehow failed to help. Carlos was my only remaining option. Also, I kind of felt like he owed me, after that thing with his racist-ass baby.

It had taken several inventive tries to get Carlos to go to dinner with me. Given that Carliss Lopes was, to put it mildly, *un pocho*, this was understandable. My breakthrough occurred when I suggested a restaurant in Berkeley. I'd explained my choice by saying that it would be more convenient for him, since he lived in the Berkeley hills. It had been an obvious pretext—I lived, and we both worked, in San Francisco—but it must have eased his concerns about being seen with me, because that was the offer he'd accepted.

Everybody makes a fuss about Chez Frottage. I think that's what it's called. The place is so fancy that they don't even have lady menus; they don't have menus at all. *They* tell *you* what you are having for dinner. In my experience, that is just a way to make you eat something disgusting. Something worse than calamari. It all tasted weirdly fine. But do you know how good a meal would have to taste to justify charging over $100 a plate for whatever some stranger saw fit to put in front of you? Well, it didn't taste half that good. And I picked up the check. More silliness—the man was a millionaire.

I was at the height of my business-eating powers. I ate an entire half a chicken using a knife and fork. Picked it clean without ever touching it with my hands. And I may have eaten an eyeball. I think it was an eyeball. I hope it was an eyeball. I ate it because the partners all seemed to believe that if you were picky about what you ate, you might also be picky about what cases you took. They were right about that.

The evening had gone well up to that point. But, even though Carliss's place was right there in Berkeley, he insisted on driving me back home to San Francisco, in that way that only a man who has drunk a $75 bottle of wine can. I hadn't counted on that. I didn't want to die on the highway, but if I offended him at the end of the night, assuming he remembered it, then I would have eaten that eyeball for nothing. I took my chances.

And now chances were that I was going to sit in a Mercedes with this man at the bottom of the San Francisco Bay forever.

We were flying across the Bay Bridge. Absolutely sailing. Benz makes a nice car; it didn't feel like we were going very fast at all. It was only when we tore past another car that I felt it, or when I peeked at the fancy digital speedometer, which at that moment calmly read 92.

"No. They'll never accept ya. Never never never ne-ver! Twenny . . . twenny got-damn years!" He fell asleep for a while. "Oh—they'll *work* with ya! Sure! But they'll *nevvver reeeeeally* accept ya."

I reviewed my life. We should have had coffee. The caffeine might have helped, but even if it hadn't, the extra few minutes might have given the wine a chance to knock him out while we were still at Chez Seddity and I could have put Carliss in a cab and gone home on BART like I'd planned and ever seen my sweet bride and kittens ever again. Instead, I'd asked for the check after the main course, nickel-and-diming, and Carliss had gone from hammered to comatose pretty much as soon as he started the car.

I gazed out at all the sparkling lights ahead in the city, behind us on Treasure Island, and on the boats and buoys we would soon be joining below. The worst part was knowing that she wouldn't survive the loss of me. Her health was just too fragile. Mama and Mr. Dr. would love to have their baby home with them, and there was nothing they wouldn't do for her. But the loss of a spouse can do in a healthy person. So this poor, sad man wasn't only about to kill me, he was about to kill Amalia as well, and probably her parents too, after a while.

I really wanted to deliver a karate chop to his carotid and push him out of the way and stop the car. The bay certainly wanted me to try. Somehow I knew better. So I just sat there and waited for the guardrail while Carliss told me things about our firm that I wished he had told me, and himself, a little sooner.

More Pamphlets.

Tuesday, September 28, 1993

Chemo is no joke.

Chemotherapy is the medieval process of poisoning the sick person, literally poisoning her almost to death, in the hope that the cancer, which has less seniority, will all-the-way die. We did chemo once a week for a month. Amalia endured "treatments" that left her olive green and motionless for days, starting to feel alive again just in time for the next one.

There were many tests. We were hopeful. Then Dr. Fallstich summoned us to her office. The first thing she did was hand us each a pamphlet entitled "After Chemotherapy." We looked from the front of the pamphlet—a beautiful watercolor of a rolling meadow—to each other. We had already figured out that the worse the news, the prettier the pamphlet cover. This one was gorgeous. The muted serenity of that cover told us that The Mass had chugged that chemo, gone for a run, then went right back to growing. The rest of the meeting was a formality.

They let us twist for a few days, and then someone mentioned high-dose chemo. I'd never heard of it. Back to Dr. Fallstich's we went. On the cover of "Preparing for High-Dose Chemotherapy" was a painting of a huge snow-capped mountain—the Alps or someplace. It was breathtaking.

"If they ever give us one with a unicorn on it," Amalia smirked, "I'm screwed."

Our laughter was genuine. Dr. Fallstich looked annoyed.

Bus Drivers.

Thursday, September 30, 1993

The San Francisco Municipal Transit System, a.k.a. Muni, hires all of its drivers from a prison work-release program. Apparently. Muni goons do their jobs terribly and with impunity. They will stop their buses, noses side by side, in the middle of the street during rush hour and shoot the shit for five minutes. If you are trying to get into your car while a bus is coming, hurry, because they really might clip you. They routinely blow past stops with people waiting at them simply because they are late. They will park a crowded bus, get out, and walk into a liquor store.

I am open to the idea that some Muni drivers are good people. But I haven't met them. In my experience, there's something about the personality type that chooses that job, like with lawyers or shrinks or prison guards. That's a generalization, but it is completely consistent with what I've seen.

The feeling is mutual. I don't know if they expect me to make trouble because I am a black man—and back then, I was a *young* black man, everybody's worst nightmare/wet dream. Or, since most Muni drivers are also black, maybe they can see my privilege. Maybe I'm not black enough for bus drivers. I don't know what it is. But it's something.

So I already had a history with Muni drivers the day I was taking the 38 Geary to the hospital and it was packed and the driver pulled over and went into a 7-Eleven.

I looked around. Most of the sheep on board were pretending that this was normal. A pale older couple was whispering and peeking in the driver's direction, but that was it.

Eventually the driver returned. He entered the bus through the open back door and pushed his way forward. I have no idea why he did this. The bus was crowded; the street was empty. The back door was closer to the 7-Eleven, but three or four unobstructed strides on the sidewalk would have taken him to the front door, which was also open, and directly to his throne. But he chose instead to do it that way.

I watched him from my spot near the front of the bus as he Godzilla'd through the people. He was big, a brother, in his fifties or maybe even his sixties. His face was fixed in a well-practiced scowl. Folks got out of his way as best they could, but clearly it was not enough for him, and he helped them the rest of the way with gusto.

When he got closer to the front of the bus I squeezed in as far as I could, sticking my crotch in the face of an older Asian woman sitting in an aisle seat. I was really trying to make room. And then I felt hands on my back. He pushed me out of his way. The fly of my jeans hit the lady in the ear.

Kill him. Just like that. Plan A was to murder this man with my bare hands in front of everybody. I didn't have a Plan B, and at that moment I didn't want one.

I turned to face his back as he stalked by. My left arm got ready to go around his throat, while my right hand prepared to take his eyes. I was going to take his eyes while I killed him. My thighs tensed up, and I took a deep breath.

And I said to his back, loud: "Don't be mad at us because you are old and you still have to work. You should have saved your money."

He didn't look up or turn or react in any way, other than to hesitate for a split second as he settled back into his seat. But that hesitation told me plenty. Plan B, wherever it had come from, seemed to be getting the job done.

I slipped through the few people at the very front of the bus and stood right next to him, facing his right side as he futzed with his seat belt. "I can see you now. 'Back in the day,' you old heads like to say. What—'72, '73? That's when all the good music came out. Al Green. James Brown. Oh, you had yourself a funky good time, didn't you? You paaaaaaar-*tayed*! Didn't you? Did you have a purple suit?" I gave him a slow up-and-down. "Yeah you did. You damn near got a purple suit on *now*. And every Friday night you went out to De Club and it was 'Drinks on me!' and you laughed and laughed and laughed. Didn't you." I was trying to sound casual, amused, like Hannibal Lecter reading Agent Starling. But even to me I sounded like I was strangling him and pulling out his eyes after all. "Well, did I *tell* you to buy everybody motherfucking drinks? Did I? . . . That's right. No, I did not. I was eight years fucking old in nineteen seventy motherfuckin' three.

But you were hot shit. Weren't you." I gave him a moment to relive his past glory. "Well, look at you now. Broke-ass motherfucker. It's obvious. 'Cause if you weren't a broke-ass motherfucker, your broke-ass motherfucking ass wouldn't be driving a motherfucking *bus* right now, would it? *Would it?* How many kinds of liniment do you need to put on those big-ass old-ass knees after sitting in that chair all day, huh? Yeah. Look at you now. Putting your hands on people. You need to keep your broke-ass hands to your mother fucking self."

I was done. I hadn't expected to get to speak my piece. I figured he'd kick me off the bus. Or try. I had not completely let go of the whole murder idea.

But he didn't stand up, and he didn't respond. And when he did finally look up at me, he didn't even seem mad. A little bit sad, maybe. But mostly blank.

I returned his gaze for a while, until I felt that we understood each other. I moved back to my previous spot, and he started up the bus and went on.

I was smiling. I think I was smiling. My face hurt. My bloodlust was satisfied, and I had used my words! Win-win all around. And I assumed that my fellow passengers had enjoyed it too. We were all in the same bus, yes? That broke-ass motherfucker had just bullied the entire bus. I stuck up for us. I said what we were all thinking. Right?

I scanned around for the gazes of silent thanks that surely were coming from every direction.

All eyes pointed studiously away from me. Didn't matter that the man had just put his hands on them. Didn't matter that what I'd said had obviously hit a nerve with him and was more than a little true. I was a bad sheep, and that is all sheep care about. No yelling in the slaughterhouse!

Fine. I bit back a "Fuck all y'all!" on the slim chance I was reading the room wrong. Just stood there and stared out the window. Even when we got to the hospital, I didn't pull the cord. I didn't trust myself to move yet.

Nurse Candy.

Friday, October 8, 1993

The intensive care unit is a big room of very sick people all trying to get out of bed.

Brenda Benson, RN, and I were kicking it in the ICU nurses station in the wee hours. Twenty years earlier we would have been smoking.

"Visiting hours" is a myth. What I mean is, it's a policy that all hospitals have on paper, but only enforce if you make them mad. If you don't make them mad, you can sleep in your wife's room every night. And if they like you, they'll hook you up with a cot. They were hooking us up with cots.

Every place is high school; hospitals are no exception. They won't kill your loved one if they don't like you, but they will go the extra mile for her if they do. And from the moment we arrived, staggering into the ER after that long death march across the street, I knew that the men and women at Ignatius Medical were going to love me. They had to. Amalia was too young, too special, too everything to die. We needed the whole staff's A-game. I was practicing better diplomacy than some diplomats. Before initiating a sensitive conversation, I would tell myself, *Mandela.*

I'd been in a deadly dull meeting with Carliss when Kate, my secretary, walked into the office without knocking and handed me one of those pink slips they put phone messages on. It was from Dr. Fallstich, calling to tell me that there had been "an event" and my wife was now recovering in ICU and I may want to come to the hospital immediately.

An event. Lawyers don't have shit on doctors.

I was there by 4:00. I thought I was too late. Her face was sunken and waxen and still. But she was only sleeping off having been poisoned very nearly to death by her own doctors. High-dose chemo is even less of a joke than regular chemo.

I couldn't be there while she got high-dose chemo. I wasn't allowed. Just being in the same room with the stuff they were pumping into her bloodstream would have made me sick. Fumes. I guess she was already so sick that fumes couldn't make her any worse.

They would run the poison into Amalia's catheter—a long, thin plastic tube that went from the outside world through her sternum and directly into a big artery by her heart. They did it that way, a poker-faced nurse had told us, because if they injected the toxic chemicals into the little vein in her arm, the stuff would eat through her vein and her arm and her skin and spill out onto the floor. She said that. The next day, a surgeon with very poor people skills showed up at our room, gave her a shot of watered-down anesthetic, and installed the catheter right there. Obviously she wasn't numb yet, and obviously he didn't care. The man sawed into my wife like a steak while she writhed and cried in her bed. If I had scalped him with his own blade it would have negatively impacted her care. So I didn't.

Death sat and waited in the corner every day of the two weeks she received high-dose chemo. She only ate when we made her, and even then she ate very little. She'd had to pee in a special chamber that had super-strong ventilation, because the steam off of high-dose-chemo pee could drop a person. I repeat: the shit was no joke. It more than lived up to the Alps pamphlet cover. And now someone had given her two drops too much of the stuff, and Death was up and leaning over her bed and breathing his terrible breath on her wasted face.

Both Mama and Mr. Dr. were there when Amalia had a seizure or stopped breathing or whatever brain-scarring nightmare had occurred to suggest that something was wrong. Now Mama was sleeping in Amalia's hospital bed upstairs. The woman was a rock, but this was simply too much, and she may have fallen out a little too. Mr. Dr. was down in the ICU flipping through his daughter's chart for what seemed to be not the first time. He was exasperated. I'd never seen that look on his face before; it's not a look you want to see on a surgeon, or on your father-in-law.

He told me what had gone down.

"Go home. I've got this," I said.

"No. We're here now. You need to work. Stay awhile, then go home and—"

I put my hand on his elbow and he jumped slightly. Also something you don't want to see your surgeon father-in-law do. "I've got this, sir. I'm rested. I don't have to choose between sleep and work today. And I keep a change of clothes at the office. Go home. Take Mama home." He did a subtle double take; maybe he didn't know that I had it like that with the Mrs. "Sleep in a real bed. Eat. Pray for your daughter. Come back at 10:00 tomorrow, and I will go straight to the office." I wouldn't stop touching him until he said "OK."

And now Nurse Brenda and I sat there, not smoking. Brenda was a good nurse. She wasn't compelled to fill the silences. We sat flipping through magazines and half-listening to all of the beeping monitors. Occasionally, she would have to go into the big room of beds and hold down one of the very sick people until the meds took over again and thwarted their escape.

"Did you know," she said, "that a quarter of a million people die every day?" I couldn't tell if she'd just read that in *Vogue* or had been walking around knowing that.

"No. No, I did not know that. But that feels right."

"Yeah. Quarter-mil at least."

Silence.

"Did you know, once you are officially terminal, you can collect your own life insurance, and spend it before you die?"

"Yeah," she said, "I knew that."

Silence.

Unfortunately, Brenda's shift ended at 2:00 a.m., and Candy Farber came on. I said good night to Brenda and moved over to the chair by Amalia's bed.

Nurse Candy was one of the only failures in my campaign to win the hearts and minds of Ignatius staff. Although it had been immediately obvious to me that she and I were natural enemies—she was skinny and fake-blond and pushy, the very definition of angry American entitlement—I wasn't going to let that stop me from trying to charm her. I had no choice. Nurse Candy, however, wasn't having it. I don't know if she had some beef with me personally or hated men or hated black folk or whatever, or if she was just an unhappy miserable cuss who treated people badly simply because she could. And I never figured it out. I do know that she was hell on my nurse fantasies. It would appear that a night strapped to a bed at the mercy of a sadistic blond nurse named Candy is actually *not* hot. I know, right? I'm as surprised as anybody.

They had Amalia intubated—hooked up to a ventilator. I don't know why. I mean, I guess that if they hadn't she would have suffocated, but I don't know why *that* was. Whatever the reason, they had a giant contraption by the bed doing her breathing for her. My love was lying there with a fighter-pilot mask over her mouth, a thick tube connecting the mask to something that resembled a 1950s sci-fi robot. Its white plastic udders lifted and sank, presumably taking her lungs with them. It was hard to imagine that that tube went through the mask all the way down her gullet. I mean, it was hard for *me* to imagine. Amalia herself seemed clear on the concept. Apparently, being physically forced to inhale is a shock every single time. She was mostly doped up and out, but each time she woke she wrote me a note about the ventilator like she hadn't already. *Hurts to breathe* or *Air too strong* or *Lungs hurt*. Nurse Brenda had assured me that the contraption was working properly. So I would read the sloppy note and nod and kiss my wife on the forehead and do a bad job of smiling.

I was dozing in a chair at the foot of the bed when all of her monitors started screaming. Like how they do on doctor shows when everybody is running with the crash cart yelling *Stat!* but the person dies anyway. I sat up. Instead of finding my wife thrashing around grabbing her heart like I expected, I found her thrashing around fighting Nurse Candy, who was doing something to her.

While I was sleeping, Nurse Candy had rolled some sort of cart up to the bed. I sat and stared. She had unhooked the hose that went from the oxygen robot to the fighter-pilot mask. My wife could no longer breathe. There was a thin plastic tube coming out of the cart, and Nurse Candy was snaking it into a small hole in Amalia's mask. *Way* in. It just kept going.

Amalia's arms shot out to each side, hands fanned all the way open. *Spasming*, my brain said. The cart rumbled and hummed. And there was a sucking sound. Coming from deep inside her. Sometimes the sucking sound would get louder, and the pain and horror on her face would magnify too.

Amalia's eyes found mine around Nurse Candy's shoulder and pleaded. Here I am not snatching Nurse Candy off my wife and punching her to death. I didn't know how to hook up the ventilator. So I held still.

I flashed back on *The Dark Crystal*—that scene where the huge evil bird people are taking the tiny fat baby people and strapping them one by one into that machine that sucks out their life essence. I saw that in the theater when it came out, alone and really high. It kind of freaked me out. It was worse in real life.

After forever, Nurse Candy slowly reeled the thin tube back out of Amalia's lungs. She re-fastened the tube to the cart. She turned off the cart and unplugged it from the wall. And only then did she reattach Amalia's breathing tube. Nurse Candy gathered up her playthings and turned and walked away. Without a word. Without a glance. Amalia was crumpled on the bed, motionless.

When I could move again, I fretted over her for a while, and then I crept across the big room to the nurse's station. Nurse Candy was sitting where I'd been sitting. She was flipping through a *Cosmo*. Even when I was standing right in front of her, she didn't look up. With Nurse Candy there was only the hard way.

"Nurse Candy?"

I sounded like a trick-or-treater. At least she didn't make me repeat it. She slapped the *Cosmo* down on her lap and rolled her eyes up at me. I thought I might have detected the beginnings of a smirk.

"Um . . . what . . . what was that?"

"Standard procedure." She stared. That was all she was going to say.

"I'm sorry?"

"Fluid. Collects in the patient's lungs. When they're intubated." Talking down to me. "We get it out." She went back to her magazine.

"Amalia."

The eyes rolled up again.

"Her name is Amalia."

Nurse Candy shrugged. "The patient's monitors went off not because of any physical distress on the patient's part but because they were disconnected. By me."

And there it was: the smirk.

She's baiting you. I'd become a fixture at Ignatius, but that was always subject to the whims of whoever was on duty. If I interfered with my wife's "treatment," Nurse Candy would boot me out and Amalia would be alone with her. I knew it, and she knew I knew it. Visiting hours loomed like a death sentence. I nodded and went back to Amalia's bed and sat down. Mandela-esque diplomacy had called for a "Thank you," but I just didn't have it in me.

About an hour later, she did it again. The cart, the tube, the pain. I was awake this time, but that made it no less shocking.

Amalia's eyes begged me. I held still some more. She remained conscious this time, and as soon as Nurse Candy strolled away, she wrote a note on the pad by her bed:

PLEASE
MAKE
IT
STOP

I went back to the nurses station. She was at the counter, her back to me.

"Nurse?"

She ignored me. I was the only person in the unit besides her who was not tethered by the wrist and whacked out on morphine.

"Nurse Candy?" Now I was begging. I was begging for my wife's life. She turned around.

"Um . . . is there any chance . . . that you could . . . *not* do that? That thing with Amalia's ventilator?" Nothing. "Please?"

"Sure." She turned back around to face the counter.

I knew I shouldn't look a gift horse in the mouth but maybe I didn't understand and also I couldn't help it. "Excuse me?"

"Sure. The procedure's not necessary." She glanced back at me. "It's for the patient's comfort." *Comfort.* And she smiled at me. Not even just a smirk. A full-on smile. And then she turned her back to me again.

Here I am not strangling Nurse Candy with the clipboard on the desk near my right hand. Her pasty neck looked like dough. Maybe it felt like dough too. I bet you can rip someone's head off with a clipboard if you pull it hard enough.

"Thank you." I returned to Amalia's bedside and sat back down.

A Loss for Words.

Wednesday, October 13, 1993

All those jokes about hospital food are true, but also they are stupid, because nobody in the hospital gives a fuck how food tastes. You eat for the same reason you do everything there: so you won't die.

This was my new home, and I was starting to settle in. I scooped up one of the big red plastic trays and some cutlery that I hoped was wet from having just been washed. I set my tray down on the little track and slid it along the counter until I caught up to the one person ahead of me in line, who was being served leftover-looking ham by an old black man. I hadn't seen him before; it was early, and usually after an overnight stay I would eat breakfast at home or in the diner next door to the office.

The old man set the plate of rainbow-colored meat down on top of the sneeze guard between them. "Thank you," the woman murmured as she picked it up. "You're welcome," the old man responded pleasantly. The woman set the plate on her tray and headed off to the cash register. I stood quietly and waited for my eyes to meet lunch-lady dude's. I wasn't sure what I wanted, other than I didn't want the ham.

Old dude walked past me and approached a man who had come up behind me in line and took the man's order.

Maybe he saw that I hadn't made up my mind yet. I took my time and settled on the fruit salad. A little overpriced, but at least it seemed like it had been made in the last week.

When dude behind me went away with his food, I opened my mouth and took a breath and tried again to make eye contact with lunch-lady dude.

This time, our eyes met. And I saw it.

The damp, red-rimmed eyes of flaming hatred that some older black people have for younger black people. Maybe older people of all races hate their younger people, but I can only speak to my own. There is this mass disappointment. They blame us for where we are today.

They're right: something happened. One minute, the tide of our long struggle had finally turned, and we were on the verge of overcoming. The next minute, Reagan got elected. Two minutes after that, *Straight Outta Compton* dropped. And then we didn't even need white racism anymore, because black folk were doing it to each other. I know that all of that happened—I saw it too—but here's the thing: I didn't do it. I was not the cause, or even one of the causes. In fact, I was pretty sure I was part of the solution. I guess lunch-lady dude couldn't know that I was part of the solution, but he sure seemed happy to assume that I was part of the problem. Granted, I was wearing jeans and a T-shirt. But what the hell are you supposed to wear in the hospital—a tux?

We were the only black people in the room.

My love was upstairs, alone. She needed me. I just wanted to grab some food and get back to her. I just wanted some goddamn fruit salad.

The old man moved away again and took the order of a woman who hadn't even gotten in line yet. So I slid my tray back down the track and followed him until I was facing the side of his shiny paper-hatted head. He must have seen me—he couldn't not have seen me—but his eyes stayed locked downward. He gave the woman her food and moved back to the other end of the counter. Again I followed. He wiped his side of the sneeze guard. Clearly, he was just going to ignore me and not serve me, like this was Selma. I was going to have to say something.

I took a deep breath. I figured I'd start with *Excuse me, I'm ready to order now* or *Hi, I believe I was next*; something like that. But when I checked the words that were waiting in my mouth, I found that they were:

I am going to wait outside. All day. I am going to wait for you in the parking lot. Or maybe across the street. And when I see you, I am going to murder you. And I am going to put your body in a dumpster. And nobody is going to care.

I was appalled. I searched around in my mouth for something else that I could use. Anything. Preferably something fruit related. But those were the only words in there right then.

Well, I couldn't say that. It wouldn't get me my fruit salad. So I just hung out awhile and let the world go by, until I felt that I could walk away. And when I could, I did.

A Working Breakfast.

Tuesday, November 2, 1993

In the ambulance with our usual crew. Siren wailing. Arturo was driving. I rode shotgun.

In the back, Julian and Kim were working on Amalia. She'd had a mishap with her catheter. It had backed up. That's what I heard Amalia tell them, at least; she wouldn't let me see. Twenty minutes earlier I had come out of the kitchen to find her sitting on the living room floor with a wad of paper towels in her hand and a three-foot-wide puddle of blood on the floor. I tried to help, but she kept turning away. I don't know why.

She wouldn't let me see or try to stop the bleeding or even sop up the blood, so I called 911 and turned off the stove and finished getting dressed. A few minutes later I let the paramedics in and I dished my scrambled eggs and bacon onto a paper plate. I brought two plastic forks but Arturo didn't want any. My briefcase was between my feet; I'd take a cab to the office after we got her checked in.

I stared out the window and chewed and enjoyed running all the reds.

I don't mention this because it was a big deal. I mention it because, at the time, it was not a big deal.

Fit to Print.

Wednesday, November 17, 1993

SFPD TO INVESTIGATE BACKGROUND OF MAN IN SHOOTING

This, in the middle of page 24 of the *Herald*. Apparently, two days earlier a retired police officer from Richmond, Virginia shot a man to death in the parking lot of the Skymount Mall at the edge of the city. The retired officer, whose name was not given, claimed that the decedent, a man from Oakland named Nathaniel Perry, had been "running in a threatening manner." That brief account was buried near the end of the article. The point of the piece was that Perry might have gang affiliations. SFPD was looking into it.

This was typical. The gang-affiliation investigation was the nineties version of "asking questions later." But it struck me that I did not remember seeing any earlier articles about the shooting itself.

I hunted around my office for old newspapers and, not surprisingly, found none. The cleaning staff at the firm was fanatical, or perhaps management was; my office was scoured at 7:00 every night (even if, as was often the case, I was still in it). My old *Heralds* were long gone. I decided to go down to the firm library on the third floor.

"Marcus! Good morning. Can I help you with something?" Paul, our librarian, smiled warmly. Two years later Paul would be dead. They would say that it was Lyme disease.

"Hey, Paul. Could you get me the last few issues of the *Herald*, please?"

"Of course. This way." He led me to the reading area, which was nicer than our house. Solid little couches and big fluffy chairs formed an oval, with delicate glass tables scattered here and there. It felt more like a place to fuck and do coke than to do legal research. I plopped down in one of the chairs. I had the whole place to myself.

The recent issues of the *Herald* were hanging on a little bamboo rack. Paul took down yesterday's issue and presented it to me like a bottle of wine. I accepted it with thanks.

I started, of course, with the back of the paper. I made it all the way to page 1 and found nothing. But I had only been skimming the headlines. So I went through it again, from the front this time, and I read a little bit of each article to make absolutely sure that Nathaniel Perry was not in there. He wasn't.

At some point, Larry Springgate entered the coke lounge. He was just another partner. Larry plucked the *Journal* off its perch, eased into a chair, crossed his legs like a woman, and read. We didn't speak. I reread the entire paper, including sports, just in case shooting black people was officially a sport now. Nothing. I went back to the bamboo racks and found Monday's *Herald*. Maybe the story had appeared on the same day as the shooting, somehow. But it hadn't.

Alone again in the lounge, I sat and thought. Today was Wednesday, and the article in the *Herald* said that the shooting happened on Monday. No time was specified, but one could reasonably infer that it took place after 12:00 a.m. Monday morning. And the laws of physics required the article to be published after the shooting. So going through the Sunday *Herald* was pointless, unless I was looking for "Nathaniel Perry to Be Shot Dead Tomorrow." I had thoroughly reviewed the Monday and Tuesday *Herald*s, and the story had not appeared prior to today.

So the editors at the *Herald* had not considered the story newsworthy until now. OK. Who knows how many such stories no one bothers to report? All the news that's fit to print, right? So the *Herald* hadn't been interested. But, surely . . .

I put the *Herald*s back on the rack and returned to the front of the library. I half-noticed Larry Springgate lurking by the entrance.

"Hi, Paul." He looked up from his reading and smiled. Paul was one of the few people in the building who didn't panic for a second when he saw me. He was clearly gay; I suspected there was a brother waiting for him at home.

"I wonder if you could get me this week's *Inquisitor*s? Do we carry that too?" Paul's brow wrinkled a bit, but I understood. Even I was whispering, like I was asking for back issues of *Hustler*. As I said, the *Inquisitor* wasn't yet the stinking piece of shit tabloid rag it is today, but it was definitely not the *Herald*. To put it in New York terms, the *Herald* wasn't exactly the *Times*, but if the *Herald* were the *Times*, the *Inquisitor* would have been the *Daily News*. Maybe *Newsday*. It's the *Post* now.

Paul got up and marched into the stacks. I followed. Larry Springgate stared.

The *Inquisitor* didn't have enough cachet to merit a bamboo display rack in the coke lounge. The issues were folded and stacked in cubbies with the ABA *Journals* and the *Congressional Quarterlys*. I felt a little sorry for them.

"Here they are," Paul said, gesturing. He didn't touch them. He didn't seem so much mad at me as saddened by the journalistic standards of the *Inquisitor*. I felt hopeful for the same reason. If it bleeds, it leads, right? I was guessing that a person shot once in the back and once in the head bleeds a bit. The *Inquisitor* couldn't resist.

"Thank you, Paul," I said. He accepted my apology and left.

I took today's, yesterday's, and Monday's issues of the *Inquisitor* back to the coke lounge. I went through the same routine, meaning I read each one backward and forward. I found the same thing: coverage of the Perry story began after the man had been dead for 48 hours.

I returned to the C-list periodicals section on my own and found the *Oakland Tribune*. The shooting happened in San Francisco, but Oakland has black people in it, and I had the distinct impression that Nathaniel Perry was black. When a police spokesman is willing to say to the press, "We don't know anything yet, but we suspect the decedent," you can bet your last money the suspicious decedent is black or Latino. And I had never heard of a white or Asian person "running in a threatening manner." So maybe some editor at the *Trib* viewed the story as local in spirit.

Even though the *Trib* was a longshot, it was my last hope, and I clung to that hope as long as I could. I actually spread the paper out on the floor, like a kid on Christmas morning, so that I could cover ground faster. At some point, Larry Springgate returned and sat stiffly on a couch. He practically had eyeholes cut into his newspaper, the same *Journal* he'd already read.

I skimmed all the *Trib*s, from the one published the day before the shooting to the one that came out hours ago, back to front and back again, twice each. Again, the story started today, with Perry dead two days already.

I sat on the floor and tried to think. What made the story newsworthy now? What was the media trying to get in front of?

"What are you *doing*?" Larry Springgate whined, finally.

"Research!" I hissed.

Larry left.

Yet Another Thousand Words.

Thursday, November 18, 1993

The video broke the next day. A Skymount Mall surveillance camera captured the whole thing.

I was in the kitchen making dinner for all three Stewarts with the little TV on for company. I'd barely been listening. Ten minutes into the 6:00 news, the anchor announced the release of a shocking video in connection with a recent "officer-involved shooting." She warned that the video might be disturbing to young children. That's what got my attention.

It's pretty grainy, and there is no sound. What I see is a parking lot, and some old white dude locking his car. A couple of people wander by. Then a young-looking black man goes whizzing past. He's looking straight ahead. Nothing in his hands. But the mall sheep shrink as he passes.

Not the old dude, though. Running dude passes by about four feet in front of him, and old dude seems to just watch him go by. But as soon as the young man passes, old dude draws and fires. You just see a little puff of smoke, like in a silent movie. The sheep all jump. Then old dude walks out of the frame. I guess that's when he takes his kill shot. The video ends. *Fin.*

The anchor never stopped jabbering, and by the time Perry was dead she was telling us about a weed conviction in '87. I turned the volume down.

That was the only time they showed the actual shooting, as far as I know. For the rest of the night, they cut the shooting. They just showed us a black man running, as if that were the crime. After a few days, they didn't even show us that.

Last Call.

Tuesday, November 30, 1993

I watched Clinton sign the Brady bill. Brady sat next to him.

This is the thing about guns: they are wrong, but they exist. The very first time I fired a gun was out in the woods of upstate New York with my thugbilly cousins, the summer before I turned 13. During the long moment I spent recovering from the recoil, I had the idea of building a time machine and going back and showing Mr. Du Pont or Browning or whoever it was the horrible horrible consequences of his invention. I would put together a slide show, or maybe a PowerPoint, of school shootings and drive-bys and crazy-ass boyfriends killing chicks who hadn't even really been cheating. The fantasy was that Mr. Smith or Mr. Wesson or whoever would be so overcome with shock and revulsion at what he saw that he would immediately reject the incalculable fortune that he would have amassed. The virtually infinite wealth that no number of generations could ever spend. And he would gladly choose not to enable the continent of his birth to sweep across the planet like a plague, terrorizing every living creature upon its surface and in its skies and in its waters, until there wasn't enough planet left to sustain any life at all. My PowerPoint of Boers massacring entire villages and three-year-olds killing their little sisters by accident and gay teenagers blowing their brains out and assassination after assassination after assassination would compel him to forego being the single most influential person in the galaxy, affecting the tide and climate of an entire world forever. But that didn't happen.

I'd been on the fence about gun ownership. But the signing of the Brady bill forced my hand. I wasn't worried about the new background-check requirements—on paper, my background was golden. But a lot of the good stuff, most notably high-capacity clips, was about to be banned. They wanted the cops and the bubbas who already had 30-round clips to keep having them, and the law-abiding types such as myself who were late to the party to have eight or so puny shots at our disposal before we had to call time out for a reload break. Fuck that.

Guns exist because guns work. The reason why I think my name is Marcus and you think your name is whatever you think it is is not because of the ships that sailed to Africa. And it certainly isn't because of the superiority of the men on those ships. It is because those men had guns. (Guns, and the vicious desperation that comes from being born in a land that can barely support human life.) If those men had not had guns, their ships would have come back empty. The other thing that happened the moment I first fired a gun was that I forgave us for our own genocide. I had not even realized that I blamed us. But I had. The missing piece was guns.

Guns work *so well*. But they are a tool, not a virtue. Those English/French/etc. thugs weren't better than my ancestors, any more than the car-jacker is better than the driver stopped at a light, or the predator is better than the runaway locked in his cellar. They just have guns is all. But they didn't want *me* to have a gun. Again: fuck that.

Fortunately, although the bill was being signed into law as I watched, it would not take effect for three full months. Some ban: *You've got three months to buy up as much of the good shit as you can get your hands on.* I knew that there was going to be a total feeding frenzy. And that it would have to include me.

Article I, section 9 of the United States Constitution begins as follows:

The Migration or Importation of such Persons as any of the States now existing shall think proper to admit, shall not be prohibited by the Congress prior to the Year one thousand eight hundred and eight, but a Tax or duty may be imposed on such Importation, not exceeding ten dollars for each Person.

What that means is, abducting Africans to torture and rape and work to death for no money is definitely legal for the next 21 years, but after that, no guarantees. The backstory is that in 1787 people saw abolition coming, possibly in the very near future, and this was a way to buy more time. "Our" Founding Fathers affirmatively made slavery legal, right there in the body of the Constitution.

People got the message. They built more ships and hired more thugs and grabbed us up by the millions. And why not? Free people! I mean, Persons. And almost half of us survived the voyage. They really came correct those last 21 years. They stockpiled us. Our Constitution told them to.

This was a lot like that.

My Cold Dead Etc.

Wednesday, December 8, 1993

The day before I was to become a gun owner, some black guy took a Glock onto a commuter train and shot up a bunch of people back east.

Mom was right—I feel a little guilty when some other black person does something bad. I can't help it. But I also know I didn't make that feeling up. It's a thing.

For centuries in this country, if any black man was accused of a crime anywhere, all black men everywhere ran a real risk of getting killed by a mob. Part of that is perceived fungibility, which is what racism is based on—we all look alike, act alike, know each other, and so on. And, until some point during my lifetime, the prevailing, out-in-the-open thinking was that if one of us did something they didn't like, any one of us (or, usually, several of us) was available to receive the retribution. We were all each other's proxy. Again, this view was considered normal and sane.

I have to say that things have changed since then. Clearly, things have changed. But I don't know by how much. I do know that back in '91, when Bush the First invaded Iraq, in certain parts of Brooklyn and Queens bat-wielding guidos were jumping any black or brown man they could catch alone. Brothers, Indians, Puerto Ricans—for a while, we were all Iraqis. So I don't think I have to pretend that mind set has completely gone away.

And then, the day before I'm planning to get me some guns while I still can, a member of my race goes and shoots up a bunch of working people.

He wasn't dead. The people he was shooting managed to disarm and restrain him before the cops could come and shoot him sixty billion times. And now he was saying that he had been out to kill white people, as well as "conservative blacks." The cameras ate that shit up. I wondered whether I was a "conservative black."

The press was acting like we'd captured the very first racist ever. *Time* magazine's cover that week featured the asshole's mug shot, digitally darkened, of course, to make him scarier. The headline under the photo: *THE FACE OF HATE.* My gut balled into a fist when I saw that cover at the newsstand outside my office. *Oh, sure. Hate got invented yesterday.* I bought three copies.

It was time for Duck Season to kick into high gear. A gun store seemed both the place to be and not. On the very next morning after the LIRR massacre I took lunch early and walked south on 2nd Street to Downtown Arms, the large, brightly lit showroom just past Market Street, a little after 11:00.

Downtown Arms was the store the respectable suits passed at top speed, averting their eyes porn-shop style. Until the Brady bill passed I'd looked away too. I don't know exactly what I'd expected, but it wasn't the professional smiling faces of the clean-cut, if paunchy, men I found there.

Everybody thinks that gun nuts are all right-wing racist kooks. And they pretty much are. But, like most stereotypes, this is both true and not true. Best I can figure, gun nuts love guns so much that it almost transcends race. Kind of like what having the same kink or owning rental property does for people—one common cause unites them beyond any rational explanation. So, sure, don't get them started on the Clintons. But the reception I got at Downtown Arms that day was undeniably better than the reception I got from the black security guards in the lobby at work. Yes, I was wearing a suit, but I wore a suit at work too. Frankly, I didn't care that they hated Clinton. Those folks could see me.

An older gent approached. White, of course, but he was smiling. "Good afternoon, sir! Help you with anything?" The smiling man sported a name badge that said *Roy* and he was also wearing a large pistol on his belt, the same belt that held up his khakis. I looked around the room. The entire sales staff was carrying. Short-sleeved button-down Dilbert shirts, Dockers, and semi-autos. With extra ammo.

OK. This is the coolest motherfucking establishment I have ever been in in my entire fucking life. And I've been to Hooters.

I didn't know it then, but I wasn't just meeting a salesman; I was meeting my mentor, my sensei, my rabbi. Roy became "my guy" the way the Johns and Dicks I worked with had a hat guy. I would talk guns and buy guns from Roy for years, off and on, until well-intentioned but utterly clueless liberals finally succeeded in shutting the place down. Today, the few remaining gun shops in the Bay Area are all in sketchy neighborhoods. Well done.

"Hi, Roy," I said. "I am looking for a gun."

"Well, OK then! Let's narrow that down a little. A handgun? Rifle? Shotgun?" I sensed not a hint of condescension. None.

"Oh, definitely a handgun." I felt kind of sleazy saying that. That's part of the liberal crazy too—a shotgun is somehow more legitimate? Do you people know what a shotgun does?

"Great! Will this be your first handgun?" It was so obviously going to be the first handgun I'd actually bought and owned, but he asked me anyway. Roy had better skills than most waiters.

"Yes."

"Big? Little?"

"Um . . . medium?"

"We can do that." Roy ambled over to a row of glass cases at the far end of the store; I followed. There were about a dozen suits milling around, mostly staring at guns inside the cases, and another dozen stereotypical gun nuts, all safari vests and plaid shirts, mostly handling the merchandise. Since the sales staff was carrying, I guess we all knew that if someone got froggy and started waving a piece around, Roy and his buddies would handle it. But nobody was feeling froggy. It was like there was a truce in effect. A time-out.

Sure, we could all end up shooting these guns at each other if society broke down but, for now, we all had a bond: we were preparing. The sheep were all outside, hoping for the best. We were at Downtown Arms, hoping for the best and preparing. I was home.

Roy stopped behind a case that held several semi-automatic pistols. They had long barrels but were slim overall. "Twenty-twos?" I guessed.

Roy smiled. "That's right. A .22 caliber is a great starter gun. A starter pistol," he said, riffing off of himself and chuckling. "But really, this is a good way to get acquainted with pistols. You could go with a revolver. Revolvers are good too, very good, and simple to learn and use. But you're a young man. You've got lots of time to familiarize yourself with semi-autos. This would be the best way to start."

I believed him. Even though it was my nature to suspect that Roy was steering me toward the small-caliber weapons to keep me harmless, or at least to ensure that I would come back to buy more, I did not really think that this was the case. For one thing, as I had predicted, we were already deep into a buying frenzy. There were 20 to 30 cats gun shopping in the middle of a workday. Business was obviously good; Roy wasn't desperate. And for another thing, I just believed him.

"A .22 sounds good . . ." I drifted down the case and took it all in. There were several finishes inside, mainly stainless steel and blued; "blued" is black. "You think maybe stainless . . . ?"

"Guns are black." I took this at face value. Even though in time I did go on to buy a couple of stainless pieces, if you ask me, guns are black. "And don't worry about the ban," Roy said smoothly. "When you are ready for something larger, we'll still have enough pre-ban inventory to get you whatever you need. All perfectly legal to sell."

Was I that transparent? I decided that I was. "And clips?"

"And clips."

A moderate amount of paperwork later, I was back in the office, the proud owner of a Smith & Wesson .22 caliber semi-automatic target pistol.

The gun was still at the store—waiting period—but I had seen and held my actual piece, identified on the receipt by serial number.

A few days later I went back, again at lunchtime, and picked it up. Having a gun in my briefcase all afternoon was badass. I considered naming it, but decided that that was probably too much.

YPDRMF.

Friday, December 17, 1993

Mr. Dr. was reading the paper; I, for once, was not. I was watching Amalia sleep and didn't notice that Mama had left the room until Mr. Dr. called to me softly: "Marcus." When I glanced up, he gestured outside with his head. "A word?"

We went out into the hallway. Mr. Dr. closed the door to Amalia's room behind us. I waited while he tried to read my face.

"Marcus. We are approaching the point in this . . . process . . . we need to discuss something. Something medical."

"OK." I was Amalia's health care proxy. We had not reached this decision lightly. One of her parents was a physician, after all, and you could probably make a solid argument that they loved her even more than I did. Ultimately, they decided to respect the office, as it were. Probably after Amalia promised them that I would listen to reason, as I was apparently doing right now.

"Do you know what a DNR is?" He didn't wait. "It stands for Do Not Resuscitate. It is an order that a patient—or her proxy—can put in place once it is certain that even the most heroic measures will only prolong life briefly, and will probably prolong suffering. Unnecessary suffering. Do you understand?"

"Well . . . I know what a DNR is. But why are you bringing it up?"

He pressed on. "Because, we wanted to ask . . . Have you considered putting such an order in place here . . . if it becomes . . . evident—"

"No. Shit no." A little loud. One or two people in the hall turned to look, but *Shit no* is a pretty normal thing to hear in a hospital. "In fact, right now I'm thinking about inventing something called a Yes, Please *Do* Resuscitate Motherf—. . . order. What I am thinking about is one of those. How does that sound to you? Sir?"

I expected him to match my anger. But his body relaxed and he smiled in a way I had only seen him smile at Amalia. "I like the sound of that fine, Marcus." He put his hand on my shoulder and glanced behind me. I turned. Mama was standing at the end of the hall. Waiting.

Ah, shit. A test. Wow. Clever motherfucker.

I opened the door to Amalia's room. "After you, Mr. Dr."

He put his hand on my shoulder again. "You can call me Papa if you like."

Fuck Hunters.

Sunday, December 19, 1993

I waited outside, in the parking lot. Go just two towns south of SF and you are in the Rust Belt. Fat men wearing baseball caps watched me as they passed. I did not return their rudeness. I had a gun on me, but we all did.

Debra arrived five minutes later. She was a good hugger, in part because her arms were so long. Debra was the size of a big dude; almost the size of The Door, with boobs. But mostly the hugs were so good because we were war buddies. Abby, her sister, was having a very hard time. As hard as Amalia. When Debra was around, I knew that somebody understood.

By the time we released our bear hugs, fat men had stopped to stare. California is basically Ohio with Oakland stuck in. "Let's go inside," she said.

We picked up our cases and went in. She held the door for me, which was noted with disapproval by a few of the heavyset gentlemen lounging on the couches inside.

"Help you," the portly man behind the counter said as we approached. Somehow he did not seem particularly inclined to help us.

"This is a stickup," Debra announced. The eavesdroppers turned to us hopefully. "You think? We're here to shoot. Please." That man would have never said *please* to Debra. Not for anything. That's what made us better than him.

The rangemaster put his hands on his considerable hips. He looked sad. "Weapons."

Debra placed her case on the counter, opened it, and turned it to face the redneck like it was a briefcase full of money. I imitated her.

The dullard's fleshy eyes widened at the sight of Debra's hardware. I took a peek. Her large case held two huge pistols, several very long clips, and some funny-looking bullets.

"Weapons and ammunition must be carried separately," the rangemaster declared, injecting what authority he could into his voice. "And that ammunition is illegal! This is felony!"

"A felony," I corrected. "Or felonious."

The chubby men behind us were all staring now. One even started to rise. Debra pulled her badge out of the back pocket of her jeans and plunked it down on the counter. The shield was heavy in its thick leather wallet; the thud of that thing on the counter carried considerably more authority than the rangemaster's panicked accusation. Debra herself didn't say a word. Instead, she began peering past the gatekeeper at the walls and display cases of the shop, clearly snooping for some sort of citable offense of her own. I looked too, though I had no idea what I was looking for. These people did need to be cited for something.

Duly intimidated, the dunce took a small step back from Deb and turned to face me. The .22 caliber target pistol placed precisely in the center of my small case might have been cool if I were James Bond.

"Well that's a puny gun!" the rangemaster said. A corpulent fellow in full hunter gear giggled.

"You got a puny gun too, Hank." Someone had emerged from the back of the shop. An Asian man, incredibly fit and wearing a tight blue T-shirt with some sort of logo over the breast. He was smiling the same wolf's smile as the other men in the place, but it was not directed at Debra, or me.

Hank puffed up even more, and bristled. But after a moment he laughed. It was a pretty convincing laugh.

The Asian man walked up to the counter. "I'll check these two in." Not a request. Hank moved slowly away, jilted.

"How you doin', Deb. How's Abby?"

"Good days and bad days, Lyle. You know."

Ah—Lyle is in The Club. Bad for him; good for us.

Lyle glanced at Debra's gear. "Nice." Then he turned to me. "It's my job to inspect all weapons before they are allowed on the range. For safety."

"Please," I said. "I need all the help I can get."

The fat men, Hank included, ignored us. Lyle took my .22 out of the case. "Unloaded?" he asked me, even as he racked the slide and checked the empty chamber himself. "Brand new?"

"Yes. And yes."

"You've never shot before?"

"No, I have . . . but not in a long time, though. And not like this." Lyle's eyebrows rose. "Out in the woods, I mean. Upstate, with my cousins. When I was a teenager. They're kinda . . ."

"I've got 'kinda' cousins too," Lyle said.

"Everybody does."

Lyle laughed and snapped the slide of my piece back into place. He looked very cool doing that. "You're fine. Lane two. Have fun, guys."

"Handle your gun a lot," Debra yelled. We were wearing those big muffs and earplugs underneath. I'd thought I remembered how loud guns were, but that had been outside. In this cramped bunker, the noise was painful even with protection. Bubbas were shooting guns constantly on both sides of us. "Load it. Unload it. Strip it. Put it back together. If you can't, read the manual. Or call me."

I hadn't handled Dookie much since I got him (yeah, I named him after all), so we took our time. Debra disassembled him a bit and we examined his guts. She showed me what to clean when I got home. She told me to stop pointing the gun at my face and staring down into the barrel. She showed me the right way to do it. I loaded up both of my clips with bullets and seated each clip into my new friend and racked all of the bullets first into the chamber then out onto the floor one by one. Pretty sure I looked as cool as Lyle did. She showed me how to clear a jam. She unloaded Dookie and had me cock and decock him a bunch of times. "Guns never just 'go off,'" she shouted. "Those 'accidental' shootings you hear about are people decocking wrong."

"Or murders." I racked the slide and held Dookie up next to my face like a movie poster.

"Yeah, there's probably a few in there." She swallowed my gun hand in hers and pointed us back downrange. "OK! You're ready to shoot."

"What about you?" I asked. Deb's guns were still in their case. I really wanted to see what they could do. Granted, we were only shooting paper, and mine could do that. But I was guessing those puppies would make confetti.

"Patience, Grasshopper. Dookie is a gun too. This counts as shooting a gun." She got behind me. "Is the safety on?" she asked for the eleventy billionth time.

"Yes."

"Good. Switch it off."

I did. The little red dot smiled at me.

"Both hands."

I turned around and stared up at her. "Are you *sure* I can't shoot one-handed?"

"I'm sure you can. Also sure you'll shoot better with two. You wanna look like John Woo? Or you wanna take down the bad guy?"

"John Woo is a director," I said. But I held Dookie like she showed me.

"Good. If it helps, we call this the 'pussy grip.' That's a good thing, right? Alright. Now breathe. Put the front sight where you want it. Breathe. Don't worry about the rear sight. You'll get shot worrying about the rear one. Just put that front sight where you want it, and breathe. Don't cock it!" she barked; she must have seen my thumb start to move. "You'll get shot cocking too. Or you'll shoot a friendly thinking you *didn't* cock it. Fuck the cock!" The three gentlemen in the next lane seemed afraid, despite the fact that each held an assault rifle. "Just squeeze the trigger the whole way. Don't pull it; squeeze."

"That's what she said."

"Yes, she did. You ready?"

I nodded.

"Take a slow, deep breath. Let it out easy. And while you do, think about what you are trying to hit, and squeeze. Don't think about the hammer or anything else . . ."

Dookie cracked, and jumped slightly. I got ready to take another shot but Debra put her hand on top of mine. "Let's see what you did with that one."

She hit the button on the wall at the left side of our lane and our paper target came speeding toward us on a clothesline like a ghost.

The target slammed up to our faces. There was a very neat, very small, very unimpressive hole in the center of the target's neck.

"The throat? What were you aiming for? The head?"

"No. The throat."

Deb leaned away and stared at me. "Why?" she asked, in a decidedly skeptical manner.

"Because aiming for the torso is bullshit these days. Too many vests. Center of mass is a myth perpetuated by the body armor industry. I was gonna aim for the head, but using just the front sight, like you said, you could go high and miss him entirely. So I figured, aim for the neck. It's about as tough as a head shot, but if I go a little high that's good for me. And if I go low, well, maybe he's not wearing a vest."

"You gave that some thought."

"Little bit."

Deb hit the button and the ghost fled backward to the middle of the range. She folded her arms. "Do it again."

I did my pussy grip and breathed and squeezed. CRACK!, Dookie said. He didn't make the satisfying *boomgrowl* that guns make on TV, but it turns out that no guns do.

"Howd'ya feel about that one?" she asked.

"Pretty good."

"Let's see."

The ghost came back. I didn't put it in exactly the same hole, which is what I'd been trying to do. My second shot was off to the right by maybe an eighth of an inch. So it wasn't one hole, but it wasn't quite two either. I'd made an infinity symbol, or a Venn diagram.

"Impressive," Deb nodded.

Dookie was incredibly easy to shoot. He had almost no recoil. Almost no stopping power either—the two pretty much go together—but he was my first, a starter pistol, like Roy said. And Debra declared me a natural. I believed her. Shooting is kind of like punching. A cross between punching and sending someone bad thoughts. All bullets are mind bullets.

We went through my box of shells. They sold .22 ammo, so I bought another five boxes, mostly to take home. And while I was at it, I bought up all of their pre-ban Smith .22 clips. I tossed my fifties on the counter like I did back when Amalia and I used to travel. *That's right—she's a cop, and I'm rich. Suck it, Cleetus.*

After we shot another box of .22s, Debra pulled out her pythons. Really they were Eagles—Desert Eagles, Israeli-made .50 caliber autos. The biggest handgun they make. Deb rocked two of them. I knew she wouldn't let me run across the range with one in each hand, shooting up everyone's targets in slow motion while doing my war cry.

She loaded them both and set one down on the counter in front of her. She checked her stance and aimed and breathed and slowly, rhythmically emptied first one pistol, then the other. Each shot thundered and kicked like I couldn't believe. It took maybe two minutes.

We didn't need to bring the target up to see what she had done but we did anyway. There was one hole punched out. Dead center, just over the sternum. Fourteen of the biggest bullets they make, all through a hole the size of a small fist.

Debra admired her work. "Armor piercing. Fuck a vest."

"I love you."

"You guys mind a little company?" Deb's friend Lyle was behind us, smiling behind some wicked sporty goggles. "I heard those Deagles talking."

For the better part of the next hour, the grown-ups shot the big guns and chatted while I watched and listened. I took in more good information about guns and shooting in that one day than most people ever learn. Turned out that both Debra and Lyle were certified weapons instructors, which explained their patience with me.

After the Deagles cooled off, we packed up our gear and left the lanes. We scrubbed the lead and other gunk off our hands in the bathroom and I bought us all Snapples from a cooler set between the paper targets and the gun-cleaning supplies. We crashed on couches arranged in a circle in the middle of the roomy shop. The place had emptied out while we were shooting. Only Hank remained, dusting suspiciously.

"Guns are hella fun. Why isn't everybody into them?" It sounded crazy, but I had to say it. If anyone would understand, it would be this crowd.

"Because," Lyle said without hesitation, "most people are taught that only Caucasians should have guns. Only hicks. Not directly," he added to my skeptical face. "Culturally. Regular urban professional types like yourself don't usually associate themselves with guns. They can't imagine themselves being all gunny like Hank here."

Though Hank had been pretending not to eavesdrop, once he was busted he smiled broadly and declared, "Mah cold dead fingers!" But then he lumbered away, back to his perch behind the counter.

"Right," Lyle said. "So the progressives and the professionals decide that guns don't fit their image, and they don't learn about them and they don't buy them. But the hicks do. It's how they were raised."

"And the gangstas," Deb grumbled.

"Yeah. And the gangsters and criminals generally. And us cops. So, in San Francisco, say, that's, what, 2,000 cops, maybe 200 on duty at any given time, protecting 700,000 citizens from 10,000 criminals. That makes no sense. That's why things are the way they are. People refuse to protect themselves."

"Cops want people to have guns?"

"People like you. We don't want bad guys to have guns. But they do anyway. Why not you? Just don't get them stolen from you."

I thought on that. "Through all that Brady bill business, it was always some guy from Montana or Kentucky someplace standing up on the House floor talking about, 'We need our guns for huntin'.' And only, um, rural types hunt." I wasn't comfortable calling Hank a fucking hillbilly to his face.

"For the most part, yeah."

"Fuck hunters!" Deb said, mostly to Hank.

"It's always seemed a little creepy to me," I agreed. "Even the ones who say they do it so they can eat it. They drive past 34 Safeways going out to the woods to wound a deer and follow its blood trail like Jason."

"Those are the guardians of our Second Amendment rights," Lyle said. "Yup."

"This country ain't right sometimes," Deb declared. We all nodded. Even Hank.

Connected.

Monday, December 20, 1993

"I remember the first time I hurt someone." Amalia sat up slightly. Mama kept staring out the window, but she was listening. The orderly left.

"I was . . . tiny. I mean like five. School was this new thing. Not, like, day care or nursery school or some shit, where you eat some paste and call it a day. Real school, the first time they really try and teach you stuff, you know?"

Amalia nodded. Mama stopped pretending and turned to us.

"I don't remember what the lesson was about. Like, what color is blue or how do you spell the word 'A' or some sh—. . . stuff. I just remember, I knew the answer. So I raised my hand and the teacher called on me and I said it.

"No problem, right? No. Problem. There was this kid. Fat fucker. Sorry. His name was Rudy. That I remember. 'Cause Rudy was, like, the first hater. That dude is famous. He was *my* first hater, anyway, and because I knew what one plus one was or whatever, that fat f—. . . he had beef.

"So class is going on, and I'm sitting there and I look over at Rudy and he's doing, you know, schoolyard sign language." I made a fist. "*I . . . am gon' punch . . . you . . . in yo face . . . at three . . . oh . . . clock.*" I showed three fingers and then pointed at the clock. "*Outside.*" I pointed at the window. "But when I shrugged 'Why?' at him, he just sat there mad-dogging me.

"So 3:00 comes and we all go outside. I don't tell anyone. The teacher or anybody. It was like, there wasn't anyone to tell. Grown-ups weren't real. We were on our own. I go out, and I'm not running and hiding but I'm not looking for him either. But here he comes. He's winded from running 50 feet. A little kid! That's not right. I bet he's dead now.

"Anyway, Rudy's all in my face, and it takes me awhile to figure out what he's talking about. Because it's the first time anyone's ever told me that I think I'm white before. And I'm trying to piece together what led him to that conclusion, and even when he tells me, I struggle for a while with that. I think I'm white 'cause I can count to two? How that meant I thought I was a white person was completely beyond me. I'm just not making the connection. And even after I decide to worry about it later, I'm still wondering why that makes Rudy mad at me. I remember wondering, If I think I'm white, shouldn't he feel sorry for me?" I laughed; Amalia and Mama smiled.

"This all takes five or ten minutes. Ten minutes of Rudy talking smack and me trying to ask questions. And there's a big crowd of kids all around us screaming. I'm not as smart as he gives me credit, because it takes me that long to realize that we are actually going to have a fight over me raising my hand in class. Like, an actual fight.

"I really don't want to fight. I want us to work it out. I'm afraid to fight. I don't want to get hurt. Rudy doesn't seem to care about getting hurt. He just keeps yelling louder and louder and calling me more and more names and the kids are all screaming and then Rudy pushes me."

I got up from my little guest chair in the corner and walked over to sit by the bed. Amalia took my hand.

"I'd pay a month's salary to see that punch on video," I said. "Because it felt beautiful. It felt perfect. I roll with the push and I use it as my windup and then I'm just coming at him. Nobody had shown me how to throw a punch. Maybe it's genetic. To this day, it's the best punch I ever threw, I think. My very first one.

"I only hit him once. An uppercut, right in his little gut. It was an experiment, to see if it would still work there, with all that cushion.

"Rudy drops. Hard. I hit him that one lick in his belly and he goes down, all doubled over. I must've caught his solar plexus. I can't always do that *now*, and I didn't even know what a solar plexus was back then. But I catch him just right. And everybody's going apeshit. For a minute I'm thinking I have to fight all them too, but when I go to leave they get out of my way. So I head home."

I glanced out the window. "There are more bullies after that. But none of them bully me for long."

Amalia squeezed my hand with her little soft one. It was skinny and green, but it was still soft. "I'm sorry, baby."

"That's not even the bad part. The thing was . . . when Rudy was in my face, I didn't want to hit him because I thought it would hurt *me*."

"What?" they both said.

"I thought that if I hit Rudy, that I would feel it too. I *assumed* it. You

know, motherf—. . . people like to act like they were never kids, but I remember. Some of it. I remember not knowing what the rules were. The rules
of the universe. And life was this big lab where you figured out where you
were. And that morning, I'd gotten up assuming that, you know, we were all
connected. I didn't see how it wouldn't hurt me to hit someone else. I only
did it to make him stop. For both our sake. I thought he was crazy.

"That moment when my fist made contact, I remember being really surprised. Maybe even more surprised than he was. Because I didn't feel it. I
didn't feel a fist in my gut. I just felt my fist in something soft. It didn't hurt
me. At all."

I turned to Mama, who looked like her brain was working very hard. "I
thought about that later. I thought about it a lot. 'Cause I was like, If people
can hurt other people, and they don't feel it, and it's always been that way the
whole time I've been here, and everyone else already knows this, then what
the fuck kind of place is this that I am in?" I looked away. "The implications
. . . I didn't want to leave the house the next morning. A world where people
are not connected at all and it doesn't hurt to hurt someone else . . . that's
fucked up." I turned to Amalia. "What kind of sick fuck would make a world
where anyone can chop someone else up and it doesn't hurt them *at all*?
Does that make sense to you? I mean, we take all this for granted now. But do
you remember not knowing it? Can you imagine not knowing it? And then
learning it? How that would feel?"

I didn't want them to laugh at me. I started to get up, but Amalia held
on to my hand.

"You were right, though." She was smiling.

"What?"

"You were right the first time." She clasped my hand in both of hers. "We
are connected." Not smiling so much now. She had leaned forward, which
was not easy for her to do, but she didn't make a face or cry out or anything.
She was one tough chick. "And, baby, you *do* feel it when you hurt somebody.
You *do* feel it. And it changes you."

My love looked very different than she had forever ago when she invited herself into my study group. But she was still beautiful. My hand melted inside of hers.

"I want you to do something for me," she said. "I want you to know that you were right the first time. Just know that."

I nodded.

She patted my hand and stared at me a moment, then lay back and closed her eyes. My beautiful angel. She was breathing kind of hard. After a while, I went and got a nurse. But the nurse said that was normal.

Buh Bye.

Wednesday, December 22, 1993

They told us that if the radiation didn't end it, they had no further treatments.

I sat in the waiting room, waiting. Waiting is a skill. When you're not good at it, you bring books and music and food and such, like you're a small child on a bus trip. After a while, though, you learn: Time passes. No matter what you do.

I sat there while they irradiated the tumor in my wife's chest, microwaving her heart in the process.

One object in the room kept drawing my attention. It sat on the far corner of the coffee table in front of me. My eye would land on it and move on. Eventually I focused on it. I meditated on it.

The object was made of wire. It was like a sculpture. A wire sculpture. Curvy waves, slopes, like a sculpture of a small hill. A small lumpy hill. I realized that the hill was actually a face. It was a life-size wire sculpture of a face, sitting on the table, staring up at the ceiling. It was more than one. It was a stack of wire sculptures of a face. The same face. Kind of unisex but vaguely masculine. It was like a mask. It *was* a mask. A stack of masks. I noticed holes, small holes, along the edges of the masks, every few inches, all the way around. And that's when I realized that what I was looking at was the thing they put over your face and screw to the table when they have to irradiate your head. When they have to do your brain. They put one of those over your face and they bolt it to the table so you don't move. So you *can't* move. The mouth of the mask was slightly open. Like in a moan, or a scream. The mask was screaming. The face was screaming.

And then something gave. Something broke in me. I did not move. I did not cry. But something came loose and floated away. It almost made a sound.

This Christmas.

Saturday, December 25, 1993

I got her a crystal unicorn. That's all. She really liked it.

Thank God, she was home. I guess we were in hospice. They didn't call it that. But we had stopped fighting the cancer, and now we were just taking care of her. Making her happy. And she was so happy. She was in love and grateful for every day. We cuddled, we laughed. There wasn't much pain anymore.

That Christmas, just us and the kittens, we unwrapped our gifts (I got myself an Etch A Sketch; the kitties got catnip, again) and we drank cocoa even though it's not that cold in San Francisco in December, and we watched *It's a Wonderful Life*.

Yes. It is a wonderful life.

Loss.

I guess there are several amazing things about death. But for me the most amazing thing is this: There is absolutely no preparing for it. No matter how old or how sick the person is. Not if you love her. Sure, intellectually, if someone is 100 years old or has stage IV lymphoma, you understand that their insurance premiums would be a lot higher than someone who does not. But, emotionally—which is all that matters—the actual death, however predictable, is always a total shock. Death is shocking. She is here. Sick, very sick, but here. And then—she is not. Not even a little. She is completely gone forever. Almost as if she had never been here at all. But you know that she was here, she was right here, in this bed, in this body. "Remains" is a really good word. She was in there. And now she is—elsewhere. Now she is *not*.

Completely gone forever.

Remember peekaboo? When you were, like, two? Remember how absolutely, completely mind-blowing peekaboo was? It was like that.

The next morning, I woke up in a different world.

The Lost Year.

I'll tell you what I can about the next year or so.

Rachel came up from LA during Amalia's last days. My mom arrived from New York soon after. Rachel had to go home about a week after the service but Mom stayed with me for a long time. All of my memories of eating include her making me do it.

I slept a lot. Sometimes I'd sleep from when it was dark to when it was dark. Sometimes I'd be awake for 24 hours, asleep for two, and awake for another 24. No matter how long I slept, or didn't sleep, as soon as I woke up it would hit me again, completely fresh. That's grief. Grief is a thing that sits by your bed and waits for you to wake up.

I remember, Mom was really cramping my style. I think that was her intention. I needed to just lay there. But she wouldn't let me. She made me take a shower. She made me feed the cats. She wouldn't stop talking to me. The only reason I went back to work was to trick her into going home.

I knew I wasn't ready to go back to work, even after months away. But I'd had no idea how not-ready I was. It wasn't because I couldn't function. I couldn't, but I couldn't function anywhere. I could have not functioned at work just as easily as at home. No. The problem was the people, and the things they said to me.

I think that people have watched too many TV movies in which someone walks up to a grieving person and says just the right words and fixes it somehow. Because they try very hard to do this in real life. But fixing the loss of a loved one is obviously impossible, and they suck terribly at it in any event. And so the only thing they succeed in doing is making the grieving person want to murder them when they walk up to you and put their hand on you and say something like *You must be relieved* or *At least she didn't suffer* or *Everything happens for a reason.* My mind has wiped itself clean of all identifying data regarding who said those things to me, I'm pretty sure for their sake.

So I stopped going to work after about a week and a half, two days after Mom finally left. I got dressed for work one morning but, instead of actually going anywhere, I called HR and I talked to someone for maybe 10 minutes and then I hung up. I got a form in the mail two days later and a week after that I filled it out, and a week after that I went out and mailed it. And the checks kept coming. One thing about working for the devil is that it comes with a generous benefits package. I never told Mom I stopped going, but I never needed money, and she never actually asked me if I was still going. And even if she had, I would have lied. I certainly lied every time she asked me how I was.

Mama and Papa were destroyed. When I saw them at the funeral, I swear to God they looked 10 years older than they had one week earlier. They just turned old. I promised I would call them, and they promised they would call me. Nobody called anybody. It didn't matter. I knew they loved me. We had seen each other's faces at the service. We knew we were all in the same place. I hoped they'd be OK. It's selfish, but I was glad I wasn't the only person who knew that the world was no longer even trying to be a worthwhile place.

I must have continued taking care of our kittens after Mom left, because they remained fed and clean. But they were as bad off as I was. They wandered the halls day and night, crying, searching for their mommy. It was comforting.

After a while, I moved into an apartment in the Haight, near Golden Gate Park. I couldn't bear the Dream Deferred House anymore. She was just so gone. If the place had been haunted I'd have bought it and never left. But it was the opposite of haunted.

The only way I can describe it is that I died too. Right then and there, on our bed, her head in my hands. I died and I never came back.

Unfortunately, the newspapers kept coming, both the *Herald* and the *Inquisitor*, straight to the house and then to the apartment; and, unfortunately, I kept reading them. Every day.

First Sighting.

O n the bus. I wasn't doing too much driving. Too much road rage. Not me; other motherfuckers. Lately, too many dudes driving out there were begging to be dragged from their cars and beat to death in front of their women. So I took the bus whenever I could. There were motherfuckers who needed to be beat to death on buses too, obviously, but I sat all the way in the back, and in those days no one sat next to me.

I was on my way to one of the infrequent tasks I needed to perform to keep the checks coming. The last time, they sent me to some dude who looked like Judd Hirsch. We sat at a cheap card table in a cold, tiny room.

"So what's your problem?" Judd asked. I glanced down at my file—it was open right in front of him—but apparently he wanted to hear it from me.

"Well . . . my wife . . . passed away. And it was hard before that too. And now I'm having trouble. Doing everything."

"So what's your problem?"

"What? I mean, I did some reading. I think it's called 'adjustment disorder.' The *DSM-III* says—"

"So what's your problem?"

And my finger was in his face. And the room was hot. And even smaller now, impossibly small, like an elevator or a phone booth. And all I could see was him. And, finally, he could see me.

"Don't ask me that again."

And then I was leaning back in my chair and my hands were on the table in front of me and I was talking. And Judd sat there and he didn't say that again or anything while I told him about the not sleeping and whatever. It reminded me of my time with Mr. O'Donnell, so long ago, except in reverse, sort of.

I didn't have to go to any appointments for three months after that. And today they were sending me to someone else.

"Whatcha readin'?" A woman in the sideways-facing seat nearest me smiled at the man across the aisle from her. She was tiny. Hippie chick. Lots of dark, crinkly hair, like Rachel. Cute. He was a jailbird. Huge. Visibly dirty. Covered in tats. It was a monster. And tiny cute hippie chick was flirting with it.

Their eyes met and the beast's face went from homicidal to bashful. If I had asked it what it was reading, it would have killed me.

"Um . . . a book," it squirmed.

"Yeah?" She leaned forward. "What book?"

The monster glanced around, then showed her the cover. Discreetly.

"Hmm . . . 'The Turner Diaries'! What's *that* about?"

"Ah . . . um . . . it's a book, by this man a lot of people really respect a lot." He peered around again, scanning for eavesdroppers, but I wasn't listening. I wasn't even there. "It's a story? But, also? It's sort of, um, a prophecy."

"Like 'Dianetics'?"

"Um . . . maybe?"

Little cutie hopped up and crossed the bus and plunked herself down next to him. She left her flip-flops on the floor in front of her seat. I was jealous. That guy? *That* guy? I wasn't looking for a girlfriend—I was lucky to be out of bed. But had the world changed so much during my absence that now huge dirty jailbirds with SS and Iron Cross tats on their necks had to beat the honeys off with a stick? *What the fuck?*, I said. I didn't really say it. I just pointed my head toward the window and watched them.

Now they were hunched together. The monster was speaking softly. I couldn't hear a thing. Jailbirds are really good at not being overheard.

After a minute, tiny hippie chick leaned back and swatted the beast on its massive haunch, a big sunny smile on her face, and said, "Oh! You're a militia guy!"

The monster froze.

"I *love* militia guys!" she announced. "How y'all are gonna blow up a bunch of folks, yeah, and pin it on the blacks. Start a race war!" She leaned in again and grabbed its shoulder. "Do you know David Duke? Patty Buchanan?"

It was pretty uncomfortable. Of course, all the sheep were staring straight ahead. But the monster was blushing. Its face was a big, sad Kabuki mask now.

Without taking his eyes off of the small hippie, the monster reached up and pulled the little cord that means you want to get off at the next stop. It stood and shuffled to the rear exit door. For a second I thought little cutie was going to follow it. But she just sat and called out, "Hey, maybe when we finally get our homeland in the northwest, I'll see you up there, yeah?" Eventually the bus pulled over and the monster got off. It didn't walk away. It just stood there with its broad back to the bus, boulder shoulders slumped under a beater.

"White power!" hippie chick yelled through the open window as the bus took off. She blew it a big kiss: "Mmmmmm*wah!*" It didn't move.

Little cutie bounced back to her seat, reclaimed her shoes, and sat there looking pleased. I think she smiled at me, but there was no way I was making eye contact.

Slip and Fall.

Wednesday, February 1, 1995

Heading out to buy unhealthy food, I slipped on some wet paint in the hallway of my apartment building and plopped down right on my ass. I wasn't hurt, but my jeans were done. Equal parts anger and amusement left me fairly neutral as I went back inside and changed. Later I called Fred, my landlord, and told him what had happened. He was really apologetic—I mean, who paints the floor?—and offered to pay for my jeans without me even having to ask. As landlords go, Fred was a good guy.

Destiny.

Friday, February 10, 1995

"Today we honor our ancestors!" the poet declared into his megaphone. "Our brave African forefathers. We are the descendants of kings! Fierce warriors and wise scholars. I dedicate tonight's reading to those brave Nubian warriors who chose to *die* rather than be enslaved! Thousands . . . millions of Africans jumped from the slavers's ships, babies in their arms, to *die* before living one day of bondage on American soil! To those immortal, courageous souls—my ancestors—I say . . ." He rattled off a long sentence in another language. Probably Swahili. Homeboy was fired up. His impeccable dreads danced.

"The first piece I will be reading for you today is—"

I raised my hand. "I have a question."

The young griot cocked his megaphone to the side so that he could see. "Yes?" I don't know why he was using a megaphone. We were in a bookstore; he could hear me just fine.

"You said you want to honor your ancestors."

"Yes! And the first piece I will read will be—"

"The ones who jumped off the slave ships."

"Yes!" I think he tried to raise his fist in defiance, but he had his megaphone in one hand and his self-published pamphlet in the other, and he couldn't seem to decide which one he could do without.

"Well . . . you know those aren't your ancestors, right?"

He stared at me. A real bright bulb, this one.

"Because . . . your ancestors are the people who had the people who had you, right? Your grandparents and their grandparents and so on?"

He didn't seem so fired up anymore. With his hair in his eyes like that, Shaka Zulu had taken on a decidedly sheepdog-like appearance. It was pissing me off.

"Right. People live, and breed, and become your ancestors. You see that, right? If they *didn't* live, if they never made it here, because they were too proud or whatever, and they took their babies with them, well, then they *can't* be your ancestors, right? Because they died. They're *nobody's* ancestors. It ended with them. That was their whole point. You see that, don't you?"

Now both his megaphone and his booklet—which inexplicably had a picture of Che Guevara on the cover—were down at his sides. He looked deflated. I stopped talking.

"Yes. Yes, of course. And I dedicate this reading to those brave Africans who chose freedom over life." He was working himself up again. "Who shed the devil's shackles and had the courage of their convictions! And chose *death*! And dignity!" Back on track now. "This first piece is entitled, 'Cubicle Plantation.'

"Our crop is paper, but we—"

I raised my hand again, but also just started talking. "So, basically, your actual ancestors—the ones who *didn't* jump off the ship, who came here and dealt with the whole *Silence of the Lambs* thing for the next few centuries— basically, you just called them pussies. Didn't you."

People gasped. One corner of the shaman warrior poet's mouth twitched. He lowered the book and the megaphone again and stared at nothing through glazed eyes. I'm guessing the room had taken on that spinning funhouse/kaleidoscope look. I know it well.

"Yeah," I continued, "I guess they were Toms or sellouts or something. Because they survived and lived and had kids who had kids who had kids who had *you*, so that you could stand there and be better than them."

My eyes felt hot. "But," I went on, "I mean, they're *not* sellouts, are they? Because sellouts get paid, right? That's the 'selling' part. And those people *didn't get paid shit!*" I was starting to foam up a little; I stopped to take a breath. "So, not sellouts. What, then. Weak? Were they weak, MC Knowledge?" I didn't remember his real name, but MC Knowledge was close enough. "Living in the fifties and the forties and the *seventeen fucking hundreds*." I couldn't stop.

"They were weak, huh? *They* were weak. Not you. *Them*. Those men and women, you know, they ate a lot of shit. *A lot. Of shit*." I leaned forward in my seat and MC Knowledge took a full step back. "What's the worst thing ever happened to you, man? A canceled hair appointment? These people— your ancestors, your *real* ancestors, my ancestors—they lived through hell. Hell. For you. So that you could stand there and shake your little fist and diss them. You think that's what they did it for? You think the thought of *this* is what kept them going?"

I stood, and everybody cringed. "You wouldn't have lasted a week. Neither would I. Those people were better than us. You don't know that?"

I walked fast out of that airless little back room and through the main room of Garvey Books and out onto Fillmore. It had been raining. As mad as I was, I had to smile. I probably didn't change MC Knowledge's life or even his mind, but his gig was ruined. Almost certainly, getting back to his mislabeled little book of suburban angst was now officially the most difficult thing he'd ever done.

Outside Garvey Books, I stood in the cool evening and tried to breathe. I'd gone to the reading to try to feel connected, but I couldn't have felt any less connected if I blew my brains out. I just stood there and breathed and at some point I realized that someone was standing next to me.

The instant I became aware of her, before I'd even had time to turn my head, she started talking. She kept staring straight ahead. So did I.

"I've got an uncle that lives in Israel now. He has to take a rifle with him when he goes out to buy toilet paper. He moved his whole family there. From Brooklyn." It was clear that she was talking to me only because there was no one else around. "They call themselves 'Israelis' now. They're from *Brooklyn*.

"My grandparents—the three I knew—were so angry. And so sad. And so racist!" She laughed. "*So* angry. Survivors, all of them. They never talked about it. The people you see, on TV, everywhere, calling everybody they don't like 'Hitler,' they weren't there. The ones who were there don't do that. They're all dead. Even the survivors. *Especially* the survivors. Dead. They don't talk about it, and nobody talks about them."

We were quiet awhile.

"So much shame. And not just survivor guilt. They don't know why they put up with it. None of us do. Some of those camps, we outnumbered the guards twenty to one. We let them march us around, beat us, starve us. Why? Even if we didn't have guns. Why didn't we try? Why didn't we storm the guards, overwhelm them? Or die trying? We were *starving*. Everybody—all of my people—we live with this shame. We're like the woman who sleeps every night with her window open, gets raped, and then goes to Model Mugging and buys a Doberman and a gun and waits for it to happen again. So she can do it differently. But it's already done. And you've got my brothers and everybody talking tough, being tough, getting ready, shooting kids for throwing rocks . . . they're all ashamed, is all. But it's just like you said, in there. We all come from them. We come from the ones who survived. We should be *proud* of them. We don't have anything to be ashamed of. *They* should be ashamed."

Finally I turned and looked at her. It was the tiny hippie from the bus. The one who had terrorized the monster.

"Would you like to—"

"Yes."

The hostess seated us at a good table, by the window. I figure they seat people at the window who they think won't look too disgusting when they eat. *Maybe we make a cute couple.*

"You're not from here." She had long hair, the thick, black, curly stuff. Some white girls get that beautiful curly hair straightened. Sarah didn't have that problem. I wanted to feel that hair on my face.

She waited. *You're staring.* "Oh. No. New York. You?"

"I figured New York, or Philly," she said. "I'm from here. A local."

"That's unusual, isn't it? A native San Franciscan?" She couldn't weigh 100 pounds. I'd never been with a tiny woman before.

"I guess. And what brought you way out here?" she asked. I was sure she could read my thoughts, or at least my face.

"A job," I replied. I had been going for the short answer but that seemed a little curt. "A good job."

"They don't have good jobs in New York?"

"You'd think. I tried. But I couldn't get *arrested* in Manhattan."

"Well . . . maybe arrested." She smiled at me. *Oh, shit—dimples.* She was definitely being flirty. But she'd flirted with that nazi too, so I had no idea what it meant. "I'm not surprised. They say New York is about five years ahead of San Francisco, right? Sounds about right." She winked. She had nice lips—not the meager portion most white girls are stuck with. Maybe it was a Jewish thing.

"Something's coming," Sarah said. "Something big. Something bad."

I nodded and stared at her mouth.

"It's so obvious. Everywhere you look. Militias taking over little towns out west. The feds won't touch 'em since Waco. And the militias know it. Then you've got this Republican takeover. This Contract on America. Everybody's pretending like they don't know what that is."

"Uh huh." *Man, this chick can make anything sexy.*

We finally picked up our menus. She leaned closer. "Hey, Marcus, look—I know this is a date and all. But I really want a spinach salad."

"I want the spinach salad too!" I laughed.

"OK! So we get what we want, and after, I'll check your teeth and you check mine? Then back to the date?"

"Deal." Now I was laughing because she had called it a *date*. Twice.

We gabbed and ate our salads, and then we stopped the *date* for a minute and checked each other's teeth. We were fine.

* * *

"Things are getting wild," she said, chowing down on her turkey burger. "Especially in the States. These last few years . . ."

"I know." What amazed me was that she knew.

"Guys on cable TV and on the World Wide Web are *promising* a race war, or some sort of civil war. So what are you gonna do? When a bully wants to fight you, you know what? You're fighting.

"Nazis are getting busted buying anthrax," she went on. "Black churches are burning. And the Y2K crash will be here before you know it. A lot of people think that's when it will go down. Whatever '*it*' is. I think about that. I think about it a lot. The people who don't are insane. And I know that's a lot of people, *most* people. They're the majority, but they're still crazy. They're like sheep." She polished off her burger.

What I wanted to say, I couldn't say.

"Let's get out of here."

We wandered a bit and found ourselves in Japantown. I couldn't help but think about Amalia and the time she backed me up in Oakland's Chinatown when we were courting. Didn't know how I felt about that.

We explored the shops that were still open, walking the wet streets, holding hands (no idea who started that), almost oblivious to the funny vibe a black/white couple gets.

One spot was about three times as large as the others and had an incredible selection of martial arts gear at beyond-reasonable prices. It appeared that we had accidentally found maybe *the* place to go for MA gear in SF. We examined everything in the well-lit store, up one side and down the other, all the while thoughtfully followed by at least two salespeople who, although they stared unblinkingly into our faces, considerately never spoke to us, even in response to a greeting or question.

Our inspection ended at a floor-to-ceiling knife display by the door. It was a wondrous thing. There were katanas and sais next to mil-spec Ka-Bar knives. There were disguised knives of all kinds—not just the usual pen knives but all manner of working office supply that also contained a sharp blade should you decide to cut someone at work.

And there were the most punching daggers I had ever seen. Illegal in California but here they were, compact and capable, under glass and about 500 watts of light. Punching daggers have a thick rubber handle, almost like a pistol grip. From the center of the handle, at a right angle, juts a thick stainless point about three inches long. You grab the grip and the blade pokes out from between the two middle fingers of your fist.

"I'd like to get you something," I said.

I bought her one. I did not get one for myself. Lord knows, given how much I love punching, a device that turns a punch into a stab is possibly my favorite thing ever. But maybe that's just it—I wanted *her* to have my favorite thing. When the watchful little lady behind the counter handed Sarah the knife, she squealed like it was a ring.

"Let's go to my place," she said, smiling slightly. "We can have dessert." I tried not to look surprised. It wasn't that I thought I was fixing to get laid. It was beyond that. She said it like I'd been to her place before.

"Sure."

Sarah lived in Berkeley. Our cars were still over near the bookstore. We would backtrack, then caravan across the bay. We didn't bother discussing the sleeping arrangements.

"This is me," she said, back in the Fillmore. We were standing in front of a cherry-red monster truck. I smiled at her sight gag. "Really," she added.

I laughed. I couldn't help it. It wasn't a true monster truck, but it was a massive Dodge Ram pickup with one of those shells enclosing the open back. Sarah may or may not have been five feet tall.

"What?" she laughed. Then she opened the door and climbed inside the truck. Literally climbed, from one foothold to the next. She did this with great authority. Once in, she smiled down at me from the driver's seat and started to close the door.

"Can I ask you something?"

"Of course."

"Can you reach the pedals?"

"See for yourself."

I peered into the cab. Yup, she reached. Just barely, but not dangerously so. Her shoes were already kicked off and lying on the floor. She had cute feet.

She gave me her address. I knew how to get there. Claire, my new (to me) 1989 Pontiac Sunbird, was only half a block away, so Sarah waited until I got there and followed me to the Bay Bridge.

It was Friday night and traffic was dense but moving. Once we crossed the bridge, the partygoers headed to downtown Oakland and the poor bastards who'd just left their law firm jobs headed for the hills. The traffic that remained on 80 East went a little bit over the speed limit in large packs of about 20 cars each, half a mile of open road between them. I don't know why drivers don't spread out and give each other more room; it would be safer. But they don't. They move in herds.

I was mid-pack, going maybe 70, Sarah right behind me. And I thought to myself, *You know what would be funny? If I lost her. We would still meet up at her place, and we'd have a good laugh.*

I sped up and changed lanes and put a few cars between us. There was a big bend ahead. I took the turn at a sober speed and as soon as I was out of Sarah's sight I gunned it. After a half-second of hesitation, Claire (the car) leaped and galloped forward, balls out, through our pack of cars and toward the next pack. *Good girl.*

I glanced in my rearview; Sarah's giant lumbering red bear of a truck was still a couple cars deep inside the old pack. I slowed us down as I approached the next pack and picked my way through, lane by lane, trying not to cut anybody off.

I glanced in the mirror again. Sarah was right behind me.

OK. I should have figured that would happen. I need to get an insurmountable lead and then maintain it. Once we were at the front edge of the new pack I charged out and tore up the highway for the mile or so to the next pack, quickly picked my way through that one, and ripped through the open space again.

A honk. Sarah was *next to* me. She smiled and waved.

God dammit! I gunned it.

We went on like that awhile—having a high-speed car chase in traffic for no reason. At one point, while I was hauling ass through a crowd of moving cars, I glanced at my speedometer. I was going a little over 90. And when I peeked back up into my mirror she was still behind me. I never lost her. I could have blown past our exit, but I knew she would follow me.

It reminded me of something. Amalia and I went to a lesbian wedding shortly after we moved to SF. I was the only guy there. During the exchange of vows, the bride—one of them—read from the Book of Ruth:

> *Entreat me not to leave you*
> *Or to turn back from following you;*
> *For where you go, I will go,*
> *And where you lodge, I will lodge.*
> *Your people shall be my people,*
> *And your God, my God.*
> *Where you die, I will die,*
> *And there will I be buried.*
> *The Lord do so to me, and more also,*
> *If anything but death parts you and me.*

At the time, that was what it felt like. It was comforting. This extremely capable woman was *with* me. She refused to not be with me. It was like our own little 90-mph lesbian wedding.

Her street was empty. I parked right out front; she pulled into the driveway. She opened the door of her little house and four dogs came charging at me and I think it wasn't so much that I froze with fear as it was that, if I was about to be mauled to death, I wasn't going to make it worse by going out like a punk. But her dogs loved me. I was already in the pack somehow. I didn't even like dogs back then.

She played her guitar for me and we talked and snuggled and even watched TV on the couch like an old married couple. We went to bed around 2:00 a.m. We didn't talk about it. We just went to bed. Fell asleep with her head on my chest.

I woke up. It was still dark. It must have been the disorientation of a strange bed, and I guess I was still half asleep, but for a moment it was 100 years ago and we were in Missouri. I didn't think it; it was. I was a farmer. Sarah had been my wife for decades. It was pitch black and dead quiet and there wasn't another human being for miles. And we were content.

I told her about it over breakfast.

"We were together in a past life. At least one." She crunched on her toast.

That was how it started.

Fuck the Police.

Sunday, February 12, 1995

I made an illegal turn. Possibly. It's confusing—sometimes left turns off Mission are permitted and sometimes they are not. Like, from 4:00 to 6:00 p.m. they are permitted. Or maybe that's when they're not. The sign is too verbose and cryptic to grok in the few seconds it takes to drive past it. Anyway, I made a left. I had no idea what time it was. Claire's clock was broken.

Then I saw them. The Cop Car Spotter in my brain has been 250% more sensitive since about five seconds after I made my sketchy turn and saw the cruiser. Which didn't help me at all right then.

They didn't flash their lights. They didn't hit their siren—not even the little *bloop* that says: *You know what's up. Let's do this.* In no way was I instructed to pull over. They just followed me. For a block, then two. Then three. When I turned, legally, onto Harrison, they turned too. They never passed me. And we were driving *slow.*

This is important: I would have taken the ticket. I didn't care about money any more than I cared about time. Maybe I would have gone to comedy traffic school. A ticket was nothing.

But I did not feel like taking a beating. Once a cop gets you, you have no control over how far it goes. I kept seeing the LAPD video playing in my head. That Klan mob beat King until they were exhausted. Half a dozen grown men wore themselves out beating one dude with clubs. I glanced in my rearview again. *They're probably calling for backup right now.* Who knows why they are so afraid of us, but they are. I was unarmed.

I made another turn. They did too. Again, if the worst thing on the table had been a traffic ticket, I'd have pulled over without them even asking. I'd have followed their directions and answered their questions and I would have signed the citation and accepted my copy and probably just paid it. But I would not be degraded because two guys were bored.

Still behind me. A short, slow parade up and down the deserted wide streets south of Market. I knew that any search of my plates would turn up nothing. Nothing that they could use. But they could see my head. In a year or two someone would coin the term "Driving While Black."

I sped up a little. Perhaps, if they weren't really following me, if they just happened to also be driving down the street at 15 miles an hour, then if I sped up to, say, 20, I could slowly leave them behind. But they sped up too. They had been maybe three car lengths behind me, and then they were still maybe three car lengths behind me.

They are baiting me. They were trying to get me to run, to do something stupid. Why my illegal turn wasn't enough, I didn't know. Maybe it wasn't illegal. Maybe I just had a guilty conscience. Cops knew about that. They counted on it, used it. They laughed at people and how easily manipulated we are. And it was happening to me right now. *I need to be cool. I need to stay cool. OK.*

I made a leisurely right turn onto some side street. I signaled first, to see if they would signal. They didn't. But they didn't have to.

As soon as I was around the corner I hit it. The side streets in that part of the city are crazy little mazes, complete with dead ends. All I cared about was increasing the distance between myself and some guys who might have been looking to boost their self-esteem at my expense.

I zoomed down a little side street. The narrow road veered left; in every other direction there were buildings. I glanced into my mirror and didn't see them. They hadn't hit the corner yet.

I made the left, fast. All that recreational action driving was paying off.

This one wasn't a side street. It was an alley. Complete with vagrants. They were milling about in what appeared to be their living room. They seemed surprised to see anyone, let alone someone in a car that was now going maybe 50. I tore into them, praying that a hobo's minimum skill set included the ability to evade a speeding car on short notice. It did. It was close, but even the old ones moved pretty good.

In the faces of the vulnerable men I shot past, I caught a glimpse of my-self. *I am in a car chase. With the police. I am evading arrest.* Those moments of clarity always came at a bad time.

Now they are really gonna beat me. "Aw," I said out loud. *For sure, now. They beat you if you run. Everybody knows that. That turn probably wasn't even illegal. But they baited you, and you let them, and now they are chasing you. And you are headed toward a dead end and it's about to happen to you now. It's your turn.*

This time, all I could do was make a right. If that was a dead end, I'd turn Claire off and hide. Maybe try to climb a fire escape. I'd watched enough episodes of *Cops* to know exactly how that would go. But the thing about fleeing is that, once you start, you really can't stop. Your body won't let you.

But the alley let out onto a wide, sunny street. I forced myself to slow down. No cops anywhere. My right hand trembled. I took deep, slow breaths.

Her Dad.

Friday, February 17, 1995

We were up late talking and she told me what her father used to do to her when she was a baby. I mean a *baby*. And for years. I won't repeat it here. I'll just say that part of me still believes that that is impossible. That nobody would do that. But, unfortunately, I know she was telling the truth. At least I'm pretty sure she was.

After she was done, we sat there for a long time.

"Do you know where he is?"

"Yes."

I didn't say it. I left it to her to say it.

Let's go. That's all it would have taken. We would have gone to where her father was and I would have put him in my trunk. That was the extent of my plan. My very worst ideas come to me on a need-to-know basis. *Let's go*, and 15 minutes later we would have been on the road, and an hour after that her father would have been in my trunk. Fact.

I knew she knew this. She knew, sitting cross-legged on her kitchen floor in the wee hours, she could have done something. She chose not to. But, even now, I hope that having the option brought her some comfort.

I Suggest.

Saturday, February 18, 1995

This was before going to clubs became a stupid thing to do. There was still a good chance of having a night of dancing and making out that didn't end with watching someone get shot. Back then, most people went to clubs to have fun, not to act like fucking idiots.

We didn't spend every moment glued together. One or the other of us would see something interesting and wander off. We danced solo, we danced with each other, we danced with other people. I enjoyed that feeling of recognition when we would come together again. It was like we had known each other a long time, and I still thought that feeling meant something.

I came out of the bathroom and "Set It Off" was playing. That's my jam. Sarah was dancing with some prep near the middle of the dance floor. I bobbed in the corner and closed my eyes and lost myself in the throb of that beat. *Set it off. Setitoff. Setsetsetitoff . . .*

Y'all want this party started quickly . . . right? Strafe asked rhetorically.

I heard something. Maybe there *was* something between us, something cosmic, because I heard Sarah's voice, clearly, over the music. My eyes opened already pointed in her direction. I didn't make out any words, but her voice was not happy. And this motherfucker—this preppie fop motherfucker with a sweater draped over his shoulders and sunglasses on his forehead in a nightclub at night—had Sarah by her wrist. And they were *not* doing the hustle.

I was moving through the crowd. *On the left!* The floor was packed, but I don't remember feeling any other bodies. *On the right!* He still hadn't let her go. Her face was rage. *On the left, I suggest, while we're left . . .* I could no longer feel my body. I could only feel my eyes. They felt hot. My field of vision had narrowed down to an oval, like a scuba mask. I only had eyes for dude.

Setsetsetsetitoff.

I came at them from the flank. I nudged Sarah aside a bit and gave the preppie rapist a big smile and I slapped him across his face with my right hand just as hard and as fast as I could. Sarah took her wrist back.

This is the thing about when a man slaps another man: it is a sign of intense disrespect. We all know that. It says, "I don't take you seriously enough to use my fist." But the *real* thing about a slap is that it hurts like fuck. It is still a hit. Even though it is supposedly kid gloves or lady treatment or whatever, done properly, a slap can rock you.

I hit the dandy with the very bottom of my hand, the palm heel. There's more padding there than over the knuckles, but otherwise it's a striking surface like any other. And I caught him on the jaw, where, if I *had* used my knuckles, he'd have woken up on the floor. My hand flew up from my side with no windup, while he was still staring, confused, at my smiling face. Total blindside.

It was a nice hit. After a little initial resistance his head swung up and to my left. Sweat sprayed off his face like he was a boxer. The shades were gone. A gold chain jumped; a pink club light hit it, and I saw a tiny medallion hanging off the chain with the name *Rich* written in cute flowing script. *Of course. Rich.* In 10 years he'd be just another Dick downtown somewhere, taking credit for someone else's work. But here, now, Rich was mine.

Rich didn't roll with the blow like he might have if he really were a boxer, and that was a mistake. He tried to stop his head from reeling back, thereby allowing me to deliver all of my energy. Then he settled for trying to whip his head back down, as if that hadn't just happened. When our eyes met again, his were blinking a lot.

So I waited. I didn't know what he was going to do. But as soon as he did it, I was going to clamp my jaws around him and ragdoll him like a dog would a squirrel. I didn't know what human movements that would translate into.

Rich blinked at me some more and then glanced away. I peeked over my shoulder to make sure he wasn't watching a buddy creep up on me. No. We were still surrounded by dancing strangers. Some were staring. But Rich and I were alone together in the way that mattered.

I could feel my face again; my smile was too wide, too toothy. I was a predator. A storm. I was Rich's misfortune.

He still wouldn't do anything. I considered slapping him again, and maybe he sensed that, because he slowly backed up and quickly walked away. Never said a word.

I turned to Sarah; another one of our little reunions. "Hi!" I was smiling for real.

"Hi yourself!" She pressed up against me; I threw my arms over her shoulders. "Thank you," she said.

"You're welcome." I scanned the room for Rich or anyone else looking for payback. "Look, I know you didn't *need* me to—"

"And I *know* that you know that," she interrupted. "I thank you because you probably just kept me out of jail."

There was something pointy in my side. "Word?" It was the punching dagger I'd bought her the night we met, gripped in her right fist, the tip gently pressed up to my guts.

"Oh, that is so sweet!" I cried. "You know, if it's like that, I kinda think *dude* owes me a thank you . . ." I started searching for Rich again.

Sarah removed the knife from my guts and got on her tiptoes and kissed me. "Dude owes you more than thanks." Kiss. "Dude needs to name his firstborn after you." Kiss. "Because if he ever reproduces"—kiss—"you are the only reason he ever got to." Kiss. "He was about to get neutered."

That's when I knew I loved her.

The music stopped for a full five seconds. And then:

Who you tryna get crazy with, ese? Don't you know I'm loco?

The crowd let out a collective *OH!* and immediately started bouncing. My first thought was that I should take the DJ's selection of "Insane in the Membrane" personally. My second thought was that I was being paranoid. Then I looked up at the DJ booth; a Latin cat in a fuzzy Kangol and Adidas sweatsuit was pointing at me and laughing. I had to laugh too. I know a displaced Nuyorican when I see one. He meant it as a compliment. If he was spinning in North Beach every weekend, he was probably more tired of Rich than I was. They behave a little bit better in the office.

Then Sarah unzipped my fly and I forgot about the DJ and Rich and everybody. We pretty much fucked standing up right there. She still had the knife in her other hand. The bouncing crowd gave us a lot of room.

Breach.

Monday, February 27, 1995

We were in love, so, naturally, I broke my lease.

Mr. Fred Meadows:

This letter is to inform you that I will be vacating my apartment effective 11:59 p.m. on Friday, March 3.

The lease that you and I entered into purports to run until the end of September. However, I advise you to forgo any contractual claims you may think you have.

As you well know, on February 1 of this year I injured myself on your property. This injury occurred as a direct result of your negligence. The full extent of my damages has yet to be determined.

Any adverse action on your part—including, but not limited to, an action to enforce the putative lease—will be construed as an act of retaliation. Such retaliation, in response to my injuries, claims, and possible disabilities, would violate the California and United States constitutions, several state and federal statutes, and public policy. (See, e.g., Civ. Code, § 1942.5; Civ. Code, § 51; Gov't Code, § 12900 et seq.; Bus. & Prof. Code, § 17200; see also Gomes v. Byrne (1959) 51 Cal.2d 418.)

We could engage in protracted litigation to sort out our claims. This would mean many thousands of dollars in attorneys' fees on your part. I of course would represent myself. But I would like to propose an alternative. We could each agree to waive any and all claims we have or may have against each other, including but not limited to any funds allegedly due under our lease. This would be my preference, and frankly it is the best you are going to do under the circumstances. I guarantee it.

Consider my offer. A failure to respond will be taken as agreement. I'll drop my keys in my mailbox on the 3rd.

Very Truly Yours,
Marcus Hannibal Hayes, Esq.

That's how much in love we were.

The Age-Old Question.

Thursday, March 2, 1995

I went to Animal Farm for litter and cat toys and when I came back out a UPS truck had thoroughly blocked me in. It was double-parked right next to Claire and the cars in front of and behind her.

I stood there a few seconds, taking it in, and then homeboy came out of the drycleaners next door to Animal Farm. A brother, about my age, in tiny brown shorts. He was walking briskly, but when our eyes met he stopped dead.

I held his gaze for a while. Then I leaned back, slowly, and lifted my head until my face was pointed to the sky. And I asked God, loudly: "Why is *ev-ry-bo-dy always* dissin' ME?"

At "ME" I stood up straight again and gave dude my biggest, wildest, googliest crazy eyes.

I read the sad story on the brother's face: *Born to good parents of modest means. Stayed out of trouble. Finished high school. Watched people fall off the edge all around him. Got himself a job. A good job, with benefits. Paid his taxes. And now, this. All for naught.* I almost felt bad.

I prolonged the moment a bit longer, then let the smile break across my face. "I'm just messin'."

He stared at me blankly for two seconds, and then started laughing. He laughed very hard. And also maybe cried a little bit. We shared the laugh. It felt good, and it seemed like it felt good to him too, mostly.

He was still cry-laughing when he climbed into his big brown truck and got the hell out of my way.

I got into Claire still smiling. Homeboy had a new lease on life. Maybe I was *his* guardian angel. Either way, he shouldn't have blocked me in.

The Boom Box.

Friday, March 3, 1995

With her four dogs and my three cats, we were the Brady Bunch, San Francisco style. Her house was bigger than my apartment, but it couldn't hold us all. It was simpler to give up both of our places and move the whole operation into a big four-bedroom house we'd found on the outskirts of the city. The owner required a one-year lease; we asked for two. That she and I would be together forever was a given. Only I signed the lease; Sarah was "off the grid."

I hadn't seen or spoken to any of my friends or family in weeks; neither had she. (Did I stutter? *In love!*) Come moving day, there wasn't really anyone we could ask to help. So, after we rented a truck, we hired a couple of day laborers outside the U-Haul lot.

Generally, I think of these men—the ones who stand outside of U-Hauls and Home Depots and such, waiting for work—as honorable people, doing unenviable but honest work to survive. And for the most part that's probably right. Maybe there were plenty of honest men there that day and we didn't see them. Maybe we ignored the honorable men and went straight to the felons. At the time, it felt only like we were passing on the older men and approaching the two strongest.

I don't remember their names. Maybe we never even got them. We just walked up to a crowd of dudes, caught one's eye, and said, "How much to help us move? You and your friend? One day's work." Sarah did the talking.

The four of us squeezed in the big truck's only seat and drove it from the U-Haul to my beautiful Haight Street flat, emptied it into the truck, drove to her place in Berkeley, loaded that in, and then headed back to the city to the new love nest.

We had a lot of stuff. Our movers, who presumably had less stuff, were openly checking it all out. Moving has often made me uncomfortable. Moving men (1) are physically strong; (2) apparently have few options; (3) see and handle everything you own; and (4) know exactly where you live.

But that day I didn't care. I didn't care generally. I had cared too much for too long. If I discovered something that mattered to me, I let it go immediately. Sarah was helping with that. A lot.

The dogs, who had been waiting for us at the love nest, were running wild around the strangers. They were well trained but didn't look it. Zoe and Helo, the border collies, kept trying to herd the men; Grace and Luther, the pits, wanted to play that game that I'd come to think of as Tug-of-War for Realsies. The U-Haul men were not afraid of the dogs. But they knew they were being watched by all of us. They spoke very little, and when they spoke to each other they did so *en Español*.

I was armed. I always had a gun on me. It's a good idea to get used to wearing a sidearm before the shit goes down and you really have to wear one. That wouldn't be all bad. Holed up in our big house after Y2K, keeping the looters at bay, while my former superiors at Clay Conti hanged themselves because all their status and power had turned out to be just a few sparks in a wire somewhere. Didn't sound any worse than anything else.

As we were finishing up the move, I mumbled some regret that we didn't own a decent boom box. I had a fancy stereo (as we had all seen) but it would be nice, I said to no one in particular, to get a high-end portable combo cassette/CD player from somewhere. Even better, I said, to get one for not a lot of money. I was burning through the money. Being in love was expensive.

"I know a guy," the one with the neck tats said. He was looking at me the same way he'd looked at our stuff. "Guy with a nice boom box for sale, cheap." The air got really still.

"Yeah?" I replied. "Cool!"

"Ye, it's real cool, mang," Neck Tat said. He and his partner, the one whose eyes never held still, shared a brief glance. "It's nice. Got the compact disc, got the tape . . . radio . . . all that. And it's only—" one last appraisal of our stuff, which now filled the dining room in head-high piles—"hundred bucks."

"A hundred bucks!" I chirped. Like a happy idiot. "That's cheap!"

"Ye, cheap," Neck Tat said. "*Mira*, meet us later, OK? So you can buy the . . . the thing. From my friend." He did the upward chin nod at me. "Lemme get something to write on." I handed Neck Tat a pen and a newspaper, and he jotted down the name and address of some hotel on Sixth Street.

Sixth Street is the shittiest street in San Francisco. It's the strangest thing. Fifth Street is fine; a little seedy, but fine. Seventh Street too: a little funky, basically regular. But Sixth Street—at least around Mission, where this place was—is an over-the-top shitbox of danger and misery. It's not just poor; it's wrong. It's like Calcutta if everyone in Calcutta were addicted to heroin.

I stared at the address. "I dunno . . ."

Neck Tat muttered something to Shifty Eyes, but all I caught was *ese cabrón.*

"See you there!" Sarah said from the doorway. I didn't even know she was standing there. "What time?"

"It'll be fun," she said later, poking me with her toe. We were lolling around on our now-ruined bed. The fact of assembling *our bed in our house* had been too much for us and we couldn't wait and we fucked on the uncovered box spring. I loved her, but to call that *making love* would be ridiculous. You ever have a lot of stray cats around your house? And at night there's all kinds of cat drama? And you hear a bunch of yowling and garbage cans falling over but you can't tell if it's cats fighting or cats fucking? That was us. I still have scars. Bites, mostly.

"Fun!" she repeated. "A little adventure." Sarah was like a tour guide through worlds located in places I'd thought I knew. My tiny Crocodile Hunter.

"Dude." I grabbed her shoulders and flopped onto the box spring, taking her down next to me. "Sixth Street? Are you familiar with—"

"That's classist," she said, crawling around on me. "It's just people. Maybe not so fortunate as *some* people"—a bite on my neck—"but *somebody* there has a boom box! With our name on it!"

"Our name, written in cooties. Other-people cooties."

"We'll do a cleansing ritual on the whole house in a few days. I've got sage in one of these boxes somewhere . . ."

"I don't know. Why did that one dude call me a goat?"

She was straddling my stomach. I sat up and we were facing each other, me between her legs. She immediately started giving me a lap dance. "We're *nesting*! It'll be the first thing we get for our new house! Together!" She put her lips on my ear and whispered: "Together." Her tongue went in and licked my eardrum. "Our." Lick. "New." Bite. "House." Chomp.

Then we were having crazy monkey cat sex again, which we both assumed settled it.

After playing with the dogs and cuddling the kitties and playing with the kitties and cuddling the dogs, we got ready and hit the road.

We parked Sarah's truck a couple of blocks away from the hotel and showed up on foot at 8:00 p.m. sharp. It was March, so it was pretty dark out.

They called this place a hotel—it had a little awning out front with *The Whatever Hotel* painted across it—but it wasn't really a hotel. It was more of a hospice. A hospice for lives.

Neck Tat and Shifty Eyes—and a couple of other guys—were standing out front in a tight huddle. Even though we'd shown up right on time, all four seemed surprised to see us.

I greeted Necky with a rowdy "Ey!" and a bro-hug. "Yeah, hey, mang!" he yelled while pushing me off him. "You unpacking all those boxes?"

I put my hand on his shoulder. "Let's go in."

Looking back, I don't think that a normal person would have gone as far as the front desk. But I couldn't wait to get all up in there.

We climbed two flights up a dirty, narrow staircase. Everything about the place assured me that no good was happening inside those rooms. All around us, people were ranting and squabbling and moaning behind thin doors. TVs blared. Babies screamed. It sounded like someone was actually having a baby in one room. We passed through a particularly foul patch at the second-floor landing. *Why am I sure that's what dead guy smells like?*

We stopped in front of a room about halfway down the sour third-floor hallway. A grimy metal badge above the peephole read *314*. The door wasn't locked; Shifty Eyes just reached for the knob and opened it. And we all went in.

I still think about the moment we walked into that room. The few seconds it took to cross the threshold from the dim hallway into some small room nobody knew we had gone to, in the middle of a giant tomb, on the sickest, most dangerous street in the city—that moment lives in a special place in my mind. I was pretty sure that everything would be fine.

Inside my leather trench, I was rocking one 9mm Smith in a shoulder holster on my left side, and another already in my hand inside the right coat pocket. My baton slept coiled in my back right jeans pocket. Sarah had selected her Ruger .380. She owned others, but back at the house she said that the .380 was all she needed, and I believed her. That was a sweet little piece. It was almost the size and weight of a 9mm Ruger, but because a .380 cartridge is half the length of a 9 and only holds about half the gunpowder, the gun shoots with almost no recoil. Bullseyes were effortless. A year later I would miss that gun more than her. She also had her punching dagger, as always.

My mind was clear. I felt relaxed and alert, like I'd been getting 10 hours of sleep a night, which I had. I felt like I'd been doing deals in shady hotels my whole life. *The Matrix* wouldn't be out for another four years. We were Neo and Trinity before anybody.

Someone behind us closed the door, and we all stood around for a moment in the tiny room, lit by a 40-watt bulb in a lamp on the floor. Sarah had gotten herself just beyond the edge of the crowd, and I was smack in the middle. The men looked at us, and we looked at them. Their eyes seemed to say, *Why aren't you afraid?* And our eyes said, *Yeah! Why?*

Finally, Necky Green said to me, "You got the money? On you?"

"Yup! Hundred bucks!"

"Oh! OK." Neckbone wiped his face from forehead to chin in one quick, hard motion. His fingers lingered on his mustache as he glanced around the room. Then he walked over to a nightstand by the ratty twin bed and produced the goods. It was basically like he'd described. A high-end Sony. Worth maybe $300 new. Somehow I doubted these guys had paid $300 for it.

Neckbone held the boom box up in front of me. With my left hand, I produced a tape from an inner pocket, popped it in, and pressed Play. *Bust a move!*, the boom box suggested. I nodded at Sarah.

I admit it: at that moment, I was the happiest I'd been in a long time. Years. *She was right*, I thought to myself. *We needed to do this.*

Sarah, using her left hand, pulled five folded twenties out of her jeans. She casually eased around the men with her back to the wall, handed Necky Green the money, and took the boom box from him by the handle. He counted the bills and stashed them. He was sweating. Shifty Eyes appeared to be in full REM sleep with his lids open. The other two men's faces were blank.

Another pause, and then Darling Necky said, kind of loud, "Um—OK! Pleasure doin' business with ya! OK!" And he looked briefly but intently into the eyes of each of the three other men. The two between us and the door stepped aside, and we walked backward past them to the exit.

"You too! Thanks! Bye!" I faced them and waved bye-bye with my left hand while Sarah got the door. Shifty closed it back, quietly, as soon as Sarah and I were in the hall.

We drove home listening to "Bust a Move" and set the boom box on the mantle, over the fireplace, where it stayed for months until one of us smashed it in a rage. We never talked much about that night. But I am sure that, if we had thought of it, we would have mounted that boom box on a plaque and hung it on the wall. Like a head.

Howdy, Neighbor!

Tuesday, March 21, 1995

Debra, her wife Camilla, and I walked six dogs around the block. Their two weighed almost as much as my four. People crossed the street.

"Hey," Camilla said, "what's up with your neighbors?"

I didn't have to ask which ones she was talking about. There's always one house on a block you would say that about. On our block that house was next door. If they hadn't been there, it would have been us.

"Oh, them?" I laughed. "They're murderers. Hell, I know better than that. I'm a damn lawyer. They are accused murderers. Suspected murderers. *Alleged* murderers. And not all of them. Just a couple. The rest are murderees, I suppose. Past, present, and future murderees. Allegedly."

Debra wasn't laughing. "Wait. Is the owner's name Galang?"

"Think so. You've heard of this place? It's an old folks' home, right?"

"Assisted-living facility," Camilla corrected. "Baby? Is that the place where . . . ?"

"Yup. Shit."

"I thought so," I said. "Most of the guys I've seen hanging around there look old, even for Asian dudes. There's one dude there about our age. I think he works there. And then there's Rita."

"Rita Galang," Deb sighed. "Aw, man. Wow."

We had just rounded the last corner. Debra was staring ahead. Rita was standing on her porch, staring back.

Rita Galang was a big piece of work. A six-foot, 180-pound Filipina in a mumu and slippers and a huge mane of mad hair like a troll doll. That I did not find her even a little bit hot says a lot.

"The cops raided that place last week," I said, lowering my voice. Rita was eyeballing us like she could hear, even though we were still almost a block away. "In the middle of the night. Like three, four cars. Parked all in my driveway with their lights flashing." I scanned the empty street. "I think they're looking at her for a murder. Maybe more than one."

"They are," Debra said in her regular speaking voice. It was hard not to shush her. "You know how every couple months someone's arrested for murdering an old woman and cashing her Social Security checks for years with the dead body in their basement?"

"For reals? Dang. Those inmates or whatever are fucked."

"They are. You steer clear."

We walked a bit. "Sometimes I hear yelling in there. And when the cops were leaving the other day I heard one of them say, '. . . because if he turns up dead . . .'"

"He won't," Deb said. She was returning Rita's death stare as we passed, which I did not care for. Staying out of trouble still seemed almost possible back then. "They never turn up. Her partner's kind of known for that."

"The dude?" I was still whispering, even though now we were back inside my house. "That one non-old dude?"

"Yeah, Michael . . . Labogin. That's the one. He's got a record." She pointed her gaze down to me. "You stay out of those people's way, alright?"

I shrugged. "I'll try."

Where the Wind Comes Sweeping Down the Plain.

Wednesday, April 19, 1995

I'll admit it: for all my talk and planning, I was caught off guard. Bit up and sore after a long night of cat sex, house to myself after Sarah left for a morning hike, all I wanted was a little background noise while I drank my coffee. Instead, I turned on the TV and learned that It had begun. Someone cut a federal building in half with a truck bomb.

The raw violence of the thing. Over time, an event like this takes on a historical sheen, and the carnage gets fuzzy. Over the next year or 10 you put a reflecting pool where all the bodies were and write poems that call the dead "angels" and their premeditated murder a "tragedy." But on the day of? The devil was in the details.

Victims were as young as three months, if you don't count the fetuses. One woman, pinned under rubble and about to be crushed by more, got to have her leg amputated without the benefit of anesthesia. Then there were the piles of parts. That's how the emergency workers sorted—literally— through the rubble on their hybrid rescue/recovery mission. They showed it on the news, for a little while. Piles of parts.

There was this foot. They recovered enough parts to build 168 people, plus a foot. They never figured out to whom that foot belonged.

Nobody knew anything, but the newscasters and commentators all agreed to assume that Arabs did it. And no one, absolutely no one, questioned that assumption.

I yelled objections at the TV.

"And so, Crystal, we would expect that any radical Muslim group claiming responsibility for the blast would do so within the next—"

"No foundation!"

"My first question, Mr. Deputy Director, is, of course, given the numerous number of militant Muslim terrorists suspected here, how does one begin the forensic investigation in a way that—"

"Compound! Assumes facts not in evidence!"

A hot blond chick reported that in a small town in Michigan a mob surrounded the house of the one Arab family who lived there and stoned it. A pregnant woman inside miscarried during the attack. I heard that story reported exactly once.

We lived in San Francisco. All of our neighbors were Filipino. I went on High Alert anyway.

There wasn't much to do. There was food and water enough to keep us all fed and clean for a week. Weapons were deployed. Doors were barricaded; windows were barred and boobytrapped. All I had to do was bring the dogs into the house. Then I went back to the TV.

Sarah would be back in a few hours. Maybe we would take turns standing watch. I would take the late shift. I had always wanted to stay up all night with guns and guard shit.

Stigmata.

Friday, May 5, 1995

Just before he became That Guy Who Got Stabbed at Altamont, he was The Only Brother at a Stones Show. Most people don't think about that, and it may have been lost on me too the day of the Ministry show. Or maybe I de-cided to go anyway because Ministry motherfucking rules.

Ministry is credited by some with inventing industrial metal. One defini-tion of industrial would be: *Very hard metal that incorporates industrial sounds and pure noise.* Another equally valid definition would be: *Music that activates the insane caveman part of your brain and makes cannibalism seem like an option.* I was listening to a lot of Ministry.

Sarah and I were the only people at the Fillmore that night who did not have a neck tat. I was the smallest dude there. Out on the floor, second row, there were tiny rocker chicks, big skinheads, huge bikers, and us. I noticed that the skin standing immediately behind me was wearing a T-shirt that bore the image of a bald eagle perched on a baseball bat in front of an Amer-ican flag. Nice. But then Al Jourgensen, the ringleader of the insane asylum that is Ministry, walked on the stage, and I forgot about baseball bat dude and presumably he forgot about me.

A low drone started up. A guitar. It got louder and louder and began to distort and pulse. It sounded how throbbing temples feel.

Uncle Al paced the stage like a tweaker, his face hidden beneath a cow-boy hat and aviator shades. He was ranting. The chatter of the crowd got louder. Al babbled and yelled, but he didn't have a mic; as close as we were, I couldn't make it out. The drone was still getting louder. It was all the way in my head. Then two sun-bright spotlights hit the drummers—two fucking drummers—who unleashed a beat so over-the-top loud that it almost cer-tainly cost me some hearing. Worth it.

Everybody's head instantly started banging to the now-recognizable in-tro beat to "Land of Rape and Honey." A sample of a speech started to play through the speakers over our heads—a call-and-response between Hitler and a massive crowd. "Sieg!" *"Heil!"* "Sieg!" *"Heil!"* This is also on the stu-dio version. Ministry, the band members, are definitely not nazis. I checked. They are anti-nazi. Ministry *fans*, however, can be a different story. Irony is easily lost on people. Fortunately, the skins behind us did not take up the chant. We all, however, gleefully sang the chorus: "*And in the land of rape and honey . . . you pray.*"

Most bands wouldn't have anyplace else to go after "Land of Rape and Honey," but when they went into "Burning Inside" a roar rolled across the hall. We burned for a good 10 minutes, after which they brought it down with "So What" and turned us all into brooding sociopaths. Then came "Jesus Built My Hotrod," which took things to a relatively lighthearted frenzy.

It was the last lighthearted moment of the evening. When "Hotrod" ended they went into "New World Order." There would be no more cooldowns.

At some point during "NWO" I became aware of a lot of jostling in the crowd and realized that I was in the mosh pit. It had spilled out around me. I got a glimpse of Sarah inching away, staying just beyond it. I was differently inclined, and let the playful aggro wash over me. At one point, I got sandwiched in by three stocky frat boys and Samsoned them all off of me in one full-body motion. One of them flew straight into a skin, and their faces met with a wet *thwock* sound.

I genuinely lost my mind during "You Know What You Are." It's weird—when your eyes roll up in your head, you can still see. I was shoving and getting shoved and hitting and getting hit. Besides the music, all I could hear was laughter. Mine.

Drinks and clothes and shoes and people were flying and bouncing over and on us. The floor was incredibly slippery; you'd see a guy or a girl go down and you'd never see them get up. The guitarist, fortunately on the other side of the stage, was hocking loogies on the crowd, who appeared to love it.

They did "Thieves." I have no memory of most of that song. Only a moment when, in the midst of the chaos, I became still. Everything was moving but nothing touched me. And I lifted my head and cocked my ear and listened to something. Something in my head. I don't remember what it was.

I lost some more time there, I think, but I remember seeing "Stigmata" coming from far away. There's this crunchy choppy kind of thing the guitarist does at the intro; it started while they were still jamming "Flashback." It was faint but growing, and when Uncle Al met my eyes I opened my mouth to say to him, you know, *Hey, cool, you are going into "Stigmata" now, I can hear it,* but all that came out was, "GAAAAAAGGHHH!!!!!"

We were on "Stigmata" a long time. Real fights broke out. No one cared. Then they went into "Psalm 69" and I couldn't tell you much of what happened after that.

Sarah drove us home. I was a dripping, grinning madman. She was fine. In hindsight, the only thing scarier than losing your mind at a Ministry show is staying calm at one.

Go Back to Sleep.

Tuesday, May 9, 1995

I thought it was the most vivid sex dream ever. Then I woke up a little more and found Sarah riding me.

The next thing I noticed (after that I was fucking) was the expression on her face. She looked *hungry*. She looked like a wild little woodland creature, feeding.

I thought perhaps it was morning. Maybe it was time to get up (despite the fact that we never had anywhere we had to be) and, being the awesome girlfriend she was, this was how she was waking me. Then I noticed it was still dark out.

Our eyes locked. She rode me some more. It felt *really* good. And she said, "Go back to sleep."

This is kind of fucked up.

I went back to sleep.

The Tae Kwon Do Incident.

Monday, May 15, 1995

I had to stop going to the dojo.

It wasn't my real dojo anyway. Those days were gone. I was on the other side of the country in some Tenderloin hole in the wall. Amalia would have wanted me to continue my training. But it wasn't working out.

This was the third dojo I'd joined in California. And it wasn't even a dojo; it was a tae kwon do school. I wasn't there long enough to learn how to say *dojo* in Korean.

The instructor was good. Cliff had been a black belt longer than I'd been alive. He was a phenomenal fighter. He was one of those people who is willing to destroy his body practicing self-defense, which struck me as ironic. After a lifetime of voluntary combat Cliff was all scar tissue and tricky joints. His gait was a series of workarounds. But he was still badass, and he was generous with his time and his knowledge.

As a dojo, it was something of a one-trick pony. Yan Su, my real dojo back east, taught not just fighting and kata but also how to live in the world. That style was a complete Way. At Yan Su we might fight for two hours, meditate for one more, and then go work at a soup kitchen. At Cliff's dojo, you paid money for the chance to consensually hit someone.

Todd, Cliff's second in command, was a total douchebag. The kind of guy who begins every other sentence with, "What you need to understand is . . ." I tried to avoid Todd.

Class began normally. We stretched and waited for Cliff to arrive. The stretching was not part of class, but that never stopped Todd from trying to lead it, ordering people to do things that were bad for them for reasons that were wrong. I tended to ignore him, even when he spoke directly to me. It was the best I could do.

We all chatted about movies while we stretched. "Indecent Proposal" came up.

"Of course my wife could fuck Robert Redford for a million dollars!" I said. "*I'd* fuck Robert Redford for a million dollars. It's a non-issue." Most folks laughed and nodded.

"Well, I guess it all depends on how much a person values his family," Todd sniffed.

I turned to face him. "You ever have a fight with your wife, Todd, and you can't work it out right away because someone has to leave for work, or has to go to bed so they can go to work in the morning? Y'ever go to bed mad 'cause you have to get up in four hours? Is that good for your family, Todd?" It was hard to call him Todd and not Dick. "You ever have to celebrate a birth-day or spend a vacation other than how you really wanted because of money? Your kids go to public school, *Todd*? Because that is what happens when you work a 9-to-5. It's built into the sentence. *Twenty years* of that, Todd, if you make $50,000 a year, which is a nice salary." I noticed that the room had gotten quiet. "Twenty years of being apart most of the time. Twenty years of snapping at each other because you're tired and worried. And 50 years of it if you are one of the many unfortunates who make only $20,000. That's your entire adult life. Under pressure." The word "pressure" echoed in the space. *Breathe.* "So, yeah, Todd, I agree—it does depend on how much you value your family." I paused. "If you think about it." I turned my back to him.

Dick—I mean, Todd—didn't say shit. Nobody did. A couple of folks were smiling though. We finished stretching.

Cliff finally arrived. We did a few basic drills, then put on our pads to spar. This school, like most, sparred round-robin style. If you have enough time, everybody gets to mix it up with everybody. Although people in your own dojo are not going to hit you as hard as a stranger would, at least you get to experience as many different body types and fighting styles as there are in the room.

Things went well for most of the class. Everybody was sparring for five vigorous minutes and then switching. It was a good workout. Then we rotated partners again and I was facing Todd.

He didn't return my bow; he just squared off. Then Cliff said, "Fight!" and Todd came at me like he had just walked in on me and his wife and he wasn't even going to get a million dollars. He was throwing full-power kicks, and a lot of them, and mainly to my head. I couldn't dodge them all, but most of what I caught I caught in the arms. Once the initial shock receded I collected myself and started countering.

After a particularly predictable roundhouse I moved in, absorbed as much of the kick as I could with my left arm, and gave him a nice right uppercut to the gut. He got that sad look on his face for a moment, but he didn't stop. I never said that Todd was a bad fighter. Only that he is a bitch.

We weren't sparring; we were fighting. At least Todd was. No one, not even Cliff, saw what was happening. The dojo is like everywhere else: nobody notices anything until it's over. We seem to be genetically programmed to overlook provocation. The sheep, anyway.

The kicks weren't really working, so Todd started mixing in some punches and the occasional elbow. He was trying very hard to knock my block off. My body was on autopilot, moving and absorbing blows and occasionally striking. I rode around inside of it and tried to find a way out.

Todd needed me to punch his brain until it wasn't mad anymore. But if I did that, I would be in trouble. I might get thrown out of the dojo. Worse, Cliff might want to teach me a lesson. That was likely; Todd was Cliff's boy. And bad knees or no, Cliff was definitely more than I could handle. He was just too skilled and too tough. No—dropping Todd was not going to help me.

But if Todd succeeded in dropping me, he would get the benefit of the doubt, because even though everybody knew that Todd was a jackass, they also knew that he had been with Cliff the longest, and that has its privileges.

Todd knew that he was behaving badly under Cliff's protection. That was the worst part. Todd was like one of those kids who says he's tough but really he just has three brothers. People like that never acknowledge their unfair advantage. They cheat, and then they parlay their cheating into a mythology of merit. It is literally insult to injury. This is what white people have done to everybody. And that was what Todd was doing to me. He was violating universal dojo etiquette and common sense and decency. And he was doing so with impunity. He was confident that he was above the rules. And he was right.

We weren't even halfway through the round. I was blocking full-power kicks and punching him in the gut. Kicking him wouldn't leave me as nimble as I needed to be while a guy with three inches and 40 pounds on me tried to turn me stupid forever. I wasn't stopping him, and I was taking lumps. Even a blocked kick hurts. Maybe I could keep myself upright. Probably not.

Todd is going to win. He is about to hurt me. Over a movie. A goddamn movie.

He threw a roundhouse with his left leg—to my ribs, for a change—and again I stepped in, but instead of just blocking it, I trapped the leg in the crook of my right arm and slid in closer. He tried to punch his way out, so I gave him an uppercut to his cup with my left, which stopped him long enough for me to get in a head butt. It didn't hurt him (we had headgear), but it got me close enough talk to him with any hope of being understood (we also had huge mouthpieces).

"Tobb," I said around my mouthpiece. "I hab a gub. Ib by bocker. A *gub*." I did. "Ib doo dutch be. Eebben bubb bore dime. I wibb *burder* doo." I spoke in short phrases so that he could get his mind around what I was saying, and also because I couldn't fucking breathe. "Abder dass. I wibb bobbow doo. Oubdide. Ad I wibb *doot doo*. Ib door *head*. Eebben bubb bore dime, Tobb. I wibb burder doo in da deet."

We were just standing there, our heads together, Todd on one leg. I pulled back and met his eyes. They were quite wide. He said nothing.

"Do doo udderdan?"

He nodded. I let go of his leg.

Todd seemed confused as to what to do. I put my hands up and nodded back. He put his hands up. Slowly. Then we shuffled around each other for two or three minutes without hitting at all. That thing about people not noticing cuts both ways. Everybody was kung fu fighting; they had problems of their own.

It occurred to me that we never agreed that I wouldn't hit him. I was tempted, but that would have been unbearably dickish. So we just circled around and eyeballed at each other. Eventually our five-minute round ended, and I made us bow before we round-robined on to other people.

I kept an eye on Todd. After only one or two more rounds he quit early, walking away from his partner without a bow or a word. I was more than a little worried about him breaking into my locker, but he just went to the edge of the dojo floor and stripped off his pads and sat with his arms on his knees and his head hung low. I understood. Been there.

Fortunately, class was almost over by then anyway. I got dressed as fast as I could and made a point of leaving before Todd did, so that he would know that I was honoring our deal and not dooting him.

When I got home, before I even went into the house, I threw the entire gym bag into the big garbage can in our yard. The bag, the gi, the pads, everything. *I don't need pads anymore. No one is ever going to hit me again.*

Licensed to Ill.

Wednesday, May 17, 1995

I don't remember exactly why we were parked outside the DMV. And I really don't remember why we were armed. Maybe in case some asshole shot up the DMV, which does happen. But we were probably just practicing. When the shit went down, we would all be armed, cruising around in trucks and dune buggies rocking firearms and, assuming *The Road Warrior* is a reliable model, boomerangs.

"Hey." She was staring at the rearview.

A cop was sauntering purposefully along the curb. Cops are masters of purposeful sauntering. There were plenty of other cars around, but it was obvious he was headed for us.

Again, that's what sucks about cops: you have no idea how far your interaction with them is going to go. There are all kinds of Supreme Court cases about probable cause and reasonable suspicion and such. And those are great. But the fact is, once a cop talks to you—once a cop *looks* at you—he has you. You have absolutely no control over how the interaction is going to go or how it is going to end. You can make it worse, I suppose, but you cannot make it better. The only thing that matters is the cop's intent. You can't know if he is going to nod or say hi or chat you up or ask for ID or frisk you or call for backup or cuff you or pepper spray you or tase you or club you or rape you with a plunger or shoot you in the back while you are lying face down or strangle you to death in front of everybody. I do agree with Chris Rock that the best way not to get your ass beat by the police is to not act like an asshole, but that only goes so far. When it comes down to it, it has nothing to do with you. And now some high school educated, breathplay-loving bully was making his way over to us for reasons known only to himself. We were wearing two guns each.

We sprang into action. Which is to say that, after a stunned moment of staring at the rearview, we scrambled around, yanking off holsters and dumping firearms and firearm accessories behind the seat.

We were sweaty and breathless when the flatfoot sidled up to Sarah's window. He smiled and peered into the truck, at us and all around. He didn't speak for what felt like a long time. I bet our faces looked hysterical, in both senses of the word.

"How you folks doin' today?" The frat boy smiled at us and spoke in that fake-casual, predatory way they do. That must be the best part of the job for them: having people in their casual clutches. You can see them savoring it. Savoring having you. As a rule, I don't like being had.

Sarah started talking. Flirting, really. I wasn't particularly up for flirting, but he wasn't talking to me anyway. The white girl was the person; I was the thing he was trying to decide what to do with.

Sarah flirts real good. I already knew this. They chatted for a minute—about what, I have no idea, because I was thinking about fishing around behind the seat for a piece. And then the flatfoot smiled again and said, "Alright then. You folks have a nice day." He patted the top of the truck and sauntered away.

"What the hell was that about?" I wondered, partly to myself, partly to Sarah.

"He was only saying hi," she said, beaming her Ivory Girl smile at me. She was still in character.

"That's some bullshit. Under *Terry v. Ohio*, an officer has to have reasonable suspicion to stop. He walked right up to us specifically and questioned us for no reason. We're not in a red zone. We weren't doing anything . . . anything *he* knew about. That was totally illegal."

"It's fine, honey! He's gone." She was still smiling.

I took a big breath, held it, then let it go slowly. "He *is* gone. Thank you for getting rid of him. It's just, knowing what I know, shit like that kind of makes me feel like a second-class citizen. I know it shouldn't surprise me, but—"

"Well, I guess that makes *me* a third-class citizen." The smile was gone. She was staring straight ahead and starting up the truck.

We rumbled home without doing whatever it was we'd come for. I really wanted to ask her what she meant by that, but we'd been through enough already.

Fight Sex.

Friday, May 19, 1995

Pretty much since we'd met, Sarah had been teaching me outdoor survival skills, and I had been teaching her how to fight. She'd thought she knew how. Her nature was violent enough, and she was comfortable with both knife and gun, but she needed a foundation in unarmed combat. A lot of people don't want to think about how heavy and sturdy human bodies are, or what it actually takes to dissuade us when we are mad. They tell themselves that, if they really had to, they could knock a dude out with one punch, like the end of a Reese Witherspoon movie.

I was showing her one thing she could do if a guy had her in a bear hug. A move with her hips that would gain her a little wiggle room.

"I don't know that I'd *want* any space," she said. "Go ahead. Grab me."

I grabbed her. A nice face-to-face bear hug. I squeezed, not so tight as to constrict her breathing, but tight enough. I was enjoying it. Sarah didn't move; I started to think she might be enjoying it too.

"Take your time," I said. "Breathe."

Then I felt it. Pain. My chest.

She was biting me.

"Ow!" I laughed. It hurt, but it was funny too. I let go. "You got me. *Osu!*"

Sarah did not let go.

Now she had me by the shoulders and was burrowing into my chest like a little weasel. It was still funny and cute—and, frankly, kind of sexy—but I was starting to worry about my actual meat. It felt like she was breaking the skin.

I moved backward, fast, but she matched my speed and dumped me face up on the bed. She was on top of me, still hanging on by her fucking teeth. She was working hard on the spot she'd initially chomped; it felt like she was trying to bring her teeth together. Now it hurt for real.

"The *fuck!*" I said.

I laid my right thumb on her left eyelid and pushed slowly but steadily up and away. She could either let go or lose the eye.

She let go and glanced up. She was smiling, with a bit of blood on her lips—the classic vampire shot. A winking vampire, because the eye I'd had my thumb in was closed.

I peered down at my chest. There was a straight-up human bite mark on my right pec. It's still visible today. If I were two inches taller I would have lost a nipple.

Why am I not pissed? And why am I so horny?

She headed for my chest again, so I went for her eye again. But instead of biting she licked. First she lapped up the blood, then she lapped up the new blood, then she lost interest in the bleeding and started licking my stomach. She released her death grip on my shoulders and slid lower. Funny—her chomping off my dick never crossed my mind.

Without looking, she reached up and clocked me on the side of my head with her half-closed right hand. Hard.

I wanted to let it slide, because she was still licking me. But then she reached up with her other fist and whomped me on the other side of my head. She caught some ear that time. *"Ow!"*

I grabbed her mean little hands and yanked her up so we were face-to-face again. I bent my right knee and pushed off against the bed, rolling us over so that I was on top. I made a mental note to show the little asshole how to do that later. Right then I wanted to sock her in the jaw. But she wasn't trying to bite or hit me anymore. She was just lying underneath me, wriggling and moaning.

It took me a minute to figure out that as long as I was pinning her arms down, things were sexy. As soon as I let even one arm go I was getting my ass kicked again. Sarah and I had a safe word and, unlike Amalia and me, we needed one. So I knew she wasn't actually resisting, because she was not saying much of anything, not "no" and certainly not "sasparilla." Once I figured it out I stopped letting her go.

I needed to get our pants down. I risked another beating by holding both of her arms with one hand while fighting our belts and jeans with the other. It worked. It occurred to me that I probably didn't have to grab her hard. I grabbed her hard anyway.

And I fucked her. Hard. Definitely the hardest I've ever fucked anyone, before or since. I'd always been a little bit careful with Sarah. She's tiny, and I'm hung. I'd have doubted she could take, or at least enjoy, a pounding like that. Hard fucking is not my thing anyway. But she took it just fine, if coming twice is any indication.

I fell asleep on top of her, still pinning her arms just to be safe. I didn't know how she was breathing down there.

We woke up, sweaty and drained, when we started getting dog noses in places people don't usually get them. It was dark out. Sarah seemed happy, and I had stopped bleeding. She blew me, and then she got up to make us pancakes for dinner.

I laid there in our bloody sex mess, petting dogs and listening to her singing in the kitchen, and I alternated between looking forward to more fight sex and praying that that *never happens again*.

Space.

Monday, May 22, 1995

I was backing into a spot and a beat-up black pickup truck came up from behind and took the space by driving forward into it. Just zipped right in. I peered into the cab of the truck through my rearview. Two heads. Baseball caps. White boys.

I got out. I wasn't exactly relaxed, but my breathing was deep and easy. I noted street conditions, bystanders, and cover as I approached the truck. About six feet away from the open driver's-side window, I stopped walking and opened my mouth.

I spoke to them because I needed the situation to escalate. Also, I wanted them to know why this was happening. It's silly; I mean, I suspect that dead people don't care why they are dead. But I knew how things would appear afterward. No matter what anybody else was going to say about "random" or "senseless," I needed these two men to understand the Cause and Effect of it. If only for a minute.

"I was parking in that spot," I said through their open window. "The spot you're in right now." I never spoke loud enough at times like that. My breathing was so steady that I couldn't project. My voice sounded very far away to me. But they heard it, and noticed me for the first time. I continued the dance. "I was backing into that spot, and you pulled into it from behind. You took my spot."

Really, all I wanted to say was, *Draw*.

My right hand was alive at my side. *Sweep the shirt back; heel of the hand against the grip; grab the grip with pinkie then ring finger then middle finger while drawing up and forward; sweep thumb upward across the safety; index on the trigger; left hand comes up under the butt and the right hand; front sight on target; squeeze.*

The men sat in the truck and stared at me. They did not move. I waited for one of them to say their lines so we could do this.

"Sorry!" the driver said after a moment. "I can move."

I waited; neither of them budged.

"We'll leave. Sorry."

I didn't know what to say to that, so I didn't say anything.

The driver started his truck, backed up slowly, and drove past me at a crawl. I watched both men's arms and made sure the truck was never pointed at me.

"Sorry!" the driver said again as they glided by.

I watched the truck as it sped up and made a right at the corner. Only then did I notice that the block was basically empty.

There was my car; there was the car I'd been trying to park behind. There were two or three cars sprinkled up and down the block, and maybe another six total across the street. Leaving at least twenty available parking spots right there on that block alone.

I stood squinting up and down the street. And I saw myself. I was me alright. But still, I was kind of surprised.

Taken for a Ride.

Sunday, May 28, 1995

Mom was in town! I had big plans. I couldn't wait to show her the house and the cats and the dogs and how happy me and Sarah were and how much better my life was now. She'd never sounded convinced over the phone.

Of course, I met her at the airport. Scooped up her bags and whisked her to my ride. She'd never seen me drive before—I'd had a license, but who drives in New York? I'd bought Claire at some point after her last visit. Everybody says that your car makes a statement about you. Claire was low to the ground and unattractive to thieves. So maybe they are right about that.

It was a 20-minute drive from SFO to our house on the southern edge of the city. I made it almost 10 of those minutes, chatting and cruising at the limit, before some shit popped off.

A young homie in a hooptie. I suppose I should say *another* young homie in a hooptie, since that probably would have described me too, but this cat was a thug, and I only looked like a thug. I saw him in my rearview, baseball cap pointing northwest, weaving in and out of lanes like Speed Racer for no reason, endangering us normal folk. The problem with normal folk is that they tolerate that shit. If the normal folk ever rose up and clubbed the assholes to death, it'd be over in a day and the world would be paradise. But they never will.

Speed Thug was now immediately behind me, having forced his car into my lane from the right, causing the vehicle behind him to slam its brakes. I calculated his next move: to my left in about two seconds. Sure enough, he swerved left out of our lane and gunned it, preparing to pass and cut me off as he'd done the others. But I swerved left too, so instead of passing me he slammed his brakes the way he'd made the others. A crash would have gone worse for him than for me.

I smiled. Maybe he would learn from that, maybe not. I had come to settle for bringing momentary discomfort to people who behaved badly. I was never going to change anybody. We are just too stubborn.

He reappeared a few seconds later. I had forgotten about him already. He came from my left. Even though there was a wide-open lane to his left, he shoved his piece-of-shit ride smack in front of us. I'm talking *inches*. I refused to hit my brakes. Instead I glanced in my mirror, hopped two lanes to my right, floored it, passed Thug Racer, and hopped back over two lanes to cut him off. This time, he didn't hit his brakes either.

The dogfight went on for miles. It was early evening; rush hour was basically over, but there was traffic. Changing lanes got kind of hairy sometimes. But Claire was my F-16, my trusty steed, and she and I were one. I was happy.

Then I glanced over at my mom.

She was clutching the little leather loop that hung from the ceiling with her right hand and bracing herself against the dashboard with her left. Her face was a wooden thing of horror called *Head-on Collision*. She was certain she was about to die.

Oh.

Shit.

Thug Racer sped by in the far left lane, staring into my car and laughing. His car was empty.

I got over to the far right lane and slowed back down as quickly as I safely could. I didn't say anything, and neither did she.

That is the only thing I have ever done that I regret. The only thing.

"*Mom!*" Sarah hollered. Mom said nothing.

My mother had loved Amalia like a daughter, but it had taken respectful time. They'd shared a common understanding of the process. It may have been a Black Thing. Whatever it was, it wasn't a Sarah Thing, because right now she was on my mom like a needy kid on Santa Claus. Amalia hadn't hugged my mom like that until Mom had hugged her first, and that hadn't been until the night we announced our engagement. This was a first meeting.

Mom wasn't returning Sarah's embrace because Sarah had her arms pinned. That was one reason, anyway. Mom's tiny too, but less tiny than Sarah, and she was holding her nose up sharply, trying not to drown.

Then the dogs came. And for the first time I noticed how fucked up it is for four good-sized dogs, including two pit bulls, to come stampeding up on a person and probe them. They did that all the time.

Sarah and the dogs swarmed my mother. Her eyes had settled on Luther. Specifically, his enormous, bulletproof pit skull, overflowing with drooly knives. Luther was smiling, but she didn't know that. All she saw was teeth. Mom was not dog people. She was barely cat people.

Sarah still had my mother in a bear hug. Luther took my mother's limp hand and held it in his wet, deadly jaws. He did that. It was cute.

It became clear that hanging back and letting the women work it out was not the right call. I hugged Sarah and Mom at the same time, then slid my arm between them and peeled Mom away. Now the dogs were jumping, snagging her cashmere sweater in dirty ragged claws. *We have bad dogs! I did not know that.* "Back back!" I barked. I tried to sound playful.

Freeing Mom was harder than I'd expected, as Sarah had her other arm. She was trying to pull her down onto the sofa. *Oh my God—the sofa's covered in fur! It's disgusting!*

The plan had been for Sarah to cook. I smiled as big as I could. "Let's go out!"

I took them to Stars, for want of any better ideas. We were walk-ins, and I was afraid we wouldn't get a table. But the man behind the little podium seated us immediately. I suspect that, even in tatters, Mom's bearing overcame that of the two ragamuffins flanking her and rated us all a table.

I did not order the calamari for old times' sake. Making conversation was difficult enough. I'd bring up a topic, squirm while Sarah rambled, and eventually try to engage my mother, who did little more than stare down at her plate. Repeat. Repeat.

And Sarah thought things were going well, apparently, because she never stopped talking and laughing very loudly and every now and then putting her hot little hands on Mom. I vowed that the remainder of my mom's visit would be just the two of us, assuming she didn't take a cab to the airport as soon as I paid the check. This introduction was not salvageable.

"I'm tired," my mother declared outside of Stars, her back to Sarah. So instead of taking us all back to the house, I drove the few blocks to the Hyatt at Union Square. I pulled up in the red zone for Mom to hop out and she sat there. My home training twitched in its shallow grave. I got out of the car and trotted around and opened Mom's door.

"Take me up to my room," she said, clutching my arm.

"I'll park and meet you inside!" Sarah yelled from the car.

But I didn't make it past the lobby. I pushed for the elevator and when I turned back around to apologize I was getting slapped in the face. It hurt a little, but mainly it was shocking. My mom had never, ever hit me before. I felt tears before I had even processed what was happening.

"I did *not*. Raise you. For *this*."

Ding! the elevator said. Shiny metal doors slid open and she stepped inside. She stood in the corner, hiding her face. I know when a woman is waiting to be out of sight so that she can cry.

I stood there touching where she'd slapped me. It felt warm. My eyes burned too. It was pretty, all of the sparkly glass through blurry eyes. I tried to focus on that.

"Where'd she go?" Sarah was standing next to me. "What floor?"

I wiped my eyes. She was wearing overalls. A hillbilly and a thug stood in the lobby of the Union Square Hyatt, the thug freshly slapped by his mother. The blank faces of the rich white people all around insisted that they saw nothing.

It Doesn't Fit.

Thursday, June 15, 1995

O.J. was trying on the gloves.

It was absurd. Imagine if someone handed you a pair of gloves and said, "Try these on. If they fit, you will go to prison for the rest of your natural life."

I'm guessing your performance would look a lot like O.J.'s.

The Juice struggled mightily to get the regular-sized glove on his hand. He couldn't seem to pull it past his thumb. The deputies on either side of him looked like they wanted to help.

"This is a shame." I hadn't realized that Sarah had come into the bedroom. She was drying a green mixing bowl with a dish towel.

"Yeah. The whole case has been a joke."

Her eyes cut from the TV to me. "There's nothing funny about this. A woman is dead." I don't know why, but for a second I thought she was going to say, "A white woman."

"That's true. Well, two people are dead. But what I mean is that the prosecution of this case has been so tainted, he could go free."

Sarah froze and stared at me.

"And, I mean . . . at this point, maybe he even *should* go free." I don't know why I said that, other than because I meant it.

She looked very angry. Not at O.J.; at me. Granted, we had our best sex when she was mad. But this wasn't the sexy mad. The bowl she was holding was large and heavy.

I put my hands up. "Look. I think he did it. Pretty sure he killed Nicole. And the other guy. But what we *know*, for a fact, is that LAPD officers got on the stand and lied. They got caught committing perjury. And in our legal system, that is supposed to matter."

"It's called framing a guilty man," Sarah said. She glanced back at the screen. O.J. was standing there with his hand in the air, the empty tips of the gloves bent where his fingers ended. Those cops really wanted to put that glove on for him. O.J. started to wrestle the other one on with his half-gloved hand.

"And you're saying that's a good thing?" I asked her. "Framing a guilty man?"

She just stared at the screen and went back to drying that long-dried bowl.

I lowered my hands. "Look. The exclusionary rule—where bad evidence gets tossed out—doesn't exist just to protect innocent defendants. It's to punish dirty cops. The only way cops won't lie every time is if it could hurt them." She still didn't respond, and I decided to believe that meant she was listening. "The Founding Fathers wrote the Fourth and Fifth Amendments because they recognized that a corrupt police force was at least as harmful to our society as assholes who kill their wife. Ex-wife. And other dude."

Sarah was completely still.

"The Founding Fathers also 'recognized' that blacks were animals," she said. Rage came up from the earth and filled me. I could feel it shooting out the top of my head. "And that women were children," she added. "It's funny that *you* should care what the *Founding Fathers* thought."

She turned and walked out of the room.

O.J. shrugged.

Good Fences.

Monday, July 17, 1995

I was playing fetch with Luther and I threw the ball and it bounced off a tree stump and ricocheted over the fence into our neighbors' backyard. Our alleged serial killer neighbors in their nursing home of horrors.

I went to their front door and knocked. Big Rita opened up.

"Hi," I smiled. I tried to sound friendly. After all, our relationship had not yet exploded into the inevitable violence you could smell, stuck inside your nostrils, whenever we were near her or her goon. "My dog's ball just bounced into your yard. Do you think I could go get it, please? It'd just take a minute." I beamed like a salesman.

And Rita smiled back, sort of. She moved her bulk aside. "Come inside!" Not so much an invitation as a command.

"Thank you so much!" I cruised into the darkness. All of the curtains were heavy and drawn. It did not smell good in there. It was that whimsical Norman Rockwell classic, *Neighbors Go In, But They Don't Come Out.*

I followed Rita through the house. The nursing home inmates—all of them chain-smoking old Asian men dressed in rags—did a double take as I passed, then turned away, bored again.

"Hi," I said to the craziest-looking one.

"It's downstairs," she called over her shoulder. "In the basement. The door to the backyard."

"OK!" That was plausible.

Rita glided down the steps in front of me. She seemed more relaxed than I had ever seen her out in the world. Her henchman wasn't around; I didn't see him, anyway. A single bulb hanging over the top of the stairs was the only light that was on.

At the bottom of the stairs, I saw a rough wall about six feet ahead, a door stuck in the middle of it. A room built within a room. In the basement.

"In here," she gestured with her chin. "Through there. Is the yard." I get so turned around without any windows that I didn't know if that made sense or not.

Rita opened the door and stood aside. "In there."

I walked up to the entrance. What little light had made it from the staircase revealed what could be a door at the back of the room within a room. Maybe it *was* a door, and maybe it was unlocked, and maybe it opened out into her backyard. Possible.

"Thank you," I said again, as I walked past her and inside.

The room within a room was big and cluttered. And it stank. Bad. My eyes took their sweet time adjusting to the dark as I walked alone through Rita's dungeon toward what indeed resembled a door.

There was only one thought in my head. If that room got any darker— say, from the door closing behind me—I was going to stop, turn 180 degrees, draw, and unload through that wooden door and those sheetrock walls, all 15 rounds, at about chest height. And then I was going to reload and shoot low. And then I was going to reload again and figure out what to do next. The moment my eyes detected any decrease at all in the little bit of light in there, that was going to happen automatically. I had programmed it in. It was a good plan.

Sometimes a room seems to get a little darker for no reason as your eyes recalibrate. I'm glad that didn't happen. I'm also glad that Rita didn't decide to joke around like she was going to lock me in with no intention of actually doing so. That would have been tragic. I just wanted my ball.

But Rita didn't move and it didn't get any darker and I walked all the way to the other side of the room and there really was a door there and even though it stuck a bit it was not locked and I opened it and walked out and was standing dazzled in a sunny backyard.

I turned and smiled at my neighbor. "Thanks again! I see the ball. I'll just get it and hop the fence back over. Bye!"

Her face was blank. She shut the door to the room within a room, and I closed the outer door behind me. Then I grabbed Luther's ball and hopped the fence to my yard.

Thinking back on this, I ask myself, *If I was willing and able to hop the fence to get back home, why didn't I just hop the fence to get my ball in the first place?*

A perfectly reasonable question. After all, if one is willing to kill, even in self-defense, then surely trespassing is an option as well. I totally get that now.

But I think that, back then, on that day, if someone had asked me that—asked me, *Why don't you just hop the fence and get the ball?*—I think I would have answered, *Because that would be rude.*

I played with Luther a few minutes more but the adrenaline crash made me tired so I went inside. I was headed to the bathroom when Sarah came absolutely out of nowhere and intercepted me in the hallway. I just turned a corner and there she was. Chick was a ninja. "Did you have fun?" she asked.

"Yeah!" I smiled. I loved Luther and he loved me.

"You . . . had fun. With that . . . *bitch*." Now I noticed that she was speaking very softly.

"What? Rita? Yeah, that was lots of fun. Crazy bitch."

"I am *not* crazy! I *saw* you!" Not so soft anymore. She was trembling. And she had something in her hand. I couldn't see what; she was turned so her right arm was completely away from me. I decided not to ask.

"You saw me . . . coming out of her place? I went to go get Luther's ball." Too late, I regretted the word *ball*. "His toy. I had to go in her yard to get it."

"You went in her yard," she said. Soft again. "You . . . fucking . . . liar. I saw you coming out of her *house*. You . . . fucking—"

"You fucking *what*?" I closed the space between us in a breath. I didn't care what she had in her hand.

She said nothing.

"You know what?" I breathed down into her face. "*Fuck* what you think you saw. Fuck *you*. You wanna act like an asshole? With me? With *me*?" The idea of any assholery between us had never crossed my mind, not really, until that moment. "Fine. Be an asshole. You know what? I'm a bigger asshole."

She stared up at me, her face stone. The hallway was small and hot and dark, like Rita's basement.

"You fucking what?" I murmured. "Go on. You fucking *what*?" I breathed and waited.

She looked away. "Nothing," she said, off to the side.

"That's right." I knew better than to gloat, but sometimes it cannot be helped. "That's right." I brushed past her and headed for the bathroom. With my back to her.

"*You fucking nothing!*" And then a tremendous bang. I didn't try to duck; it was too late. But it was only the slam of the bedroom door. I turned around. She was gone.

I took my leak and went back outside. I sat on our front steps to watch the sun go down and let time pass.

A few of the inmates I had seen on my way down to Rita's dungeon were sitting out on their front steps having a smoke. They stared and spoke openly (though not in English) about me. I guess they hadn't expected to see me again.

Gun Sex.

Sunday, August 13, 1995

I only kept a gun under my pillow sometimes. And even then, mostly because I thought it was funny. I didn't really think I would ever have to jump out of bed half asleep and start firing into the darkness. Not really. Pillow Gun was a whimsical affectation. And, again, I didn't always sleep with him.

So I just happened to have had a loaded Smith .45 under my pillow when Sarah climbed onto my sleeping morning wood. And I guess that's how I woke to find my woman riding me while pointing a gun at my face.

When you wake up and you are fucking your girlfriend and she has a gun to your head, you keep fucking. Trust me. It is the best option by far. The piece was definitely loaded—it was, after all, mine—and in her right hand, finger on the trigger, muzzle about two inches from my face. Her eyes were closed. She was really wet. Honestly, it wasn't that hard to keep fucking. Honestly, it was pretty hot. Honestly, it was the single hottest fucking thing I have ever done in my entire fucking life. Or had done to me.

She probably came once while I was still asleep, which is what woke me up. Soon she came again, and then I did. She dropped my piece on the carpet (didn't appreciate that; I loved Pillow Gun) and collapsed across my face, still wrapped around my cock. I guess she fell asleep. I know I did. Woke up sometime later, still being smothered. Eventually she woke up too, and we kissed good morning and got on with our day. We never talked about it. I wasn't positive she even remembered it.

She continued to molest me in my sleep, which was cool. I stopped sleeping with Pillow Gun though.

Our Bad.

Wednesday, August 16, 1995

"Well that's just fucking ridiculous!" I said, half to the TV, half to Grace. Grace sat up and looked at me with her ears held in that way that means, *I do not understand, but I agree with you. Also, I love you. Also, would you like to go to the beach again?* And then she lay back down.

The federal government had just settled with Randy Weaver—the nazi who lost a gunfight with the FBI a few years earlier—for $3,000,000. And an apology.

Three men stood at a podium, announcing the settlement. The tall one on the left, a US attorney, was reading a statement that he had obviously been ordered to read. He never even glanced up at the cameras. Whoever had written the statement had used the word "regret" too many times, in my opinion. When the government lawyer was done, he timidly pushed the podium mic toward the tieless, angry-looking man in the middle. Dirty crazy-eyed bearded angry man stared down but said nothing. He just shot his beams of hate down at the mic in silence. And so Gerry Spence, standing on the angry coot's other side, jumped in. Gerry Spence was the absolute best you could get now that Johnnie Cochran was in trial. A super-rich rock star in a fringy suede jacket, Spence's homespun act was legend. And this cracker had him. Stunning. Gerry bent down toward the mic and announced that he was just an old country boy. I turned off the TV.

"Just ridiculous," I repeated. With my mouth stuffed full of Kettle Chips, I sounded like Daffy Duck.

Grace peeked up from the rug and assured me that I was still subject to field execution by local, state, and federal authorities at any time, without notice or apology.

"Got that right," I said. "Where's Eleanor Bumpurs's apology, huh? Where's Edmund Perry's apology?"

Grace didn't know.

I wiped my hands on my jeans and stood up. "Walkies!" Helo, Zoe, and Luther materialized, leashes in grinning mouths. We all five went to the beach. I needed air.

Everybody Loves a Girlfight!

Friday, August 25, 1995

I heard the commotion—I heard *something*—for a while before I noticed it. Maybe I thought it was a TV. Or maybe angry voices just didn't register for me anymore. But when I became aware of them I got up and peered out of the big bay windows at the front of the house. The voices were coming from the left.

Sarah and Big Rita were mixing it up on Rita's porch.

I *say* that everybody loves a girlfight, but really I think that only applies when you don't care about either of the girls. The only reaction I remember, besides a desire to make it stop, was that I was impressed. Sarah was holding her own against a woman almost twice her size.

I ran out of the house in my boxers. Fortunately, the dogs were locked in the backyard; things would have gone differently if Luther and the rest of the pack had seen what I saw.

Rita and Sarah were still toe-to-toe when I got there. They were doing the one where you each get a big hank of your opponent's hair in your left hand (and they both had a lot of hair) and throw wild hooks at the attached head with your right. And all the while they were both talking smack— Sarah in English, Rita in Tagalog. I'm still surprised I didn't think it was at least a little bit hot. First Nurse Candy, now this.

They didn't break it up just because I told them to. And I didn't have the wingspan to push them far enough apart to make them let go of each other's hair. As soon as I got them a little bit separated the kicking started, so that backfired. Ultimately I had to pick Sarah up from behind and snatch her from Rita like a purse. This didn't go particularly smoothly, but taking Rita down would have gone worse. Her henchman was never gone for long.

After a few wild seconds I was able to wrench Sarah away and set her down several feet from Rita. They had stopped fighting but continued cussing each other out. Rita switched to English. There wasn't a mark on either of them.

"What's the rhubarb?" I demanded.

Rita took three big steps backward through her open front door and made a snatching motion at us. "Come inside!" she hollered.

I peered in, past Rita; eyes peered back.

"Come inside!" she commanded again.

She didn't say, *Come in, neighbor—let's talk* or, *We have to live together; sit down and have a beer with me.* Nothing like that. Whatever she now wanted to do to us required us to be inside her house; that was all. It sounded much worse than the time I went to get Luther's ball.

I started to walk in, but Sarah grabbed my arm and pulled it back hard. "*Fuuuck YOU!!!*" she screamed in a demon voice, then turned and stomped away, dragging me with her. Surprisingly strong for a 100-pound person. I glanced back over my shoulder at Rita. I wanted to say something diplomatic, like *I'm sorry*, but I wasn't sorry, and the expression on Rita's face suggested that it would've made no difference.

We were safely back at home. "So . . . what the hell was that about?"

"I was telling that *bitch* to stay away from you."

At first I thought she was protecting me. Then I remembered our chat in the hallway a few weeks back. *Oh.* "Seriously? Seriously, you think Rita and me are fucking? Really, baby?" I could not ignore this. This is how motherfuckers die. Motherfuckers like me, anyway.

She let me lead her over to the couch. We sat down and I held both her hands. I made a quick tactical decision not to go the "I love you" route. That argument is too vulnerable to the (usually screamed) counterargument that I do not, in fact, love her. So I decided to appeal to logic.

"Baby? *When* am I fucking Rita? Can you just tell me that? When are we fucking? You and I wake up together and run around all day together and spend every minute together and go to sleep together. Just, physically, when is there time for all this fucking?"

Sarah seemed to be formulating a response to that question so I kept talking. "And . . . and do I seem to you like someone who isn't fucking enough? You don't think you are fucking me enough? *Really?* Or are we too vanilla?" I got a little smile with that.

I was on a roll. "And . . . and Rita? Really, baby? Why would I want Rita? Why the hell would I want a giant crazy Filipina with all that hair and all those tattoos and . . ."

I went back to the other approach. "Baby. If I ever look hard up to you— hell, if I ever *don't* look totally fucked out and drained to you—fuck me. OK? Please? If you ever find a moment where we are not fucking, let's fuck. OK?" I kissed her hand. "OK?" I kissed her other hand. "OK?" I kissed her neck.

We fucked.

If women ruled the world, we would have as many wars as we do now. They would just be for different reasons.

Cop Killer.

Friday, September 1, 1995

I love Dolores—the colorful double-wide Mission District street with the hilly rows of palm trees running down the center. It's the one street in San Francisco that tells you, *See? You really do live in California.* At least, Dolores tells you that during the three months a year it tops 65 degrees. The rest of the time she still says it, but mockingly.

In San Francisco summertime comes in the fall, and it was a beautiful fall/summer day. I felt like Ice Cube rolling through those palms, or maybe Sonny Crockett. (Because, really, does anybody feel like Tubbs?) And so it is possible that at the intersection on 18th I may have gone through a stop sign.

My cop radar was better by now, but he totally snuck up on me. The siren derailed my inner "Today Was a Good Day" video. One *bloop.* It was less creepy than silently following me around like those other cops had done, but this time I had to stop.

I signaled and eased Claire into the nearest safe spot. I did not panic. Of course, I had a gun on me. Shooter—my day-to-day carry piece—was snug in his concealmeant holster. I had my usual long shirt over it too, but my concealment system broke down once frisking was involved. No way you miss a pistol in a frisk.

I didn't know why the cop would order me out of the car, let alone pat me down. But if he did, I had a plan. I'd read somewhere that, once it is clear that you are about to be frisked, you should fess up that you are armed. As an attorney I would say that confessing is a bad idea 99% of the time, but that other 1% would include just before you get searched by a cop while you are wearing a weapon. Better to give him a heads up. That's what I was going to do, if I had to. And it would be fine. I'd *make* it be fine.

I pulled up the parking brake. *My record is clean. The schools, the grades, the internships, the jobs—I can use them to make a weapons charge go away, if I handle it right. It's possible. Anyway, it's the nineties—everybody carries. The guy's only doing his job. This is just business.*

I sat with my hands on the wheel and waited. Seemed like a full minute, or even more. *Dude is taking his time.* I watched him in my rearview, sitting in his cruiser. Maybe he was running my plates, finding nothing, running them again. Good. *Just business.*

Eventually, the lone officer slid out of his cruiser and squinted in my direction. He stuck his nightstick into its loop and sauntered up. He was smiling. He seemed to be having a good day too.

"Hi!" the officer said.

"Hi." I tried not to sound like I was mocking his friendly tone. He had me, for now. I reminded myself that I was that one-in-a-million exception that cops must dread: a young black man who, on paper at least, is firmly screwed into the power structure. And the gun on my hip—that was just what we in my profession called a "bad fact." That's what I told myself.

"How are you today, sir?"

"Fine. You?"

"Good, good," Officer Friendly said, all the while his eyes sweeping around, seeing what they could see. He was chewing gum. With his mouth open. He was smacking his gum. And he did not lean over toward my window; he stood straight up and peered down. He was still smiling, but his hand rested on his gun, and his gun was in my face. This, I did not care for.

The cop said:

"Son, didja see that stop sign? Back there?" He gestured slightly with his head.

I thought to myself:

Did he just call me "son"?

He wasn't much older than me. Back in the day, men his age addressed men my grandfather's age as "son." It was practically "boy." *Son?* My face felt hot. *Maybe he called me "sir" again. Yeah, probably. Why would he call me "son"? Who says "son"?* I looked around. We were stopped right in front of Dolores Park. Everyone was strutting around half naked or posing on blankets in the grass. They were still in San Francisco, and suddenly I was in Birmingham. Or was I? I calculated a 50% chance I'd heard him wrong, so I told myself again that he'd said "sir," and I put on my most earnest, disarming smile.

And I said:

"Not really, officer. I don't know what to say. I'm sorry?" I did my best to appear helpless. Maybe it didn't work. Or maybe it did. Because Officer Friendly smiled even wider.

And he said:

"Well, then, boy, tell me this: Are you a good guy? Or a bad guy?"

And I thought,

I am going to kill this motherfucker.

He had me. I was in his world. He was the authority; I was the mythical Young Black Male, inherently worthless and as good as shot and dead and forgotten. Which was exactly why he would never expect me to draw right now and shoot his hand and both his legs right here from the driver's seat. Then I could take my time and pop him a few more wherever else I felt like, as long as I saved one or two for his misshapen head. I didn't care who saw.

My smile never faded. *Yeah. This fool, this person, this fellow human being, he got up this morning and drank his orange juice and he drove around listening to the radio and he saw me and pulled me over and he was just having a little fun with me and he is about die out here on Dolores in sunshine and pain and fear. This boy is about to eject you from the game. You are seconds away from the Cosmic Penalty Box and you don't even know it.*

As soon as he told me to step out of the car, he was dead.

About 10 seconds had gone by since this man had committed suicide. His question was still hanging in the warm air.

"Well . . ." I said, "I like to think of myself as one of the good guys."

It was a real smile now. My purpose had found me.

C'mon. Say your line. Say, "Step out of the car, son." Please. Please say it.

But he didn't say his line. Instead he said, "Good! Good for you."

He took a step back, hitched up his gun belt, and got one last eyeful of my interior. "You watch those stop signs, now." I was expecting another *boy* at the end, but it was implied.

"Um . . . OK."

He drove off. I sat there for a long time and watched the preening people, none of whom had noticed us. I tried to figure out how things could have gone so wrong so fast, and then turned back into nothing just as quickly.

I would like to think that Officer Dead Man had sensed that he was in danger. But no. When cowards realize they are afraid, they make things worse. He never knew.

My hands were shaking. I leaned back and closed my eyes.

Maybe *he* had a guardian angel. Maybe his guardian angel told him, in that intimate, believable way that only guardian angels can, that he needed to get away from me and climb back into his ride and go home to his beat-up wife and kids.

That was probably it.

My Nowhere Place.

Saturday, September 9, 1995

We were the last people on Earth, talking and fucking in the dark. Nights like that made me forget about the other stuff.

She'd just come back from the bathroom. I was incredibly thirsty, sweating across a corner of the bed and staring at the ceiling. I was thinking of making the journey into the kitchen for a cold glass of sugary crap but as soon as Sarah came back in she got down between my knees and started sucking my limp dick.

"My dad didn't die the way I said."

She blew me a bit longer. Then she got up and sat in the chair in the corner. She crossed her legs. She looked like a naked shrink.

I sat up. "It isn't true that I never knew him," I said to the floor. "Not really. I was young, but I'd been born."

She was silent and still. *Breathe. You have to do this.*

"He died when I was four. And not in the ring. He died at home."

"I know he died at home. You never told me he died . . . in the ring? Boxing?"

"I didn't tell you that? OK. Good." There had been so much lying over the years, and so many sex confessions over the last few months, I could no longer keep up with my stories. Still, it was doubtful I'd told her the truth. I'd have remembered that.

"Good. But I didn't tell you when, I think." I paused, hoping for another interruption. Silence. "I was . . . four. I was four. I was there. I don't remember. Heart attack. That's what I heard. He just died. My mom came home from work and found us. He just died. That's what she says. I don't remember."

More silence. *Fuck.* Her poker face was as good as mine. *Fuck fuck fuck.* "OK. I was eight. That is the truth. He died in his sleep, in the bed at least, when I was eight and he was 29."

"The same age you are now."

"Yes . . . whoa. I didn't even realize . . ."

"And you don't remember? You don't remember *that?*"

"No." I looked up. *Do it.* I stared right at her face. "But I don't mean I don't remember that day; I don't remember that *year.* I don't remember the third grade."

"Well . . . that was a long time ago . . ."

"No. I mean, it was a long time ago . . . but . . . I *never* remembered it. I didn't remember third grade when I was in fourth grade."

Still and silent again.

"And it's not the only time that's happened. Three or four times, I've lost . . . chunks . . . of time. Months. Once when I was a teenager. Once in college." I had to turn away again. "It's like amnesia, or a blackout. A few times in my life I woke up and I know I'm me but I don't know where I am or how I got there. But I know I'm *supposed* to be there, that it's my life. All the information is in my brain. Names and phone numbers and everything. I just have to . . . kind of do a walkthrough. To trigger it all. So I start from there. I get up and I go wherever I am supposed to be and I figure out what my life is. And I keep on going."

More silence. It was like an interrogation.

"I think it just happened a little while ago."

Then she was across the room and I was in her arms. "You don't know how you got here?"

"No, not *that* recently. After . . . after Amalia died." I almost never talked to Sarah about Amalia. I was afraid she would get jealous and try to make me choose in some way. And choosing a dead person when you are still alive is just foolish. "I remember . . . the end. I pretty much remember a little while after. Then . . . spots . . . here and there. Then I just woke up one morning, and it was like I said.

"It's not a *bad* thing. Not really. I've never woken up in prison, or next to a dead body, like in the movies." I laughed; she smiled. "I think . . . I think I am the same person. I never find myself in a life I don't like, or that isn't me. I think that I just . . . go away for a while."

"To your happy place," she said. I thought of Mr. Dr. Stewart—Papa— and immediately felt guilty.

"I guess. I don't know what it is. My nowhere place."

She leaned away a bit and stared into my eyes. "What would you like me to do?"

"Oh! Nothing! Seriously. Please don't treat me differently because of this." *Impossible.* "It might never happen again. And even if it does, it won't happen for a long time, if it only just happened a year ago."

"But if it *does* ever happen again, it's good that I know about it, even if it doesn't happen for 20 years, right? So I can help you."

Because we will still be together, she was asking. "Yes."

She held me tight again, and rubbed my back in big circles with her palm. It felt like she was burping me. I dug it.

"Here's the thing, though." My lips dragged against her neck. "I never told . . . Amalia any of this. Not any of it. I don't know why. I couldn't. I mean . . . I didn't get to. I didn't get a chance." The rubbing stopped. She was still and silent again, and I couldn't see her face. "I didn't have time. I thought I was going to be with her forever. But we didn't get enough time, and I didn't tell her. I never told her."

I guess I cried. She started rubbing me again, and humming. I have to say, it really hit the spot. Then she blew me, still humming, and that hit the spot as well.

Maybe Sarah was a little jealous of Amalia. Maybe she liked having something on her, knowing something about me that Amalia never knew.

Who am I kidding? She loved it.

Publish or Perish.

Tuesday, September 19, 1995

15. Leftists tend to hate anything that has an image of being strong, good and successful. They hate America, they hate Western civilization, they hate white males, they hate rationality. The reasons that leftists give for hating the West, etc. clearly do not correspond with their real motives. They SAY they hate the West because it is war-like, imperialistic, sexist, ethnocentric and so forth, but where these same faults appear in socialist countries or in primitive cultures, the leftist finds excuses for them, or at best he GRUDGINGLY admits that they exist; whereas he ENTHUSIASTICALLY points out (and often greatly exaggerates) these faults where they appear in Western civilization. Thus it is clear that these faults are not the leftist's real motive for hating America and the West. He hates America and the West because they are strong and successful.

I ate my bagel and drank orange juice out the carton while I read this shit. It wasn't that he didn't have a point. It was that he was a madman, a murderer, a serial bomber, and they had published his manifesto in the *New York Times* and the *Washington Post*. Because he told them to.

It was dense and rambling and insane. I read every word.

140. We hope we have convinced the reader that the system cannot be reformed in such a way as to reconcile freedom with technology.

The only way out is to dispense with the industrial-technological system altogether. This implies revolution, not necessarily an armed uprising, but certainly a radical and fundamental change in the nature of society.

They are publishing mad bombers in the Times. *They are publishing mad bombers in the* Times.

212. Would society EVENTUALLY develop again toward an industrial-technological form? Maybe, but there is no use in worrying about it, since we can't predict or control events 500 or 1,000 years in the future. Those problems must be dealt with by the people who will live at that time.

The bagel was gone. The OJ was gone. The Unabomber was still going strong.

They are winning. The lunatics are winning.

Sankofa Is a Tough Movie, Mang.

Tuesday, September 26, 1995

The Lakeway Theater is an Oakland art house that only shows movies—I'm sorry, *films*—the owners consider radical. This week's screening: *Sankofa.*

And homeboy kept looking at me. Two men in the row in front of us, a few seats to our left. The one on the right was turning around and staring at me.

Sankofa isn't just a movie about slavery. It *is* slavery. Watching *Sankofa* on the big screen is like taking magic peyote and going back in time to find yourself and your parents and your children on a plantation being tortured forever. *Sankofa* is a tribulation, a rite of passage, kind of like I imagine my first trip to Africa will be. And every time someone in the movie mentioned Uncle Toms or house [negroes], this guy twisted around in his seat and stared at me, and at my white girlfriend next to me. Every time.

I don't know how many times he did it, exactly. But, again, he did it each time Toms or house [negroes] came up, and in *Sankofa* they come up a lot. After about 45 minutes, my brain told me: *Next time, I am going to do something.*

A little later, someone in the movie made a comment—something like, "That house [negro] is so in love with Massa that he won't let the rest of us get free." And the brother turned around and looked straight at me. And smiled.

I waited a minute. Then I got up and went to the Men's. I drew my 9mm and racked one into the chamber. I took the safety off. I did not cock the hammer—that would have been crazy. But, set up that way, a pistol works like a revolver: just point and shoot. The Lakeway men's room has no lock on the door and no doors on the stalls, but fortunately no one walked in on me. I eased Shooter back into his holster and returned, quietly, to my seat.

I sat in my big cozy chair and waited in the dark. For what, I did not know. Much of the rest of *Sankofa* was lost on me. I am good with that.

I looked around. I love the Lakeway. It's a big theater, one of the last grand old theaters in Oakland. It has a chandelier hanging high overhead and angels painted on the walls. Only one screen. It was not crowded. We were surrounded by a handful of what would later be termed "the liberal elite." Homeboy and his man and I were just about the only black people in the room. The only Latinos were ushers. There were no Asians.

Homeboy kept up with his turning-around shtick too, but it didn't matter anymore. Even if he had never done it again, at that point it wouldn't have changed a thing.

Sankofa finally ended, and the survivors sat stunned while the credits rolled. The dim houselights came on. As Homeboy and his buddy stood up, he turned and gave me one last triumphant look. I stood up too.

I felt a big smile on my face as I moved toward him. "Ey, mang. Was that you?"

His little smirk wavered, but he said nothing.

"Was that you?" I repeated. "In the movie." I gestured up at the screen. "The brother on the horse, in the field, with the whip. The deputy overseer. That was *you*, right?" I'd had no idea I was going to say that.

Only then did I get a good look at his face. It had a soft quality I'd neither noticed nor expected. I'd assumed I was dealing with badasses; we were in Oakland, after all. Maybe he was a badass with a soft face. Maybe he was a jock at Cal. But that didn't matter anymore, either. Whoever he was, he had earned this.

"That was you, right?" I bared my teeth.

I watched Homeboy's face go through changes. From arrogance to confusion to surprise to hurt and, finally, to anger. I was waiting for him or his friend to draw so I could murder them both.

Homeboy's buddy appeared to be in shock—mouth open, eyes wide, fingers splayed. First *Sankofa*, now this. He'd had no idea this was happening. Sarah almost certainly hadn't known that anything was going on either, but that didn't show.

Now Homeboy was fighting back tears. That didn't mean he wasn't going to go for a piece. Far from it. But he was also trying to find words. Trying to get his brain and his mouth working together again. His lips were moving but no sound came out, and his eyes struggled to focus on me. He looked like how I'd felt when hospital lunch-lady dude begged me to murder him, so long ago.

The only two words Homeboy could find in his mouth were *fuck* and *you*. "F-f-fuck . . . you!" he sputtered. "Fuck YOU!" He obviously wanted to elaborate, but it just wasn't happening right then. A scan of his profile was inconclusive as to whether he was carrying. But by then it seemed more likely than not that neither of them was going to draw. And if they didn't draw, I couldn't murder them.

"Coulda *sworn* that was you! My bad." I smiled at him for another second and then started shuffling out of my row, Sarah in front of me.

They followed us out. They kept their distance—maybe 20 feet. But Homeboy was still making his historic "Fuck you" speech. I thought we made for an interesting parade going through the lobby, though most people seemed genuinely not to give a shit. Perhaps this was a typical reaction to *Sankofa.*

I just wanted to go home. My murder trance was fading, and I was hungry. But there they were. The buddy was still, unwisely, going along for the ride. Homeboy didn't seem so much mad at me as drawn. Maybe he was in shock too.

Sarah's truck was three blocks away.

"F-fuck you! Fuck your mother!"

What?

I was glad for him that his mind was coming back to provide him with new material, but I had to wonder what kind of mind it was to begin with. I mean, who goes out of their way to try and shame somebody like that all through a movie that puts you through a lifetime's worth of shame already? He ruined his own *Sankofa* experience ruining mine. What was that about?

"Fuck you and your white bitch!"

"Hey," Sarah said. The parade kept moving.

Has he always been this way? Of course he has. No one just becomes like this. This guy is Black Police, Oakland version.

"Fuck you, [negro]!"

And what makes him so sure that Sarah and I are fucking? Or that we shouldn't be? He has no idea where I've been. This motherfucker doesn't know me. But he feels qualified to judge, to rate my life at a glance. To disapprove. If Amalia were still here, I'd have been sitting in there watching Sankofa with her. And Homeboy would have seen her with me instead of Sarah and he would have approved. He would have smiled at me for real and nodded and given me his blessing. He would have let me know that he approved of Amalia being alive.

At some point I had turned around. I was heading back toward them.

They both stopped dead, Homeboy's mouth frozen in the midst of making the *f* sound. They had lagged about 30 feet behind by then. I walked fast.

I was aware that my new aggressive posture might force one or both of them to finally draw. They didn't. I drew anyway.

It was like being on the other side of a mirror. This time, I was the one bearing down on someone with a gun in his hand. I could only imagine how slowly it was all happening to them. Like me back in Alphabet City, they didn't budge, except that Buddy's head slowly cocked to the side, just a bit. Grace would do the same thing when I made her ball disappear.

Closer. *Am I their guardian angel? What if I am?* Closer. *Homeboy has been rolling like this for 20 years or more. It has taken a long time for his comeuppance to arrive. I owe it to him to make it good.*

This is the thing about pistol whipping someone: they let you. I understand. You see someone coming at you with a gun in his hand and you assume he is about to shoot you to death. So when he raises it over his head, it's like, *Yay! My assailant is an idiot. He does not realize that he is holding Death in a Can; he thinks it is but a simple club. I will not disabuse him of this notion.* The mind works like that. It's not entirely wrong, either. A pistol whipping is a compromise, a settlement. You just don't get to agree to it first.

I brought Shooter's butt down right smack on top of Homeboy's head as hard as I could. If I'd wanted to be a dick about it I'd have raked the front sight across the eyes. But I just wanted this brother to understand that he had miscalculated. That was my job.

I think he got it, because his eyes rolled up in his head and his whole body went limp and he poured face down onto the pavement and promptly set about bleeding. Heads bleed a lot.

His buddy watched the blood collect in a crack. "What . . ."

I pointed Shooter at the back of Homeboy's head. Homeboy didn't notice, but Buddy did. He blinked. "No."

"Your man. He brought this on himself. He did this. Don't forget that.

Don't let *him* forget it." I swung Shooter over to Buddy. "And you might want to choose better friends."

"Oh. Alright."

Homeboy started moaning. I backed away. About halfway back to Sarah I turned and walked quickly but calmly forward. After a while I realized that I was walking down the street with a gun in my hand, so I stuck it in my pants. Then I pulled it out again, put the safety on, and stuck it back in my pants.

Once Sarah saw that I was finished, she turned and continued walking to the truck. I caught up with her as she was climbing in.

She started it up. "Could've been worse," was all she said. I nodded.

She pushed the tape into the deck. *Olde School Classics, Vol. I.* We drove home to P-Funk and Cameo. Gangster shit.

You Must Acquit.

Tuesday, October 3, 1995

Where were you when O.J. got acquitted?

I was at home—not a shocker; I hadn't had a job in forever. The puppies and I were in the bedroom, watching the verdict on the big TV, lest we miss some detail.

I had watched most every day of the trial, even though the sight of lawyers working that hard triggered flashbacks. I needed to see how that complex equation worked out: *Dead white woman + black male defendant + probably did it + money + fame + world's greatest living defense attorney + incompetent prosecution + perjurious police witnesses = ?.* Even if it wasn't really the trial of the century, it was at least the social experiment of the decade. White girls were pleading guilty to murder and being sentenced to time served. Obviously, equal protection wasn't possible in America but, surely, all our centuries of struggle amounted to something.

We'll see, the puppies said.

CNN was bugging the shit out of me. They kept cutting back and forth between that LA courtroom and the student lounge at Howard University. Lanky young black people in sportswear sat in front of a TV three times larger than mine. CNN's panel of pundits never stopped chattering. At one point, it seemed like they forgot to switch back to the courtroom feed, and we watched the young, gifted, and black chillax for five minutes straight.

"The *fuck*," I asked Zoe.

Finally, the verdict. O.J. was standing, swaying like he might pass out. Johnnie was at his side. I couldn't imagine what it felt like to be either one of them.

Off camera, a lady with a blaccent read the verdict aloud, rapidly and without inflection: ". . . We the jury in the above-entitled action find the defendant Orenthal James Simpson not guilty of the crime of murder . . ."

Now O.J. really looked like he might fall out, but he was smiling.

The camera cut away to the Howard break room again.

"God fucking *dammit!*" I howled. Zoe barked.

A very tall youngster wearing a loose-fitting tank top and large shorts jumped out of his seat and started pumping his fist in the air as if O.J. just caught a Hail Mary in the middle of the courtroom. Not that I didn't understand the youngster's reaction, but he was an idiot. He had a fucking news camera in his face.

"You see that?" Sarah was standing behind me, by the door. Five seconds earlier she had not been there. Even the dogs were startled. "They're celebrating over there. They're celebrating."

"Yeah." Now two young sisters were holding hands and jumping up and down. "That's kind of messed up."

"Kind of?" Sarah took a step back and put her hands on her hips. "*Kind of* messed up?"

"Yeah. There's nothing to celebrate here. Maybe the system worked, but this whole thing—"

"What the hell do you mean, 'the system worked.'" She should've looked hot to me with her eyes narrowed like that, but she didn't. *This woman—she is in my house, and she's no better than the pundits.*

"The system," I repeated. "Presumed innocent. Burden of proof. Shit like that." I stood and gestured at the TV. "Reasonable doubt. Johnnie caught at least two of those cops in lies. On the stand. That's doubt."

Which only seemed to make her hate me more. I was getting tired of trying. "You know, the jury got an instruction that if they didn't believe something a witness said, they didn't have to believe anything that witness said. All juries get that instruction. It's just common sense. If someone lies to your face under oath, that person is a liar, and you don't have to believe liars. They chose not to believe liars. That's all."

The malice shot from her eyes unabated. *She doesn't care about the law. You knew that. She just wants her lynching.*

"I'm not saying he didn't do it," I went on. "The husband always did it." I took a step toward her. She did not budge. "But, here, in America, you still have to prove it. In court. That's a good thing." I jerked my head toward the TV. "Maybe those kids are celebrating because they just found out that the Constitution actually applies to them. You know, it didn't always."

"Are we talking about *slavery*? Again?" And she laughed. "You are obsessed with slavery. Racism. You all are. That was 200 years ago!" She laughed some more and then, just like that, turned grim again. "It still doesn't apply to me," she said, very low. "Your *Constitution*. Men kill us. Nobody cares."

"Nobody cares? Are you fucking . . . are you kidding me?" I risked taking my eyes off of her to glance at the television, where George Will and Pat Buchanan were taking turns announcing the end of the universe. "Obviously, this is the exception that proves the rule. My people are celebrating a fluke."

I took another step. "And, 'men kill us'—who's 'us'? Who is 'us' supposed to be?"

One last step and I had closed the distance between us. "O.J. could have cut off a sister's head on video." The words oozed out of my mouth and rolled down her mad little face. "And it would have never gone to trial. And you wouldn't even remember."

Her expression changed, and she turned away and quickly scanned all around the room, at the floor and the other surfaces nearby. *Looking for a weapon? Please. Oh, please. I'll give you one free hit with whatever you find. Let you get in a good wound. To show the cops. After.*

Her face shot back up at me again and she became very still. There was a slight chance that I had said all of that out loud. Just in case, I decided to deescalate. I moved backward, away from her, more, more, then turned slightly away. She stared at me for a long time. Then she stormed out of the bedroom.

When I heard a huge crash somewhere in the house, I wasn't surprised.

I sat back down on the bed and faced the bedroom door and waited. I surrounded myself with dogs, so that if she came back in waving a gun, she might hesitate. She did love our puppies. But after five minutes she still had not appeared.

Sarah's silence emboldened me. I crept out of the bedroom. The lights were on in the kitchen, at the end of the hall. I assumed that was where she was. "Hey," I called. "You ever ask yourself *why* CNN sent a news crew to Howard in the first place? If I am the only one who sees it that way?" No response, which for some reason emboldened me further. I eased up closer to the entrance. I couldn't see inside; most of the kitchen was around a corner. "Yeah," I called out. "International news networks sent camera crews to an all-black university on the biggest news day *ever*. Trial of the century. And *I'm* the one who's obsessed? *We* are? That's what that tells you? You didn't think about that?" I was riling myself up. "You didn't *think?*"

I burst around the corner into the kitchen with no idea where she would be waiting for me or what she would be holding.

But she wasn't in the kitchen.

Fuck. She's behind me.

I spun around. But she wasn't behind me. She wasn't anywhere.

I ran to the living room and peered out the bay windows over our drive-way. Her truck was gone. And there was now a sizable dent in Claire's passenger-side front door.

Ninja.

I searched the whole house anyway, just to make sure she hadn't moved her truck around the corner and snuck back in and hidden somewhere, waiting for me to go to sleep.

Some time later, the dogs found me lying on the floor in the downstairs hallway and settled on top of me in a pile. And then, one by one, the cats came and lay down on top of the dogs.

It felt good in that pile. I kind of wished that Sarah were there. Also, not.

But Thanks for Calling.

Thursday, October 5, 1995

The telephone is a little bell that rings when I am sitting on the toilet.

Fuck the phone. I never, ever would have invented an alarm in my house that you can activate from your house. People ask if they've called at a good time. What are the odds that it's a good time? I'm just sitting around, waiting for phone calls? Why wouldn't I be in the middle of something when you randomly decide to bother me?

Mother fuck the phone. I want to go back in time and kill the parents of the guy who invented the phone. I doubt it was Bell. Bell and Edison and those hacks lost more infringement suits than Led Zeppelin. The brilliant, robbed, died-penniless-and-insane brother who *really* invented the phone? Fuck that dude. I'm glad he died.

Funny thing was that I hadn't even known that I hated the phone until recently. Some months ago I realized that I have always resented those bullshit fire drills. I had also realized that I don't like eggs. Because of what they are. Eggs have always grossed me out, yet I'd eaten them anyway. Until recently. I was discovering all kinds of things about myself lately.

I had our answering machine set to eight rings, after which it played the entire introduction to "More Bounce to the Ounce." Then a beep. No words (other than *Mooore boooooounce!*). If I had chosen to say anything, it would have been, "Hang up. Hang up without leaving a message." But eight rings and 60 seconds of *Mooore boouuunce* said that just as well.

But whoever it was didn't hang up, and was still talking on the machine when I strolled out of the bathroom.

"Marcus." It was Rachel. "Marcus. Pick up. Pick up." She waited. "Marcus." We hadn't seen each other since she turned my suicide watch over to Mom and went back to LA. I don't think we'd even spoken. I'd been kind of busy.

I stood there a moment and stared down at the machine, the way people are positive you are doing even when you are not. I was giving her one more chance to hang up. But instead she said, "Marcus. Pick up. The phone."

"Rachel! Baby!" As it often did, my dope-ass answering machine message prompted me to go play "More Bounce to the Ounce" on our boom box. "How you doin'?"

"*I'm* fine. How are *you*. Really."

"Whaddya mean?"

"I mean, how *are* you," she barked over the music. "I had a bad feeling. About you. Are you OK. What's wrong." Her questions lacked the usual question inflection; everything she said sounded like an order. I figured she must be halfway to partner at—wherever she was—and no longer needed to ask things.

It was touching as fuck. Rachel was one of those people in my life I could go for years without seeing or talking to, but when we finally did talk we would click like no time had passed. It was a friendship that did not expire or grow stale no matter how long you neglected it. That's what I told myself.

I settled into a beanbag chair and told her some of what I'd been up to lately. She did not interrupt. She let me talk a long time.

"Do you need me to go out there."

"Why?" I laughed. "Dude, I just told you! We're fine."

Silence.

"Have you talked to Alejandro lately."

"Um . . . well . . . lately . . ."

"I am going to call him. I'll give him your new number. I had to get your new number from your mother." *New number? Oh, yeah.*

"It's great to hear from you . . ." I tried.

More silence, which was worse than the scolding.

"Marcus. You say you're fine. Fine. I'm calling Alejandro. And I am going to say something to you now. Maybe it isn't a good time, but it's always a good time and a bad time to speak the truth. OK."

"Did you just make that up? About the truth? 'Cause it was awesome."

"Are you listening, Marcus."

"Yeah?"

"I do not like to pursue people. I am not in the habit of pursuing people. I live my life in such a way that I don't have to. I left the firm because being there required chasing after partners and I *do not do that.* I pursued Judah, but only until he started pursuing me, and then I married him, and that was that. Tracking you down like this is *not* how I do things. I require a two-way street. A *two-way* street. Do you hear me."

I did. "Yes."

"Listen to me. I share a *toilet.* With a *man.* So that I do not have to pursue *anyone.* That is how serious I am."

I knew better than to laugh. "I *do* understand, Rachel. And I'm sorry."

"Fine."

"I'm sorry."

"You said that."

"I promise I will call you more."

"Or at all would be fine. Do you still have my number. I did not change it without telling you. I left it with your mother but do you have it."

"Actually, you'd better give it to me again."

I started rummaging for a pen. Then the dogs began barking downstairs, and under that I heard an engine outside. "Oh! Sarah's home!" I said. First I was happy, then I remembered how things had been lately. Then I remembered how jealous she was. I tried to imagine still being on the phone when she walked into the house and telling her, "Hi, baby! My smart sexy friend that has known me longer than you called!" and I just couldn't see it. So I hung up.

Missed.

Friday, October 6, 1995

We'd argued about something. I don't remember what. We were fighting almost every day now, and the fights were getting worse. Things would get serious very quickly. Grave, even. So, when some mundane discussion about housework or politics or whatever it was went suddenly sideways and, just like that, murder was in the air, I left. I grabbed my keys and I walked out. No plan. No jacket. I was lucky I was wearing pants.

I drove to the Fillmore District and parked. It was Friday night. I wandered streets full of couples on dates and young men up to no good. When it got chilly I ducked into the Kabuki Theater and caught a new movie called *Seven*. It helped a lot.

I got home around midnight. Sarah ran into the garage one second after I stepped out of Claire and when I saw her streaking toward me my first thought was that she had a knife. But her hands were empty. She got up on her tippy toes, threw her arms around my neck, and whined into my ear while she sucked it. "Oh, my love! *slurp* I was so worried! I just knew that you were dead somewhere! *lick* I called the police *chomp* but they wouldn't take a report yet. *slurp* Oh, baby! I'm *so* sorry. *lick* I'm sorry, baby!"

"I'm sorry too," I said, horny.

We almost did it in the garage but there was sawdust and metal shavings on the floor, and she was too little for us to do it standing up unless I held her the whole time, which I didn't feel like doing. So we crashed through the back door of the garage and did it in the hammock in the yard. It wasn't exhibitionistic so much as lazy, and stairs just aren't happening when your pants are down around your ankles. Nevertheless, at one point I opened my eyes and pretty much everybody I'd ever seen going into the houses on either side were lined up in their respective yards, staring over fences at us from the dark. Rita's old inmates were smoking, of course; mostly all I could see of them was the glow of their butts. I tried to tell myself that the two thin shadows at the other fence were somehow not the teenagers who lived there, but when Sarah hauled off and smacked me dead in my face just as I was about to come, I hoped that might scare them straight, as it were. And a minute later I grunted out, "And don't . . . do . . . *drugs!*" for good measure. They might have just been grunting noises, though. Then I fell asleep, and for all I know she fucked me again.

The next day started out normally. We were rearranging the furniture for no reason. Soon, things were tense. We were trying to get a dresser through a narrow doorway we'd been lucky to get the thing through once, and Sarah was insisting that we carry it without first removing the large mirror that was screwed onto the back. Whenever I moved, Sarah wasn't strong enough to match the action, and the mirror bowed and sagged, promising to mutilate us both.

The phone rang.

"Gah!" I had no intention of answering the thing. But Sarah stopped moving.

From the living room: *Click. Mooore bounce.* Best song ever? I say, Maybe. We waited.

"*Much more bieeeee-younce!*" Roger eventually concluded. *Beep.*

"Yeah this is Sergeant Eric Tucker, SFPD. I am trying to return your call.

I don't have time to listen to your music. I am trying to follow up on your call of yesterday evening . . ."

"You gonna pick that up?" Sarah asked. I note in hindsight that she didn't tell me to pick it up. She always liked to give people a choice. Satan does that. I do too.

"Alright," I said.

The phone was a cordless, and was still sitting on top of the dresser. We set down the furniture and I picked up the phone.

"Yellow!" I sang. I didn't give a fuck about Sergeant Tucker. If he didn't like my answering machine message he could come over here and change it. If he had a warrant. If he didn't have a warrant, Sergeant Tucker would have a problem.

"Yeah, I'm calling about a report we got last night, about a missing person? Are you that person?" He sounded so bored. This must happen a lot.

"Yup, that was me," I said. Maybe Sergeant Fucker wasn't so bad. It was nice of him to follow up, even if it was his job. "Thanks for—"

The most shocking scream I have ever heard in my life. I won't bother trying to spell it.

When you hear a scream, from a man or a woman or a baby, it's mostly voice. Air moving through vocal cords. That's almost all of it. It sounds different coming out of different people. But what all screams have in common, all real screams, is an undertone. You know this undertone. Everybody does. It's primal. A scream is a sound, but underneath the sound is a vibration that says to the brain stem of every living thing, *Oh shit!* This scream was mostly that. It was, by far, the best scream I have ever heard, before or since. Janet Leigh in *Psycho* comes in second.

I freaked out from the scream and when I was done freaking out she was still screaming. She was staring at me, mouth open, arms at her sides, and this horrible electrifying horror-movie scream was pouring out. And her face was empty. She ran out of air, took a deep breath, and screamed some more. She never took her eyes off mine.

"Everything good over there?" Sergeant Tucker asked. Now he sounded amused.

I tried to think of a lie but I couldn't. There was no lie for this. "I don't know why she's screaming," I told him. "She's just standing there, screaming. We had a fight last night . . . uh, an argument. I guess she's still mad . . . ?"

"Want me to send a car out?" You could hear his smile. Fucker.

What a question. Do you tell the cops *not* to come? You certainly don't tell them *to* come, do you? Sarah was still screaming. *What would an innocent person say?*

"That won't be necessary." This was the best I could come up with. And for some reason I said it like a Bond villain: *nesssssry.*

Sergeant Fucker didn't give a fuck. "Well, call back if you change your mind." He hung up.

I put the phone back down on the dresser. Sarah stopped screaming.

We stood there a moment, that vibration echoing through the house. We wouldn't see a cat for the rest of the day.

And then I asked. I'm glad I asked, and I'm surprised I did. Because if I had to ask, clearly, I did not want to know.

"Why did you scream bloodcurdling screams once you knew I was on the phone with the police?"

"I wanted them to arrest you. I think you should get raped. I was hoping they would come and arrest you, and you would get raped in jail."

She said it like she was telling me that after we rearranged the furniture we should go out to eat because we'd be too tired to cook.

What did we do then? I don't remember.

Ruffneck.

Sunday, October 8, 1995

I was minding my own business, driving Sarah's truck across the Bay Bridge to Berkeley. We'd agreed that I should probably get used to driving the truck, in case she were wounded in the course of the Y2K race war and I had to get all of us and our gear to safety.

Back then, minding my own business largely consisted of playing a game I called How Bad Do You Want It? Sometimes I called it Offensive Driving. Basically the game involves inviting another driver to have a fatal collision. It's way fun.

Say you and I are driving side by side on a two-lane street that, after the next intersection, becomes a one-lane street. I am on the left; the one remaining lane will be mine. Your right lane has cars parked in it immediately past the intersection, which at this point is half a block away.

Likely, you will intend to accelerate and cut in front of me, since your lane ends and you, unlike me, are going somewhere. That you made a poor choice of lanes is irrelevant. Perhaps you stayed up late and then overslept and are now running late for work. This is my problem. By no means does your failure to think ahead mean that you should peacefully merge into my lane behind me. Why would it? Obviously, you are entitled to scoot in front of me. Because you are more important than me, aren't you? Yes, you are.

When you speed up to get in front of me, as is your birthright, I speed up too. But I don't speed up any more than you do, or even as much. I only speed up a little bit. And so you might go from being right alongside me to two feet ahead. Not enough to cut in. This will probably encourage you to speed up a little more. I certainly hope it does.

We are almost at the intersection. You are making progress, now half a car length ahead. You speed up, and so do I, and so on, and soon, if all goes well, you are now going about 40 and headed toward the back of a parked car only a few yards ahead.

To the extent that you have any options left, you can: (a) step down on that other pedal—you know, the big wide one that you hate—and get your savage soccer-mom ass the fuck in line; or (b) you can just go ahead and plow into the parked car, hopefully launching into the air and bursting into flames on impact.

Unfortunately, all of my playmates so far had chosen the humiliating option of acting like normal, civilized people. Who knows, maybe they learned something. Probably not.

There are many opportunities to play How Bad Do You Want It? Double-parked cars work well, as do big slow semis on the highway. Due to the increased speeds and aggro on highways, one would expect a better result. But, as on surface streets, in all the times I had played on the highway not one of my subjects had chosen the Bruckheimer Option. I remained hopeful.

So I was minding my own business as we all sped across the bridge and I wouldn't quite let the ancient green two-door to my left get into my lane. It wasn't even really conscious, except that I noted it was even funner in a truck. Up ahead, the Foster Farms semi was getting closer.

"Mah bay bee takes the mornin' train," I said.

The green hooptie almost succeeded in passing me but ultimately hit the brakes maybe five feet behind the semi. Five feet! Closest one yet! I even saw a little tire smoke.

Sheena and I continued our duet: *"He works sooooo hard!"* "Yeah I do!" I heard an engine, but we were on a bridge. There were engines everywhere.

So when the killers were upon me, it was almost like when a little devil pops up on your shoulder. I glanced over and there they were. Car full of heads. It was my green hooptie. The car was old, but only on the outside. The insides grumbled and snarled.

There were two, maybe three hulks in the back. No one was riding shotgun. The driver appeared to be about my height and skinny. Barely out of his teens. Dark and wiry. He was wearing a beater—a real beater, not a beateresque light-gray Gap tank top like me. He had a blue bandanna tied Aunt Jemima–style on his sweaty head. And yet he did not look ridiculous. He looked like the real deal. I felt a little envy. *I could never get like that. I started too late.*

I'm sure his potnas were impressive too, but this Alpha took all my attention. He was doing the most incredible thing. We were moving well over 70 miles an hour in light traffic. And he lined up his car right next to mine, maybe six feet to my left, and kept it there, perfectly matching my speed. Effortlessly. He only glanced at the road long enough to zip around some poor car in front of him. The rest of the time, he stared up at me. He had to crane his neck a bit to see me in the truck. His car seemed to drive itself.

After waiting for me take in the full splendor of his uber-thuggosity, and sizing me up as the poseur I was, he spoke: "You trippin'?" Conversationally, but his voice carried. He sounded like Eazy-E.

"What?"

"You trippin'?" he said, exactly the same way. He peered up at me earnestly.

There was something about it. Yes. We were having The Talk. We were having the pre-violence talk that I liked to have. I was on the other side of it.

It appeared that I had finally found someone to play with. But it was all wrong. Maybe if we sat down in a coffee shop, I could explain How Bad Do You Want It? to Alpha Jemima and how getting in line is the cornerstone of civilization. I could draw on the placemat how to merge in behind someone. But as it was—zooming down a highway, not looking where we were going— even the shortest explanation was too long. Lord knows, "*You* bumped into *me*" hadn't gone over too well a billion years ago. And I was in the wrong then too. I didn't want to get into it with folks who were only correcting me for my incivility. Those were my people.

In the six or seven seconds I'd spent pondering my situation, the .45 Smith I kept in the glove box—possibly the same model The Door had chosen not to use on me—found its way into my hand and switched its safety off. But it was never supposed to be like this. Even if this was quickly turning into a matter of self-defense, I had started it. That was more than just a bad fact. I couldn't get past it, morally. It was true what I'd said to Officer Friendly: I liked to think of myself as one of the good guys. If I was going to go out in a blaze of glory, I wanted to take someone with me who had it coming. Maybe these guys had it coming, sure, but not because of anything they had done to me. They hadn't done anything to me. Yet.

We were off the bridge now and heading east on 80 through Oakland. I kept glancing at the road. Alpha Jemima didn't. He was still hawking on me, waiting for an answer to his trick "trippin'" question. He wasn't going to leave it alone.

My pistol was in my right hand, low and out of sight, pointed at him through my door. Big Roller was loaded with heavy, high-pressure semi-wadcutters—no hollowpoints for the car gun. My slugs would slice through the truck door no problem. Even if I didn't hit Alpha, the attack would buy me a moment to take a proper shot or three through my window. It was safe to assume that Alpha was armed, but he had both hands on the wheel. His boys were probably strapped as well, but none of them was waving a gun at me, for now.

A.J.'s awesome driving was making it easy to aim a gun at him, even though we were now pushing 80 miles an hour. He was lining up his body with the muzzle and keeping it there. Very helpful. After I made the most of my surprise first shot I would empty the rest of the clip into the car, then try to get away. If they stayed with me, I still had Shooter on my belt and, even better, I was in a truck. It's so easy to kill with a car that motherfuckers do it by accident.

And then she came to me. The only thing I can liken it to is the end of *Star Wars* when Obi-Wan appears in Luke's cockpit and tells him to use the Force. Only it was Amalia, riding shotgun like she used to, and instead of "Use the Force, Luke" she said, "Apologize, Marcus."

Oh. I was wrong; I would apologize. Yes. They were thugs and I was me but we were still members of civilized society. Also, I was about to get into a life-and-death fight with men who would be dead in a year anyway. And if I killed all four of them the cops would spend about 15 minutes searching for me. But I didn't want to do it if I didn't have to. *Apologize!* That was the way out of this. So simple. So elegant. Classic Amalia. I took a deep breath and let it out laughing. For the first time in a while, I realized, I felt sane.

I turned my head back toward them to say sorry. Then I lifted Big Roller up to my window and fired a shot at the car.

OK. This is why they make you wear protective goggles at the range: Because when you fire a gun, even a pistol, even a top-shelf pistol by a venerable American institution, hot dust and bits of fucking metal and shit explode out everywhere. And while the *crack* of a real gun is not as cool as the *boomgrowl* of a movie gun, it is about 6,000 times louder, especially when you don't have sense enough to shoot lefty but, rather, hold the gun in your right hand about twelve inches from your face, inside a truck.

There was no time to see if I'd hit anything; I could hear tires squealing, and I had a feeling they were mine. Apparently I had drifted two lanes over when I let go of the steering wheel to brush burning shit off my face. I dropped Big Roller into my lap and grabbed the wheel.

I wanted to stop, but I did not want to be executed, not by Jemima or by the CHP, so I kept moving. At least I was in the fast lane now. I glanced in the rearview; traffic was snarled up a ways back, but there were no green hoopties or patrol cars to be seen. My right ear was ringing, loud.

I blew through Berkeley, giving Alpha a chance to give up and go the fuck back to Oakland. Eventually it felt safe to take an exit, duck down a side street, and pull over.

That was a bad idea.

I took Big Roller out of my crotch, decocked him, put his safety back on, and put him back in the glove box. My ear was still ringing. I pulled down the visor and looked at myself in the mirror. There was dust on my face. Gunpowder, I guess. And there was a good-sized cinder in the inside corner of my left eye. A black crumb embedded in the pink webbing by the bridge of my nose, a drop of blood underneath it. It stung. *Did I almost lose an eye?* It's weird—we can explore space, build supercomputers, and alter genetic structures, but guns are still these messy, loud blunderbusses. I picked the cinder out of my eye and wiped my face with a wet nap and prayed that I would live to see the ray gun.

Why didn't I just listen to Amalia?

I should have been scared. If I had been afraid of those men, that never would have happened. But the last time I could remember really being afraid was when I thought that Amalia might die.

I can't tell Sarah about this. She'll go find them in Oakland and shoot them. Or tell them where I live.

I started the truck up again.

It was a good question. I am trippin'. I am trippin' hard.

It's a Thin Line.

Monday, October 9, 1995

I was washing dishes. I looked over my shoulder for no reason and Sarah was standing in the kitchen doorway, glaring at me. Until recently, her death stare had been reserved for Rita. It was almost like she was trying to block the exit. Which was pretty funny, because she was so tiny. And also not funny, because I knew her.

"You got something to tell me?" she said, finally.

"Um . . . I love you?"

"You wanna tell me about that hole?"

A sex game? No. She's serious.

"What hole, baby?" I was trying not to sound mad. But already I felt annoyed.

"The *hole*," she growled, stalking toward me. "In my *truck*. On the *driver's* side." She obviously read a lot of significance into that, and yet, somehow, no significance at all into the fact of mortal-enemy murderers living in the house on one side, teenagers in the house on the other side, and a world of assholes all around. All she could see was me.

I turned off the faucet and faced her. "You think I did something to your truck? Why would I do that? 'Cause you kicked Claire's door in?" We'd never talked about that. "Why would I do some passive-aggressive shit like that?" I needed to stop talking; I was working myself up.

"Well, then how the *fuck* did it get there?"

"*How the FUCK should I know?*" I yelled. Which was fine, sort of. We yelled a lot. But I was still holding a dish—a large dinner plate. And I must have gestured, perhaps wildly, while I was talking. Because the soapy plate flew from my hand. Not at Sarah, fortunately, but straight up, where it shattered against the ceiling. Then most of the pieces of the plate collided with the blades of the ceiling fan spinning over our heads and shards of porcelain rained down upon us. The animals that had been sleeping nearby hauled ass.

It was obviously an accident. Obvious to me. There weren't any more sharp objects around Sarah's bare feet than there were around mine. But Sarah marched quickly back out the kitchen door. I tried to tell myself that she had stormed out in a huff. But I know the *Wait right here motherfucker* walk when I see it. The odds of her coming back shooting were significant. This had all the hallmarks of a tragic misunderstanding. I considered climbing out the kitchen window, but there was no time. She was too fast.

She returned a few seconds later, our boom box held high over her head. She looked like John Cusack at the end of a movie we'd just watched on TV. She walked right up to me, grunted slightly, and hurled that boom box straight down. It exploded on the floor in front of my feet. I made no attempt to get out of the way, so she must not have been aiming for me.

In less than 60 seconds things had gone from domestic bliss to domestic violence. Plastic guts were still skidding across the room as I considered my next move. I saw her also considering my next move, and *her* next move. And I was considering her next move too.

But she didn't do anything else. Instead, she stared at me with real hatred, the kind of look you can't take back. And she said, "I better not see any more holes." And she backed out of the kitchen.

Our poor dogs were peering at me from the hallway. Grace, the sweet pit Sarah had rescued from God knows what, was trembling. They deserved better.

Guns, schmuns. When you're *really* mad—when it's personal—you don't want to shoot anybody. You want to cut his throat. You want to beat her to death.

A little later, I snuck outside to take a peek at the truck. Like she'd said, there was a small, round hole in the rear panel, driver's side, just above the tire. I was grateful that Alpha Jemima missed my wheel. Things would have gone differently.

Calm Down, Sir.

Tuesday, October 10, 1995

It was time to go.

Things were out of control, even for us, the Fighty McFuckertons. Interestingly, my wake-up call had not been a moment of near-violence but one of self-reflection. The night before, I'd found myself idly wondering if I would be able to snap her neck before succumbing to whatever fatal injury I would soon receive. The fact that we were having makeup sex at the time did not help.

Leaving was not enough. After all, Nicole left O.J. Sarah would definitely hunt me down; despite everything, our lesbian wedding vows were somehow still in effect. I had to slow her down.

I settled on taking her ammo. If I took her guns, she would press charges. Guns are not cheap. But bullets are, relatively speaking, and they were the part I was worried about.

Bullets may be cheap but, thanks to the Brady bill, they are well regulated. All gun shops now required and logged picture ID, and all had security cameras. If she was going to shoot me for not loving her anymore then cry to the cops that she didn't mean it, better she should have to explain video of herself buying a box of shells the day before. Even a little white girl might have some trouble with that.

Today Sarah was at the Federal Building in Oakland, gaming the Social Security Administration. They were searching people and cars now, of course, so she'd had to roll completely unarmed. Perfect time to make my move.

I had packed the night before, during the wee hours while she snored, and hidden the suitcase in the garage. Now I moved my bag into the front hall. Pretty much all I had left to do was disarm her, collect my kitties, and maybe write a note.

I tore through her shit. I located her .380 and her two backup pieces. Then I found two more guns she never told me about. I unloaded all of them and put them each back where I found them. I found her ammo stash. When I discovered a second ammo stash I knew I would have to search the whole house. I moved all the ammo I'd found so far into the closet of the spare bedroom.

I heard a key in the door. She was back early.

I ran in circles for a few seconds and then ducked into the spare bedroom and closed and locked the door.

From downstairs: "Marcus?" Sweetly.

Then she was right outside the room. Trying the door.

Silence.

"What?" This from the bedroom. "Shit! Marcus!"

Silence.

Trying the door again. Harder. It was dismaying how her comings and goings were completely silent. She would just appear out there.

Then the thumping started. "Marcus." *Thump.* "Open the door." *Thump, thump.* "Marcus." *Thump.* "Give me back my stuff." *Thump, thump.*

Fuck.

I didn't want to talk to her, even through the door. She might convince me to let her in and give her back her stuff.

The thumping got harder. I had to do something. Our house was full of crowbars.

The phone still sat on the dresser.

"911 what is your emergency," the most bored person in the world recited.

I told her.

"And where are you, sir?"

By now I was hiding in the closet with the ammo. I said so.

She stopped being bored long enough to laugh, then told me to stay on the line.

Eventually, I peeked out of the closet and saw flashing blue lights reflecting off the bedroom window. I ran to the window to yell to them, like they were firemen instead of cops.

Sarah was out there already talking to them.

I went outside. "Thank God you're here!" The line didn't sound right, even to me, but it was how I felt. Right then, I took back every bad thing I'd ever said or thought about the police. The police were my friends. I'd called, and they had come. To protect me.

"Calm down, sir," one of the officers said as he put his hand on his pistol.

Sarah turned and faced me. She slipped me a little smile while the two armed men regarded me and put a face to whatever she had just told them. She hadn't even known I'd called the cops. She was straight improvising. This was what I loved about her.

The cops pushed past me and inside my house without a word.

Sarah had been pretty honest with them, apparently. Once we were inside, she repeated her position that her ammo was her property and that I had taken it without permission. I related my discomfort with her being armed at that moment.

They asked Sarah if I'd ever hit her; she told the truth and said no. I understood, completely, why they'd asked her that. They were responding to the proverbial Domestic Disturbance Call. We all think we know how those go. And I understood when they asked her the exact same question again three minutes later. Sometimes victims of domestic violence need to be coaxed. Mind you, she didn't have a mark on her, whereas I, while not visibly bruised, had a human bite mark under my shirt. They never asked me. But she was tiny, she was a chick, so whatever.

They split us up and spoke to us separately. Her cop pressed her in the kitchen. All I clearly made out was Sarah saying, "No. Nothing like that."

"This is a big place," my cop said to me, scanning around. "How can you afford the rent?"

They asked Sarah to lock the dogs in the kitchen and told me to sit in the living room. Sarah moved about freely. When one asked me if there were any weapons in the house, I noted that we had both already told them so, and then I explained exactly where each one was. The cop immediately called for backup. Soon, four more cowards arrived, and most of them started to search the house.

All of the cops were white; all were male but one. A petite female cop with a blond ponytail sticking out the back of her police hat. When you hear the words "affirmative action," you probably imagine some incompetent black guy with a job he can't handle and that should have been given to some other, qualified (i.e. white) person. The actual data tells us that the affirmative action poster child is much more like this cop: white, female, blond, cute. That's what passes for affirmative action these days: cute white chicks getting preferential treatment.

Real-Life Affirmative Action Poster Child struck a pose while she talked into her radio. She was wearing a vest. Apparently SFPD didn't have a vest small enough to fit her, and swimming in her too-big vest she resembled a blue suit of armor. I prefer my cops big. Male or female, but big and tough, please. Big enough to beat my ass without the benefit of a weapon. This cop would have no choice but to shoot me, and she knew it.

Legally Blond stood in the hallway, conferring with the first two officers on the scene (*shit—my house is "the scene" now*). When she wasn't barking orders at them she was shooting daggers at me. Finally, she approached Sarah.

They smiled warmly.

They stood in the front hall and talked about me while I watched. Blond Justice put her arm around Sarah's waist. She moved her head close to Sarah's and they whispered secret things. From time to time they glanced at me. We can add that to my list of things I'd have thought would be hotter. Flashing lights glided past the bay windows—more backup. Three more cops walked into my house through the open door. They did not acknowledge me.

Does SFPD really have this little to do? How many unsolved stabbings am I going to read about in the back of the paper tomorrow?

At some point I noticed my suitcase.

Sarah was standing right in front of it. The place was cluttered; she hadn't noticed it. Yet. Once she did, I would be dealing with the person I didn't want to have any bullets.

I sat there and willed Sarah not to notice the suitcase. It worked for about five minutes. Then some cops passed the two of them in the hallway, and they scootched a little to let them by. Sarah backed into the suitcase and almost fell over it. Blond Justice caught her arm when she stumbled. Sarah turned to look at what she'd tripped over. It was going to be a glance, but when she saw what it was, she froze, body twisted, head down. She stood and stared and I couldn't breathe. Finally, she raised her head and gazed down the hall at me. I could see the crazy in her eyes from across the house.

Blond Justice was still steadying her; Sarah clutched at the arm and shrank. Then she said something, and Blond Justice put her arm around Sarah again and hustled her out of my sight.

Blond Justice came back a few minutes later. Alone. She snapped a quick order at two lazy stormtroopers that were standing around, and they followed as she quickstepped into the living room straight for me. Her little hand was, of course, on the butt of her oversized security blanket. I wondered if she was going to draw it. She didn't. Instead, she pointed at the floor and said, "Down."

It really wasn't enough information, not for someone who had never done it before. I got down on one knee and held my hands up, Al Jolson style. "Like this?" One of the goons took semi-pity on me and semi-gently helped me into the position: completely prone, flat on my face, hands behind my back.

Somebody cuffed me.

I was lifted by the cuffs to my feet. Given that my arms were behind my back, this hurt a great deal. I didn't give anyone the satisfaction of hearing me cry out. No rights were read. Somebody unceremoniously robbed me, emptying my pockets while threatening me with what they'd do if anything in my pockets cut their hands. Then someone shoved me out of my living room through the hall and out the front door and down my front steps to one of the six or eight cop cars badly parked around my driveway. No one told me to watch my head, like they do on *Cops*, but I watched my head get more than a little bumped on the way in. Someone slammed the door.

They left me in the back of the cruiser, cuffed and alone. The car smelled like fresh vomit. The glass between the backseat and the front had a big crack across it—from kicks, maybe?—but someone had since installed a thick wire grate in front of the cracked glass, so there was no longer any hope of escape that way. The windows to either side of me had wire built into the glass. There were no handles, locks, or knobs on either of my doors in the back. It was pretty creepy.

My eyes got accustomed to the dark and I noticed graffiti here and there inside the back of the car. *I dint do it*, someone had written in what looked like blood on the window to my left. In the cracked glass in front of me some-one had etched, *FUCK KNEE GROWS*.

I thought about that. Some dude got himself busted. He was sitting in here under arrest, like I was now. Either the cops had uncuffed him or he had uncuffed himself; the glass was already cracked, or perhaps he had cracked it. There was no wire grate yet. He had a sharp object in his possession. Of all of the options that lay before this man, he had chosen to spend precious minutes doing that. A real mastermind, that one.

Next door, Rita and Michael stood on their porch, basking in it. It must have been nice for the wolves to be at someone else's door. Rita was almost pretty when she smiled. Maybe those psychos had left me alone because they knew it was only a matter of time until I self-destructed. Maybe we were so crazy that serial killers kept their distance. We were amateurs. Funny thing was, if I *had* killed them, the day I went to get Luther's ball, say, and the cops found a dozen corpses stashed around the house, they would have called me a hero. They'd have let me *drive* this car, with the siren on. It's all about context.

But I had bigger problems. They had me. Really *had* me. I felt the beginnings of panic, so I took a big breath of vomit air, held it, and let it go slowly. Then I took another. I needed to be calm enough to take any opportunities I got.

Cops streamed in and out of our house. Most of the ones coming out carried ammo. I guess you could say we had a "stockpile." We kept it in military ammo cans—those big green metal rectangles with the flip tops—because that is what they are for. They keep your ammunition dry and safe. I didn't really intend to stockpile per se. We'd pick up a box or two every few weeks or so, and we didn't go shooting much anymore. But watching the ants march out with our property, I knew that they would say I had been deliberately stockpiling ammo for something. Not that *we* had been stockpiling. Me.

One cop, at his limit with just one ammo can, actually took the time to walk up to the car I was in, peer in at me, and whine through the slightly open passenger-side front window, "Why do you have so much ammo?" I wanted to say, *Because guns don't work without it,* but I knew I couldn't say that so instead I said, "I don't know what to tell you." The weakling cop trudged away with his burdens.

I had been in my cage for maybe a half an hour when another cop came by the car to get something out of the trunk. A brother.

I watched him through the rear window. He tried to open the trunk but it was locked and I guess he didn't have the key because he walked over to the passenger side and opened the front door and leaned across the seats to pop the trunk using the latch near the floor on the driver's side. He paid me no mind. He would be gone again in a second.

"Excuse me? Officer?" He didn't react at all. The trunk was now popped, and he was starting to back out of the car. He still hadn't acknowledged me, but I knew he could hear me because I had heard the weakling cop. "Officer? Do you know Debra McGee?"

He had almost completely exited the car, but at that he froze and turned and looked me in the face for the first time. "Yeah?"

"Would you please call her and tell her that this is happening, please? Please?"

He said nothing, and his face never changed. He pulled himself back out of the car and slammed the door.

I felt pretty good about the exchange. Black cops were for some reason particularly unpopular in hip-hop at that time, but still I hoped. It was something.

I figured that was probably the only break I'd get, so I settled into my seat and took in my surroundings again. *FUCK KNEE GROWS.* I stared out the window again. Rita was smiling at me. I smiled back. Kind of meant it. She had, after all, punched Sarah in the head. I closed my eyes.

The door slammed and I jumped. Two cops sat in front; one started up the car. Had I actually gone to sleep? It was completely dark now. My house was still a buzzing hive. I did not see Sarah. Maybe she was upstairs, fisting Blond Justice in our bed. I kind of hoped so.

I didn't want to show weakness by saying anything, but when we got on the highway I cracked: "Where we goin'?" Of course they didn't answer. No one had read me my rights, or said much of anything to me after "Down," so I wasn't even sure I was officially under arrest. Granted, I was chained up in a rolling cell, but I wondered if a court would find that I was being detained in the constitutional sense. I mulled over that awhile, until I remembered that the question was moot because the Constitution did not apply to me. I was right all along.

Two exits later we were back on surface streets in the South of Market District. Still not a word from either of my abductors. Maybe the jackbooted thugs were taking me to 850 Bryant—jail, or, as the rappers call it, County.

They were. We pulled into an underground garage and one of them dragged me out of the car and shoved me toward a freight elevator. I was in the belly of the beast, but at least I wasn't at the dump, or on some pier.

The freight elevator doors opened into a dirty, crowded office. One of the klansmen plunked me down in a chair by a desk and left me there. I sat for a while and watched other manacled black men get led around. It was a lot like *Sankofa.*

Most of the prisoners looked like criminals, for what that's worth. I probably looked like a criminal too. OK, I definitely did. But a few of them didn't look like criminals at all. A few looked like how I felt. Their frozen haggard faces said, *But I did everything right! I did everything you told me to do. This happens anyhow?* Yes, yes it does. You cannot escape your destiny, young Skywalker.

On TV, some pig sits down at a typewriter on the desk and barks, "Name." That never happened. Maybe, since they'd stolen my wallet, someone got it off my license. What happened instead was nothing, until a huge pig scooped up my arm as it waddled by and pulled me back over to the freight elevator. We went up, up, up. I'd have thought they'd keep us down below, in the hold. But instead they keep us in the tower. Maybe those are the most difficult floors to escape, or to evacuate in a fire. I didn't know. It was all new to me. I'd made it to almost 30 without any of this.

The elevator doors opened onto a small bulletproof waiting area, though you could see the cells in the back. The fat pig pulled me past the coward behind the glass who buzzed us in, then it finally uncuffed me and shoved me into a cell. I was not alone.

Although, yes, I had tried my whole life to avoid what was happening, that doesn't mean I hadn't thought about it. I'd probably thought about it every day. But as soon as Officer McPigwich closed the cage door and left, I understood that I'd never had any clue what it was really like.

There were six other men in the large cell. Half wore baggy orange sweatshirts with matching pants—the jail uniform, I guess. The black-and-white-striped getup must cost more. The other three were still in their real clothes, like me. All of us were black. I wondered if this really was a representative sample of the penal system's inventory. I had not seen anyone but brothers getting pulled around downstairs.

At first I was tense, waiting for other inmates to try to jump me like Sarah wanted or take my shoes or whatever. But they all pretty much ignored me, and each other. I guessed I was the only first-timer. The big man who pulled his sweatpants down and took a noisy dump in the exposed toilet was my pick for most frequent flyer. There was no sink.

I spent my time not afraid but disgusted. No rats, but there were plenty of droppings in the corners, and squads of roaches on the walls. It was quiet, save the occasional clang or buzz. In my limited experience, jail isn't so much dangerous as it is gross and boring.

I was there a long time. I don't know how long, because there was no clock, I hadn't worn a watch in years, and even if I did wear one they'd have taken it when they robbed me.

They stuck two more men in the cell with us: first a black man who was dressed like a pimp, and later a black man wearing a janitor's uniform. Initially I thought he was there to clean up, which, although welcome, seemed odd. But he had no mop, and once inside he just sat down on a bench and looked sad.

I may have fallen asleep again.

The next time someone came, they came for me. A bored frat boy opened the cage and gave me that annoying finger-beckon cops do. I wanted to ignore it but all that would have gotten me was a closed cell door. So I rose and followed. Frat Boy Pig turned his back on me and walked out to the elevator. We rode down, down, down, and exited into a lobby.

"Go," it said.

One hundred and thirty years earlier, a little girl named Azzie McCoy was out in a field working, like she was every day. All of her friends and family were working around her. And some asshole—who probably looked a lot like that cop—rode out to them on a horse and said, Y'all free now. Git. Those were his exact words. We have passed them down. The asshole rode off, and Great-Great-Grandma Azzie and her people got. They just walked away. So did I.

It was late. There was a cop standing on the big front steps outside. "Debra says she'll call you," he said as I passed. It was the black cop I'd asked for help in the car. It took me a minute to process his words, and by the time I finally said "Thank you" he was already walking back up the stairs to be with his buddies.

I had no money; my wallet, and my keys, were taken and gone. I didn't dare go back in and ask for them. Cell phones didn't really exist yet, and if they had they would have taken that too. So I walked. I walked home. It no longer was a home, but it was someplace.

Ten minutes on the highway is hours on foot, and I didn't exactly rush to get back to *the scene*. By the time I could see our house at the end of the block it was almost starting to get light out. In a way, it seemed safer to be in there now than it had that morning, as our drama was now a matter of public record. I naively assumed they'd taken her guns as well.

The front door was open; the lights were on. The house was trashed. It was impossible to tell how much of it had been done by Sarah and how much had been done by her goons. It seemed like everything I cared about was gouged or smashed or, in the case of electronics, doused. That last was definitely Sarah's touch. I wandered from room to room, marveling like a hurricane survivor. Yup, the cat was definitely out of the bag about us now.

The cats.

Now I ran from room to room, eventually into the kitchen. It was the only room that hadn't been destroyed. Nia was sitting on a counter, cleaning. She knew she wasn't supposed to be up there. Suki was asleep by the oven. Finding Jimi was harder. After a while I spied him squeezed behind the refrigerator. He was still scared, but I coaxed him out with tuna juice and got most of the dust out of his thick fur with damp paper towels. Then we all had tuna.

I went back to the front door and closed and locked it. She wasn't in the house. Almost all of her stuff was gone too. I wanted to destroy the few possessions she'd left, but what would be the point? It would be pointless. There was no point.

I stomped a doll's head flat and tore out the pages of her poetry notebook, carefully dipping each page in the toilet before placing it in the bathroom garbage. Maybe I'm biased, but her poetry really sucked.

I found a very old photo of her on the floor in the hall; like the notebook, it must have fallen out of a box during her chaotic, vandalicious exodus. Perhaps Blond Justice had carried this box, couldn't see over the top of it, and tripped. It was a school portrait, from third grade or so. I set the photo down on the coffee table and rooted around until I found my hole punch. Then I went back to the photo and I punched out young Sarah's eyes. I put her eyes in the toilet and stuck the improved photo on the refrigerator, under a magnet bearing an advertisement for a funeral home.

There was a blue clog under the bed. I spooged into it and buried it in the backyard in the still dawn while birds sang and early-rising old men smoked and watched.

Then I lay down on the floor next to our bed. The actual bed was wet—with what, I didn't want to know. After a while, the kitties joined me. We lay there for a long time. I don't think anyone fell asleep. Rays of sun started peeking in. Nobody purred.

V

The Morning After.

Wednesday, October 11, 1995

My suitcase was gone, but I didn't have to move. By 11:00 I'd made an appointment with a locksmith for noon. I called the guy whose van I'd seen all over the city, the one that bore a creepy silhouette on its side. Above the creep was the question: *Does he still have a key?* And below the creepy ex-boyfriend, the name of the company: *AND STAY OUT!* Sarah hadn't even bothered with the charade of leaving a key. And Stay Out! appeared to specialize in such matters.

Mr. And Stay Out! looked like an Asian Mario Brother. I had him replace every cylinder in the house. While he worked, I unburdened myself.

"Hmm," he said, twisting his screwdriver. "How long did you two know each other before you moved in together?"

"'Bout three weeks."

"Hm."

I wanted to call Debra and thank her, but I knew she'd understand if that waited until I was out of the woods. Checking in with a lawyer, sooner than later, seemed like a good idea. I found Rachel's number and called her that afternoon.

Lawyers have a reputation for being judgmental. This is unfounded. How could a judgmental person make their living defending whoever walks in off the street? No, lawyers are opinionated, but not judgmental. Quite the contrary. We are profoundly disinterested. We do not give a shit.

Luckily for me, Rachel was at her desk and had a few minutes to talk. She listened to my entire report, interrupting two or three times to ask good questions. When I was finished, I waited while she ran it all through her computer.

"You're not in any real trouble," she said, finally. "She doesn't know about anything serious. Not serious enough for the police to investigate. Unless she lies. But you were always vulnerable to that." *Because Sarah is a white girl*, she meant. I nodded, then remembered she couldn't see me.

"Going forward," she continued, "you need to stop acting like a chick."

I had a series of flashbacks of squaring off to fight any number of men to the death. "Excuse me?"

"Sounds to me like you do what you feel. Like a chick. Which is fine, as long as it doesn't get you into trouble. But it almost did. And next time it will. So stop."

You can't pay for counsel like that. I tried. She wasn't having it. Later attempts to thank her were ignored. Rachel did not give a shit. Man, I love lawyers.

I dragged the wet mattress out of the house and left it on the curb. The kitties and I had lunch and a snuggle on the couch. Then I drove to the Ace Hardware on Mission.

I was greeted by a tattooed and pierced butch-looking goth chick in a blue work shirt with the store logo on the front. "Help you?"

"Me and my girlfriend just broke up, and she took all her tools. Fuck that. I need tools."

Goth chick escorted me up and down the aisles. We loaded up a cart while I made a speech about not needing some damn woman in my life to have tools and being a grown-ass man who can have his own goddamn tools. Goth chick just nodded. I bought a socket wrench set, two sets of screwdrivers (flathead and Phillips), four hammers, several monkey wrenches (monkey wrenches just seem extra tool-like to me), a saw, an ax, a weed whacker, and the biggest pair of bolt cutters in the world. I haggled on principle and got out of there for $300 even.

Served.

Thursday, October 12, 1995

Much more bi-younce! Beep.

"Marcus? It's Alejandro."

He didn't say anything else. I thought the machine would hang up on dead air, but it didn't. They both just waited. *Why couldn't Sarah have smashed the phones?*

I picked up. "Alejandro?"

"Rachel called me. She's worried." He sounded different. Older. I wondered if I did too.

"Well, I don't know why! I told her I was fine."

"You did?"

"Yeah. I told her what happened."

"Yes. How are you feeling?"

I took in a breath to repeat the word *Fine*. Then I remembered that my life had gone to shit, again, and I didn't say anything.

"Marcus . . . are you OK?"

"Yeah, man. It's just drama, you know? Rough patch is all. Little setback." I made myself laugh. "You know those mornings when the first thing you do when you wake up is promise not to die?"

Alejandro didn't say anything.

"You don't? Me neither. I was just testing you."

"Marcus?"

"Yeah?"

"Are you OK?"

"Yeah, mang!"

Nothing.

"Sure. I guess."

Waiting me out. Fucker.

"Shit, dude, I don't know! Does it matter?"

* * *

Just before dinner I ran out to the 7-Eleven. A sister in a tight black dress was at the counter buying a lottery ticket when I went up with a six-pack of root beer and a large tub of Vaseline in a basket.

She turned and gawked. "Marcus? Marcus Hayes?" Bare arms came up to hug me. I didn't recognize her, but I still went in for the hug, because, you know.

Fwap! the manilla envelope smacked into my palm.

"You've been served," she winked.

In the few seconds it took me to realize what just happened, the hottie handed the pimply cashier a dollar, strutted out, and climbed into the passenger seat of a red sports car taking up two spaces just outside. She and the truly scary-looking white dude at the wheel took off.

The cashier and I stared at where she used to be, our respective gifts in hand.

I turned to him. "OK. That was badass."

"Yeah," he said.

You Are Here.

Friday, October 13, 1995

The beautiful sister leaned back and smiled. "So, how is Alex?"

Alex? I fidgeted in her guest chair and tried to relax. *If I ever called Alejandro "Alex" he would figure out how to punch someone in the face and then he'd do it.* "He's fine. I guess. I haven't really been in touch, you know, lately. But . . . when this came up . . ." It's awkward admitting to being a bad friend, but an attorney intake session is modern-day confession. "He said he knew somebody."

"Alex knows everybody." *He does?* Her smile broadened on just one corner of her appealing mouth. "Did he tell you how he knows me?"

"Um. No. But I think you just did."

She laughed, leaned forward, and narrowed her eyes. I was in love with Simona Reece Guerrero Downs, Esq. Retaining all of her ex-husbands' names helped her keep track of them, she'd said. *Simona Reece Guerrero Downs Hayes* had a nice ring.

"About this . . . Usually, I'm on the criminal side of things. But a restraining order hearing is a hybrid. And down the road the DA could file. I think you are going to need representation there." I trusted that she wasn't gouging me, because I trusted her, and because apparently Alejandro Velez was some sort of sex angel in disguise, like the bespectacled stripper in the first half of every Van Halen video ever, and Simona was repaying a favor performed over a long weekend in the Poconos. I say I was in love, but really I was grateful beyond words.

"Why would the DA file charges against me? On what grounds? I heard Sarah tell the cops that I never hit her. Which is the truth," I added. "I'll testify to that. And anyway, *I'm* the one who called the cops. *I* am the complainant." I considered showing her my bite marks, but decided that was too much information for a first meeting.

Simona leaned back again and regarded me with amused surprise, as if I had just popped into my chair from out of nowhere like on *Bewitched.* She opened her mouth, then closed it back. She opened it again but she scrapped that too. Her brow furrowed. In retrospect, I understand. When someone says something much stupider than you would have expected, it is difficult to respond. You don't know where to begin.

Finally, she placed one long finger on the slim closed file in front of her and slid it across her desk to me. "Document on top."

It was the police report from the night of—of whatever that was. I scanned the form boxes that made up the first three lines of the report. Most notable:

VICTIM 1: SARAH A. STRAUSS

SUSPECT 1: MARCUS H. HAYES

My eyes moved back and forth between those two boxes. It's funny to me now, how much they did not compute. I looked up at Simona. She stared back. "But . . ." She said nothing. I looked back down at the boxes again. And then I knew where the fuck I was.

Numbers Game.

Monday, October 16, 1995

Like everyone else, I watched the Million Man March, even though we didn't know what we were watching.

The pundits assured us that it was the end of the world. Every network had a full panel of professors and other experts on black people. You could trust that they were experts because they were all white.

I for one was pleasantly surprised. My relationship with the Nation of Islam began and ended with the scented oils I'd bought from the brothers on Sixth Avenue. Of course they tried to recruit me, both in New York and Oakland. I was young, angry, and black. But I wasn't much of a follower.

They didn't get me, but they got a bunch of other cats. And it was beautiful. We'd come from everywhere. Sure, there were brothers selling T-shirts, and I'm sure that someone had to prevent at least one fight (if there'd been an actual fight it would have been broadcast), but mostly what I saw was more brothers than I'd ever seen in one place, including Africa. And we were happy. I was starting to wish I'd gone.

Certainly Minister Farrakhan was happy as he took the podium. I didn't trust him but he had a nice smile. He drank it in. It was his moment. This was history.

He began:

In the name of Allah, the beneficent, the merciful. We thank Him for His prophets, and the scriptures which they brought. We thank Him for Moses and the Torah. We thank Him for Jesus and the Gospel. We thank Him for Muhammad and the Koran. Peace be upon these worthy servants of Allah.

Wow. The air was heavy and electric. I sat down on the bed and was covered in cats in five seconds.

He cleared his throat a little while longer, and then he talked about Lincoln. He talked about Clinton. He talked about Jefferson. Suki fell asleep. And then he said:

There in the middle of this Mall, is the Washington Monument, 555 feet high. But if we put a one in front of that 555 feet, we get 1,555, the year that our first fathers landed on the shores of Jamestown, Virginia, as slaves. In the background is the Jefferson and Lincoln Memorial. Each one of these monuments is 19 feet high. Abraham Lincoln, the 16th president. Thomas Jefferson, the third president, and 16 and three make 19 again.

What? Jimi asked with his ears.

What is so deep about this number 19? Why are we standing on the Capitol steps today? That number 19—when you have a nine you have a womb that is pregnant. And when you have a one standing by the nine, it means that there's something secret that has to be unfolded.

The minister beamed. Jimi ran away.

He was only getting started but he'd lost me already. I got up. I was glad I was home.

I went into the kitchen and opened three cans of wet food. Jimi reappeared and joined the mob demanding that I give the food to them. I emptied the cans into three bowls and put them on the floor.

"Some redneck blows up a building, kills and maims hundreds of people, they call it a tragedy," I told them. They ignored me. "A few thousand brothers mingle, it's the Apocalypse."

I watched the kitties eat and listened to the panicked nasal voices talking over the minister.

"Those stupid motherfuckers deserve whatever they get."

Be Seated.

Monday, October 23, 1995

In court again. Simona sat to my right, in the aisle seat, her legs crossed like a dude.

The hearing had been continued—postponed—four times, because Sarah had not shown up. Everyone, including the judge, promised me that if I failed to appear, even once, the court would immediately issue a restraining order for Sarah and a bench warrant for me.

Simona bumped my knee with hers and stared forward. I followed her eyes. A sour woman in a saggy brown suit was working her way down the back row of the jury box, which currently held random audience members since I did not enjoy the right to a jury trial.

"That's your DA."

The woman picked a seat and heaved a massive briefcase onto the chair to her left.

"Susan Brick," Simona said softly. "She's who will file criminal charges against you. Or not. Her call. She'll want to see what comes of this first. Like we talked about—anything you say here is in play in the criminal action." I hated the way she said *the criminal action*.

While we spoke, I watched Brick. She never once even glanced in our direction, which told me that she knew exactly who we were.

"I feel like O.J."

Simona said nothing.

A lifetime trying not to end up here. I scanned the room. *This is exactly what Mom didn't want for me. My suit and good lawyer change nothing.*

When she took me to start kindergarten they told her, "He's too little. He's only four. Come back in a year." And she said, "He'll be five in two months. A year from now he will be almost six. You are enrolling him today." She wouldn't leave. And they looked at her like how people look at me now. Then they enrolled me.

I sat in court and thought about every grade-school report card, which always contained nothing but "E"s but also always had some vague claim of "behavior problems" in the Teacher's Comments. I remembered the fuss my mom always made about those. She would respond in the Parent's Comments, asking for supporting facts and quoting prior contradictory statements and requesting a meeting to discuss my "alleged behavior problems" in person. At first that confused me, then it embarrassed me. Now I know what she knew: they were building a file on me. So that one day when some drifter fired her privilege at me, the Bricks of the world would have dirt in which to bury me.

It was getting hard not to cry a little. I didn't feel fear so much as shame. I couldn't remember the last time I'd felt shame, either.

Mom protected me as long as she could. But when it came time for me to protect myself, I failed. No. I refused. Which is worse. I looked around again at all the miserable, dirty people. I was one of them. *In two years I have squandered more opportunity than all of these people will ever see ever.*

We were in the back row, at my request, so that I would see everyone who came in. Nevertheless, at some point I turned to my right and Sarah was sitting a few feet away, directly across the aisle. She was staring at me.

I guess Simona felt me jump or something, because she glanced over to where I was looking. She bumped my knee again, hard this time. I broke eye contact with Sarah and tried to face forward.

She looked good. Cute. She was wearing overalls. In court. *Fucking hill-billy.* A fucking hillbilly who was trying to have me locked up and worse but I still thought was cute. Her hair was in a big bun. She'd gained weight. Not too much, but I pictured her in whatever hillbilly-ass rent-free situation she had weaseled herself into, crying and stuffing Ring Dings in her face, and it pleased me. I looked great. I'd been hitting my heavy bag for about an hour every day.

The doors behind us swung open so fast I felt a breeze and a thug rolled in, clutching a mistreated document. He scanned the area, exchanged waves with another thug across the room, and threw himself down into the little seat directly in front of Sarah.

I felt suddenly and inappropriately protective. I started peeking at him as well as at Sarah, and eventually Simona gave up trying to stop me. Dude didn't like having a male face pointed in his direction—I know that because I don't like it either—and he started returning my gaze, even when I was looking at Sarah. Then I started looking at him more because he was looking at me, and soon I was staring at both of them, and both of them were staring at me.

The judge shuffled in, and a deputy called us to order. This is who was there: the judge; some court employees; Simona and me; the thug; the other thug; Sarah; and 40 abused women. The sight of Sarah among those women was another round of *Which of these things does not belong.* The abused women all looked like zombies, or survivors of the camps. Their eyes. All of them, regardless of their age or race. You could have issued a TRO based on their eyes.

Then there was my Sarah. Twitchy. Hostile. She had a lot more in common with the thugs than their girlfriends. I couldn't tell if anyone could see that, or cared.

One by one the dead-eyed women rose and stood at a little podium between the two big parties' tables in front of the judge. They answered a few questions, and then the judge—an older white woman who could have played a judge on TV, or Barbara Bush—would make the same speech issuing the same order: a three-year stay-away against some dude. One of the women was trying to get away from the thug; he stood at the other podium and sucked his teeth (but said nothing) while someone who had gotten old well before her time told on him.

In that case, Judge Bush's speech was a little different, because this was the first case she'd called where the dude had bothered to appear. "Now, Mr. Jackson, just so we're clear. You have heard the terms of my order. If you do not follow it, and if you do not follow it *exactly*, you are going to jail. Do you understand me?" Mr. Jackson sucked his teeth again, which I guess the judge took as a yes. "If you contact Miss Decker in any way, or any of her family, or if you have anyone contact her or any of her people, I will send you to jail." She glanced down at a file. "Uh, *back* to jail. Do you understand?"

Jackson stared defiantly at the judge but said nothing.

"Do you understand, me, Mr. Jackson?"

The tension got pretty thick. The two deputies flanking the bench started to move toward Mr. Jackson.

"Yeah. Yeah, I understand," he said eventually. The deputies who were headed for him relaxed.

"Lovely. Next case."

Romeo and his girlfriend left, seemingly together.

"Hatfield?" the court clerk called out. Another exhausted woman stood and walked down the aisle like the bride in some sad reverse wedding. Sarah spoke up.

"Judge? What about the Strauss case? Strauss versus Hayes? I am Sarah Strauss? I've been waiting . . ."

"I'll get to your case, Miss Strauss," the judge said without looking up.

"But I've been waiting since 9:00."

"Miss Strauss," Barbara Bush said to her, "I just told you that I will call your case when I get to it on the calendar."

"*This is bullshit!*" Spit flew out of her mouth. "I've been waiting . . . and he's right here!" Sarah hopped out of her seat and pointed at me, the real killer. "He's sitting right here! And . . . and *I'm afraid!*"

The dead-eyed women, including the one frozen in the aisle, all shrank and turned away.

"Miss Strauss," Judge Bush said, "*sit down.* You will wait until we have dealt with the matter I just called, and then I will call your case next. Alright?"

"Bullshit!"

I watched the deputies; they hadn't budged.

"Miss Strauss. Sit."

"I'm afraid!" Sarah demanded again. But she sat the fuck down.

They swore in the abused woman and asked her some questions and gave her the restraining order and sent her on her way. "Give me the Strauss file," the judge said to her clerk.

The clerk picked through the stack of files on her desk, pulled out one from near the bottom, and handed it up to Judge Bush. The judge opened the file and began to review it.

"Now?" Sarah called out.

The judge sighed. "Sure. Case C-975309. Sarah Strauss versus Marcus Hayes. Step forward, Miss Strauss."

Simona stood. "Your Honor? Simona Reece Guerrero Downs for the respondent. This matter is contested."

The court clerk and the court reporter glanced at each other and nodded slightly. The communication was clear: *Oh, good. Simona is here. She'll tell us what's what.* Credibility. I had credibility literally on my side.

"Alright," Judge Bush said, almost warmly. "Good morning." She turned to her staff. "Marty, we are going on the record. Annie, let's get the parties sworn in. Miss Strauss, are you represented today?"

"Yes," Sarah declared. Which was surprising, because now no one was sitting anywhere near her. But she turned her real killer pointer to a young white woman in a black suit seated in the far left corner of the front row.

"That's my attorney. Right there." The young woman did not speak.

"Is that so, counselor? Are you ready to proceed?"

The suit stood without acknowledging Sarah. "Wilma Harris, Your Honor. About that. I withdrew from this matter four days ago, on Thursday. But—"

"I did *not* accept your resignation!" Sarah hollered. The abused women cringed again.

"Counsel?"

"That was her position, yes. On Friday I moved ex parte to be relieved as counsel. The motion was granted that same day."

Annie handed the judge a piece of paper. The judge glanced at it.

"Indeed it was. Miss Strauss . . ." Slowly now, as if speaking to an idiot. "Miss Harris is no longer your attorney. Are you ready to proceed *in pro per*— ah, representing yourself?"

"Yes, judge, I'm ready. I don't need her." Sarah shot her patented Hate Stare at the back of the suit.

"Fine." Judge Bush gestured at the two large tables behind the podiums. "Please have a seat at the table to your left and be sworn. Mr. Hayes—"

"I would like to take the witness stand, please," Sarah said.

Annie and Marty looked at each other again. A different kind of look this time.

"What? Why?"

"Because I am the witness, judge. I am the victim."

"Fine. Take the stand."

Annie approached Sarah carefully. "Raise your right hand? Do you solemnly swear or affirm that the testimony you're about give will be the truth, the whole truth, and nothing but the truth, so help you God?"

Sarah looked right at me. "I do."

Yikes.

The judge addressed Sarah with a new patience. "Miss Strauss, why have you applied for a restraining order against the respondent?"

"He hit me," she said triumphantly. She threw her shoulders back and stared up at Judge Bush. "Because he hit me."

There it is. That's it, then.

The young lawyer hopped up. "A word, Your Honor?"

"Denied!" Sarah spat from the witness box. "I fired you."

"Chambers." Judge Bush was already up and walking toward the door she'd come in through. Sarah followed close behind, and her ex-lawyer gathered up her papers and started to head backstage as well. When Simona stood up, I did too.

"Not you," Simona said.

I sat back down. Brick, the DA, picked up her briefcase and headed into chambers uninvited. The women went to go talk about me. Brick shut the door.

"We're in recess," Annie said.

I must have sat there an hour, though I made a point of not checking the clock. I was still good at waiting.

I had been in a few courtrooms, but never like this. The view was all wrong. Back here, in the peanut gallery, the trappings of government power— the Great Seal of California, the signs telling you to sit down and shut up, the trigger-happy deputies—are all pointed at you. Up close, you are in the protected area, and that power is pointed at the others behind you. And now I was the other. I was a party. I was—*ugh*—the public.

I thought about the cops asking Sarah 16 times if I had hit her. I wondered what she said after I left. I wondered what her TRO application said— it had been filed under seal. Even Simona couldn't get it. Did Sarah change her tune the night of, in the days since, or just now? And did it matter?

I thought about Emmett Till. I've thought about Emmett Till possibly every day since Mom told me about him when I was 12. It was her way of beginning The Talk. White people mostly agreed that tearing a kid to pieces was an excessive response to the charge of whistling at a white woman. But even as a child my reaction was to the charge itself: I didn't buy it. My suspicion was that some white girl woke up that morning and decided to kill somebody. This of course has since been confirmed.

Funny how little I actually learned from that.

Eventually, the backstage door opened again and all the players came out and resumed their marks. Simona patted me on the shoulder.

"Back on the record," Judge Bush said. "Having taken *in camera* testimony in chambers, I am issuing mutual restraining orders in favor of and against both of the parties, Miss Strauss and Mister . . . ah, Hayes. The parties will have no contact . . . other than that required by law . . . for a period of three years. All conditions of the temporary order are extended for that period. We're done here."

Bush called the next case, but Simona sat calmly. I followed her lead and went back into waiting mode. Sure enough, a minute or two after Sarah jumped up and stomped out, Simona got up to leave.

Debra was standing in the hallway in her formal dress uniform, complete with medals. *Standing by to testify. Oh, wow.* She passed the time glowering at a woman who was ignoring her crying baby.

I walked up to her and hugged her, making sure she knew it was me before I touched her.

"Thank you" was all I could say into her chest. "Thank you."

Simona and Debra nodded at each other, and the three of us headed for the elevators. I felt like I had an escort out of the building. And like I needed one.

Back out in the sun, Debra and Simona exchanged brief but cordial goodbyes. I couldn't tell if they already knew each other or if Simona had contacted her to ask her to testify on my behalf or if Debra had found Simona and volunteered. All I knew was that things had happened behind the scenes to save me. Without my knowledge. Despite me, even. Once again, I had failed to throw it all away.

I stared at Simona and blinked and blinked. *I don't understand myself at all.*

"Did you drive here?"

"I took the bus."

"Come on."

She led me to a black BMW in a reserved spot in the courthouse lot.

"You're lucky your girlfriend can't control herself," she began, glancing at me as she started the car. "If you'd acted like that, you'd be in a padded cell on a 5150 right now. Believe that." She gave me a smirk. "Of course, if you acted like that, I would have never taken your case, Alex or not."

"Why did the judge take it in chambers?"

"She said she wanted to protect the parties' privacy, and, what was it . . . ? 'Dignity.' Yes. She wanted to preserve your girlfriend's dignity." She laughed.

"Dammit. I wanted to get up there and sling some mud, on the record."

"How nice for you. She has mud too. You know she does." I breathed through the embarrassment and tried to enjoy being exposed. It took me back to the early days with Amalia. "Judge Davis finally let me see your girlfriend's application. It contained some interesting accusations."

If she was waiting for me to confirm or deny, it was going to be an uneventful ride.

"Fortunately for you, they were not all true. A few were demonstrably false. Like her claim of abuse. That's why Harris was there. Her lawyer. Your girlfriend told her she intended to lie on the stand. Harris had to alert the court, to cover her ass. She didn't want to get caught up in a perjury charge."

"That's what happened in there?"

"That's one of the things that happened in there. Your girlfriend is wild. Which worked in your favor, today. If she had held it together . . . You were not supposed to leave that building."

I felt dizzy. I closed my eyes and slouched down in Simona's incredibly comfortable shotgun seat.

She took all surface streets; the drive was leisurely. Maybe I dozed. I sat up again a bit later.

"So, all of that was off the record? What Sarah's lawyer said about her? And whatever else Sarah did?"

"Yes."

"So it's like it never happened?"

"You are free, Marcus." Simona kept her eyes on the road because she was driving, which I appreciated. But it wasn't hard to imagine the eyes I'd be getting if she weren't. "So, clearly, it happened."

"What about the DA?"

"Brick?" Simona snorted her amusement. "She had enough too. She won't be filing any charges."

"But what about Sarah? I mean, she did do it. Commit perjury, I mean."

We were in front of my house. Simona put her ride in park, turned slightly, and gave me the "stupid motherfucker" look she had been saving up.

I pressed on. "That much is definitely on the record. 'Question: *Why do you want a restraining order?*' 'Answer: *Because he hit me.*' That happened. I saw the reporter take it down. Under oath . . . That's perjury. She lied under oath. And she admitted she lied, in front of the DA. That's a fucking felony. Sarah committed and confessed to a felony in front of a DA and a judge? That's an easy conviction. Prosecutors are conviction *junkies*. Nobody's going to snag that one?"

Simona faced forward in her seat again. Apparently if you get stupid enough you become invisible. "Goodbye, Marcus. Stay out of trouble. If you can."

I got out of her car. As I passed her open window, I stooped slightly and opened my mouth to thank her.

"You won't get a bill," she cut me off. "Your parents-in-law took care of it."

Then she was gone.

My Dick Is Trying to Kill Me.

Tuesday, October 24, 1995

"What?"

"I said, my dick is trying to kill me. I only just realized this."

Alejandro was a patient man, but I was pushing it. I heard a baby getting fussy somewhere in his house. He hadn't even mentioned they'd had a kid. I guess we didn't really talk about his life.

"I mean, if I want to fuck you, you are probably insane."

You could hear him deciding to hang up.

"I mean, I've come to suspect that I am attracted to crazy women. Not just a little bit attracted, and not just a little bit crazy. Put me in a room full of all different kinds of women, and I will almost certainly fall in love with the most batshit one in there without even trying. That's what I am afraid of."

"Oh. That."

"This morning I go downtown to pick up my file from Simona, your . . . um, your friend. I don't feel like dealing with parking downtown so I take Muni. So I'm down in the Balboa Park Muni station waiting for the train. And I notice this woman, and immediately I feel *really* drawn to her. Powerful. I can't even see her face. I don't know if it's her clothes or what. But dude I'm about to talk to this chick. And then I see her face. And she's crazy like a shithouse rat. It's just right there on her face. Too much meds? Too little? I don't know. But she's ready to jump in front of the train, or push somebody, and I'm ready to make babies."

"That's when I realize that my dick is trying to kill me."

"Amalia wasn't crazy." It was the first time I'd ever heard anything like anger in Alejandro's voice. I loved him for it.

"No. Amalia was not crazy. I think that's why I locked that deal in quick—I got lucky, and I knew it. But Sarah was not my first rodeo. I don't know why. I may have learned it in childhood."

"Hm."

"Yeah. I wonder if maybe early on I decided that the ones that scream and throw things can bear children."

"I used to think that," Alejandro said. "I thought the unstable ones would be more adventurous in bed." I wanted to ask him if Simona had been part of that research, but I didn't dare. "Yes, I used to think that." He lowered his voice. "My wife has since clarified the matter." The baby fussed again. "I should go."

"Dude, it's a terrible thing to realize that all the late-night hangup calls and the threatening letters made from the cut-out newspaper letters and the dead roses on your doorstep and the rocks through your window were coming from your dick all along. I trusted my dick. I thought we was brothers."

"I have to go."

"Kiss that baby!" I said. I don't know if he heard me.

There Goes the Neighborhood.

Wednesday, November 1, 1995

The sun was in my eyes. An old woman was staring at me.

She started pretending to fold laundry. But her face was still right up on my ground-floor window. She had been watching me sleep. It almost seemed like a loving thing. But after she recovered from her embarrassment she spit on my window and muttered something. Both seemed full of bile.

Right. I was in my new apartment.

The rent on the Love House was $1,700. Back when I was in love and fucking daily and had a chunk of cash in the bank and 40% of my salary still coming in and was fucking and, most importantly, in love, no amount of money seemed like too much. And even though $1,700 a month still didn't seem like too much for what I was getting, I was no longer in love. Or fucking. Also, I was broke. I'd gotten my last check from the firm long ago, and my stash was going fast. As expensive as falling in love is, falling out of love puts it to shame.

So I wrote the landlord a scary lawyer letter and found a new apartment. The kind of apartment that would be rented to a black man with no job and no income and no disclosed rental history and three cats and three months rent in cash. It wasn't exactly a basement apartment—it was street level, looking out into a courtyard—but it had all the charm of one.

Sayeed, my new landlord, hadn't given a damn about my siddity airs and my hopelessly inappropriate questions. ("Does the building have a laundry room?" I had asked. Sayeed waved roughly at the clothesline outside my door. "I see. And where is the gym?" He waved at the clothesline again.) Fortunately, he hadn't cared about anything but the wad of cash literally in my hand while we spoke. And even that had been a bluff. Coming up with first, last, and deposit cleaned me out. It was safe to assume that I would be seeing little of the deposit back on the Love House.

I sat up in the bed, surrounded by boxes, sun streaming in through the curtainless window onto me and my morning wood. It had been a long night of solo house moving, back and forth in the car. Anything that didn't fit in the car was abandoned.

The old woman's eyes met mine again. I smiled and waved. She turned away and called to someone across the courtyard. "*Mira*," she said. Then she said a bunch of stuff I didn't understand, though I did recognize a few words, including the one at the very end of her little speech, holding out the vowels like the town crier—"*Ne-griiiiiii-tooooooooooo!*"

I laid back down. On the one hand, I'd have bet my life that I was the only person on the block with an undergrad degree, let alone a doctorate. On the other hand, maybe they did need to worry.

The crone continued to announce my arrival. *Mayate* kind of sounds like a sports car.

Lesson.

Thursday, November 2, 1995

"It has occurred to me that some of the conflicts in my life may have been avoidable."

The monumental nature of this revelation seemed lost on Rachel. But I'd promised I would keep her posted, and this was big news.

"At the time, certain . . . events . . . did not seem avoidable. Quite the opposite—they seemed inevitable. Either someone was demanding something of me that they were never going to get, or someone needed to learn something and it was up to me to teach them." I flashed back on that frat boy, years ago, standing there with his windpipe all stove in. "Sometimes the lessons are hard. But I know that, in a very real way, I have left everybody better than I found them."

"What the fuck are you talking about."

"It's OK. I got off track. My point is, even the times some dude was in my face, asking for it, I could have done something other than what I did. I could have walked away. That's what everybody else does, right? People don't stand up to bullies. They just go home. That's why we have tyranny and exploitation and a dying planet. But my point is that I *could* walk away. Y'see?"

Nothing.

"OK. Remember the last time someone said something stupid to you and all of a sudden you had this urge to hit them in the head with a bottle?"

"Yes."

"And you didn't do it, right?"

"Not so far."

"Well, that's what I mean. That. I'm gonna do *that*."

"Marcus. What have you been up to out there."

"Up to? Uh, well . . . living. Learning."

"And what have you learned."

"Dude, I just told you!"

Pause. "Is that it."

"Man, I'll be lucky if I learned that."

The Terrorists Win.

Saturday, November 4, 1995

Goddammit. God damn it.

He was dead. He stood up for peace and they murdered him. His own people shot him in the back.

It was night in Tel Aviv, and it was chaos. Police cars and ambulances sparkled everywhere, too late.

Rabin had just finished speaking at a peace rally. He was walking to his car when some asshole came up behind him and put two in his back. He was gone for sure.

People everywhere. Some were wailing. Some were mad. I knew that some were glad. Not a week earlier, the right wing was in the streets, protesting peace with Palestine. Protesting peace. Many of the protesters held pictures of Rabin sporting a Hitler mustache. The man was basically the anti-Hitler, but that didn't matter. All you had to do was draw that little 'stache on someone and they were dead. I wish I was allowed to hate like that.

The camera cut to a podium at the edge of the scene; some guy was speaking frantic Hebrew at a small cluster of mics. "There was no conspiracy," a monotone interpreter said. "This is not a conspiracy. One shooter, and we have him. There is no conspiracy."

I turned off the TV and got in the bed. It was noon here, but every other reaction that crossed my mind was now verboten. The kitties and I cuddled and listened to the world outside.

Even if I have to change my ways to survive, that doesn't mean I was wrong about this place. Earth is exactly what I thought it was.

Safety Net.

Thursday, November 16, 1995

I was out of money.

Fair enough. I hadn't had a job in forever. And I had no prospects, or even a plan. I would try to imagine going back to a firm, and it just wasn't happening.

I had $620 in the bank and $37 in my pocket. After December rent of $595, that was $62 total for enough food to last me and the kitties I didn't know how long. And so, after doing a little research, I found myself at the Human Services Agency of San Francisco, also known as the welfare office.

I stood in the middle of the large, grimy space and got my bearings. I was doing it again: living the life my mom had suffered and struggled to spare me. I couldn't have been any more ashamed. On the other hand, I didn't have any money. That takes care of a lot of shame.

When you are about to get out of prison, they tell you: *Go straight to the welfare office. Go there before you get a place to sleep or fuck a woman or find the punk you think snitched. Walk there straight from the Greyhound station, trash bag luggage still in hand, and start the paperwork going, so you can get your first check as soon as possible.* I didn't hear anyone actually say that while I was locked up, but I was sure they must say it all the time, because everybody in the welfare office looks like they got out this morning.

In fact, the vibe in the welfare office was thicker than it had been in jail. Maybe that was because you could actually get away with something at the welfare office. We were not locked in, and there were zero guards. Almost all the dudes were brothers, and all were ready to fight. We were outnumbered by women three to one. They were almost all white, and all had babies. They were ready to fight too. They looked like every chick on *Jerry Springer*. I was in love with all of them.

I had to wait in three different lines before I was waiting in the line where you give your application form to somebody. Long ago someone had glued to the floor, behind a faded yellow line, two paper shoeprints signifying that the person at the front of the line should go only as far as the footprints AND NO FURTHER UNTIL CALLED. For the benefit of the dim, this directive was echoed on dozens of crudely handwritten signs covering the walls. There were signs everywhere, even more signs than in court, prohibiting all manner of normal human behavior. One sign said NO READING. *No reading? Seriously?*

Those design elements that had not been inspired by the criminal justice industry were borrowed from banks and "urban" liquor stores. For example, the clerks behind the counter were encased in Lucite. Even if you were bold enough to defy the paper shoeprints, you still couldn't have done anything to the clerks, because they were literally bulletproof. If the thickness of the glass didn't tell you that, their boredom in the face of the unchecked prison vibe did.

My current line trailed up to a long row of about 20 windows, three of which were staffed. The one to the far left appeared to open up; a large dirty blonde with two babies in a double stroller and two toddlers on foot began her slow caravan to some other line. The mother fumbled with a stack of loose papers while the larger toddler struggled to push the stroller. Together, the two babies plus the stroller almost certainly weighed as much as he did. And he had to reach up to grab the handles. But clearly this was little dude's job, and he managed. The caravan pushed on.

I waited. Once I was at the yellow line, I did not approach the window before I was called, because something told me that I should go NO FURTHER UNTIL CALLED. But finally I thought I heard a "Next!" from that direction. It was difficult to hear through all that glass.

Her name tag said that she was "Tiffnie."

"Good morning, Tiffnie!" I like addressing clerks by name. It's friendly, while at the same time it points out that if I need to complain about you I already know your name. Tiffnie did not seem impressed.

I began the process of transmitting my paperwork to Tiffnie. Perhaps at some point a fellow applicant had squirted lighter fluid through a slot in the glass and set someone on fire. That had been all the rage at New York subway token booths several summers earlier, and the response was the same bank-like feature I saw here. There was a clear Lucite cube built into the Lucite wall. You open a little bulletproof door, stick your documents into the cube, and spin the cube around so that the door faces the clerk. Actually, you can't spin the cube yourself; the clerk does that. Then she opens the little door, glances at the upper-left corner of the top of your six applications, and tells you that you don't qualify.

"Don't qualify for what?" It was the welfare office. None of us qualified; that was why we needed welfare.

"Your assets. Exceed our maximum."

I stood there, struggling to understand those five words. I had $600 to my name. *Didn't I mention that? Did I add two zeroes by accident?*

Eventually, all those years of the Socratic method paid off: I formed a question. "What is the maximum?"

"Two hundred dollars," Tiffnie said with a straight face as she shoved my papers into an overstuffed bin. "Come back then."

Are you fucking kidding me? But I had exhausted Tiffnie's patience. She was staring past me, at the yellow line with the shoeprints. I turned to see who was next. A member of the Aryan Brotherhood stared back, a wad of papers crushed in his fist.

"Next!"

The newly released AB enforcer began stomping toward us. I cut my losses and fled.

Hustler.

Monday, November 20, 1995

Plan B was to straight-up rob people. I would revolutionize the robbery industry by targeting people who had money. Maybe I'd work the Oakland hills; maybe Sausalito. Some guy walking his dog in a place like that would have enough on him to keep me going for a month, once I figured out how to fence jewelry.

That was Plan B. Plan A was this.

I stood at the end of the long hallway on the second floor of the Superior Court. I didn't know what kind of cases I should be looking for, or how to spot them. So instead I scoped out certain kinds of people. They were not hard to find.

All up and down the hall, dozens of small groups conferred, trying one last time to settle out of court. At least 80% of those groups fit the following description: a greasy man in a cheap suit, usually white, speaking gruffly to one or more even shabbier people, usually not white. Bad lawyers bullying poor people.

A biker and his old lady were being yelled at by a man who looked like Danny DeVito. The biker was wearing his "good" Harley shirt, all eagles and lightning and purple. The old lady had opted for the hooker-at-church look. They seemed like good prospects, but I couldn't trust that I didn't just want to fuck the old lady. My dick was still out to get me. I moved on.

A tall, sad-looking black man in a brown Kangol, brown rayon button-down shirt, and brown Hammer pants was being mistreated about halfway down the hall. His bully was particularly sweaty, with eyes that darted all around while he barked. The brother's attention was alternating between the lawyer's loud dripping face and a piece of paper in his hand that baffled him.

These two will do nicely.

I approached and interrupted with all the legitimacy I had left. "A word?" I said to the brother in the Kangol. He stood mightily confused for a moment, then followed me across the hall.

"You look like you're getting railroaded over there."

Kangol nodded many times.

"What kind of case?"

"Ar, rah—they're evicting me?"

"Unlawful detainer?"

"Yeah. That."

"You got roaches?"

"Yeah."

"Mice?"

Kangol lit up. "Yeah!"

"You tell your landlord about it?"

"Uh huh!" He seemed impressed at my ability to divine his new and unique situation.

"How many months of back rent you owe?"

"Only three . . . and a half . . ."

"And what's the rent?"

"Four hunnit."

"Hm." For a second I considered finding out where he lived, walking away, and getting the place after they kicked him out. Four hunnit would be easier to rob each month than six hunnit. Then I remembered the roaches and the mice.

"OK. I can get you out of this. Or damn near. I can help you, a lot, right now. Do you believe me?"

Kangol nodded.

"For a hundred dollars cash right now, I can tell you what to say to that *fuck* over there." Those last few words I said loud enough for the fuck to hear. He was even sweatier now. Maybe he thought I was with the State Bar. "You got a hundred dollars?"

Nodding.

"On you?"

"Yeah."

I waited. Kangol reached into the front pocket of his Hammer pants and pulled out a respectable wad, peeled off two fifties, and handed them to me. I wondered too late if we should have been more discreet; I was not at all sure that what I was doing was strictly ethical.

"Best hundred you ever spent," I said, tucking it away. "You got a pen?"

Ten minutes later, Kangol was back before Sweaty McShyster. He still clutched the papers—the summons and complaint in his unlawful detainer—but they were now turned over to the other side. That side had been blank. Not anymore. We'd even rehearsed a few times while the fuck stared. Now I stayed close while they conferred. Not close enough to get roped into their conversation, but close enough to hear.

"Counselor. I am advising you of my intention . . . to move . . . the court . . . for leave . . . to file . . . ah . . . affirmative . . . defenses. And . . . counter claims. For breach of . . . the . . . ah, rah . . . implied warranty of hab . . . habit-bility." *Close enough.* "And for retal-tory eviction." He was pretty proud of himself.

"Do you even know what those words mean?" Sweaty asked. Rarely had I heard more contempt in a person's voice. Even lately.

"Yeah," Kangol said. He seemed to suddenly remember that he was a foot taller than his adversary, because he closed the distance between them and towered. "It means I *told* that motherfucker you work for about the goddamn rats and the goddamn roaches. And the busted heater. And the motherfucker sicced *you* on me. That's illegal."

The pale wet face fell slack.

"You wanna talk settlement? *Counselor?*" A bit of spittle flew out of Kangol's mouth and landed on the shyster's nose. I smiled. Hammer Pants was going to be all right.

My client and I walked out of the courthouse together after filing the hand-written Stipulation of Settlement in the clerk's office. He had until the end of next month, six more weeks, to move out. And he didn't have to pay any rent—not past, not future. If he didn't move out, Sweaty, Sketchy, and Fuck

LLP could have judgment entered against him for all five months' rent—$2,000. Sweatstain had insisted on that, and I didn't fight it very hard. If Kangol was stupid enough to blow a deal like this, then fuck him.

We stood around until the shyster came out, shot us a fearful glance, and scurried away. I didn't want him following me. Learned that from Simona.

We watched him go, and I turned to shake hands and say goodbye. Then I was getting hugged. A full-on embrace. My head came up to dude's neck, so I got a snootful of cologne with a touch of funk while I was mauled. I did not back him the fuck off of me. Client relations are important.

"Thank you. Thank you. Thank you."

When he was finished, I wiped my face and said, "You *are* going to move out, yeah?"

"Yeah."

I believed him. "Then you're good." I reached out for my shake, though it was pretty anticlimactic now. "You take care."

"Thank you." Kangol took off. He was practically skipping.

Shit. I laughed out loud. *Law is easy.*

So much for Plan B.

Crash Test Dummies.

Friday, November 24, 1995

In the three weeks I'd been living in the Mission District, San Francisco's Latino neighborhood, I'd had more racial slurs hurled at me than in 20 years of living in New York, if you count slurs *en Español*. I would be walking by some dudes, not staring at them or anything, and more often than not one of them would hock a loogie at the sidewalk and a *mayate* at me. Spike Lee on Telemundo. It would have pleased me to know that in 15 years my new neighbors would lose their precious barrio to white 25-year-olds with stock options and bad fashion sense. Meantime, I kept to myself.

I had a new hustle but I was still poor, and driving home with a trunk full of groceries felt like the exciting privilege it was. The day was cool but sunny. I was blasting Cypress Hill. *Here is something you can't understand: how I could just kill a man*, they said.

We didn't think about it, but New York in the seventies and eighties was a high point for non-white race relations. To the Puerto Ricans I'd grown up with, I was basically a Puerto Rican who spoke bad Spanish and drank weak coffee. Life in the Mission was a crash course in both the current state of affairs and the sometimes all-important East Coast/West Coast distinction. I learned many things. I learned, for example, that Mexicans are not Puerto Ricans.

Not everything I learned was negative. I also learned that there were women in the world with names like Sad Girl or Little Shorty who hid hard bodies under baggy sweats and wore dark red lipstick and a shitload of eye shadow and got tattoos in remembrance of dead people. Goth chicks, basically. *Tough goth Latinas? That's a thing?* And I learned that I desperately needed one. I also learned that I wasn't going to get one. Ever. I almost had a better chance of getting an Asian chick.

But, most importantly, I was learning to be a cholo. For me this represented progress.

Every culture has its thugs, but each culture's thugs are different. For a while, I was like a skinhead, or a homie—loud and eager to engage. But now I had a record. A change was in order.

I'm ignorin' all the dumb shit! Cypress Hill announced.

I liked cholo style because it reminded me of cats. Cats are fast, but they choose to go slow. Cholos are ready to handle shit, but when they are not handling shit they seem relaxed. They know how to be still, how to laugh, how to not constantly boil with rage. Those were all things I needed to learn.

Back when I was a skinhead homie, I always drove like someone was chasing me. Now I drove super slow. *Make me speed up, ese*, my Inner Cholo said.

I was still a quarter of a block away from the big intersection of 24th Street and Mission; the light ahead had been green for some time. And I decided it was better to hurry up and reach a green light going maybe 30 than to hit the intersection at lowrider speed (half that) while the light went from yellow to red. An orange light, Sarah used to call that. Or was that Amalia? Anyway, stopping at the yellow and waiting for the next green never occurred to me; my cholo style was still a work in progress. So I sped up to make the light, which had indeed turned yellow by then.

Nearby, a kindred soul was deciding that that exact moment was a good time to make a U-turn. The signs prohibiting it were large and everywhere. He too had been on Mission, headed toward me; now, as I joined him in the intersection, his passenger side faced me, blocking my entire lane.

Hummin'! Comin' at ya!

Sure, I saw what was happening. I had maybe two seconds, after the car swung into the path of oncoming traffic, when I could have driven around it, or stopped. I'm quick, and 30 mph is still pretty slow. Two seconds was plenty of time to avoid a crash, but I didn't *have* to avoid it. I was not obligated to. I wasn't in the wrong; the other driver was. Undeniably so. It is not my responsibility to protect another driver from the consequences of his or her poor judgment. And no one would ever be able to prove that two seconds was enough time for me to stop. It wouldn't have been enough time for the sheep. That's why they are constantly running over innocent dogs and cats: *I was driving my car at the speed of my choosing and I looked ahead and saw another living creature in the road and I had a few seconds but I'm too slow and also I didn't completely care so I killed it with my car.* They say that, and the other sheep nod like that is a decent or reasonable thing to say. They might use the standard shorthand—*I couldn't stop*—but it means the same thing.

If the sheep are allowed to do so much damage thoughtlessly—and they are—why can't I do a little damage deliberately? Harm is harm. No one being hit by a car is ever thinking, *Well, as long as this is a genuine accident it's not so bad.* I'm careful, the natural consequence being that I do less unintended harm than someone who is careless. That should count against me? I say no. I do not relinquish the amount of damage that I, as a human being, am apparently entitled to do. And if I can't do my share of damage by accident, then I am entitled to make up the difference on purpose. All I want is my fair share.

Claire came at the car with a calm fearlessness. It was a Mercedes. I peered inside. Dude at the wheel; chick riding shotgun. They weren't even looking at me.

What does it all mean? a sample asked.

Time slowed. We were 20 feet away, then 10, then five. My windows were open, but all the background noise faded out. I leaned back and tried to relax.

The sound effect that they use in movies for a car crash is about as accurate as the one they use for gunfire. I'd expected *screeeeeeeeeeeeeeeeeeeeeeeeee-CRISH!* There was, of course, no *screeee*; I hadn't used my brakes. And there was no *CRISH*. It was more like a *WHUMPF*. It sounded like a door slamming.

A door did get slammed. Claire hit the Benz's rear door and kept on going. By the time we stopped, her bumper was damn near in their backseat.

But there was no one sitting there, and the people in the front didn't get that banged up. I'd expected heads shattering windows. But all I saw was a couple of people getting jostled. Somebody spilled a large drink on dude, though. What looked like a cherry Big Gulp (definitely not blood) was dripping off his chin onto his nice white shirt. So there was that.

The woman was pissed. Even with her back to me that was obvious. She never even turned around to see what could have killed her. She was too busy chewing out her man. *She told him not to do it. She told him not to make that U.*

Dude opened his door, but he didn't get out of the car right away. I heard him try to calm her down first in Spanish, then in English. Neither worked. I think he called her Leticia. I love that name.

We were stuck together. I didn't care for that. Dude looked over Leticia's shoulder and saw me just as I was putting Claire in reverse. He started motioning. You know the gesture—you wave your outward-facing palms side to side while shaking your head *no no no*.

Say some punk try to getcha for your auto? Cypress Hill queried. *Would you call the one-time, play the role model?*

"No." I gave Claire some gas.

The Benz screamed. Claire and I backed up about six feet, dragging the Benz with us for the first two. Fortunately, Claire had butted but she didn't bite; we didn't have any shreds of Benz attached to us. That might have interfered with her tires. *Good girl.*

Once we were clear, I turned Claire off and got out. And I began that little dance people do after an accident where they meander over to the part of their car that was hit and begin inspecting it casually.

Even after the dragging, it took dude another minute to get out of the Benz, and even then Leticia was still talking at him. Mostly curses. Dude was in trouble.

"Hi!" I smiled. "Looks like we had a little fender bender, huh?"

He made it around to the crushed side. His mind was blown. He stood still and stared at it awhile, hand plastered to his face, and then he walked past it and stared at it from the other side. It was still crushed. He looked up at me, and then he looked down at it again. Half the Benz's ass was just gone.

He'd had a chance to grieve; it was time to move on. I made a little "tsk" sound at his devastated luxury sedan, and then I turned and regarded my car. My old domestic beater. My beautiful hooptie I'd bought for $5,000 cash.

Claire was fine. Almost completely unharmed. She had a good-sized scratch right in the middle of her big metal bumper, but that might have been there already.

"Hmm," I said to the scratch.

I approached my bumper and examined it from different angles, the way dude had done. My movements felt very tai chi. I *tsk*ed and *tsk*ed. When I was sure that dude had observed my performance, I turned back to him.

"Well!" I said. "Guess we're going to have to exchange information!"

"Wha?"

"Exchange information. For our insurance people!" I gestured at the insurance people out there somewhere. I hadn't made a student loan payment in years, but a brother always kept his car paperwork straight. Anything else would have been rookie shit.

"I don't have insurance . . ."

"I'm sorry?"

". . . and this is not my car."

"God dammit, Erik!" Leticia snapped through her open window. I guess she'd told him not to do that too. I still hadn't seen her face. But she was Latina, she had long black curly hair and big gold hoop earrings, she cursed a lot, and she was mad. I wanted to marry Leticia. But first I had to fuck Erik.

"Not your car? Oh my."

Spurred on by fear of his woman, Erik tried another tack. "Yeah," he said. "Yeah. No insurance." Bolder. "What you want to do?"

I chose not to see it as a rhetorical question. "Well . . . I guess you and I can work this out without involving any third parties. You know. Directly?"

A cop car drove past and slowed. The passenger cop glanced at the accident. He looked singularly uninterested. I waved and smiled and the car went on.

"I'm *real* sorry about your car," I lied. "But you know you're not supposed to be making any U-turns here, right?" I glanced up at one of the huge red-and-white signs hanging directly over our heads.

"Yeah." Deflated again.

"I would be happy to just get reimbursed for my repair work . . ."

Erik looked at the old scratch on my bumper, looked up at me, then looked at "his" caved-in Benz. At my scratch again, at me, at the Benz. We looked at Leticia's shiny hair. Then he looked back at me.

"I need my car for work," I lied. "It has to look nice." Claire still had the dent where Sarah had kicked in the passenger-side front door. "I could go get an estimate for my body work and let you know the number, and if you forwarded that amount straight to me, I wouldn't have to contact my insurance people and give them your license plate number . . ." A little ham-handed, but I wanted this done with.

"No—I mean, OK." Erik's palm was plastered to his head again. "Yeah. Yeah."

"Great!" I went back to my car and got a pen and a scrap of paper out of the glove box. I pointedly wrote down Erik's license plate number, then handed the paper to him. "So if you could give me your address, I can forward the estimate to you . . ."

Leticia sucked her teeth loudly, without turning around. Erik flinched.

"Perhaps your phone number?"

Leticia was silent.

Erik wrote down a phone number, and then seemed to have a revelation. A wicked smile appeared. "Now you can give me *your* address," he said. "To send you the money."

I was well aware that, even though I was a lawyer dressed like some sort of rock-and-roll gangbanger, Erik was probably not an accountant dressed like a coke dealer. Not with his ruined $500 silk shirt and $1,000 gold rope chain and borrowed, uninsured Benz and superhot girlfriend who didn't make eye contact. I saw *Scarface*. My tiny basement apartment could be overrun by a Colombian hit squad with little difficulty. My neighbors would hail them as liberators.

"Okey doke!" I took back the piece of paper and ripped it in two and wrote my full name and actual address legibly and in large print on his half. I handed it to him. "Here y'go. Now, I will get an estimate ASAP, and I'll call and tell you what it is. And I'll need cash in the mail within—oh, let's say a week. Then I'll keep my insurance out of it and nobody has to know, OK?"

Erik had a funny expression on his face. Good enough.

"One week!" I repeated. My smile was at maximum. "OK?"

"Yeah."

I made Erik shake my hand, then left him to deal with Leticia. I envied him more than a little.

I spent much of the next morning canvassing the local auto body repair shops for estimates on my $100 dent job. (The fender scratch wasn't even worth that.) As I'd hoped, my neighbors wanted to gouge me not only physically but financially as well. Some of those quotes were profound insults. When the owner of Como Nuevo Auto thrust the yellow estimate form at me with "$450.00" written at the bottom and underlined three times, I looked up and let him see sadness on my face. I wanted him to be happy.

I headed back to my car, assuming that Como Nuevo was the best I was going to do. Then I glanced across the street and saw the biggest "It's STILL Army Street" sign ever.

Some months earlier the city changed the name of Army Street, one of San Francisco's auto rows, to Cesar Chavez Street. In America, when you are badass, you get a street named after you. No big deal, one might have thought. One would be wrong. Motherfuckers lost their minds when they heard the change was in the works. Dirty white men took to the streets. They lost; City Hall did it anyway. As dirty white men are wont to do, they refused to acknowledge their defeat. The "It's STILL Army Street" placard is the Confederate flag of San Francisco.

This particular flag took up most of the picture window at All-American Auto. The rest of the window was covered with old newspaper front pages. Most of the photos on the front pages were of Reagan.

All-American Auto was extremely promising. But I wasn't ready. I went home and changed.

For the first time in my life, I wished I had a bow tie. But I didn't, and I wouldn't know how to tie one if I did. So I went with a black suit and no tie. It would look like I'd taken the bow tie off.

I pulled into the garage and got out. "As-salaamu alaikum!" He didn't turn around. There was no way the owner of All-American Auto had any idea that was even a greeting, so I restated. "As-salaamu alaikum, my brother! Good day to you!"

Picture George Carlin, if George Carlin was neither smart nor funny and had been drinking since he was ten years old. Picture dirty hate. He was beautiful.

He regarded me, but he didn't talk and he wasn't going to. What he is doesn't talk to what I am. I'd been there before. It was fine. This wasn't a job interview.

"Yes, yes, good day to you, my brother. I am in need of your assistance. Driving home from the Million Man March some weeks ago, oh, the glorious— were you there? Did you attend the beautiful spectacle that was the revelation of Minister Farrakhan's dream made flesh? No? I am truly sorry you couldn't make it. No doubt you watched it on the television. In any event, on my return home from that blessed gathering of black male power, I had a slight collision with another Nubian vehicle . . ." I reached out and herded Dirty Hate over to the dent in my door, careful not to touch him for any number of reasons. He stared down at it. Dirty Hate hated my car too. Claire was a race traitor.

"No one was hurt. But, as you can see . . . how can I go forth and preach the gospel of the Honorable Elijah Muhammad in this condition? I ask you?"

His face twitched. Dirty Hate was almost ready.

"Help a brother out!"

Now he was ready.

Dirty Hate stared at the dent a bit more. He pulled a wrinkled pad out of his back pocket and jabbed at the top sheet with a pencil. He ripped the sheet off and extended his arm without looking at me. Then he spit on his own floor.

"$700.00" was all it said. No description of labor or time; no list of parts. Just a number. That would do.

"Splendid! More than reasonable. Let me just—I would like to minister to this area a bit, while I am here, perhaps enlighten your neighbors? I will drop off my vehicle before you close tonight. At what time do you close, my brother?"

But Dirty Hate was already walking away.

Exactly one week later, there was an envelope in my mailbox with no return address and nothing in it but cash. Erik was a bad driver, but he took that loss like a professional. And I got to live indoors another month.

History Is Written.

Sunday, May 19, 1996

"We now return to 'Ruby Ridge: A Star-Spangled Tragedy.'"

My eyes moved from the TV down to the newspaper at my feet. *FREE-MEN STANDOFF ENTERS THIRD MONTH.*

Scott Glenn or somebody was on one knee in a fucked-up cabin making a speech about freedom to a little Aryan boy.

History is written by the victors.

I'd have turned off the TV, but Jimi was sleeping on it. It was warm.

What's Your Excuse.

Friday, June 7, 1996

The bus smelled funny. Well—I wouldn't call it *funny*.

It wasn't armpit, which I would have expected; and it wasn't ass, which I would have feared. It wasn't any sort of artificial smell, like cologne. It was a natural smell, an earthy smell. A bad smell? Certainly not a good one. But could be worse. More unexpected than truly bad. It was faint, but that only made it harder to place.

Maybe it was just that I hadn't been on a bus in a while. Maybe the smell was just bus. If this used to be familiar, I had blotted that out. I didn't miss riding the bus. But I had things to do downtown and didn't have the heart to deal with parking. Plus, driving was a little too much fun lately.

I sat all the way in the back of the bus and mulled it over. There was a window right next to me, but I closed it. The fresh air was hindering my investigation.

Was it feet? No. Rotten produce? Rancid coffee grounds? Negative. Oysters? Any sort of shellfish? Nope. Vomit? Thankfully, no. Weed? No. A dead mouse? No. The smell an alcoholic has coming off his skin all the time? *Maybe.* I made a triumphant fist. We were getting somewhere.

The Geary Boulevard bus stopped at Divisadero, and a single person got on and dumped a handful of change into the fare box. An old man. He eased himself into the nearest old-people seat, almost directly across the aisle from the driver. The driver waited until he sat down before taking off.

"Oh . . . my . . . goodness," the old man said, loud, as the bus squeezed back into traffic. "A nigger. Driving a bus. What a shock."

I was certain I'd heard him wrong. I rewound the tape in my head and replayed it. The tape was obviously defective. Everybody told me I was paranoid; this one was easy to write off. The man was, after all, all the way at the other end of the bus. I tried to focus back on the smell.

"Nigger, do you know how lucky you are to be driving this bus? This is a good job, boy! You're lucky to have it." The bus driver didn't respond or react in any way at all, which only confirmed that I wasn't hearing what I was hearing.

"Because this is *my* country. You're in *our* country, boy. White men. This country was put here for the *white* race." The old man dry heaved, twice, but it passed.

"White men made this country. You're only here because we brought you here. Do you know how lucky you are to be in my country, boy? We did you a favor! You could be back in Africa with all those other crazy niggers, chop-pin' each other up. We civilized you. So know your place!" The driver still did not respond, and the old man smiled widely. I spotted no teeth. "Yeah, you know your place. Good boy. You're one of the good ones."

I had to seriously consider the possibility that I was having an auditory hallucination. I calculated a 61% probability that if I walked up to the front of the bus and brought both my fists down on the top of that old man's head as hard as I could, later, when I told the cops what I'd heard, that driver would point at me and say, *That poor man said no such thing! He didn't say anything. You just walked up and killed him.*

"You people should be so grateful to us, saving you from yourselves. But instead all you do is make trouble. You come over here and wear your god-damn pants down around your knees and shoot the place up. Don't you people know you ain't in Africa no more? I got damn dogs act better'n the best of ya."

There was a 24% chance that the two men were friends. Maybe they had that friendship that white people always fantasize about in movies, where, because the two men were in Vietnam or something, the white one can drop N-bombs like a Tourette's patient and the brother just laughs because he somehow knows that white dude doesn't really mean it. But even 24% was high, because the brother wasn't laughing or responding or doing anything. It was more likely that I was psychotic, which was almost the more attractive option. But those odds had dropped from 61% to 35%. I could see the old man's craggy lips moving.

"This here country—the whole country, nigger!—is here for the *white* race. It was built for the benefit of *white* people. *Only.*" The hallucination stared challengingly down the length of the bus; I and the five or six others on board quickly looked away. "You don't count. Niggers don't count. The spics don't count. The chinks *can* count but they don't count neither." The old man laughed, which turned into a retch. He swallowed a few times.

"I say this is *my* country, boy! Y'hear? You're just here for cheap labor! And cheap pussy! And for my entertainment! You remember that, now."

The old man slowly reached up and pulled the little string.

The bus rolled up to the Van Ness stop. The old man stood and blocked the entrance while he turned to face the driver. "Nigger, never forget you are in my country, and you mind your place, and you thank your black heathen nigger god that you got *any* place here. You drive this bus and you watch yourself, nigger."

The driver waited for the old man to get off the bus. He even operated the little hydraulic lift that lowered the front of the bus so the old man wouldn't have so far to climb. The driver never said a word, even after the old man crept off and new, baffled passengers began to board.

Quite a few folks were getting on at Van Ness, and the bus was still sitting at the stop as the old man backtracked past my window. I opened it. "You're right," I said to him. He looked up.

"You're right. This country was made for white people. For the use and benefit and prosperity of white people. And *only* white people. Every little thing about it. You are absolutely right about that." By now the new passengers had all paid their fares and boarded. Most had even sat down. But the bus didn't move.

"So how do you explain yourself?" I asked him. "You were born in this country, yeah? This town, probably. Grew up in San Francisco in, what, the forties? Boom times. Jim Crow, still, even here. You were a young white man in a world where every opportunity was openly, expressly reserved for young white men. So, what happened?"

The old man stared but said nothing.

"How do you explain being what you are today in a country where you were born a king? You're supposed to be a captain of industry right now. A leader. A titan. But instead you are a bum. You are a white man in America. You got a thousand chances. What did you do with them all?"

"Hey," one of the bus newcomers said to me.

"Look at you. You're not even average. You're nothing. In a country entirely dedicated to your personal success, you have succeeded in becoming a dirty, poor, alcoholic nothing. Smelly drunk garbage. What is *wrong* with you?"

I was done. I gave the old man a moment to explain himself but he had nothing to say, so I closed the window and faced forward. My eyes met the driver's in his rearview and I nodded. Slowly, the bus revved up and pulled back into traffic.

A couple of sheep peeked at me, but nobody said shit.

I watched the driver in his mirror. He looked like the driver I'd had to tell about himself after he shoved me, a lifetime ago. He looked a lot like that guy. In the rearview, anyway. It was the same route.

I closed my eyes and pretended I was somewhere else. Whatever that smell was, I couldn't smell it anymore.

What Happened.

Wednesday, July 24, 1996

"How are you?" Mom asked.

"Fine," I lied.

"Are you alright?"

"Yes," I lied.

"How are you *feeling?*"

"Fine," I lied.

"Did you see that therapist your friend found for you?" She sounded afraid to ask. She needn't have been. I was lying.

"Yes."

"Goooood," she sighed. "Good."

A long pause.

"You know, honey, you know, as long as you are talking to someone . . . you may talk about your past a little bit. Your . . . your childhood. And . . . if you do, I want you to know some things . . . Some things that might help . . . explain some things?"

She sounded so meek. But there was nothing to do except wait for her to work up her nerve and say whatever she'd called to say.

"Your father. Died. You know that. I know you don't remember. I told you. I told you that he died . . . naturally. In his sleep. Well. He died. In his sleep. But.

"But not exactly. Naturally. It was an accident. An accident."

I waited.

"There was gas. A leak. I came home and . . . I could smell it from outside the apartment. I went inside and it was full of gas and all I could think of was you. I knew you were in there. Your father was in there too, but . . . all I could think of was you in there.

"I couldn't find you. It stank and my eyes were watering and I tried to hold my breath but I couldn't stop calling your name. Your father was in the living room. He was lying on the couch. He had his back to me. He wasn't moving. I got so dizzy I had to go back outside and I screamed for help but then I went back in. I wasn't going to leave you in there, Marcus. Even if I died in there with you. I wasn't leaving without you."

I stayed quiet.

"I found you in your room. Your room was at the end of the hall, in the back. Do you remember? We moved to Seneca Avenue after . . . You don't remember. You don't remember any of this.

"Your door was closed and your windows were open. First I thought you weren't in there and I lost my mind but next thing I knew I was at the closet and there you were. You were hiding in your closet. On the floor. In the back. You had a scarf over your face.

"You were calm. I thought you were sick, or hurt. The gas. But you were fine. I carried you out.

"I held you and I talked to you but you weren't afraid or hurt or anything. By then the neighbors had come out. I gave you to Mrs. Panzer and I went back in to see about your father. But he was . . . gone. He was dead.

"It was the stove. There were police, and then there were detectives.

The detectives examined the stove a long time. They said the gas line came aloose. They did things to the linoleum—to see if it had been moved recently, they said. It hadn't. They even made me try to stick my arm back there! To see if I could reach the gas line. I couldn't. I could see the line hanging there, but I couldn't get my arm back there. The space was too narrow.

"And then everyone was leaving. They still didn't know how it happened. One of them shrugged. The other one said, 'Accident, ma'am.' I guess one more dead black man wasn't worth being late for dinner. And they left. And I never saw them again.

"I fretted over you all night, but you were fine. You weren't scared or upset.

"You didn't even cry."

I stayed quiet. The great thing about not saying anything is that people tend to fill in the blanks with whatever they need.

"I know you can't remember anything about that time. You told me that you can't. Not any of the friends you had made. For months after. I thought they would have to leave you back, but you always did your schoolwork just fine. I figure they didn't teach you anything you didn't already know until high school." She laughed.

Try law school, I thought, but I was busy not saying anything.

"Why am I telling you this now?" She laughed again. "You might need to know. I don't know why. You seem to me the closest you've ever been to being ready to face . . . whatever it is that's . . . what it is that you struggle with. So now I'm telling you. I'm telling you," she declared.

"Your father had . . . changed. Life was harder than he expected it to be. He was all swagger when I met him, and I liked that. I was young. We were both young. He was a lot of . . . talk. Plans. But sometimes plans don't work out. You know that. You always have. I've always known it. But your father . . . he didn't.

"He had some disappointments. Graduate school. Art school. Jobs. A business. Some of his plans seemed like a good idea to me, and some didn't.

Maybe I would have done them differently, if I was him, or not at all. But he was my husband, and, back then . . . He had his plans and his talk and I went out and got a job at New York Tel.

"He got bitter, Marcus. And he got mean. Abusive, they call it now. Everybody talks about all this now. But back then—nobody talked about it. I tried to talk to *my* father about it . . . oh, Lord. I tried to leave, Marcus. I was going to take you and go back home. I didn't mean to tell you that. But I called Daddy and I told him what was happening and all he did was quote scripture at me. 'Cleave unto your husband,' he said." She laughed a laugh that bore no mirth. "I never tried telling anybody else after that. If your own daddy . . .

"He started to hit me. Sometimes. He didn't beat on me, not like he could have, but it was bad. Scary. I tried to keep you from all that. I thought I did. And then. One day.

"After work I picked you up from the day care center like always and we went home. Your father was drunk. He'd been home all day. I took you to your room and I told you to play. And I closed the door. Because I could tell. It was going to be . . . bad.

"I changed my clothes and made dinner as fast as I could but nothing was good enough for him that night. I was in the kitchen cooking and he sat down at the table and he talked. He said . . . things . . . He was so *mean*.

"I knew I should keep my mouth shut. But, Marcus, you don't know what it was like. I'd gotten a few promotions by then. I started out as a rep and then I was a supervisor and then I was an assistant manager down at headquarters. It was 1974. I was one of the only black women who didn't have a broom in her hand, anywhere down there. It was *hard*. I grew up in Alabama, Marcus. I grew up with Jim Crow. Work was worse than that. But I did it. I did it for my family. I did it for you.

"And then I came home to this. I stood up to men all day. I was tired. He was just another man, to me, for a minute. So . . . he said something, and I said something back. Then he said something and I said something and he threw his glass at me. And I threw a pot . . . a pot of boiling rice, Marcus. At him. And then he was up and he was so fast and he had me by my throat.

"I thought we were fighting, but we weren't fighting. He was big and strong and I was nothing. I tried to make him let go but he wouldn't. He was hurting me and I couldn't breathe and then I couldn't hear and I started see-ing spots. He was wringing my neck. And I started going away. I was dying. And then he dropped me on the floor and left. And when I sat up, you were standing there in the kitchen. I think he stopped because you came in.

"You saved my life. He was going to kill me."

She was quiet for a really long time.

"And the day after that I came home from work and he was dead."

Quiet.

"They said it was the stove."

It was time for me to talk. "Oh. Wow. Oh, my mama. Thank you for tell-ing me this. I *did* need to know it," I lied. "I will tell Dr. Partikian all of this at our very next session," I lied. "OK? We're gonna sort all of this out. OK?"

She was trying to not let me hear her cry, so when I lied and said I had somewhere to be, she was glad to hang up.

"It'll be fine," I said. "I'll talk to you soon. I love you."

That last part was not a lie.

Bicycle.

Monday, August 26, 1996

I was walking up Van Ness, on the right side of the street. One second before I reached California, just shy of where the buildings end a few feet back from the curb, I stopped walking for no reason. And then some asshat came blast-ing by on a bicycle from my right. He was just suddenly there, from around the corner on California, riding on the sidewalk. I had not seen him or heard anything before I stopped walking. My body sensed something my brain had not. If I hadn't stopped walking, he would have plowed into me from the side and hurt me bad.

But he didn't hit me. Instead he cruised by me from my right side to my left, less than a foot in front of me. He was moving at a good clip. On the sidewalk. I think he was trying to make the light.

Before he passed me, time slowed down and my arms woke up. A guy on a bike is hell on wheels going forward, but sideways not so much. Shoving him would have been like doing a fast push-up. There was a tall, thick pole on the corner, a streetlight I think. With his forward momentum, that pole was in exactly the right spot to catch his head. It would change him. Even though the people across the street waiting to cross California would see the whole thing, no one would be able to dispute my claim that he had surprised me and my arms automatically shot out in front of me to ward him off. And he'd be ruined.

I remember each frame. His face, with that indifferent expression, on his exposed, helmetless head. His infantile skater getup. His chopper-style bike. If any part of him had touched me, even just brushed me, I was going to do my push-up and play billiards with his brain. Hopefully, he'd get to his feet and want to fight.

But he didn't touch me. And I let him go.

He never knew what almost happened. It's too bad for him if he's riding around today not knowing something like that about his own life.

Let's be clear: a grown man who rides a bicycle on the sidewalk with no concern for pedestrians needs a head injury. He *needs* one. But I didn't have to be the one to give it to him. I was retired. Somehow, I was doing what folks consider the right thing. And it was getting easier.

I called Rachel and told her all about it. She wasn't as happy for me as I'd expected. She said she had to go. Maybe I called during dinner.

VI

Two Things.

Two things happened that were not good.

The first was Christmas. Amalia died in January, but it's like those events happened to somebody else. The few memories I have are almost in the third person. The rest are just gone. Burned away. You know how in those old films of the first A-bomb tests, the actual explosion is just white? What was happening exceeded what film can capture, so what it captured was nothing.

But that last Christmas together, I was all there. Maybe the last time I was ever all there. The last time I was ever really happy. It's almost too much to bear. I could have blotted that out too. I could have checked out, gone to my nowhere place. I'd hurt less now. But I knew that it was some of our last time together, and I made myself be there. I pulled my heart and my mind wide open, as wide as they would go, to take in all I could. I needed to stock up on her. And I did.

That was Christmas '93. Every Christmas after that was as bad as Christmas '93 was good. On Christmas '96 I did not get out of bed. I did not answer the phone. I did not drown my cats and hang myself. That's what I did that day. It took some doing.

The other thing that happened came in the mail the next day. No return address. Postmark was somewhere in Oregon. It was a photograph. A snapshot of a baby. Maybe a year old. Looked to be a boy. Mixed. Cute.

My first thought was whether I could use this to have her thrown in jail. She was in violation of the restraining order. *Nobody cares.* My next thought was, *Why didn't she have an abortion? She's had nine already. Why wouldn't you have abortion number 10?*

So, that happened too.

One More Thing.

Monday, January 13, 1997

I called my mom. Still hadn't told her about the photo.

"How are you, honey?"

"Foine," I lied.

"That's good. How are you doing?"

"I'm doing pretty good. I'm OK."

"I'm glad to hear that, baby. Because, honey, I have to tell you something."

I was in the kitchen. I heard the front door open and, a moment later, close.

"I haven't been feeling right lately. So I went in to see my doctor. It was almost time for a checkup anyhow."

Slow footsteps grew louder.

"Dr. DeSalvo examined me, and he felt something. A little lump, under my arm."

Death stood in the doorway. *Oh. You.*

"He thought it might be a lymph node. So he checked other ones. And some of them were swollen too."

Death entered the kitchen and sat at the dining table.

"I'm going in for more tests in early March. I wanted to get in sooner but I would rather see the best doctor, and that's the soonest I could get. Dr. DeSalvo said that since I haven't been feeling bad for long, and since he didn't notice anything a year ago, we are almost certainly not talking about fast growth. And there's always a chance that my lymph nodes are just inflamed . . ."

She said some other things after that, and I must have said some things too. But all I really did was watch Death looking at me. And I tried to imagine how unspeakably beautiful the cover of the "So You Just Lost the Only Person You Care About in This World" pamphlet would be.

Another Slight Relapse.

Friday, February 21, 1997

The sun had started to set, but it was in no hurry—the sky was all yellows and reds and sometimes almost purple. Long clouds made their way across a low sky. It was a moment of beauty and peace that even I could see, despite my worries. Claire and I were rolling down Dolores. "Be Thankful for What You Got" was playing on the radio. I was digging the scene in a gangster lean.

It had been a long, productive day. I did two evictions in civil court, and finally worked up the nerve to go to 850 Bryant, where the criminal court is. It is also where they had me locked up. I didn't take any cases but I did do some recon.

I'd just passed the stop sign at the top of the big hill on 18th Street and was coasting briskly past Dolores Park. The next stop sign was at the following intersection, but with the park immediately to my right that intersection was two long blocks away.

I enjoyed the view of the city. And then I saw him. Officer Friendly. I knew it was the same fuck that had stopped me for no reason and stuck his gun/crotch in my face, because he was doing it to someone else. Standing in the street, hand on top of the parked car like it belonged to him, all smiles. Either this was how he consciously toyed with his prey, or he didn't see anything strange about shooting the shit with someone while detaining them against their will with the implied threat of deadly force. Either way he was a predator.

Since noticing him, I had closed the distance between us by half. The car he'd pulled over was not far from the stop sign on 20th. I hadn't used my brake in a while. I was coasting at a goodly clip. And I knew that I was going to kill him.

I moved over to the right lane. Cruising like a missile. Seconds were minutes. *I am really doing this.* He was peering straight down—he must have stopped a chick and was taking in the cleavage. And there was nothing he could do. Soon, even if he ran, trying to get around the car and out of the street, he would only make himself a bigger target. I edged over to the right as far as I could without sideswiping the parked cars.

I don't know why he glanced up. Maybe because there was a Pontiac speeding toward him. And while I was probably correct that at that point any attempt to get around his victim's car would have only gotten him more hit, I hadn't anticipated what Friendly did do, which was to smush up against the car completely flat in a move any bullfighter would have respected. His face was turned toward me, his mouth still in a smirk. He hadn't had time to change his expression.

My fender was almost on him when he did his bullfighter move. Inches away. There was no way I could adjust my trajectory enough to hit him properly without then crashing into the parked cars, and I wasn't interested in sticking around after. But in that amazing slo-mo I did have time to make one executive decision. I bumped the wheel to the right, just a bit, and corrected again. Claire scooted over two, maybe three inches. And an instant later my right-side mirror caught him in the ribs.

I knew I got him good when the mirror snapped. The whole thing, even the metal casing the mirror was in, popped off and bumped against the side of car, tethered by some wire.

"*Yeah!*" I hooted.

With surprise on my side, there was a chance that no one had caught my plates. What I needed was to not get into an accident at that next intersection—obviously, I wasn't going to heed the stop sign after all—and then I'd be over the crest of another hill and out of sight.

There was no time to look in the rearview. I was no more than two seconds from the intersection. I saw some movement through the trees on 20th Street, to my right. Oncoming cars.

Since keeping a low profile was already out of the question, I hit my horn, hard. What I was afraid of is known as the California Stop, a.k.a. the

California Roll, which is basically people not stopping at stop signs. Usually there is not a car fleeing through the intersection the other way. Right then, the California Roll wasn't going to do anybody any good.

Claire had a real horn. She said exactly what I meant: *HEY! SOME ASSHOLE IS BLASTING THROUGH THE INTERSECTION! FUCK YOUR RIGHT-OF-WAY! STOP IF YOU WANT TO LIVE!*

The two cars doing serial California Rolls bumped slightly when the first one stopped. I'm sure they didn't mind. Death was passing through. And he was laughing.

It felt like Claire left the ground as we went over the lip of the next steep hill, but I think that the wheels hung on and just the body lifted. We were still booking, and now we were also bouncing. Claire didn't have any sort of gangster-type suspension. I was just driving too fast.

I slowed down and calmly put a few more blocks between me and the new improved Officer Friendly. Then I made a right onto Cesar Chavez Street, a.k.a. It's *STILL* Army Street.

I was moving down Still Army Street at a nice pace, but so was everybody else. Eventually I cut over to a smaller street, then a smaller one, trying to make sure I wasn't being followed but also trying to get the hell home. Every once in a while I would remember breaking my mirror off in that cop's ass and I would laugh and laugh.

I didn't have a parking space; I had to park on the street. Claire didn't have any blood on her, but her right rear door handle had shreds of blue trouser stuck to it. *Ouch.* I removed the shreds and what was left of my mirror and hurried inside.

I paced the tiny apartment and debated turning on the TV. I wanted to know, and I didn't want to know. And what was I going to do—leave town? I'd be taking me with me.

All three cats were piled into the same small cat bed and watching me stalk back and forth, only half interested.

Fuck.

Finally, I walked up to the cardboard boxes of unpacked shit I kept stacked up near the bathroom. I pulled out the third box from the top and opened it. After all this time, I still knew exactly where it was. I took the little pad out of the box and a pen from my pocket. *At least let me start a new page.*

I did. Across the top, I wrote the word "DAYS."

And under that I wrote "0."

Acknowledgments.

My love and thanks to the following for believing in this book: Arthur W. * Ashaki J. * Ashley C. * Ben W. * Benita D. * Betty T. * Bob W. * Brian E. * Carol M. * Chad F. * Chris von T. * Christine C.S. * Claudia J. * Cliff F. * Cristina F. * David K. * Dawn S. * Deborah D. * Deborah R. * Deirdre H. * Dexter C. * Diem J. * Ed N. * Elisa S. * Elizabeth J. * Elmaz A. * Emmett T. * Erin N. * Frine E.G. * Glenys R. * Heidi L. * James T. * Janelle Y. * Jasmine D. * Jasmine F. * Jenna von T. * Jeremy L. * Jessie W. * Jill B. * John P. * Jono S. * Juan A.V. * Julian S. * Kelli S.K. * Kendra L. * Kim D. * Larry C. * Laura A. * Lisa L. * Lisa S. * Lorien S. * Lynne U. * Marc D. * Marissa J.V. * Mary S. * Melanie S. * Mikayla C. * Nadine D. * Patti W. * Pervanche M. * Peter J. * Phil O. * Ray L. * Rita H. * Scott A. * Scott D. * Scott W. * Shane B. * Sharline C. * Sonya M. * Stacie H.T. * Stephanie M. * Tananarive D. * Tara B. * Tara D. * Tarik R. * Todd S. * Tomas M. * Wendy M.

Thank you to Akashic Books—Johnny Temple and Ibrahim Ahmad especially—for seeing as I did that Akashic is where this book belongs.

A special shout-out to Mat Johnson, who helped me so much for no reason.

And an extra-special shout-out to my agent, Danielle Chiotti, who kept pushing long after I had given up.

~@.